DAUGHTER
OF THE
MOON
GODDESS

DAUGHTER
OF THE
MOON
GODDESS

A NOVEL

SUE LYNN TAN

HARPER Voyager
An Imprint of HarperCollins Publishers

DAUGHTER OF THE MOON GODDESS. Copyright © 2022 by Sue Lynn Tan. All rights reserved. Printed in Canada. No part of
this book may be used or reproduced in any manner whatsoever without written permission except in the case of brief quotations embodied in critical articles and reviews. For information, address HarperCollins Publishers, 195 Broadway, New York, NY 10007.

HarperCollins books may be purchased for educational, business, or sales promotional use. For information, please email the Special Markets Department at SPsales@harpercollins.com.

Harper Voyager and design are trademarks of HarperCollins Publishers LLC.

FIRST EDITION

Designed by Angela Boutin

Map illustration by Virginia Norey
Frontispiece © hikolaj2/stock.adobe.com
Cloud illustration © chic2view/stock.adobe.com
Cherry blossom illustration © paprika/stock.adobe.com

Library of Congress Cataloging-in-Publication Data has been applied for.

ISBN 978-0-06-303130-2
ISBN 978-0-06-323748-3 (international edition)

22 23 24 25 26   FRI   10 9 8 7 6 5 4 3 2 1

To my husband, Toby—my first reader and partner in life.
This would not have been possible without you.

And to my children, Lukas and Philip, for letting me work
some of the time.

DAUGHTER
OF THE
MOON
GODDESS

PART I

1

There are many legends about my mother. Some say she betrayed her husband, a great mortal warrior, stealing his Elixir of Immortality to become a goddess. Others depict her as an innocent victim who swallowed the elixir while trying to save it from thieves. Whichever story you believe, my mother, Chang'e, became immortal. As did I.

I remember the stillness of my home. It was just myself, a loyal attendant named Ping'er, and my mother residing on the moon. We lived in a palace built from shining white stone, with columns of mother-of-pearl and a sweeping roof of pure silver. Its vast rooms were filled with cinnamon-wood furniture, their spicy fragrance wafting through the air. A forest of white osmanthus trees surrounded us with a single laurel in its midst, bearing luminous seeds with an ethereal shimmer. No wind nor bird, not even my hands could pluck them, they cleaved to the branches as steadfastly as the stars to the sky.

My mother was gentle and loving, but a little distant, as though she bore some great pain which had numbed her heart. Each night, after lighting the lanterns to illuminate the moon, she stood on our balcony to stare at the mortal world below. Sometimes I woke just before the dawn and found her still standing there, her eyes shrouded in memory. Unable to bear the sadness in her face, I wrapped my arms around her, my head just coming up to her waist. She flinched at my touch as though roused from a dream, before stroking my hair and bringing me back to my room. Her silence pricked me; I worried that I had upset her, even though she rarely lost her temper. It was Ping'er who finally explained that my mother did not like to be disturbed during those times.

"Why?" I asked.

"Your mother suffered a great loss." She raised a hand to stall my next question. "It's not my place to say more."

The thought of her sorrow pierced me. "It's been years. Will Mother ever recover?"

Ping'er was silent for a moment. "Some scars are carved into our bones—a part of who we are, shaping what we become." Seeing my crestfallen expression, she cradled me in her soft arms. "But she is stronger than you think, Little Star. Just as you are."

Despite these fleeting shadows, I was happy here, if not for the gnawing ache that something was missing from our lives. Was I lonely? Perhaps, although I had little time to fret over my solitude. Every morning my mother gave me lessons on writing and reading. I would grind the ink against the stone until a glossy black paste formed, as she taught me to form each character with fluid strokes of her brush.

While I cherished these times with my mother, it was the classes with Ping'er that I enjoyed the most. My painting was passable, and my embroidery dismal, but it did not matter when it was music I fell in love with. Something about the way the melodies formed, stirred emotions in me which I did not yet comprehend—whether from the strings plucked by my fingers, or the notes shaped by my lips. Without companions to vie for my time, I soon mastered the flute and qin—the seven-stringed zither—surpassing Ping'er's skills in just a few years. On my fifteenth birthday, my mother gifted me a small, white jade flute that I carried everywhere in a silk pouch that hung from my waist. It was my favorite instrument, its tone so pure even the birds would fly up to the moon to listen—though part of me believed they came to gaze at my mother, too.

Sometimes, I caught myself staring at her, entranced by the perfection of her features. Her face was shaped like a melon seed and her skin glowed with the luster of a pearl. Delicate brows arched over slender jet-black eyes which curved into crescents when she smiled. Gold pins gleamed from the dark coils of her hair and a red peony was tucked in one side. Her inner garment was the blue of the noon sky, paired with a white and silver robe that flowed to her ankles. Wrapped around her waist was a vermilion sash, ornamented with tassels of silk and jade. Some nights, as I lay in bed, I would listen out for their gentle clink, and sleep came easy when I knew she was near.

Ping'er assured me that I resembled my mother, but it was like comparing a plum blossom to the lotus. My skin was darker, my eyes rounder, and my jaw more angular with a cleft in the center. Perhaps I resembled my father? I did not know; I had never met him.

It was years before I realized that my mother, who dried my tears when I fell and straightened my brush when I wrote, was the Moon Goddess. The mortals worshipped her, making offerings to her each Mid-Autumn Festival—on the fifteenth day of the eighth lunar month—when the moon was at its brightest. On this day they would burn incense sticks for prayer and prepare mooncakes, their tender crusts wrapped around a rich filling of sweet lotus seed paste and salted duck eggs. Children would carry glowing lanterns shaped as rabbits, birds, or fish, symbolizing the light of the moon. On this one day a year I would stand upon the balcony, staring at the world below, inhaling the fragrant incense which wafted up to the sky in honor of my mother.

The mortals intrigued me, because my mother gazed at their world with such yearning. Their stories fascinated me with their struggles for love, power, survival—although I had little comprehension of such intrigues in my sheltered confines. I read everything I could lay my hands on, but my favorites were the tales of valiant warriors battling fearsome enemies to protect their loved ones.

One day, while I was rummaging through a pile of scrolls in our library, something bright caught my eye. I pulled it out, my pulse leaping to find a book I had not read before. From its rough stitched bindings, it appeared to be a mortal text. Its cover was so faded, I could barely make out the painting of an archer aiming a silver bow at ten suns in the sky. I traced the faint details of a feather within the orbs. No, not suns but birds, curled into balls of flame. I brought the book to my room, my fingers tingling as they clutched the brittle paper to my chest. Sinking down on a chair, I eagerly turned the pages, devouring the words.

It began as many tales of heroism did, with the mortal world engulfed by a terrible misfortune. Ten sunbirds rose in the sky, scorching the earth and causing great suffering. No crops could grow on the charred soil and there was no water to drink from the parched rivers. It was rumored that the gods of heaven favored the sunbirds, and no one dared to challenge such mighty creatures. Just when all hope seemed lost, a fearless warrior named Houyi took up his enchanted bow of ice. He shot his arrows into the sky, slaying nine of the sunbirds and leaving one to light the earth—

The book was snatched from me. My mother stood there, flushed, her breaths coming short and fast. As she gripped my arm, her nails dug into my flesh.

"Did you read this?" she cried.

My mother rarely raised her voice. I stared blankly at her, finally managing a nod.

She released me, dropping onto a chair as she pressed her fingers to her temple. I reached out to touch her, afraid she would pull away in anger, but she clasped her hands around mine, her skin as cold as ice.

"Did I do something wrong? Why can't I read this?" I asked haltingly. There appeared nothing out of the ordinary in the story.

She was quiet for so long, I thought she had not heard my question. When she turned to me at last, her eyes were luminous, brighter than the stars. "You did nothing wrong. The archer, Houyi . . . he is your father."

Light flashed through my mind, my ears ringing with her words. When I was younger, I had often asked her about my father. Yet each time she had fallen silent, her face clouding over, until finally my questions ceased. My mother bore many secrets in her heart which she did not share with me. Until now.

"My father?" My chest tightened as I spoke the words.

She closed the book, her gaze lingering on its cover. Afraid that she might leave, I lifted the porcelain teapot and poured her a cup. It was cold, but she sipped it without complaint.

"In the Mortal Realm, we loved each other," she began, her

voice low and soft. "He loved you, too—even before you were born. And now . . ." Her words trailed off as she blinked furiously.

I held her hand to comfort her, and as a gentle reminder that I was still here.

"And now, we are parted for eternity."

I could barely think through the thoughts cramming my head, the emotions surging within me. For as long as I could remember, my father had been no more than a shadowy presence in my mind. How often had I dreamed of him sitting across from me as we ate our meals, strolling beside me beneath the flowering trees. Each time I awoke, the warmth in my chest dissolved to a hollow ache. Today, I finally knew my father's name, and that he had loved me.

It was little wonder that my mother appeared haunted all this time, trapped in her memories. What had happened to my father? Was he still in the Mortal Realm? How did we end up here? Yet I gulped back my questions, as my mother wiped her tears away. Oh, how I wanted to know, but I would not hurt her to ease my selfish curiosity.

TIME TO AN IMMORTAL was as rain to the boundless ocean. Ours was a peaceful life, a pleasant one, and the years passed by as though they were weeks. Who knows how many decades would have swept by in this manner if my life had not been tossed into turmoil, as a leaf torn from its branch by the wind?

It was a clear day, the sunlight streaming through my window. I set aside my lacquered qin, closing my eyes to rest. As had happened before, silver flecks of light drifted into my mind, tugging and teasing at me—just as how the scent of osmanthus drew me to the forest each morning. I wanted to reach out to them but recalled my mother's stern warning.

"Don't go near them, Xingyin," she had pleaded, her skin ashen. "It's too dangerous. Trust me, they will fade."

I had stammered my promise to her then. And over the years, I had kept my word diligently, too. Whenever a glint of silver beckoned to me, I thought furiously of other things—a song or my latest book—until my mind cleared and they faded away. Yet it was harder each time, the lights blazing brighter, their call more tantalizing. The urge to reach out, almost overwhelming.

How brightly they glittered today, as though sensing my wavering resolve, the restless churning in my blood. I had felt this more often of late, a part of me yearning for . . . something which had no name. A change, perhaps. But nothing ever happened here. Nothing ever changed.

The lights did not seem dangerous. Was my mother mistaken? She had cautioned me against countless things, as harmless as climbing a tree or running through the halls, maybe recalling such perils from her mortal childhood. I drew closer to the radiance in my mind. Closer than I had ever been before. Something clutched at me, dragging me away—was it fear or guilt? But reckless now, I tore through it as though it were cobwebs. I was at the brink, teetering on the edge. A current raced through my veins, whispers coiling between my ears. Leaning forward, I reached out—only to see the shimmering silver scatter as the starlight at dawn.

My eyes flew open, my senses tingling. I had no idea how long I sat there, lost in a daze. Beyond my window, the evening sun infused the sky with threads of rose and gold. The thrill gone; remorse sat like a stone in my chest. I had broken my promise to my mother. And worse yet, I wanted to do it again.

Those lights were not dangerous, they were a part of me—I knew that now with startling certainty. Why had she warned me from them? *I will ask her,* I decided, rising to my feet. *I am old enough to know.*

Just as I reached the entrance, a strange energy thrummed through the air, raising the hair on the back of my neck. Immortal auras—unfamiliar to me—shifting and mingling as the clouds in the sky. I could not tell how many, although one seemed to blaze brighter than the rest, far stronger than my mother's or Ping'er's.

Who had come here?

As I flung the doors open, my mother flew into my room. I stumbled back, knocking into a chair. Did she discover what I had done? Was she here to scold me?

I hung my head. "I'm sorry, Mother. The lights—"

She grasped my shoulders. "Never mind that, Xingyin. A visitor has arrived. She mustn't know that you're here. That you're my daughter."

My pulse raced at the thought of meeting someone new. Then, her meaning sank in—as did her tone—and my excitement crumpled like a sheet of paper. "You don't want me to meet your friend?"

Her hands fell away from me, the planes of her face hardening until they seemed carved from marble. "Not a friend. She is the empress of the Celestial Kingdom. She doesn't know about you, nobody does. And we can't let them find you!"

Her words—tumbling out in a rush—startled me, despite the excitement which sparked within. I had read the Celestial Kingdom was the mightiest of the eight immortal lands, nestled like a precious teardrop at the heart of the realm. Its emperor and empress lived in a palace that floated upon a bank of clouds, from where they governed over the Celestials and mortals, and watched over the sun, moon, and stars. In all our time here, they had never deigned to visit our remote home, so why now?

And why did I have to hide?

A strange flutter in the pit of my stomach spread icy tendrils through my core. "Is something wrong?" I asked, hoping she would deny it.

She touched my cheek gently. "I'll explain everything later. For now, stay in your room and don't make a sound."

I nodded and she left, shutting the doors behind her. Only then did I realize that my mother had not answered my question. I opened a book, dropping it down again after reading the same line thrice. My fingers plucked a qin string, but then pinched it to muffle the note. As I stared at the closed doors, a burning curiosity engulfed me, consuming my fear. Slowly, I walked toward it, sliding it open a crack. Just one look at the Celestial Empress and I would return to my room. When would I get another chance to see her, one of the most powerful immortals in the realm? And she might even be wearing her Phoenix Crown, said to be crafted from feathers of pure gold and embellished with a hundred luminous pearls.

As silent as a shadow, I tiptoed down the long corridor that led from my room to the Silver Harmony Hall—the grandest room in our Pure Light Palace—with its marble floor, jade lamps, and silk hangings. Wooden pillars set into ornate silver bases added a touch of warmth to its pristine elegance. This was where I had always imagined we would entertain our guests, although we never had one until now.

Just around the corner, a soft voice drifted through. I strained my ears to listen.

"Chang'e, have you been well?" The Celestial Empress's cordial address surprised me. She did not sound so very fearsome.

"Yes, Your Celestial Majesty. Thank you for your concern." My mother's voice was unnaturally bright.

A brief silence followed this exchange of courtesies. Crouching down by the wall, I craned my neck to peek into the room. My mother knelt on the floor, her head bowed low—while across from her, seated in my mother's own chair, had to be the Celestial Empress.

She was not wearing a crown, but an elaborate headdress crafted with jeweled leaves and flowers which clinked as she moved. As I stared at it—enthralled—a bud unfurled, blossoming into an amethyst orchid. Over her fingertips glinted pointed gold sheaths, curved as the claws of a hawk. The silver embroidery on her violet robe caught the fading light streaming through the windows. Unlike my mother's delicate and calm aura, hers was strong, pulsing with heat. She was dazzling, but her glossy lips against her white skin made me think of freshly spilled blood on snow.

As befitting her exalted position, the empress had not come alone. Six attendants stood behind her—along with a tall immortal man, his complexion darker than the rest. Flat pieces of amber adorned his black hat, his inky robes were fastened with a bronze sash, and white gloves covered his hands. I knew nothing of the Celestial Court, but the way he carried himself seemed to indicate he was of a higher rank than the others. Yet there was something about him I did not like, and as his pale brown eyes sliced across the room, I recoiled, pressing my back against the wall.

After a brief pause the empress spoke again, her voice now

cooler than a piece of unworn jade. "Chang'e, a peculiar shift was detected in the energy here. Are you cultivating a secret power or harboring a forbidden guest, violating the terms of your imprisonment?"

I stiffened, my shoulder blades clenching at the way she spoke. An eagerness seemed to coat each word as though she reveled in the idea of my mother's wrongdoing. Empress or not, how dare she speak this way? My mother was the Moon Goddess, worshipped and loved by countless mortals! How could she be a prisoner? This place was more than our home; it was her domain. Who lit the lanterns each night? Who did the trees sway and sigh for as she walked past? How could she do anything here that wasn't her right?

"Your Celestial Majesty, there must be some misunderstanding. My powers are weak, as you are aware. And no one else is here. Who would dare come?" my mother replied steadily.

"Minister Wu. Share your discovery," the empress commanded.

Footsteps shuffled forward. "Earlier today a significant shift in the aura of the moon was detected. Unprecedented, in all my years of study. This can be no coincidence."

In his smooth voice, I sensed an undercurrent of excitement. Did he relish my mother's troubles, as the empress seemed to? Anger seared me at the thought, despite my prickling unease. That rush in my veins earlier when I had touched the lights, the whispering in the air . . . had that somehow drawn them here?

"I hope our leniency has not made you bold," the empress hissed. "You were fortunate before, to have been imprisoned here in comfort for stealing your husband's Elixir of Immortality. You escaped the lightning whip and the flaming rod then.

But that will change if we discover you're engaging in further deceit. Confess now and we *might* be merciful," she lashed out, shattering the tranquility of our home.

My fist flew to my mouth, smothering my gasp. I had never asked my mother how she ascended to immortality, sensing it caused her pain. Yet ever since I read the tale of the sunbirds, one question kept winding through my mind: Where was my father? To hear he had been bestowed the elixir, and my mother was accused of stealing it . . . something twisted in my gut. *The empress was wrong,* I told myself fiercely, burying a treacherous kernel of doubt.

My mother neither flinched nor denied these vile accusations. Was she accustomed to such treatment from the empress? As I peeked into the room again, she folded over to press her forehead and palms to the floor. "Your Celestial Majesty. Minister Wu. Perhaps this phenomenon was caused by the recent alignment of the stars. The Azure Dragon's constellation has entered the path of the moon, which may have distorted our auras. When it passes, things should return to normal." She spoke like a scholar who studied the skies, though I knew she had no interest in such matters.

A long silence followed, punctured by a rhythmic tapping— the empress's pointed gold sheaths digging into the soft wood of the armrest. Finally, she rose, her attendants gathering behind her.

"That may be so, but we will come again. You have been left alone for far too long."

I was glad for them to leave, despite the threat that lurked beneath the empress's tone like a silk cord yanked tight. Unable to bear listening to more, I crept back to my room and lay on the bed, gazing out through the window. The sky had darkened into the elusive violet-gray of dusk, when the last of day gives way to night. My mind was numb, though I still sensed when those unfamiliar auras faded away. Moments later, my mother pulled the doors apart, her face whiter than the stone walls.

My doubts vanished. I did not believe the Celestial Empress. My mother would never have betrayed my father. Not even for immortality.

I scrambled up from the bed, coming to her side. I was almost as tall as her now. "Mother, I heard what the empress said to you."

She threw her arms around me, clutching me tight. Against her shoulder, I sagged with relief that she was not angry, though her body was tense with strain.

"We don't have much time. The empress could return at any moment with her soldiers," she whispered.

"What can they do? We did nothing wrong." My stomach roiled, an unpleasant sensation. "Are we prisoners? What did the empress mean about the elixir?"

She leaned back to look into my face. "Xingyin, you're not a prisoner here. But I am. The Celestial Emperor bestowed the Elixir of Immortality upon your father, for killing the sunbirds and saving the world. Houyi did not take it, though. There was just enough for one and he did not want to ascend to the skies without me. I was with child, our happiness seemed complete. And so, he hid the elixir, only I knew where."

Her voice broke then. "But my body was too weak to bear you. The physicians told us that you . . . that we would not survive the birth. Houyi did not want to believe them, he did not want to give up—bringing me to one after the other, searching for a different prognosis. Yet deep down, I knew they spoke the truth." She paused, a tautness around her eyes like she was reaching into her memories, those which hurt. "When he was called to battle, I was left alone. The pains began then, far too early, in the deep of night. Such agony tore through my body, I could barely cry out. I was so afraid of dying, of losing you."

As she fell silent, the question burst from me, "What happened?"

"I took the elixir from its hiding place, uncorked its stopper, and drank it."

In the stillness of the room, all I could hear was the beating of my own heart. My hands were no longer warming my mother's but were as cold as hers.

"Do you hate me, Xingyin?" she asked in a shaking voice. "For betraying your father?"

The empress's words were true. For a moment I could not move, my insides curling at the revelation. If my mother had not taken the elixir, perhaps we might have survived. My family, unbroken. Yet I knew how much she loved my father, how greatly she mourned his loss. And no matter what, I was grateful to be alive.

I swallowed the last of my hesitation. "No, Mother. You saved us."

Her gaze was distant, veiled in memory. "Leaving your father . . . oh, how it hurt. Though I must admit I did not want to die. Nor could I let *you* die. Only later did I learn that gifts from the Celestial Emperor came with unseen strings. That such decisions were not for mortals to make. The emperor was enraged that it was *I* who became immortal instead of your illustrious father. The empress accused me of using trickery to obtain immortality which I had not earned."

"Did you explain?" I asked. "Surely if they knew it was to save us—"

"I dared not. The empress seemed hostile, as though she bore some grudge against your father. She even accused him of ingratitude for spurning the emperor's gift. I knew then, she had sought to punish rather than reward him for killing the sunbirds. She would not hesitate to harm you. How could I tell them of your existence? To shield you from their wrath, I kept your birth a secret. I confessed my theft. As punishment, I was exiled to the moon—an enchantment cast upon me which binds me here for eternity. I cannot leave this place, no matter how much I want to." In a low voice, she added, "A palace you cannot escape is a prison nonetheless."

I struggled to breathe, my chest heaving like a fish flipped out of the water. I had thought our lives so peaceful, so safe from all the dangers in my books. To learn we had incurred the wrath of the most powerful immortals in the realm shook me to my core.

"But why did the empress come today, after all this time?"

"Our auras emanate from our lifeforce, the core of our magic—those lights you see in your mind. Since you were born, we did our best to conceal your power. Despite our efforts, the empress sensed you today."

My throat closed tight. "I didn't know. This is all my fault." How stupid and reckless I had been! Because I was bored I had ignored my mother's warning, broken my promise, and hurled us into the gravest of danger.

"I am to blame, too. I told you *not* to reach for your magic, but I should have explained why—that it might alert the Celestial Kingdom to your presence." She sighed. "It would have happened eventually; with every year you grow stronger. If they find you, our punishment will be severe—I have no doubt. I fear less for myself, but what they would do to *you*, an immortal child who was never meant to be."

"What can we do?"

"The only thing we can. You must leave this place."

Fear glazed my skin like ice forming over a lake. To never see my mother again . . . I was suddenly afraid to let go of her. "Can't I stay with you? I'll hide. Train me, so I can help."

"We can't. You heard the empress's words. They will be watching us even more closely now. It's too late."

"Maybe you convinced them, maybe they won't come back." A desperate plea, a childish hope.

"I may have bought us a little time. But the empress would not have come on a whim. They will return. And soon." Her voice thickened, clogged by emotion. "We can't protect you. We're not strong enough."

"But where will I go? When will I see you again?" Each word was a blow, giving shape to the forming nightmare.

"Ping'er will bring you to her family in the Southern Sea." She spoke brightly now, as though trying to convince us both. "I hear the ocean is beautiful. You will have a good life there, free from the cloud that hangs over us."

Ping'er had shared with me all she knew of the lands beyond, stirring my imagination, which hungered for adventure. The great sea was divided into four domains stretching from the eastern shore to the southern ocean, from the cliffs in the west to the waters in the north. I had been transfixed by her tales of the creatures who lived in the glittering cities underwater or upon the golden shores. How I had dreamed of exploring them.

Yet *never* had I imagined fleeing my home to do so. What use were adventures when there was no one to share them with?

My mother's hand closed around mine, dragging me back to the present. "You must never tell anyone who you are. The Celestial Emperor has informants everywhere. He would take your very existence as an unforgivable insult." She spoke urgently, her eyes boring into mine until I choked out my promise to her.

Leaning toward me then, she fastened something around my neck. A gold necklace with a small jade disc. It was the color of spring leaves, with a carving of a dragon on its surface. My fingers rubbed the cool stone, feeling a thin crack in the rim.

"This belonged to your father." Her eyes were as dark as a moonless night. "Don't tell anyone who you are. But never forget either."

She held me close, stroking my hair. I kept my head down—cowardly—not wanting to see her leave, wishing this moment could last forever. Her knuckles brushed my cheek once, and then there was nothing except an aching emptiness.

Sinking onto the floor, I wrapped my arms around my knees. Oh, how I wanted to scream and howl, and beat my fists against the ground. My hand flew to my mouth, muffling my hoarse sobs, but my silent tears . . . I let them stream down my face. In the single night it took the moonflower to bloom and wither, my life had been upended. My path, which had seemed a straight road, had taken a turn into the wilderness—and I was lost.

The room was dark, night had fallen. The moon was still cloaked in shadows as the lanterns had yet to be lit. Moonrise would be late in coming tonight.

Urgency jolted me into action. I did not wish to be discovered if Mother and Ping'er would be punished. While death was rarely inflicted upon immortals, the empress's threats of lightning and fire made my body clench in terror.

Ping'er helped me wrap my belongings into a wide piece of cloth. "Not too many, and nothing too fine to avoid arousing suspicion." Her eyes were rimmed red, but seeing my stricken expression, she added, "You'll be safe in the Southern Sea, as well-hidden as one star in the heavens. My family will look after you and teach you all you need to know."

She knotted the ends of the cloth together, forming a bag that she slung over my shoulder. "Shall we go?"

I did not want to. Yet numb to everything, I nodded. What else could I do? I could not even blame the vagaries of fate when it was *I* who had brought this upon us.

As Ping'er and I hurried through the entrance, heading east into the osmanthus forest, I glanced back, one last time. Never had my home seemed more beautiful than in this moment when I was pressing each curve, each stone into my mind. The thousand lanterns illuminated the soil, the silver roof tiles reflected the stars. And on the balcony where I had stared at the world below, there stood a slender figure in white.

My mother's gaze was not fixed on the Mortal Realm, but on me, her fingers lifted in farewell. Ignoring Ping'er's urgent tug on my sleeve, I sank to my knees, folding myself over to press my forehead to the soft earth. My lips moved in a silent vow: that I would return, that I would set my mother free. I did not know how, but I would try with everything that was in me. This would *not* be our end. As I followed Ping'er toward the cloud which would carry us away, pain struck my heart so sharp and clear—it fractured—only kept whole by a slender thread of hope.

2

I inhaled the bracing air, so fresh yet hollow without a trace of spice. As the cloud darted through the sky, I stumbled, grabbing Ping'er's arm. How eerie the night was without the lanterns' glow. Only this morning, fear had been a foreign emotion to me, and now I was choked with it. Fortunately, the cloud's dewy folds did not give way beneath my feet, but was as firm as the ground—if not for the surging wind all around.

It would be a long journey to the Southern Sea— beyond the Celestial Kingdom, past the lush forests of the Phoenix Kingdom. Farther than the Golden Desert even, the vast crescent of barren sand that bordered the feared Demon Realm. How would I ever find my way home? It struck me then, perhaps they did not think I ever would.

A sea of lights glimmered in the distance, drawing me from my bleak thoughts.

"The Celestial Kingdom," Ping'er whispered.

As a sudden gust sprang up, she glanced over her shoulder, the color draining from her face. I whirled, my gaze probing the night. A large cloud soared toward us, the shadowy forms of

six immortals upon it. Their armor gleamed white and gold, although their features were obscured by the dark.

"Soldiers!" Ping'er gasped.

My heart hammered. "Are they searching for us?"

She pulled me behind her. "They wear Celestial armor. They
must be here at the empress's command. Stay down! Hide! I'll
try to outrun them."

I pressed myself down as flat as I could, burying myself in
the cool tendrils of the cloud. Part of me was glad to not see the
soldiers, and yet my skin crawled with dread of the unknown.
Ping'er's eyes were closed as a thin stream of light shot from her
palm. Until tonight, I had never seen her use magic—perhaps,
there had been no need for it before. Our cloud dashed onward,
but all too soon slowed again.

Sweat beaded her skin. "I can't make it go faster; I'm not
strong enough. If they catch us . . . they'll discover who we are."

"Are they near?" I twisted to peer behind, wishing I had not.

Steel glinted from the soldiers' hands, drawing ever closer.
Soon, they would overtake us. Someone might recognize Ping'er,
questions would be asked. I was a clumsy liar, without the practice which welled from need—one stern look from my mother
was enough to spill the truth from my tongue. Monstrous visions crowded my mind: of soldiers storming through my home,
dragging my mother away in chains. A crackling whip of lightning lashed across her back, splitting her skin as blood spattered
the white silk of her robe. I gagged, hot bile rising in my throat.

My nails dug into the flesh of my palm. I could not let them
catch us. I could not let my mother and Ping'er be hurt. But
weak as I was, there was only one thing I could think of, which
might very well be the last thing I ever did.

Gritting my teeth until they ached, I forced the words out. "Ping'er, set me down here."

She stared at me as though I had lost my mind. "No, this is the Celestial Kingdom! We must reach the Southern Sea. We must—"

My calm shattered. I tugged her arm with a frantic strength, pulling her down. "We can't outrun them. Once they capture us, they'll punish us all. I . . . I think we should split up. You must stay on the cloud; I can't control it. Ping'er, at least this way we have a chance!" What choice did we have? None which might give us both a hope of escaping. Yet, try as I might, I could not stop myself from trembling.

She shook her head, but I pressed on. "I'll be safe in the Celestial Kingdom, as long as they don't realize who I am. I promised Mother I wouldn't tell anyone, and I won't. I'll find someplace to hide. Maybe you can outrun the soldiers without me?" My words fell out in a rush. In a moment it would be too late, the decision wrenched from us.

Fire blazed through the night, streaking toward us. It struck, our cloud shuddering as it swerved sharply. Heat flashed over my skin as Ping'er raised her hand, gleaming with light which extinguished the flames. With a cry, she fell beside me.

"They're attacking," she said in disbelief, even as she pressed her glowing palms into the cloud, speeding it along.

Terror gripped me but I could not succumb. Not now, when every second mattered. "Ping'er, it's the only way. We can't let them catch us." I spoke firmly, urgently—no longer a child pleading to be heard. "This is my choice, too."

Something hardened over her face then, a grim determination. She pointed to a thick cloudbank in the distance. "Over there—I'll drop down as low as I can. I'll shield you from the fall."

Despite her reassuring words, something unsettled me. Her breathing came harsh and labored. Her skin was damp to my touch. Was she sick? Impossible. Immortals did not suffer such ailments. "Ping'er, are you hurt? Did the fire—"

"Just a little tired. Nothing to worry yourself over."

I rolled on my side, peering over the edge as the cloud hurtled on. My mind leapt to the perils ahead—beyond the emptiness beneath, to those glittering lights weaving across the darkness. Beautiful. Terrifying. Scrambling up, I threw my arms around Ping'er, hugging her tight. Wishing I did not have to let go. Wishing for so many things, none of which would ever come to pass.

She clutched me with a raw desperation as we dove into the cloudbank. Droplets of icy water brushed my skin, the moisture clinging to my clothes. As we plunged lower, the chill bit deep, right into my bones. My legs quivered as I uncoiled them to stand. Ping'er's skin was like ash gone cold as she wrapped an arm across my shoulder. The air shimmered as a feathery tingle glided over me.

"The shield will cushion your fall. But you might still feel pain and you must be careful at all times." Her hands shook as she slung my small bag over my arm.

"Will you try to return? Once the danger passes?" I clung to this frail hope, trying to gather the scraps of my courage. Trying not to fall apart.

Tears pooled in her eyes. "Of course. But if I don't—"

"I'll find my way back. One day, when it's safe to," I said quickly, to assure us both.

"You will. You must, for your mother." She drew a sharp breath. "Are you ready?"

I was wound so tight I thought I might snap. No, I would never be ready . . . to leap into this unknown, to sever this final cord to my home. But if I didn't leave now, if I yielded to my clawing panic, if I let myself sink into the shadow of doubt— what little resolve remained would vanish. Facing her, I forced my stiff legs to take a step back to the edge. I would rather see her a hundred times over than the gaping hollow below.

"Now!" She cried out in a sudden burst of strength, her eyes blazing.

My legs staggered back—just as Ping'er's head rolled to the side and she collapsed into a crumpled heap upon the cloud. But I was falling, too, through the black void of the sky. The wind struck all thought from me, swallowing the cry that erupted from my throat, whipping my face and limbs until they were raw. My clothes sucked forward in a cloud of silk. I could not breathe through the air slamming against me, my lungs afire. A roaring in my ears blocked out everything except my pounding heart.

Yet ahead of me, shrinking to a speck was Ping'er's cloud, gone still. Her body was huddled where she had fallen. Had she fainted? *Move!* I screamed in a soundless cry, as the soldiers raced toward her. Terror shriveled my insides as I stretched out my hands—a futile gesture—grasping wildly at . . . at something within me. My skin tingled, hot then cold, as a glittering surge of air hurtled across the emptiness toward Ping'er's cloud. It shimmered brightly, before bolting away, vanishing into the distant horizon.

I crashed into the ground, pain erupting across my body. The air knocked from my chest, I could only lie there as tears flowed from my eyes, mingling with the sweat that slicked my skin. A weariness gripped me. As my fingers grasped soft grass beneath me, I drew a trembling breath, the scent of flowers filling my nostrils. Sweet, yet I was numb to it. Pressing my palms to the ground, I pushed myself up—sore and aching—but otherwise unharmed. Ping'er's enchantment had shielded me from the worst of the fall.

I thought I was saving her, but she had helped me get away, careless of her own safety. Had she escaped? Was my mother safe? Was *I*? My breaths came short and fast—I was drowning, struggling for air. Immortals did not suffer from illnesses or old age, but we could still be hurt by the weapons, creatures, and magic of our realm. Fool that I was, I never imagined such dangers would touch us. And now . . . I curled into a tight ball, arms wrapped around my knees, a thin, keening wail slipping from me like that of a wounded animal. *Stupid*, I cursed myself again and again for bringing this upon us, until at last I clamped my lips shut to muffle the sounds.

I did not know how long I lay there, my throat racked raw with swallowed grief. And yes, I feared for myself, too, as thoughts of cruel soldiers and vicious beasts crowded my mind. Who knew what lurked in the dark? I was unraveling, a tangled wreck, but then a beam of light fell across me. Lifting my head, I stared at the moon—the first time I had seen it from afar. Beautiful and luminous, and comforting, too. I breathed easier, finding solace in the thought that as long as the moon rose each night, I would know my mother had lit the lanterns and was well. A memory crept into my mind, of her walking through the forest, her white robe gleaming in the dark. My bruised heart cramped with longing, but I steeled myself against sinking into the abyss of self-pity again.

Bright flickers from below caught my eye, shimmering lights dancing within their inky depths. Were these the ones I had glimpsed from above? Only then did I realize the ground was like a mirror, a reflection of the stars weaving across the night. Their unfamiliar beauty seared me, a stark reminder that I was no longer home. I slumped back down, clasping my arms across my body. Staring at the moon until my pain subsided and I finally fell into a dreamless sleep on the cold, hard ground.

SOMEONE WAS PATTING MY arm. Was it my mother? Had all this been a terrible dream? Hope flared, shattering the haze of slumber. My eyes opened, blinking in the brightness of day. The swirling lights had vanished and reflected in their place were the rosy clouds of dawn.

A woman crouched beside me, a basket by her side. Her hand, which rested on my elbow, was as warm and dry as the surface of a paper lantern.

"Why are you sleeping here?" She frowned. "Are you all right?"

I lurched up, suppressing a gasp from the ache in my back. I could barely manage a nod to her question, numb from the memories which crashed over me.

"Be careful here. You should go home. I heard there was some disturbance last night and soldiers are patrolling the area." She picked up her basket, rising to her feet.

My insides knotted. *Disturbance? Soldiers?* "Wait!" I cried, unsure of what to say, yet not wanting to be left alone. "What happened?"

"Some creature broke through the wards. The guards gave chase." She shuddered. "We've had fox spirits in recent years. Though I heard this might have been a Demon, trying to snatch Celestial children for their evil arts."

One of those monsters from the Demon Realm? It hit me, then, that it was *I* the guards were searching for. That I was the supposed Demon. I would have laughed aloud had I not been stricken with fear. Ping'er must not have been aware of the wards. "Did they catch anyone?" My voice came out feeble and thin.

"Not yet, but don't worry. Our soldiers are the finest in the realm. They'll capture the intruder in no time." She gave me a reassuring smile, before asking, "What are you doing here at this hour?"

I sagged with relief. Ping'er had gotten away! Yet I must have lain here for hours and she had not come back. That gale which had burst through the skies, sending her soaring away—did it take her too far?

A thought nudged me. Had that power, somehow, come from *me*? Could I do such a thing again? No, how ridiculous to think so. Besides, nothing good had come of my magic so far, and I could not risk drawing any attention to myself. I started, realizing the woman was staring at me, her earlier question left unanswered. She did not suspect me because she expected some fearsome beast or fiend, but I dared not give her any reason to doubt me now.

"I have nowhere to go. I . . . I was dismissed from the household I worked in. I fell, and fainted." My words were clumsy, my tone halting. My tongue unused to uttering such brazen lies.

Her face softened. Perhaps she sensed my misery, spilling from me like a river swollen with rain. "By the Four Seas, some of these nobles are so ill-tempered and selfish. There now, it isn't so bad. You'll soon find another place." She cocked her head to one side. "I work at the Golden Lotus Mansion. I hear the Young Mistress is looking for another attendant, if you're in need of a position."

Her kindness was a warmth in the winter of my misery. My mind raced. Wandering alone by myself would surely arouse suspicion. I wasn't sure how I could think of such mundane things, but something hardened inside me. Grief was a luxury I could ill afford after wallowing in it half the night. If I fell apart now, it would all have been for nothing. I would find a place here and somehow, I would make my way home—whether it took me a year, a decade, or a century.

"Thank you. I'm grateful for your kindness." I bent from my waist in a graceless bow, as we never stood on such ceremony at home. It seemed to please her as she smiled, motioning for me to follow her.

We walked the rest of the way in silence, past a grove of bamboo trees and across a gray stone bridge that arched over a river, before arriving at the gates of a large estate. A black lacquered plaque was displayed just below the roof of the entrance, gilded with the characters:

金莲府

GOLDEN LOTUS MANSION

It was a sprawling estate, a cluster of interlinked halls and spacious courtyards. Red columns held up curved roofs of midnight blue tiles. Lotus flowers floated upon the ponds, their fragrance heady and sweet. I followed the woman through long corridors lit by rosewood lanterns, until we reached a large building. Leaving me by the doorway, she approached a ruddy-faced man and spoke to him. He nodded once, before coming toward me. I stood straighter, instinctively smoothing out the creases in my robe.

"Ah, this is well timed!" he exclaimed. "Our Young Mistress,

Lady Meiling, admonished me just last night for not having found her a replacement. Although one wonders why she can't make do with three attendants," he muttered, as he fixed me with an appraising stare. "Have you served in a large household before? What are your skills?"

I swallowed hard, thinking of my home. I had not been idle, helping out whenever I could. "Not as large as this one," I finally ventured. "I would be grateful for any position you can offer. I can cook, clean, play music, and read." My skills were far from impressive, but my answer seemed to satisfy him.

The next few days were spent learning my tasks, from how to brew Lady Meiling's tea to her liking, to preparing her favorite almond cakes, and caring for her garments—some adorned with such exquisite embroideries they seemed to quiver beneath my touch. Other duties included polishing the furniture, washing the bedding, and tending to the gardens. I was kept on my feet from dawn till night, maybe because I had no powers to speak of that might have eased my chores.

It was the rules here which chafed more than the labor: dictating the depth of my bows, requiring me to hold my tongue until spoken to, to never sit in my mistress's presence, to obey her every command without hesitation. Each rule ground my pride a little more into the dirt, widening the gulf between mistress and servant—a constant reminder of the inferiority of my position, and the fact I was no longer home.

These might have stung more, yet my heart was already leaden with grief, my mind sunken with worries far greater than aching feet or palms scraped raw. And in a way, I was glad my days were crammed even with such drudgery, leaving me little time to dwell on my misery.

When the chief steward finally deemed my performance satisfactory, I was assigned to Lady Meiling, along with her other attendants with whom I would be sharing a room. She was supposedly a demanding mistress, but I hoped among the four of us we might suffice. When I arrived with my bag, the other attendants were getting dressed, slipping on willow green robes over their white inner garments. One of the girls helped another tie a yellow sash around her waist. A pretty girl with dimples slid a brass lotus-shaped hairpin into her hair, which all of us were required to wear. They were a lively trio, chattering among themselves with easy familiarity. Despite the misery that weighed on me, a spark kindled in my chest. Perhaps I finally had the opportunity to make the friends I had long wished for.

The girl with the dimples swung toward me. "Are you the new girl? Where are you from?"

"I . . . I . . ." The story Ping'er had helped me concoct flew out of my head. Under the weight of their stare, heat rushed into my cheeks.

The others giggled, their eyes gleaming as rain-washed pebbles. "Jiayi," one of them called to the girl with the lotus pin. "She seems to have lost her voice."

Jiayi's stare raked me, her mouth curling as though seeing something which displeased her. Was it my plain hairstyle or the lack of ornaments dangling from my waist, wrists, and neck? Or was it that I lacked her poise, her assurance of her place in this world? All of which heralded the simple truth that I was an outsider, that I did not belong.

"What do your parents do? My father is the chief guard here," she declared with a distinct air of superiority.

My father slew the suns. My mother lights the moon.

That would wipe the smug expression from her face, yet I stifled the reckless impulse. A moment's satisfaction was not worth being branded a liar or thrown into a cell. Not to mention the danger to my mother and Ping'er, if they believed me.

"I have no family here," I said instead. A safe answer, though one which would earn me more of their contempt—I could already see it in the looks they exchanged, now they knew I had no one to protect me.

"How dull. Where did the steward find you? Off the street?" Jiayi sniffed, turning away. One by one the rest followed suit, talking among themselves once more as gaily as a flock of birds.

Ice glazed the pit of my stomach. I was not sure what they expected of me—only that, somehow, I had been found lacking. Unworthy. I walked woodenly to the far corner and lifted my bag onto the empty bed. The girls laughed, sharing a joke among themselves, their merriment driving the sting of my isolation deeper. As a lump formed in my throat, I hurried outside to gather my composure. I hated running away, but I would hate more crying in front of them.

Save your tears for something which matters, I told myself fiercely before returning to the room. They swung to me at once, the sudden silence jarring. Only then did I notice my cloth bag was unknotted, its contents strewn across the floor.

The air was thick with hostility as I crawled around to retrieve my possessions. Someone snickered, my ears burning at the sound. *Childish. Petty,* I seethed. But oh, how the humiliation seared! How privileged I had been to have only known love and affection until now. In my childhood, I had been terrified of the vicious monsters I read about in my books. Yet I was learning that as much to be feared was a scythe-like smile and words that cut deep. Never had I imagined people like this existed—those who took pride in treading on the dignity of another, those who thrived on the misery of others.

A small voice inside me whispered that I was indeed picked off the street, with no skills or connections to speak of. Perhaps if I held my tongue and kept my head down, they might eventually accept me as one of them. I was so tired, I just wanted to let things be. What did it matter if they won? Who cared for dignity or honor? It was nothing compared to all I had lost. But something within me cried out in protest. No, they would not shame me. I would not pander or flatter to gain their friendship. I would rather be alone than have friends as these. And though I felt lesser than an insect in this moment, I raised my chin to meet their stares.

Scorn was stamped across Jiayi's pretty features, yet there was unease, too, in the way her eyes flicked away. Did she expect me to slink aside and fade into the shadows? I was glad to have disappointed her. They had wounded me, but they would not have the satisfaction of knowing it. Their unkindness only had as much power as I gave it, and I would wrench back my tattered pride from beneath the soles of their feet because . . . it was all I had left.

3

The pavilion overlooked a courtyard of wisteria, the trees draped with clusters of lilac blossoms. I stood behind my mistress, Lady Meiling, who wore a pink brocade dress with gleaming flowers on the flowing sleeves and skirt. It was exquisite, the embroidered petals blushing a deep red before turning silver once more. My eyes widened. Lady Meiling possessed countless outfits, but this was a rare one. Only the most skilled seamstresses could enchant their creations to respond to its wearer's powers.

In addition to serving Lady Meiling and keeping her rooms and courtyard pristine, I was assigned the care of her garments—her robes, cloaks, and sashes of silk, satin, and brocade. At first, it seemed a pleasant if somewhat tedious task. But I soon learned I bore the brunt of her considerable displeasure whenever anything was misplaced, for the slightest scratch or speck of dust. To make matters worse, Jiayi selected our mistress's attire each day, adding to my workload with her never-ending stream of complaints and demands.

Perhaps sensing my distraction, Lady Meiling's lips pursed as she glanced my way. "Tea," she said curtly.

I hastened to refill her cup, the fragrant steam curling in the air.

A strong gust of wind blew through the courtyard, showering petals across the grass. Lady Meiling smoothed down her fluttering sleeves, her brow puckering as though vexed the wind had dared to disrupt her morning.

"Xingyin, fetch my cloak," she demanded. "The peach silk with the gold hem. Make sure you get the right one."

I bowed, fighting the urge to grind my teeth. Lady Meiling was young, but she possessed the imperious temperament of a thousand-year-old matriarch.

Just a few months had passed since I came here, but the warmth of being among loved ones had already faded to the echo of a memory. As promised, I kept my identity a secret—yet it was never far from my thoughts. At night, I listened out for the deep and steady breathing of my roommates before letting my mind drift to the shining halls of my home. That's when the nightmares began, of my mother and Ping'er being captured by soldiers. Of returning home to find it deserted and left in ruins. It was no wonder that I often awoke drenched in sweat, gasping through the cramp in my chest.

The other attendants disliked me, thinking my situation beneath theirs. Their contempt only steeled my spine, although they made life hard for me in countless petty ways: ruining the things in my care, mocking my every word, carrying untrue tales of me to our mistress. She sent me to kneel in the courtyard so many times, I felt I was one of the carved stone lions that guarded the entrance. I should not complain; this was better than imprisonment or being flogged with flaming whips. Yet more than the discomfort, it was the indignity which stung. Each time I sucked back my tears, swallowing them all until I could almost taste the difference between the bitter tang of humiliation and the salt of sorrow.

I hurried to Lady Meiling's room and searched frantically for her cloak. Her patience was short and her temper as incendiary as those firecrackers the mortals set off during festivals. Finally, I spotted it flung onto a chair. Picking it up, my relief vanished at the sight of the dark blot seeping through the fabric, the ink still glistening. Without thinking, I dropped it back down before it stained my skin.

"What's the matter?" Jiayi entered, a smile playing on her lips as she stared at the ruined garment. "If you don't look after our Young Mistress's clothes properly, you only have yourself to blame."

As her hand flicked out in a disdainful wave, I stiffened to see one of her fingers darkly stained.

"It was you," I said flatly. It should have come as no surprise.

Her cheeks reddened as she tossed her head. "Who would believe you anyway?"

My temper, simmering over the months of indignities, roiled over. "Such tricks don't make you better than anyone, they make you *less*," I hissed.

Jiayi took a step back. Was she afraid I might attack her? All I wanted was an apology, an admission of her guilt instead of hiding behind her mocking smiles and accomplices.

But I was denied even that, as Lady Meiling stormed into the room. "What's taking you so long? I'm almost frozen from the wind!" As her gaze slid to the cloak on the floor, her mouth fell open.

Jiayi recovered her composure first, her eyes wide and guileless as she picked up the garment and shook it out to better display the mark. "Young Mistress, Xingyin spilled ink on it. She told me not to tell you because she was afraid."

I breathed deeply, fighting for calm. Lady Meiling would never side with me against her favorite attendant. Not without proof—which I had, this time. "Jiayi is mistaken; I did no such thing. It was stained before I got here. Young Mistress is welcome to inspect us for stains."

Jiayi paled as she buried her hands into the silken folds of the cloak. She need not have bothered as Lady Meiling's eyes pinched tight, like a cat who had been stroked the wrong way. She disliked me, perhaps influenced by the stories the others told her.

"Jiayi is your senior in this household. Apologize to her at once. Then clean this and make sure it's spotless." She snatched the offending garment and tossed it at me. It struck my cheek, slithering down to pool by my feet.

I could not speak, my gut recoiling from the injustice. My arms remained wooden by my sides in defiance of her orders. A wild urge gripped me, to hurl the garment back at her. To pour freshly ground ink over Jiayi's own robe. To storm out . . . but here the fantasy ended. Where could I go?

As Lady Meiling's lips clamped into thin streaks, I dropped my head, forcing out an apology. Grabbing the cloak, I ran from the room, unsure how much longer I could contain myself.

I wanted to be alone, far from the chatter of the other attendants. I was beginning to understand why my mother preferred solitude during the times that burdened her heart. With a bucket and a bar of soap, I made my way to the nearby river. Clusters of bamboo grew all around, lush emerald green as they stretched proudly toward the sky. I sat by the riverbank, scrubbing the cloak, my chest so tight I could barely breathe. How I missed my home! The vow I had made to rescue my mother crushed me with its sheer futility. How could I ever help her, powerless as I was? My future stretched before me, lonely and bleak—a lifetime of servitude without hope of betterment. An unwanted tear welled up in the corner of my eye. I had learned to swallow them, inhaling sharply or blinking them away. But as I was alone, I let it trail down my cheek.

"Why are you crying?" A clear voice rang out, startling me.

I spun around, only now noticing the young man sitting on a rock a short distance away, an elbow resting on his raised knee. How could I have missed his aura, which pulsed in the air? Strong and warm, as bright as a cloudless noon. His dark eyes gleamed from beneath sweeping brows, and there was a radiance to his skin like it had been glazed by the sun. His long black hair was gathered up into a tail, spilling over his blue brocade robe, which was fastened around his waist with a silk belt. A yellow jade ornament swung from his sash, its tassel reaching to his knees as he jumped down and strode toward me. As he returned my gaze unreservedly, heat crept up my neck.

"It can't be that hard to clean some dirty clothes," he remarked, staring at the bundle in my hands.

"How would you know? It's a lot harder than it looks," I retorted. "And I would never cry over this. It's just . . . I miss my family." The moment the words slipped out, I bit my tongue. It was the truth, but what had possessed me to speak of such things to a stranger?

"If you miss your family, just go back to them. Why would you leave? Especially for work such as this." He gestured at the sodden garment dismissively, the corners of his lips curving up.

Was he mocking me? I'd had my fill of such treatment today.

His arrogance, the careless way he spoke, snapped my frayed nerves. What did he know of my troubles? Who was he to judge?

I cast a pointed look at his finery. "Not everything is that simple. Not everyone is as fortunate to do as they please. And I'll take no advice from someone who has never worked a day in his life."

His smile vanished. "Your attitude is rather insolent for an attendant." He sounded more curious than offended.

"Being an attendant doesn't mean I don't have my pride. The work I do is not a reflection of who I am." Turning my back to him, I scrubbed at the cloak with more vigor than before. I had wasted too much time already; Lady Meiling would be furious if I took too long—which would mean another night of kneeling on the cold, hard ground.

There was no reply and I thought he had left, tired of teasing me. Yet I twisted around to find him still there.

"Looking for me?" he laughed. As a heated denial rose in my throat, he added quickly, "Are you from the Golden Lotus Mansion?"

"How did you know?" I rose to my feet, wondering if he was an acquaintance of Lady Meiling.

He leaned forward then, his outstretched hand grazing the side of my head. I recoiled and swatted him away, knocking out the brass lotus pin from my hair. Before I could move, he bent down and picked it up from the grass. Without a word he wiped the pin against his sleeve, sliding it back into my hair. Dirt smeared his robe, which seemed not to bother him in the least.

"Thank you," I said, finding my voice. No, he could not be my mistress's friend. None of them would ever help an attendant.

"Your pin," he explained. "Don't all the attendants from there wear the same one?"

I nodded as I sat down, plunging the cloak into the stream again, cursing inwardly at the stubborn ink. Instead of leaving as I expected, he settled down beside me, his legs dangling over the edge of the bank.

"Why are you so unhappy?"

It had been so long since I had someone to talk to, someone willing to listen. My caution—so carefully cultivated here—thawed in the spark of his warmth. "Each morning when I awaken, I don't want to open my eyes," I began haltingly, unused to unburdening myself.

"Maybe you should sleep more if you're so tired."

He grinned but I scowled at him, in no mood for humor. How silly I was to think he might have cared. I grabbed the cloak and bucket to leave, as he scrambled to his feet.

"I'm sorry," he said stiffly, as though unaccustomed to apologizing. "I shouldn't have made fun of you when you were trying to tell me something important."

"No, you shouldn't have." Yet there was no rancor in my voice; his apology had blunted my resentment. It was heartfelt and kind, both of which I had encountered little of since leaving my home.

"If you're still willing to tell me, I would be honored to listen." He inclined his head with unexpected formality.

I snorted. "I would hardly describe this as an honor, but I appreciate your clumsy attempt at flattery."

"*Clumsy?*" It was his turn to scowl. "Did it work?" he asked, unrepentantly.

I could not suppress my smile. "Unfortunately."

As an awkward silence settled over us, I plucked a long blade of grass and wound it between my fingers.

"So, why do you dread each day?" he probed.

I tied a knot in the grass, and then another. It was easier to look at it than at him. "Because I have nothing to look forward to. I'm a failure and no matter what I do, how hard I try—nothing will ever change. Have you ever felt this way? Helpless?" At once, I chided myself for being a fool. Someone like him would never understand.

"Yes," he said simply.

"You do?" It was not that I doubted him, but he seemed to be one of those golden creatures who possessed more than their fair share of blessings. I knew nothing of him except his appearance and fine garments, yet his assured manner heralded privilege louder than bloodlines or titles.

He leaned back, resting his palms on the grass. "Everyone has their own troubles; some lay them bare while others hide them better. For myself, I do what I can to stretch the boundaries which chafe, even if it's just a little each time. Who knows when the slightest shift might make a difference?"

What he said struck a chord in me. I had berated myself for being weak, but had that been an excuse for doing nothing? These past months I had been a shadow of myself, hollowed by grief and self-pity. It was true that I possessed no powers to speak of, no friends or family to aid me. But I was *not* helpless, not even when those soldiers had chased Ping'er and me. I had taken a wild chance then, rather than await certain capture. So why not here? Where shelter came at the price of my dignity and dreams? I might not find a means out now, but through small nudges, little steps—I might carve my way after all, one that might lead me home.

A giddy relief swept over me, unexpected yet welcome. I was grateful to him, this odd-mannered man—at times offensive, yet courteous and kind. Oh, my situation was still dire but my spirit, while bruised, was unbroken. Perhaps all it had taken was finally being seen as a person again. As *myself*. To be reminded there was life beyond the Golden Lotus Mansion once I broke this cycle of misery, which I had somehow trapped myself into believing was my only path forward.

"I would leave tomorrow, but I have nowhere to go," I muttered fervently.

"What about your family? Your friends? Can't they help?"

My face shuttered. My mother and Ping'er were lost to me. "I have no one."

"Have your parents . . . passed?" he asked tentatively.

I shuddered at the thought, wishing I had not spoken of my mother. The mortals believed it courted bad luck to even speak such things aloud. Too many fears still shrouded my heart, of too many things which could go wrong.

His expression softened. "I'm sorry," he said gently, taking my silence as an answer.

Guilt lay heavy on my tongue. I did not want to lie to him, yet I could not tell him the truth. But worse still was claiming his sympathy which I had no right to. I opened my mouth to correct him, to utter the words that would dispel his compassion and leave him a disinterested stranger once more—but the sound of footsteps cut me off.

It was Lady Meiling, stalking toward me in a rustle of brocade. I leapt to my feet, fighting the familiar dread spreading through me. The air shifted with the heat of her aura, anger rolling off her in waves. I was well versed in the stages of her temper and from the scarlet mottling her cheeks, she was truly furious.

"Xingyin! How long does it take to clean one small stain?"

I winced at the sharpness in her tone, even as something

hardened along my spine. No apology sprang to my tongue, nor did I drop my gaze.

My silence seemed to enrage her further. "How dare you sit here, idling about and chatting to strangers?" She cast a scornful look at my new acquaintance, but then a strange and wonderful thing happened. Her face drained of color, a gasp sucked from her lips. Dropping to her knees, she cupped her hands together, holding them before her as she folded over in a formal bow—to the young man who had risen to stand beside me.

"Lady Meiling greets His Highness, Crown Prince Liwei." Her voice turned as sweet as honey. "If we had known you were honoring us with your presence, we would have prepared a proper welcome."

I would have followed her to sink to my knees, too, but all I could manage was to stare at him in disbelief. Why didn't he tell me who he was? *He had not lied either*, I reminded myself. Gone was the gentle young man I had confided in; in his place was a lord, secure in his might. He stood with his hands clasped behind his back, his expression aloof. If I had seen this side of him earlier, I might have fled.

He nodded to her with cool formality. "Lady Meiling, what has this attendant done to earn such a harsh rebuke?"

A soft sigh slid from her as her shoulders drooped. How frail and lovely she appeared right now, like a rose stripped of its thorns.

"Your Highness, I have always treated those who serve me as though they were my own family. What you witnessed was just a slip in my temper, caused by this attendant's repeated offenses."

Strangled sounds emerged from my throat which I choked

back down. Prince Liwei's expression was inscrutable. Did he believe her? And why did my spirits sink at the thought?

"How has she offended you?" His tone was pleasant, yet he did not give Lady Meiling permission to rise.

"She spoiled my favorite garment and tried to lie her way out of it."

"I did not lie!" I cried out, all decorum forgotten.

Prince Liwei's back stiffened a little. Did he regret being drawn into this trivial squabble? Such were my days at the Golden Lotus Mansion; an incessant stream of pettiness which wore away and gnawed at me. But no more, I decided. My encounter with the prince—inexplicable though it was—had reminded me that I did not need to meekly walk the path set before me. I would seek and use all the advantages I could find, even that of his position now.

"Did you see her ruin your garment?" he asked Lady Meiling.

She hesitated. "No, I heard from—"

His hand flew up, cutting her off. "Lady Meiling, you appear quick to cast blame without proper investigation." He took the cloak from me and looked at the blot, which all my efforts so far had failed to lessen. The air warmed as golden light streaked from his palm into the silk. The stain disappeared, the cloak drying as though it had never been wet.

His magic was strong! As was the ease with which it flowed from him. How I wished I could do that. The gale which had sprung up to snatch Ping'er to safety seemed a distant dream. If it had come from me, I had no idea how to do it again. When I closed my eyes, I still caught tantalizing glimpses of the lights within me, but they darted away the instant I reached out. My attempts were halfhearted at best—the sight of them stabbed me with fear and remorse. If only I had not drawn the empress's attention, I would still be home. Maybe Ping'er would have eventually taught me how to use my powers. I thought, bitterly, what use was magic when it was untrained? And there would be little hope of advancing my skills as long as I remained here.

In the Golden Lotus Mansion only the most favored servants were taught to channel their magic to perform rudimentary tasks, to aid their chores. The guards were instructed in attack and defense enchantments, from raising shields of protection to casting bolts of fire or ice. While the rest of us were expected to labor as the mortals did. Admittedly, most of the other attendants possessed a weak lifeforce, unlikely to ever become strong enough to ascend the hierarchy of immortals.

Perhaps it was true for me as well, but deep down, I did not think so. It was my powers which had drawn the Celestial Kingdom's attention. It had been my bane, but perhaps I could turn it into an advantage—if I found someone willing to train me.

Prince Liwei passed the now pristine cloak to Lady Meiling. "I trust there will be no need to berate anyone further." His tone hardened. "Any senior attendant in your household, or even you yourself, could have fixed this without resorting to these measures. Such behavior from a position of privilege does not reflect well upon you."

Two red spots burned in Lady Meiling's cheeks. A petty part of me relished watching her get reprimanded, but what would happen when the prince left? As a new voice rang out, that of Lady Meiling's father, my anxiety increased threefold.

"Your Highness." He hurried to where we stood, likely alerted to the Crown Prince's presence by a vigilant attendant. Sinking to his knees, he performed a formal obeisance, touching his brow to the ground. "If my daughter or this servant has offended you, I plead for your forgiveness."

"I was disappointed to see how Lady Meiling treats those in her household," the prince said. "Such behavior has no place in my court. When I return, I intend to rescind the invitation to your house for the selection of my companion."

I stifled a gasp. Lady Meiling had spoken of little but this, ever since she was chosen as a candidate. The Crown Prince had arranged this competition to choose a study companion, one who would learn alongside him. Was this what he meant by stretching the constraints which chafed him? Was he tired of his friends in the palace? It was said the prince wished to open the opportunity to the entire kingdom but was overruled. Now each candidate had to be sponsored by a noble household, who then proceeded to put forth only their kin.

Lady Meiling's father blanched. It would be a terrible humiliation to be struck off the list and there would be endless gossip as to why his daughter had been found wanting. "Please forgive her, Your Highness," he implored. "My daughter would be a true flower to grace your court, should she be fortunate enough to join it."

A bold idea formed in my mind. Audacious even, but I might never have such a chance again. To no longer be at the mercy of a capricious mistress, to study with Prince Liwei, to learn to harness my powers . . . my mouth went dry at the thought. Perhaps then, I could help my mother.

I sank to my knees, performing a clumsy bow. "Your Highness, please don't withdraw Lady Meiling's invitation. But—" The words stuck in my throat like a firmly lodged fish bone.

He waited, his patience calming my scattered nerves. My tongue darted over my lips as I gathered the courage to say, "I wish to participate, too."

Lady Meiling and her father spun to me, their eyes bulging.

To them, I was nothing, undeserving of such an honor. I wanted to sink through the ground, unused to putting myself forward this way—but Prince Liwei's opinion was the only one that mattered.

He blinked, seemingly taken aback for the first time since I met him. "Why?" he drew out the word.

Lady Meiling's father had hoped to knit closer ties with the royal family. There was even talk of her winning the prince's affection. I cared little for all that. It crossed my mind to flatter him, but I decided to speak from the heart. It was what I had done before I knew who he was. "Your Highness, it would be an honor to be in your company, but that is not why I want this—"

He tapped his chin, his lips twitching. "You *don't* want to be in my company?"

"No, Your Highness. I mean, yes! Yes, I do want to be in your company," I stammered. "But more than anything, I want to learn *with* you, from the greatest masters of the kingdom." Silently, I cursed my fumbling words. *He would refuse*, I thought in despair. But it would have been worse *not* to have tried.

He stilled as though weighing my answer. Finally, he said to Lady Meiling's father, "I will allow your daughter to keep her place, on one condition: that you sponsor this attendant's participation as well."

Hope soared in me like a kite swept up by the wind.

"Your Highness, she is just an attendant," Lady Meiling's father protested.

"What we do is not a reflection of who we are." Prince Liwei echoed my earlier words, his gaze steely beyond his years. "Sponsor them both or none at all."

"Yes, Your Highness." Lady Meiling's father bowed, as Prince Liwei walked away, disappearing into the bamboo forest.

A tense silence followed his departure. I picked up my things, intending to make myself scarce when Lady Meiling's father waved me over.

"How do you know the Crown Prince?" he demanded.

"I only met him today," I replied honestly.

He squinted at me, stroking his beard. "Why is he so interested in your well-being?" he wondered aloud, observing nothing in my appearance that might have prompted the Crown Prince's defense.

From the corner of my eye, I caught a glimpse of Lady Meiling's face, still red from fury and humiliation. Reluctant to salt her wound, I chose my words with care. "He saw me crying and I think he felt sorry for me." It struck me, then, this was probably the truth.

He nodded, dismissing me with a flick of his hand. Pity for someone like me was something he could comprehend.

I bowed and excused myself, my steps lighter than a gliding feather. I was no deluded fool; it would take a miracle for me to win. But there was a deep satisfaction in reaching out to grasp this opportunity. Even if I lost. Even if I was turned out of the Golden Lotus Mansion. This sliver of hope was a breath of fresh air in my stagnant existence. Spurred by new resolve, I walked back with my head held a little higher. I was no longer a child willing to drift with the tide—I would steer against the current if I had to. And if I won, by some miraculous stroke of luck, I would never be helpless again.

4

I found no rest in sleep, my mind plagued by visions of failure. Throwing the covers off, I rose to ready myself. All the candidates had been given a set of garments and a sandalwood tablet engraved with our names. I slipped on the apricot silk robe, tying the yellow brocade sash around my waist. Then a diaphanous coat, the shifting hues of dawn. Flowing sleeves grazed my wrists, the skirt coming down to my ankles. My fingers ran over the material, light and soft, with a subtle shimmer in its threads. I had not worn such fine silk since my home. Lacking the skills to try anything more elaborate with my hair, I pulled it into a tail that swung across my back.

Picking up the wooden tablet, I fastened it to my waist, tracing the characters of my name carved into it:

星银

Silver star, the constant companion to the moon. *Mother,* I thought, *I'll make you proud of me today.* I made my way to the doors, eager to escape the stony stares from the other girls who were just rising from their beds.

"Don't get too used to the Jade Palace. You'll be back here soon enough," Jiayi called out tauntingly.

I halted by the entrance, not turning around. "Thank you for your kind wishes, Jiayi," I said, in as pleasant a tone as I could muster. "When I return, it will be to pack my things. Do take care of Lady Meiling's garments better, in the meantime. For your own sake, be sure to keep them away from the inkstone."

I strode away, my back pulled straight—yet glad she could not see my face. Despite my bold words, a part of me was certain her mean-spirited prediction would hold true. However, since the day by the river, I was no longer content to feign indifference nor hold my tongue against insult.

Outside the mansion, it struck me that I did not know the way to the Jade Palace. Even if I could bring myself to ask Lady Meiling, she would never aid me. I raised my head to search the skies. The Jade Palace floated on a bank of clouds above the kingdom. It would not be hard to find.

Whenever I'd ventured outside before, I'd never had the time to linger. All around were the magnificent estates of the most powerful immortals of the realm. Some were built from rare woods with tiered roofs of glazed tiles, while others were crafted from polished stone with elegantly upturned roofs. Trees and shrubs abounded in jeweled tones of crimson and amethyst, emerald and vermilion. The Celestial Kingdom was like a garden in eternal spring; the flowers did not wither and the leaves did not brown. Today, the ground gleamed a brilliant blue, mirroring the clear heavens above as though earth and sky were one.

The stairway of pure white marble leading to the palace disappeared among the clouds. As I walked up the steps, gripping the railing, my eyes were drawn to the intricate phoenix carvings on its balusters. Reaching the top, I stilled at the sight. Amber columns held up a magnificent, three-tiered roof of grass-green jade. Gold dragons perched majestically in each corner, luminous pearls clutched within their jaws—so lifelike, I could almost feel the wind rippling through their manes. The white stone walls were flecked with crystals which glittered like stars against a sea of clouds. Flanking the entrance were bronze incense burners studded with precious gems, from which tendrils of sweet smoke curled.

An enormous plaque of lapis lazuli hung over the entrance, etched in gold with the characters:

玉宇天宫

JADE PALACE OF IMMORTAL HEAVEN

As a waiting attendant gestured at me, I followed him through the red-lacquered doors, trying not to gawk at the ceilings painted with flowers in cobalt, scarlet, and persimmon. We crossed winding corridors and large pleasure gardens, golden pavilions and lotus-filled ponds, before emerging in a courtyard teeming with immortals. I craned my neck to read the wooden plaque painted with the name of this place:

恒宁苑

COURTYARD OF ETERNAL TRANQUILITY

Although today, the residence of the Crown Prince was anything but tranquil. While the sun was not yet high, the air thrummed with immortal auras. All the other candidates had already gathered—cultivated and plucked from the most illustrious families in the kingdom. All eager to be planted in the Crown Prince's garden, just as I was, I admitted to myself. Although I felt as out of place here as a weed among the orchids, just as whenever I compared myself to my mother.

Beyond their lineage, the other candidates were undoubtedly bright, cultured, accomplished. *Powerful.* While we were all attired similarly, jade and gold gleamed from their hair, jeweled ornaments dangling from their waists. Their slippers were thickly embroidered with silk thread, some encrusted with lustrous pearls. Many stared at me curiously and when my eyes met Lady Meiling's, her lips puckered as though she had bitten into a sour plum. She turned away with a forced laugh, her words drifting to me as she made no attempt to lower her voice.

"That girl over there, the one who looks like a mortal peasant. She used to be my attendant." Lady Meiling paused, letting the gasps quieten before she continued. "The worst one I ever had, both stupid and dull."

"How did she get selected?" a slender man asked, glancing at me.

Her nose wrinkled. "She begged Prince Liwei for the chance, and he took pity on her. He probably only allowed it because he knew she could not win."

My fingers dug into the skirt of my robe, crumpling the delicate silk. She meant to wound me, to shake my confidence, perhaps. Little did she know how deep her jibes went. But I would give her no satisfaction, my desire to win hardening instead. I would feel no remorse for my supposed temerity in climbing above my station to reach for the prize. What did I care for such rules anyway? I was not brought up to revere their titles or rank, and I would certainly not start now—not when winning would transform my life, not just gild an already bright future.

A gong was struck, its brassy tone reverberating loudly, silence trailing in its wake. Attendants hurried into the courtyard, clearing the path to the raised dais in front of the pavilion where thirteen desks were arranged. An odd number, and I guessed I was the late addition. Whispers rustled through the crowd as the immortals sank to their knees, touching their foreheads to the ground. I followed suit hastily as the Crown Prince entered, accompanied by his mother and their attendants.

"All may rise."

The familiar sound of his voice calmed my nerves. As I rose, I glanced eagerly at the dais. Was this the same young man who had cleaned the dirt from my hairpin and listened to my troubles? A collar of gold gleamed at his neck, beneath a blue brocade robe embroidered with yellow dragons. A silvery glow emanated from their jaws, as though they were breathing mist and cloud. Flat links of white jade clasped his robe around his waist. His hair was drawn into an immaculate topknot, encased in a gold crown set with a large oblong sapphire. How grand, he looked. Majestic, even. And yet he was also just as I remembered, with his thoughtful expression and dark, intelligent eyes.

My gaze shifted to the brilliant vermilion robes of his mother beside him. The scarlet phoenixes on her garments stretched their graceful heads, their crests almost entangled in the long necklace of jade beads around her throat. As my gaze drifted up to her face, my blood froze to ice.

The Celestial Empress.

The one who had threatened and terrified my mother, forcing my flight from home. Anger sparked, thawing my fear, my emotions warring within. My fingers curled into tight fists as I forced my mouth into a bland smile. How senseless of me to have missed the connection! Was my mind dulled from grief and those months of sleepless nights? My instincts yelled at me to leave, but I could not reveal myself now. Besides, the empress did not have the slightest inkling of my identity. More importantly, necessity outweighed my fear—I *needed* this opportunity to have any hope of making something of myself. Even if it brought me closer to those I dreaded. Those I despised. Slowly I unclenched my hands, letting them hang limp by my sides.

At Prince Liwei's nod, the chief attendant called out, "For the first two challenges, all candidates will participate. Only the winners will move on to the third and final round. His Highness has determined that no magic is permitted; these are tests of skill, learning, and ability, of which he prizes most." He paused. "The first challenge will be the art of tea brewing."

I breathed out, feeling my tension ease. Part of me had feared being set some impossible task that I would fail before it began. But my relief was short-lived as the candidates hurried into the pavilion in a swirl of silk and brocade. I dashed to my assigned desk, trying to calm my thumping heart. I could brew tea, I had done so countless times before—for myself, my mother. Even for Lady Meiling.

Except, what was all this on the table before me? My head began to throb at the bewildering assortment of items. Over a dozen teapots in varying sizes, of clay, porcelain, and jade. A large tray was crammed with jars of tea leaves: black oolong curls, pearls of jasmine, and leaves of golden-brown and green. In a corner was a pile of bricks and cakes of pressed pu'er. Tiny porcelain bowls heaped with dried flowers were lined up beside them. I picked up a few items and lifted them to my nose—earthy and heady, flowery and sweet—the aromas only confounding me further. I could barely identify a few; Longjing tea, jasmine, and wild chrysanthemum, among them.

My spirits sank as I looked around. The other candidates were sniffing the teas expertly before making their selections. A few picked more than one type, perhaps disdaining a single blend as too humble? Those quickest were already pouring out their teas, while I had not even made my choice. Seizing a fragrant cake of pu'er, I pried off a wedge with a silver needle and dropped it into a porcelain teapot. I had little experience brewing this, but I heard the finest leaves were pressed into these forms and aged for years, decades even. As I waited for the water to boil, I glanced around again—only now realizing those who chose pu'er all used clay teapots, some tossing out the first steep. Struck by sudden doubt, I discarded my first choice, deciding to stick with what I knew best—my mother's favorite Longjing, the Dragon-Well tea. Steam hissed from the bronze kettle and quickly, I poured the boiling liquid over another tea set to warm it, to better awaken the flavor in the leaves. Without a pause, I tossed a fistful of the bright green leaves into the teapot and filled it with hot water. Replacing the lid, I waited impatiently for it to steep. Twenty seconds. No more, as I was almost out of time.

I poured the tea into a porcelain cup, a murky brown soup. My gut twisted as I lifted the lid to inspect the dregs. *Careless,* I cursed myself. In my haste, I had placed the Longjing into the same pot as the pu'er. When mixing teas, I had been cautioned to take care with the water temperature and the ratios to balance their flavors, whether delicate or strong. From the heavy and dull aroma emanating here, I had gotten it all wrong.

Someone cleared his throat—the chief attendant, waving me over impatiently. I was the only one who had not served my tea and now, there was no time to brew another. My hands were stiff as I carried the tray to Prince Liwei. With every step, my grand dream of distinguishing myself here faded further into oblivion. Worse yet, what if His Highness spat out my tea? The empress would be furious, I might be ejected from the competition at once—deemed as unworthy and unfit as everyone here believed me.

As I placed the tray before Prince Liwei, his eyes warmed in recognition, flicking down to the sandalwood name tablet by my waist. Without hesitation, he lifted the cup to his mouth and took a long sip. I was standing in front of him so only I saw the slight wrinkle across his brow, the quirk of his lips. It was gone in an instant, but my spirits plunged. There was no way I could imagine that to be an expression of pleasure. However, to my astonishment, Prince Liwei lifted my cup into the air.

"This one. I've never tasted such a unique blend before." He nodded to an attendant who recorded my name.

The Celestial Empress leaned forward. "Liwei, are you sure? It's such an odd color. Let me try it."

A shiver rippled down my spine. How well I remembered her voice, melodious yet sharp.

As Prince Liwei handed her the cup, it slipped from his fingers, striking the ground with a crash. The porcelain shattered, dark liquid pooling on the stone floor, the remnants of my unfortunate concoction. A crowd of attendants rushed forward to clean up the mess, but the empress ignored them, glaring at me as though it were I who had dropped it.

When the chief attendant announced me as the winner of the first challenge, I slumped with relief, taking no offense at the shocked whispers. For, despite Prince Liwei's words, I doubted my tea deserved the honor. Yet somehow, I was ahead in the competition and that was what mattered.

In front of the pavilion, a painting of flowering osmanthus

trees was unveiled for the second challenge. As the audience sighed in admiration, we were asked to compose a couplet inspired by the scene. I stifled a groan. It had been a long time since I'd held a brush, much less composed anything. I tried to conjure up elegant words and flowery phrases, but my mind remained as blank as the untouched paper before me. I closed my eyes, the smell of ink sharper in the dark—heavy, with a faint medicinal undertone. I could almost imagine myself back in my home, the cool air blowing through my window, rustling the thin sheets on my wooden desk.

It was years ago, when my mother had begun teaching me to write. I remember how her sighs had echoed through my ears. While she had been patient, I was a challenging student, particularly for the subjects that did not interest me.

"Xingyin, hold the brush firmer," she had admonished me for the tenth time. "A thumb on one side, your index and middle fingers on the other. Straight, don't let it slant down."

Only after she had been satisfied, did she allow me to dip the stiff, ivory brush hairs into the glossy ink. As I swirled it harder against the inkstone, she had warned, "Not too much. Your lines will be clumsy, the ink will bleed."

I had imagined the elegant characters I would form, but my enthusiasm soon waned after making the same wobbling stroke again and again. "What's the point of learning this?" I asked impatiently. "It's not like I'm going to become a scribe or scholar."

She had taken the brush from me then, drawing the character 永 in steady, precise movements: "Forever," the word composed of the eight brushstrokes from which all characters were formed. "You'll never grow if you only do what you're good at," she had said. "The most difficult things are often the most worthwhile."

Reluctant to leave the haven of my memory, I opened my eyes

slowly. The other contestants wrote with a frenzied calm, bent over in concentration. I stared at the painting, no longer thinking of what might please the judges, but how much I missed my mother until it hurt. Lifting my brush, I wrote the following lines:

花瓣凋零，芬芳褪尽，曾映骄阳，却落泥霜。

The blossoms fall, their sweet fragrance is lost,
Once warmed by the sun, now sunken in frost.

When my couplet was read aloud, there were a few nods and appreciative murmurs. Mine was far from the best, but I was just grateful to not have disgraced myself. After the empress selected Lady Lianbao's as the winner, I clapped along with the audience.

As the painting was carried away, several attendants entered, bearing large trays piled with food for the afternoon meal. I lost count of the staggering number of dishes as the tables heaved under platters of prawns simmered in golden butter, roasted pork, chicken braised with herbs, delicate soups, and vegetables artfully shaped into flowers. It smelled delicious yet I could only manage a few bites before my stomach churned in protest. I laid my chopsticks down, looking up to see Lady Lianbao pushing the food around her plate with as little enthusiasm. There was an incessant flow of chatter around us, but all I could think of was what would come after—the last challenge which only we would participate in. When our eyes met, I shot her a tentative smile, which she returned after a moment's hesitation.

After the plates and remaining food had been whisked away, the clang of the gong rang out once more. The chief attendant announced loudly, "For the final challenge, Lady Lianbao and Attendant Xingyin will each select an instrument to perform a song of their choice. The winner will be chosen by Her Celestial Majesty and His Highness."

My heart leapt. Finally, something I possessed some skill in! The desks had been cleared and a vast assortment of instruments laid out. Lady Lianbao bowed to the dais, before selecting the qin and taking her seat. She played a beautiful melody—a classic about the leaves in the mortal world changing their color from jade to russet—her fingers plucking the strings masterfully. While I admired her ability, my confidence dipped with each perfect note.

It was my turn. As everyone swung toward me, my palms broke out in a sweat. I wiped them against my skirt, trying to calm myself. I had only ever performed in front of my mother and Ping'er. A most amiable audience, a most forgiving one. With wooden steps, I made my way toward the center of the pavilion. My eyes darted over the zithers and lutes, glazing over the chime-bells and drums . . . but there was no flute. I paused before the qin, the only one familiar to me here. However, it was not my best instrument and Lady Lianbao had played it far better than I ever could. To select it would be to choose defeat, and a lifetime in the Golden Lotus Mansion would not bring me one step closer to my dream.

Grateful that the long skirt hid my shaking legs, I bowed to the dais. "Your Celestial Majesty, Your Highness. There is no flute here. May I play my own instrument?"

The empress pursed her lips. "The rules cannot be broken." Her tone was sharp with disapproval.

I kept my face lowered so she would not see my stifled fear and resentment. "Your Celestial Majesty, the rules only stated that I had to select an instrument to perform. It did not specify from where."

Someone gasped. I glanced up to see the chief attendant take a hasty step away.

The empress glowered as she tossed her head back, the jade beads around her neck clicking furiously. "You insolent girl, how dare you argue with me?"

"Honorable Mother, it's our mistake that no flute was provided," Prince Liwei interjected. "I don't see why it matters if she plays her own. Are not our instruments of equal standard to any other?"

The empress leaned forward as she addressed me in a chilling tone, "Your flute will be inspected. Should we discover any enchantment upon it, you will be whipped until you cannot walk for attempting to cheat."

"There will be no whipping today," Prince Liwei said tightly. One of his hands was clenched in his lap.

She did not reply, gesturing toward someone behind her. "Minister Wu, conduct the inspection."

An immortal with pale brown eyes stepped out from the crowd, the amber in his hat gleaming like drops of gold. It was him; the minister who had discovered the shift in the moon's energy, who had alerted the empress and brought her to my home. Perhaps he was merely a vigilant courtier, but my gut clenched at the sight of him. In my shock at seeing the empress, in the tumult of the day—I had not realized he was here, too.

I could feel the empress's gaze upon me, everyone was staring at me as I fumbled with the ties of my pouch. If they believed me nervous, I was glad for it—better that than the simmering fury which threatened to erupt. How dare she accuse me of cheating? Perhaps, in her mind, someone like me would have no scruples. Perhaps, I thought viciously, she only suspected me of what *she* was capable of herself.

I bowed, raising my arms to offer up my flute. An attendant rushed to take it and passed it to Minister Wu. His expression was one of bored disinterest, a far cry from the eagerness he had shown in my mother's troubles. Did he find today's proceedings tiresome? Did he resent being ordered around by the empress? Nevertheless, he performed his role admirably, inspecting my flute with meticulous care. How I hated seeing my precious instrument—my mother's gift—between his gloved fingers.

Finally, he turned to the empress. "There is no enchantment."

Her displeasure was evident in her curt nod. "Proceed," she ordered.

As the empress's attendant returned my flute, my fingers closed tight around it. I breathed deeply, trying to loosen the tightness in my chest, still burning with the humiliation of her accusation. Closing my eyes, I tried to shut out the indifferent strangers around me, searching for the melody I wanted—of a bird's desperate hunt for her stolen children, until she froze to death when winter came. One of sorrow, grief, and loss, to channel the emotions swirling through me. As a stillness swept over me, I lifted the flute, rejoicing in the familiar press of the cool jade against my lips. How I had missed this. The song began playfully, with joyous notes rippling through the air, soaring clear and pure. Slowly, the melody morphed into jagged uncertainty and terror, before plunging into the abyss of despair.

The last note faded. With trembling hands, I lowered the flute. Ping'er had praised my playing, but would it be deemed lacking here? I glanced up to find the empress white-faced and furious—surely, that was a good sign, though I could not read Minister Wu's expression. A clap rang out, joined by others, the sounds crashing together like thunder. A fierce gladness coursed through me that regardless of the outcome, I had tried my best.

Prince Liwei and the empress conferred for a long time. As the last performer of the day, I had remained in my seat before them and caught snatches of their conversation.

The empress tried her utmost to sway her son. "Lady Lianbao's heritage is impeccable. She is well-educated, intelligent, graceful, and musical. How can you prefer a mere attendant to her? She looks so common and that mark on her chin is a sure sign of an ill-temper."

I clasped my hands in my lap, squeezing my fingers together.

"Honorable Mother, if we chose someone based only on their heritage, there would be no need to hold this event today." His tone was respectful yet firm.

Silence hung in the air as they stared at each other. I saw little resemblance in their features, for which I was glad—a warmth to Prince Liwei's face, instead of the cold, stark planes of the empress.

Finally, she sighed, an exasperated sound. "Such a trifling matter does not merit my time. I expect you to obey us in more important concerns." Without another word, the empress rose and left the courtyard, her attendants hurrying after her.

When my name was announced, I did not hear the cheers and well-wishes. My heart swelled with relief, yet I still feared this was just a dream. Across the crowd, my restless gaze sought Prince Liwei's. Only after I saw his answering smile did I dare to hope, as the first flower springing forth after a long winter.

5

The sun was low in the sky by the time I packed my belongings at the Golden Lotus Mansion. I could have left the next day, but I had no reason to delay; there were no farewells to make, no one I would miss here. In the days after the competition, Lady Meiling and her other attendants had kept me busy with an endless stream of unpleasant and humiliating tasks. I would have liked to say that such maliciousness slid off me as water on oil, that the joy in my heart left no room for bitterness to fester. But I was neither so magnanimous nor forgiving. I had learned by now that nothing irked my tormentors as much as indifference. And so, I had smiled at their commands, bowed and complied, all the while imagining their dismay when I left for the palace, to never return.

As I walked up the white marble stairs which led to the Jade Palace, my feet were lighter than the clouds that drifted above. To my surprise, I found the chief attendant waiting by the entrance. His lips thinned in disapproval at the sight of me, or perhaps he did not appreciate the lateness of the hour.

"Her Celestial Majesty asked that I instruct you in your

duties." Without waiting for my response, he strode through the red-lacquered doors, leaving me to hurry after him.

Gripped by anxiety before, all I could recall was a blurred haze of vibrant color and exquisite beauty. Calmer today, I studied my surroundings, discovering that the Jade Palace was the size of a small city and laid out with methodical precision. The soldiers were housed in the outermost perimeter along the palace walls, while a little farther in were the rooms of the attendants and palace staff. Ringed by flowering gardens and carp-filled ponds was the Outer Court, the quarters of honored guests and select courtiers without an estate of their own. The Inner Court was where the royal family resided, their sprawling courtyards clustered around the heart of the palace: the Imperial Treasury, the Chamber of Reflection, and the Hall of Eastern Light.

Lost in this maze of winding paths, each hall and chamber with its own name and designated purpose, I recalled the simplicity of my home with a pang. While the grounds of the Pure Light Palace were vast, our needs were undeniably more modest with no courtiers to entertain, the uncomplicated meals which we prepared ourselves, and a wild forest in our backyard.

As we walked, the chief attendant droned on about the rules of etiquette. "You must kneel when you greet His Highness and whenever he issues you a command. At all other times, bow from your waist when he speaks to you. Always address His Highness using his title and never his name. If you have the good fortune to meet Their Celestial Majesties, kneel and press your forehead to the ground until they give you permission to rise. If you walk past someone of higher rank, stop and bow. Speak in a soft tone, dress neatly as befits your station—"

I listened attentively at first, but my attention soon wandered to the ornately carved ceilings and pillars along the corridor.

Gilded phoenixes were interspersed with crimson peonies and emerald-green leaves. The walkway cut through a garden which I longed to explore, shaded with magnolia and crabapple trees—

I stopped, realizing that I had lost sight of the chief attendant. Spinning around, I found him standing a short distance behind, his arms crossed over his chest as he glared at me with intense displeasure.

I bowed—low. While I was unfamiliar with the nuances of palace hierarchy, the chief attendant evidently believed himself my superior. "Thank you for your guidance," I intoned as respectfully as I could, all the while wondering how many rules I had missed, and if they were of any importance.

To my relief, he unfolded his arms and continued walking. "Should a noble have assumed this position, they would not reside within the palace, instead arriving each morning to accompany His Highness and returning home each evening. However, given your situation, we needed to make some adjustments." Here the chief attendant sighed as though *he* had made some onerous concession. "With these additional benefits in mind, in addition to your duties as Prince Liwei's learning companion, Her Celestial Majesty has commanded that you serve him as well."

I looked away to hide my confusion, aware of his watchful gaze on me. Was I a glorified attendant, or a disgraced companion? This was not the prize I had won, and I did not think another would be treated so—certainly not Lady Lianbao. Did the empress hope I would take offense and refuse? I was not as weak-willed as that. Despite the shade she had cast over my achievement, I would not storm out in a fit of pique. After serving Lady Meiling, this was no hardship. Moreover, I preferred to earn my keep instead of feeling indebted to Their Celestial

Majesties. Perhaps I should have resented my reduced status more, but for this opportunity I would sweep the floors here every day if I had to.

"I would be honored to serve His Highness," I said.

The chief attendant pursed his lips. "You are honored indeed. Do not forget that. You are to awaken each morning before His Highness rises and help him to dress. You will prepare his tea and arrange his meals. While at mealtimes you may dine with His Highness, serve him before yourself. Do not eat until he takes the first bite. You will accompany him to his classes and training, where you will study alongside him—placing his learning needs above your own, of course."

"Of course," I repeated tightly, biting back the choicer words that sprang to my tongue.

Fortunately, we soon entered the Courtyard of Eternal Tranquility. How serene it was, without the crowd of spectators and anxiety knotting my insides. Jasmine, wisteria, and peach blossom trees bloomed in the garden, their fragrance delicate and sweet. A waterfall rumbled into a pond which thronged with yellow and orange carp. Overlooking it was the pavilion where the selection had been held, except now a round marble table and several stools were arranged within.

"This is your room." The chief attendant stopped outside the closed doors of a small building. "One more thing, I urge you to maintain an attentive and respectful manner at all times, creating a harmonious environment for His Highness. During his bath—"

I inhaled sharply, the breath hissing between my lips. "I need to help His Highness with his bath?"

He drew himself up, shooting me a censorious look. "When His Highness is taking his bath, use that time to prepare his books and materials for the following day." He enunciated each word with painstaking clarity, no doubt taking me for a fool.

I mumbled my thanks, grateful when he left. Sliding the doors open, I entered. The room was spacious and well-furnished with a large wooden bed draped with light blue curtains. Silk scroll paintings hung on the walls, depicting scenes of violet-gray mountains and cypress trees, pheasants and peonies. A large window opened to the courtyard and beside it was a desk, stacked with paper, a set of writing brushes, and a porcelain inkstone. A silk lantern was already lit, throwing its radiance against the dwindling light. I perched on the bed in disbelief, pinching the flesh of my arm. It stung; this was real. I wanted to laugh aloud as I fell back onto the soft mattress. The serenity of this place, broken only by the rhythmic flow of water and the wind rustling through the trees, reminded me of home. And after living with those who had found my every word and gesture wanting, it was a relief to be alone once more.

UNDISTURBED BY PAST NIGHTMARES, I slept through the night until sunlight streamed through my window. The curtains fluttered in the morning breeze, laden with the scent of flowers. There was an unfamiliar lightness in my spirit—the lack of dread, I realized. I had not been aware of the tension coiled within me, until it was gone. Piles of silks and brocade were stacked in the cupboard, and I pulled out a white robe which I fastened around my waist with a length of green satin. Its flowing skirt was embroidered with butterflies and when I ran a knuckle across the smooth stitches of a wing, it fluttered. An enchanted dress. Did this mean my lifeforce was strong? Would I soon learn to use it? My skin tingled at the thought.

Leaving my room, I crossed the courtyard to Prince Liwei's chambers—the large building across from mine. The wooden doors were lacquered a rich red, latticed with a pattern of circles, interspersed with gilded camelias. Raising my hand, I knocked gently. When there was no response, I rapped harder. After waiting a short while, I slid it open, anxious to not be late. It was dim inside, thick brocade drawn across the windows and around the rosewood bed in the far corner. Prince Liwei must still be asleep. My heart beat quicker as I stepped into the room, a floorboard creaking beneath my feet.

"Your Highness, I was instructed to wake you at this hour." My voice came out thin and uncertain, his title stiff against my tongue. Recalling the chief attendant's lecture, I sank to my knees, folding myself over until my forehead thumped clumsily against the hard floor.

Silence greeted me in return. I shifted, wondering how one might "respectfully" awaken a prince. The bed curtains rustled, a moment before they were pulled away. Lifting my head, my eyes locked onto his. Heat rushed into my face when I realized he wore just his white underrobe.

"Tea," I blurted. "Do you want some tea, Your Highness?"

He propped himself up on one elbow, yawning as his hair fell loosely across his shoulders. "What are you doing on the floor? Rise, there's no need to kneel. You weren't nearly as respectful when we first met."

"Only because I didn't know who you were. You shouldn't sneak up on people without warning or a procession, or . . . whatever you usually do. It's most inconsiderate and unfair of—" Too late, did I shut my mouth. He had a knack for needling me.

He grinned, looking unexpectedly pleased. "I'm glad the person I met by the river is still here. You seemed different a moment ago. So . . . deferential."

I bared my clenched teeth in more a grimace than a smile. "Tea, Your Highness?"

"Ah. Yes please." But then a strange expression flitted across his face. "Could you ask someone from the kitchen to prepare it? I'm not sure I could drink your 'unique' brew a second time."

Caught between laughter and mortification, I hurried to the kitchen, retracing my steps from yesterday. A rich and savory aroma wafted from the simmering pots of porridge, the pans sizzling with crescent-shaped dumplings. Distracted, I almost collided into an attendant carrying a steaming bowl of soup. He shot me a fearsome glare, his mouth opening to scold me, but someone grabbed my arm and pulled me away.

It was a girl in the purple robe of a kitchen attendant. Her cheeks had the rounded curves of an apple and her black hair was coiled into a bun.

"Best to stay out of his way. He thinks he's better than the rest of us because he serves the empress." Her chestnut brown eyes darted to me. "I'm Minyi. Are you new? What do you do? Whom do you serve?"

I paused, taken aback by her inquisitiveness. But I detected no malice in her, just curiosity and an openness which reminded me of Ping'er. "Prince Liwei," I replied.

"Ah, so you're the one who displeased Her Celestial Majesty."

My mouth went dry, the smell of food now turning my stomach. How quickly the news had spread.

She patted my hand. "Don't worry. Her Celestial Majesty

disapproves of almost everyone. Now, was there something you or His Highness needed?"

"Just breakfast. And tea, for His Highness," I said, recovering myself.

"Was there anything *you* wanted?" she asked.

When my gaze strayed to the dumplings, she winked. "I'll make sure you get an especially large serving this morning."

"Thank you." I bowed to her, but she pulled me up.

"No need for that. You're Prince Liwei's companion." She rubbed her chin in contemplation. "Maybe I should bow to you."

"Please don't," I said with feeling, before thanking her once more and leaving.

In Prince Liwei's room, I helped him to dress, holding out a sky-blue brocade robe as he slipped into it. Around his waist I knotted a black sash, to which he fastened an ornament of yellow jade and silk.

His dark hair flowed loosely down his back as he sat before a mirror, holding out a silver comb. "Would you help me?"

I hesitated, before reaching out to take it. I had only ever done my own hair, in the simple style which required no skill whatsoever. In the Golden Lotus Mansion, it was Jiayi who had the intimate task of dressing Lady Meiling. I ran the comb through Prince Liwei's strands with rhythmic strokes, my mind working furiously as I tried to recall the men's styles from the Golden Lotus Mansion. His hair was heavier than mine, silken and lustrous, spilling down his back like polished ebony. Finding a knot, I dug the comb deeper, accidentally ripping out a few strands.

He inhaled sharply, turning to me with a pained expression. "Xingyin, have I offended you in some way?"

The comb fell from my hand with a clatter. Perhaps I had attacked his hair with more vigor than intended. "I'm sorry, Your Highness."

With deft fingers, he pulled his hair into a smooth topknot, which he tucked into a silver headpiece and secured with a carved jade pin. Catching my eye in the mirror, he arched an eyebrow. "Are you? Sorry enough to help me with my hair every morning until you get it right?"

Was that a command? Recalling the rules of etiquette, I knelt in acknowledgment, but he reached out, placing his hands beneath my elbows to lift me up.

"Xingyin, we'll be together every day. When it's just the two of us, there's no need for such formality. You don't need to kneel or bow every time I say something, or you'll spend most of the day with your head on the ground. And just call me Liwei. When we met, I felt there were no walls between us. That you were someone I could speak freely with. I'd like us to be friends, if you want that, too?" he asked gently.

My eyes collided into his. How warm his smile, like a ray of sunshine had slid into the solitude of my soul. He was not at all what I expected of a prince, but so much more. I wondered what the chief attendant would make of this. Not that it mattered.

"Yes, I would," I replied.

After our morning meal, we left to our first lesson. I followed Liwei through the seemingly endless corridors, into a large garden. Graceful willows ringed a lake, a red wooden bridge arching over the water to a small island. A single pavilion was built upon it with an upturned roof of glazed green tiles, blending seamlessly into the verdant surroundings. I inhaled deeply the fresh air, tempted to linger, but Liwei strode ahead through a circular gateway of white stone adorned with a lacquered plaque which read:

崇明堂

CHAMBER OF REFLECTION

An apt name for a place of learning, one I hoped to live up to. As we sat down at a long table and took out our books, I looked around the room. The gray marble floor, plain wooden beams, and sparse furnishings were a stark contrast to the rest of the opulent palace. Shelves were crammed with scrolls, and books were piled onto the tables which had been pushed against the walls. The tall, latticed windows opened out to the garden, the cool air drifting into the chamber.

An elderly immortal entered. Liwei whispered to me that he was the Keeper of Mortal Fates who would teach us the history of the realms. His white beard hung past his waist and his wrinkled hand grasped a jade staff.

I had seen those creases on Ping'er's face before, as she tucked me into bed those nights my mother lingered too long on the balcony. My finger had brushed the lines at the corners of her eyes. "Ping'er, what are these?"

"A mark of the years," she had replied.

"Are you older than Mother?" I was surprised, as my mother seemed so grave and solemn.

"By a hundred years at least. Up until adulthood, our lives follow a similar pattern to those of the mortals. After that, our ages cease to matter. An immortal who is a thousand years old may appear the same as one who is thirty. The strength of our lifeforce determines our youth."

I raised myself up on an elbow, alight with curiosity. "Life-force?"

"The core of our powers, which determines how much energy we possess to be channeled into magic. I have these lines because I'm not as strong," she said.

"Will Mother have these lines? Me?" I had asked.

"Only time will tell." Before I could ask more, Ping'er had hurried from the room, closing the door firmly after her.

The memory tugged at my heart. Until the empress's arrival, this was the first and last time Ping'er had spoken to me of magic. Now I knew the secrets she had kept that night, those of my sealed powers. This discovery might have upset me more had I learned it before the empress's visit. But I found it no longer mattered—not now, after the storm had broken and swept me away. Though I could not help wishing that I had known of its existence, that I might have done something to prevent it.

The Keeper of Mortal Fates picked up a book, flicking through its pages. "How old is he?" I blurted to Liwei as I stared at his snow-white hair.

The Keeper glanced up with a pained expression. "Do not comment on another's age. It's not considered good manners anywhere, especially in the Mortal Realm." His manner was stern yet not unkind, as though warning me of others who might take offense more easily.

I murmured a hasty apology. But the moment the Keeper turned away, Liwei leaned closer to whisper, "Some immortals choose to no longer preserve their youth."

"Because we prefer to preserve our wisdom," the Keeper snapped. "Your Highness, I urge you to set a better example for your study companion."

I nodded somberly, ignoring Liwei's glare—although I admittedly had a part in his rebuke. It was refreshing to hear someone, other than me, reprimanded for their conduct.

When the Keeper of Mortal Fates left, a tutor arrived to teach us about the constellations, then another, about herbology. I was struggling to sit still during the lengthy lesson, delivered by an unsmiling immortal with a pointed chin and pedantic air. As my eyes glazed over the pictures of flowers, all of which were beginning to look the same, my hand flew to my mouth to stifle a yawn.

Perhaps sensing my wandering attention, the teacher swung around. "Xingyin, what are the properties of this plant?" His tone was biting as he tapped the page in front of me with a slender bamboo cane.

I bolted upright, staring blankly at the picture of an unremarkable pale-blue flower with pointed petals. "Star-lilies," its title read. Unfortunately, no other information was forthcoming.

"Umm," I glanced wildly at Liwei. He widened his eyes at me, before closing them and letting his head droop to one side.

"Sleep!" I cried out, catching his meaning.

The teacher's mouth pursed. "Correct. Though bitter, this wildflower can be a potent sleeping drug when consumed with wine."

"Thank you," I whispered to Liwei.

"You're welcome." A small smile played on his lips.

I had just put away the books from the last lesson when a grim-looking immortal strode toward us, his boots clicking against the marble floor. His lean face was unlined save for a deep crease in his brow and his dark hair was pulled into a topknot. His armor was crafted from flat pieces of shining white metal rimmed with gold, laced tightly together like scales over his shoulders and chest, reaching down to his knees. Red cloth covered his arms, gathered into thick gold cuffs around his wrists. A wide strip of black leather encircled his waist, set with a disc of yellow jade. Strapped to his side was a large silver scabbard, from which protruded an ebony hilt. The aura which rippled from him was as steady and strong as a sturdy oak of many years.

A Celestial soldier, just as those Ping'er and I had fled that night. A chill settled over me, my fingers curling on the table. "Why is he here? Is there some trouble?"

"General Jianyun is the highest ranked commander in the Celestial Army. He's here to instruct us in warfare."

"Your Highness." He greeted Liwei with a bow. As his gaze slid to me, the lines across his brow deepened.

"General Jianyun, this is Xingyin," Liwei gestured to me.

I bowed to the general, but he did not respond. Beneath his piercing glare, I fidgeted, unsettled by the memories his presence evoked.

"Are you interested in warfare?"

I stiffened at his sharp tone even as I floundered for an answer. I had given little thought to the grand schemes of kingdoms battling for dominance, for glory, power, and pride. My desires were humbler, smaller. All I wanted to learn was how to defend myself and protect those I loved.

"I don't know yet. This is my first lesson," I replied. As his expression darkened with disapproval, a spark of defiance kindled in me. "I am keen to learn. But a student's interest also depends upon a teacher's skill."

His eyes bulged. I held my breath. Would he toss me out of the class? I would have deserved it, too, for my impertinence.

To my surprise, General Jianyun grinned instead. "Does Her Celestial Majesty approve of your companion?" he asked Liwei with mock incredulity.

"My mother does not involve herself in such matters" was all Liwei said, as he flipped his book open.

Though the general's expression was one of disbelief, he said no more on the subject.

By noontime, my head throbbed from learning and my hand ached from writing. When we were dismissed for the afternoon meal, I was glad to escape to the kitchen. Carrying the tray laden with food, I headed toward the pavilion outside the Chamber of Reflection. A small sign hung over it, painted in broad black strokes with the characters:

柳歌亭

WILLOW SONG PAVILION

"A beautiful name." I laid out the steamed fish, tender snow pea leaves, and eight-treasures chicken on the marble table.

"A fitting one, too," Liwei replied, placing a finger to his lips.

I did not understand his meaning, but followed his lead to remain silent. When a breeze blew, the willows swayed, dipping their branches into the clear water. As their delicate leaves rustled against each another, the air filled with sighing whispers—an exquisite though melancholy melody. How it reminded me of the wind blowing through the osmanthus trees, the clink of my mother's jade ornaments.

"Did you enjoy our lessons?" Liwei asked, breaking my reverie. He served a little of each dish onto my plate, in blatant disregard of convention.

"Some more than others," I replied, recalling the tedious lecture on plants and herbs. "Especially General Jianyun's."

"I thought you would fall asleep in that class."

"Why? Should girls only draw, sing, and sew?" I asked, thinking of Lady Meiling's lessons, and my own with Ping'er.

"Of course not." His tone was grave as he leaned forward like he was about to impart some great wisdom. "What about having children?" There was a teasing glint in his eyes.

I choked on a piece of chicken I was chewing, with the added indignity of having Liwei slap my back to dislodge it. Eager to change the subject, I said, "Well, I can't draw, and you wouldn't want me to sing."

"Will you sew my clothes?"

"Not unless you want clothes with holes where they shouldn't be."

His fingers tapped the table contemplatively. "So, you can't draw, sing, or sew. What about—"

"No!" I burst out, louder than intended, fighting down the flash of warmth across my skin.

He blinked, shooting me a look of innocence. "All I was going to ask was whether you would play your flute for me."

Flute? I cursed inwardly, my wandering mind.

"What did you think I meant?" He shook his head in mock disapproval.

"Just that. Nothing else." I grasped at the lie.

"How else might you compensate for your shortcomings? It appears you have many indeed." As Liwei's lips twitched, I suspected he was enjoying this far too much.

"The same way you can compensate for yours," I retorted.

"Mine?" He sounded stung. A part of me wondered if anyone had ever spoken to him this way. "Name one."

"Your manners?" I offered. "Your sense of superiority? Your habit of interrupting your teachers? How you say such outrageous things to amuse yourself? Your—"

Liwei held up a hand, looking pained. "*One* was enough."

I tried to keep a straight countenance through the mirth which bubbled up in me. How at ease I felt, my heart lighter than it had been in months. "Besides, I don't believe playing music was included in my list of duties," I added.

He picked up a glistening piece of white fish, inspecting it for bones before placing it on my plate. "You're not very accommodating."

I shot him my sweetest smile. "It depends on how you ask."

He laughed, but then cleared his throat. "I'm sorry for my mother's order, that you were asked to attend to me as well. You don't have to. I'm perfectly capable of looking after myself, when I want to."

"I really don't mind," I said. "I'm glad to earn my keep. And if I don't, someone might report back to Her Celestial Majesty." She would be keen for the slightest excuse to dismiss me—of that, I was certain. Part of me was relieved that the empress showed me no generosity, because it meant I owed her nothing. And Liwei did not make me feel like I was attending to him, but rather assisting him. A small distinction, yet it made a world of difference to my pride.

"Thank you," he said, rising to his feet. "Now, we must hurry. We have a long afternoon of training before us."

My curiosity was pricked. "What training?"

"Sword fighting, archery, martial arts. If you aren't interested, I can have you excused," he offered, with a magnanimous sweep of his hand.

I forced myself to breathe deeply, to stem the exhilaration rushing through me like water streaming down a mountain after a burst of rain. My appetite was whetted after General Jianyun's lesson and I was eager to learn more about the skills which could help me become stronger. Powerful enough to withstand the winds of change or to shift its course, instead of yielding under the slightest breeze. My imagination soared, unfettered, as I fantasized about flying home and breaking the enchantment that bound my mother to the moon . . .

My voice shook with excitement. "Liwei, I'll play the flute for you whenever you wish—as long as you *don't* excuse me from those lessons."

6

Camphor trees ringed an enormous grassy field, throwing their shade upon us. All around were soldiers, clad in shining armor of white and gold. Commanders shouted instructions to their troops—some fighting with swords, others with red-tasseled spears. On a raised wooden platform, rows of soldiers followed the steps of an instructor. Their movements were as graceful and well-synchronized as a dance, though far deadlier—I thought—as a woman flung a large soldier onto his back. Several target boards were set up on the edge of the field where the soldiers were practicing archery.

As I watched them, a soldier released an arrow—slicing through the air, plunging into the center of the board. Struck by admiration, I clapped until my palms throbbed.

"You're easily impressed," Liwei told me.

"Can you do better?" I demanded.

"Of course."

The certainty in his tone took me by surprise. But then General Jianyun appeared, striding toward us.

"Your Highness, what do you wish to practice first?"

"Archery," Liwei replied at once.

At the general's command, the soldiers cleared the round target boards—each painted with four rings that culminated in a red center. Liwei selected a long, curved bow from the weapons rack. Almost effortlessly, it seemed, he drew an arrow and released it at the target. Before I could blink, another whizzed past me. Both pierced the center with loud thuds.

I stared at the board, stunned by his accuracy and swiftness. "You did not exaggerate."

"I never do," he said. "Do you want to try?"

My hands reached out, but I snatched them back with a furtive glance at the soldiers surrounding us. I had never held a weapon before, much less one which seemed to require such precision.

Liwei spoke quietly to General Jianyun, who left with the others. When it was just us, I breathed easier. He passed me a bow, smaller than the one he had used.

"Mulberry wood. This is a good one to start with as it's lighter," he explained.

My fingers tingled when they touched the lacquered wood, closing around the silk-wrapped grip. The bow did not feel unfamiliar to me, but as though I had wielded one a hundred times before. Had it been so with my father, the greatest archer who ever lived? If my mother had not taken the elixir, if we had remained in the world below, he might have taught me to shoot like him—though I doubted I could bring down one sun, much less nine. My heart ached, a futile pain with no remedy. All the wishing in the world would not bring my family together again.

"Xingyin, are you ready?" Liwei called out.

I nodded, moving across from the target, a distance away, as he had. Liwei stood just behind me, guiding my hands as I raised the bow. "Breathe deeply from your core. As you draw the string, pull your strength from across your body, not just your arms." He tapped my shoulders and lifted my right elbow up. "Hold these in a straight line."

My arms strained to hold the position, the string biting into my thumb and fingers.

Finally satisfied, he stepped away. "Adjust your arrow until its tip aligns with the target. When you release it, only that hand should move—keep the other steady on the grip. And don't feel disheartened if you miss. It's your first try."

Something burned in the pit of my stomach. A desire to do well, to live up to my father's name. Even if no one ever knew it but me. My eyes narrowed on the target in the distance. Everything else shifted into a blur, the board shining as brightly as a beacon in the dark. Holding my breath and keeping as still as I could, I released the arrow. It tore through the air, hitting the target's outermost ring with a thud.

"I hit it!" A raw thrill coursed through my veins.

Liwei clapped, his mouth curved up. "You have a good teacher."

"Hah! I'll be better than you soon," I bragged, shameless in my euphoria.

"Care to wager on that? Three months from now, we'll have a contest. The loser will have to do the bidding of the winner for a day."

"Don't I have to do your bidding, every day?" Somehow, I managed to say that with a straight face.

"Without complaint, without argument, without hesitation," he added, after a moment's deliberation.

"But within reason," I countered, the bow in my grip giving

me a newfound confidence. And I could not back down now; he would tease me mercilessly.

"Agreed." His grin widened. "Are you afraid of what I might order you to do?"

"Far from it," I told him with an equally broad smile. "I'll enjoy ordering Your Highness around."

"You haven't won yet," he reminded me, before heading toward the soldiers practicing with swords.

"Neither have you," I muttered to myself.

I decided to remain by the archery boards. My fingers itched to hold the bow again—to feel the raw exhilaration as the arrow sprang free, the satisfaction when it struck true. Plucking another, I drew it through the bow, trying to recall Liwei's instructions.

"You shouldn't have taken that wager. His Highness is an excellent shot," someone remarked from behind me.

My concentration broke, my body jerked. The arrow flew wide of the target.

I spun around to find a Celestial soldier watching me. She was striking, with light brown skin and a smattering of freckles across her nose, her eyes slightly upturned at the corners. Her full lips were twisted into a grimace as she inspected my arrow, buried unceremoniously in the dirt. "Yes, you definitely should not have accepted that wager," she repeated.

Was this another Jiayi, concealing malice beneath a veneer of civility? My nod was cool, dismissive, even. "Thank you for your concern. I'll be fine."

I thought she would leave, but she folded her arms across her body. Did she intend to watch? Maybe hoping I would humiliate myself?

I turned my back to her, wishing she would go. Drawing another arrow, I released it. It struck the board, quivering from the ring closest to the center. More likely through fortunate coincidence than my untrained abilities, but I couldn't resist saying, "Maybe His Highness is the one who shouldn't have accepted."

"Not bad for your third try." Her compliment took me by surprise. More so, when she wrapped her hand over her fist, inclining her head to me. "I'm Shuxiao."

My mind went blank; I was unused to such civility. In the Golden Lotus Mansion, I had never been accorded such courtesy. While here, it was Liwei upon whom all attention was fixed.

She tilted her head to one side, perhaps wondering at the awkward silence. Hastily, I returned her greeting. As I straightened, I thought furiously for something to say. The weather would be too dull. We had no friends in common, or rather I had none to speak of. And I couldn't ask after her family when I was unable to speak of mine.

"Do you enjoy being a Celestial soldier?" I finally managed.

"Who wouldn't?" she said with a straight face. "It's marvelous being ordered around most of the time, expected to obey without question, getting thrashed during training, and feeling lucky when you don't wind up dead from an assignment."

I recoiled. "It sounds . . . dreadful."

"I haven't told you the best part. Do you see what we have to wear?" She poked at her armor. "It's heavier than it looks, if that's possible. And when we walk, we clank like pots and pans. It's a good thing we're taught to conceal the sound from our enemies."

"Why do you do it?" I couldn't help asking.

She shrugged. "Who wouldn't want to serve the Celestial Emperor and our kingdom?"

Was that catch in her voice earnestness or sarcasm? I couldn't tell and decided it would be wisest to remain silent as she selected a bow from the rack.

"I heard you study with His Highness. Do your parents serve at court?"

I shook my head, moving aside to make space for her, hoping she would ask me something else. Anything else.

She raised her bow, adjusting her aim as she inspected the target. Her arrow whistled through the air, striking the board near the center.

"A good shot," I remarked.

She grimaced. "Archery is my bane; I've practiced so much and still can't hit the center. Swords, I prefer. Or spears." She peered at me, not to be diverted. "Are you a Celestial? Is your family from here?"

I stared ahead with feigned concentration. "My family is no more." The lie came easier to me now, though the shame burned just as hot. I had little choice but to maintain the pretense, as Liwei believed my parents deceased.

She was quiet for a moment, before reaching out to pat my shoulder. "I'm sorry. I'm sure they would be proud of you."

My chest tightened. How wretched I was to claim her sympathy under false pretenses. And yet, how desperately I wished her words were true. I could not help wondering how my mother would feel, now that I served the household of the emperor who had imprisoned her.

"The courtiers were grumbling about a 'nobody' winning the position with Prince Liwei," she added. "Highest compliment in my opinion. How did you do it?"

"Luck," I said with a flippancy I did not feel, irked at the same time. I would not be a "nobody" forever. They would know my name one day, and those of my parents.

"Where is your family?" I tried to shift the conversation away from me.

"We're Celestials, but my parents don't serve at court. My father claims it's too dangerous. Fractious, with everyone scrambling for favor. He prefers a quiet existence." She wrinkled her nose, adding, "Although with six children, our home is anything but peaceful."

"Six!" I gasped.

"It's not as horrible or wonderful as you might think. When we get along, my brothers and sisters are the best friends in the world. But when we fight . . ." she shuddered, her features twisting into an expression of horror.

"Perhaps your father should have escaped to the Celestial Court after all," I told her.

A wide smile stretched across her face. "My mother wouldn't let him."

For the rest of the afternoon, we practiced together. The youngest of her sizable family, Shuxiao had been surrounded by companions since birth. She possessed a vitality about her, an ease of manner which drew others close. Many soldiers called out or waved to her as they passed by. Some included me in their greeting, believing Shuxiao and I were friends.

And indeed, after today, we were.

By the end of the day, my fingers were blistered. My arms ached and my back hurt. I had not touched a sword or uttered a whisper of magic. Nevertheless, as we left the field, I could not wait to come back.

In Liwei's room, I set out the books for our lessons tomorrow. When he returned from his bath, he wore just a short white robe draped over loose-fitting black pants. His long hair, still damp, hung down his back. I expected to be dismissed, but he sat down at the table and looked at me expectantly.

"Which song will you play?"

His earlier request had flown out of my mind. I was tired, my sore limbs longing for bed—but I sat beside him and took out my flute. A lilting melody rippled through the air, of spring awakening, the rivers thawing and flowing with life once more.

When I finished, I laid the flute down.

"It's amazing how this small instrument can bring forth such music." After a moment's hesitation, he added, "This song is happier than the one you played before. Does it reflect your mood?"

"Yes. This has been one of the best days of my life, and I have you to thank for it." My words were plain, but heartfelt. I missed my home, my mother, and Ping'er still—yet I no longer felt I was drifting alone and untethered in this world.

Liwei cleared his throat, the tips of his ears reddening. Rising to his feet, he strode to his desk. A scroll painting of a girl hung on the wall beside it. Dark eyes gleamed from the perfect oval of her face. She sat beneath clusters of blooming wisteria, holding a bamboo embroidery frame.

"Who is she?" I asked.

He stared at it in silence for a moment. "She used to live in the courtyard near mine. When I was a child, I visited her often. She was patient, even when I tangled the threads which she wove into her embroideries."

I imagined a young Liwei, brimming with mischief. "You said 'used to.' Where is she now?"

A shadow fell over his face. "One day, I came to her courtyard and found it deserted. The attendants told me she had moved away. No one would say where she had gone."

I wished I could ease his sadness. He sat down at his desk where a tray of drawing materials was laid out: a few sheets of crisp paper, a large purple jade inkstone, and a sandalwood stand from which brushes of bamboo and lacquered wood hung. I watched curiously as he selected a brush, dipped it into the glossy ink and drew on the paper with deft strokes. After a few minutes, he offered it to me.

"It's for you," he said, when I made no move to take it.

I stared at the paper. My face looked back at me, a remarkable likeness, gazing into the distance as my fingers rested on the flute. My hands trembled as I took the picture from him.

"You draw very well," I said softly. "Though you don't need to do this every time I play for you. It may not be a duty, but neither is it an exchange."

"How else might I compensate for my shortcomings?" he asked with a straight face. "After all, I have so many."

I laughed, recalling our earlier conversation. "Just this one, then."

He smiled. "Good night, Xingyin."

I rose to my feet and bade him good night. As I shut the doors behind me, I found Liwei still bent over his desk, his brush in his hand. My heart filled with an inexplicable warmth as I turned away to stare into the sky above.

In the clear and cloudless night, the moon was dazzling, its light unhindered. As I walked to my room across the courtyard, its radiance lit my way, brighter than a string of lanterns.

7

I slipped into my new life, the days morphing into weeks.
Each morning, we had our lessons in the Chamber of Reflection, while in the afternoons we trained with the Celestial
Army. My mind was opened to new worlds and knowledge, but
it was the training on the field which stirred me most. I learned
to wield a sword proficiently—to slash and thrust, block and
parry—although my abilities still trailed behind Liwei's. Eager
to catch up, I studied the fighting techniques late into the night,
repeating the moves in the quiet of my room until they came as
easily to me as grasping my chopsticks or forming a note on my
flute.

Sometimes I wondered, why did I feel such exhilaration when
an arrow struck true? Or when an opponent was brought down
by a well-placed blow? Was it because I had been so weak before, that I now rejoiced in my newfound strength? Or had this
urge—this desire to win—always run in my veins?

The prospect of training my powers filled me with both excitement and dread. As a child I had fantasized about summoning

firebolts and flying through the skies. But after the disastrous consequences of my first brush with magic, I would have been glad to never touch it again. Liwei would have excused me, yet an immortal without magic was like a tiger without claws. We might be physically strong, but we might as well be mortal. If I ever wanted to help my mother, I had to embrace my power. And though it frightened me, a part of me hungered for this, too.

Our instructor, Teacher Daoming, was the guardian of the Imperial Treasury and its hoard of enchanted artifacts. She only ever seemed to wear robes of dull gray, her black hair coiled into a tight bun from which silver pins protruded like a fantail. Her wide eyes were the hue of almonds, and her pale skin was unmarred by lines from either frown or smile.

I had no magical training, whereas Liwei had already progressed to advanced enchantments. For the first few weeks, all Teacher Daoming allowed me to do was meditate—with sparse instructions to keep my eyes closed, my mind empty, and my spirit "as calm as a windless dawn." I approached these exercises with enthusiasm at first, anticipating the discovery of some hidden power or enlightenment—but soon became bored with sitting cross-legged on the floor for hours on end. Whenever Teacher Daoming saw so much as a wrinkle appear in my brow or a quiver in my leg, she smacked my arm with her fan, snapping such vague things as:

"Clear your mind of distraction!"

"Focus on the awareness of your energy!"

"Seek the light through the dark!"

I would grit my teeth in mounting frustration, swallowing my ire as I imagined Liwei summoning bolts of flame while I was sitting here getting hit with a fan.

Meditating, for me, was particularly exasperating. In archery the goal was clear, the results, instantaneous. I knew what to do to improve and how I might get there. Whereas meditation was a nebulous, mysterious thing. A path with endless winding destinations, where you might spend hours wandering and end up just where you started.

One day, while I was sitting as still as I could and trying not to doze off, a shadow fell over me. I lifted my eyelids a crack, to find Teacher Daoming standing there.

"If you're worrying about whether you're doing it right, then you're not," she sighed.

My eyes flew open. "I'm not very good at this," I admitted. "Besides, how will meditating help? All it does is make me fall asleep."

Teacher Daoming shook her head as she sank down beside me. "Ah, Xingyin. Calming your mind is a crucial skill that extends even beyond magic. You are impatient, rash, passionate in your endeavors. You, more than anyone, need to learn how to untether your mind from your feelings. Steady your thoughts and observe, before you plunge ahead. When emotions cloud us, disaster soon follows."

She smoothed her robe over her knees. "There is no target in meditation. No judgment. It is the peace, the connection and oneness with yourself that is the key." She paused. "I sense your lifeforce is strong. However, it's been suppressed since your childhood, which is why you have trouble grasping your magic. It was crudely done and would never have worked had you been older and trained properly. Meditation will help break the seal on your lifeforce, to unleash your abilities. But only if you let it."

I stared at Teacher Daoming, my mind whirling. My mother had not wished my magic to strengthen. She and Ping'er must have done what they could to shroud my powers and conceal my existence. I bit my lip, clenching down hard. My mother wanted a quiet life for me, a happy one. After her decades of heartache and terror, she must have thought peace was the best gift she could give me. Perhaps I had wanted it, too—until this fire was lit in me to be more than I was, to be all that I could.

Teacher Daoming continued, "You have great potential. However, before you can harness your powers, you need to understand them. Before you can unleash your energy, you must learn how to grasp it. I hear you're skilled in archery. Could you shoot as you do without becoming one with the bow?" She touched the side of my head gently. "Some knowledge beats in our hearts, while others are learned by the body and mind."

Her words echoed those of my mother, a lesson I should have learned long before. Because some things came easily to me, I grew impatient at those which did not.

A wave of emotions swelled in me—shame at my conduct, gratitude for her patience. I shifted to my knees and stretched out my cupped hands, bowing low. "Teacher Daoming, I ask your forgiveness. I was impatient and resentful. Arrogant, in thinking I knew better. From now, I promise to follow your instructions to the best of my abilities."

Her smile infused her face with sudden warmth. She was beautiful, I realized then, though not in the same way my mother was. One had to look a little closer to find the grace in her movements, the strength in her bearing, the delicacy of her features. Hers was a quieter beauty, but no less luminous once it was uncovered.

"I'm glad to hear that. My fan is getting worn out." Without another word, she rose and walked away.

I choked back a laugh, even as I instinctively rubbed my arm. Perhaps Teacher Daoming was not as intimidating as I had thought. And perhaps, I might not be as terrible a student as I had feared.

MY PROGRESS WAS QUICKER now that I no longer resisted the lessons. Still, it took weeks more before I gained sufficient skill in meditation to advance to using my powers—what I had both craved and dreaded since leaving my home.

According to Teacher Daoming, the lights I glimpsed swirling through me was my spiritual energy. While casting enchantments drained us of it, as water trickling from a bucket, it could be replenished through rest and meditation. Without this, our bodies would be no different from a mortal's and our lives as frail as theirs.

"Never drain your energy, Xingyin," she cautioned me.

"Why?"

"Trying to draw more than you possess will leave you unable to sustain your lifeforce—which is the core of your powers, the source of your energy." She spoke slowly, holding my gaze to ensure I was paying attention. "That is death to an immortal."

Cold sweat broke out over my palms. I had always thought learning to use my magic meant I would be strong. Fear, a distant thing of the past. Never did it occur to me that there would also be danger in using it.

"How does that happen?" I asked.

"Trying to cast too powerful an enchantment, trying to sustain one for too long, or trying to undo something you can't."

My thoughts flew to my mother and the spell which bound her. "Are some enchantments unbreakable?"

"All enchantments can be broken if you know how. If you're strong enough. If you're the right person to do it," she said. "You don't want to end up hurling your power into a void and getting too caught up to stop."

I released a drawn-out breath. It was possible. That was what mattered. As for how, I would figure that out later.

IN THE BEGINNING, I was unable to cast even the simplest enchantment—the lights still eluding my grasp. Yet as the weeks passed, I edged closer until I sensed a stirring deep within, like an unfinished chord on the cusp of harmony.

One evening while Liwei was having his bath, I found his tea had gone cold. While he would not have cared, it was a cool night, ideal for a warm drink. Closing my eyes, I searched inward for my energy—silver bright, glittering as stardust. It flickered as I reached out, struggling against that unseen force tugging me back. Sweat broke out over my brow, my fists clenching under the strain—but I shoved through, snapping the hidden restraint to grasp the lights. For a moment they wriggled in my hold like the slippery scales of a fish unwilling to be caught, but then something shifted deep within, imbuing me with a sense of oneness as though I had finally connected to some vital part of me. My skin tingled like I had been doused in ice water. This was no accident. The lights stilled, yielding to my command as a stream of glowing energy surged from my fingertips toward the teapot. Steam curled from the spout, the water roiling with heat. I laughed, giddy with the success of my first enchantment.

Under Teacher Daoming's guidance, I learned to coax a breeze from the air, freeze raindrops to ice, raise protection shields, and—yes—even summon the bolts of flame I had dreamed of. Many immortals chose not to exert their powers for mundane things that could easily be done without. Yet in those early days

I practiced whenever I could, no task too small nor tiresome. Once, I unthinkingly summoned a hairpin, which plunged into Liwei's topknot with more force than intended. His head jerked back, a startled breath hissing from him, though he smiled as he glanced my way. No longer was I fumbling in the dark to grasp a sliver of light—my energy darted readily into my grasp, my magic flowing unbound.

Several months into my training, Teacher Daoming brought me to the lush garden just beyond the Chamber of Reflection. It was a windless morning, the lake as still as a mirror. As she raised her hand, five luminous spheres formed in the air. Tongues of flame leapt in one, translucent water lapped in the other. The third contained a chunk of coppery earth, and a hazy mist swirled in the fourth.

Fire, Water, Earth, Air. The four elemental Talents of magic that I recalled from her previous lessons. I peered at the last globe, glowing a rich crimson. "What is this?"

"Life magic, to heal the body's wounds and ailments. One of the intrinsic Talents." She stiffened a little, her lips pressing into thin lines.

"*One* of them? What are the others?"

She fixed me with a hard stare, ignoring my question. "Xing-yin, which is the strongest of the elemental Talents?"

I passed my palm over the spheres, the heat mingling with the coolness from the different energies. Fragments of lessons flashed across my mind. Earth might douse Fire, but Fire could scorch Earth. Air might fan a flame or extinguish it. My thoughts wound together into a maze of contradictions.

"It depends on the strength of the Talents pitted against each other," I finally answered.

Her brows snapped into a frown. "That is half an answer."

I lowered my head, wishing I had listened more attentively in her class.

She continued, "Each Talent has its own strengths and weaknesses. All four can be equally powerful. What matters most is the strength of the casters, their lifeforce which determines how much energy is at their disposal and the skill with which they wield it." As she passed her palm over the first two orbs, fire leapt high, engulfing the sphere of water. In the next moment, water surged to drown the flames.

"Those strong enough to specialize, first need to discover their Talent. Most immortals are drawn to one, maybe two. Prince Liwei's Fire and Life magic are his strongest, while our emperor is one of the few accomplished across the Talents, even able to channel Sky-fire."

"Sky-fire?" I repeated. It was the first I had heard of it.

"Lightning, as wielded by immortals. A rare and powerful magic. Not an element in itself, rather a unique convergence of one's magic."

With a flick of her finger the flames rekindled. "For some, their Talent is innate. For most of us, it stems from our natural environment—perhaps because we unconsciously absorb the energy from our surroundings. Those living in the forests and mountains are more skilled in the arts of Earth and Air. Phoenix Immortals are adept in Fire magic and Sea Immortals cast the most powerful Water enchantments. The Talents of Celestials have always varied across the elements." She turned to me with a grave expression. "Which is yours?"

A thrill raced through me. Teacher Daoming believed I was strong enough to advance! Most immortals possessed enough magic to cast a repertoire of minor enchantments—lighting fires, healing minor injuries, calling a shower of rain. However, true power lay in the mastery of a Talent and for that, one needed a sufficiently strong lifeforce. It was said that some advanced enchantments were so powerful, they could drain a weaker immortal's energy with a single casting.

Following her instruction, I reached toward the glowing orbs and released my energy in a cloud of gleaming silver. The Earth, Air, and Life spheres died out at once. Fire flared higher but a gust of wind surged from the translucent orb, extinguishing the flames before it hurtled across the garden. The willow trees bent sharply, whipping the lake into waves.

With a sweep of Teacher Daoming's hand, the wind calmed and died. Her lips curved into a rare smile, as my heart pounded like a drum. The wind had wreaked utter destruction upon the once tranquil garden; scattered leaves blanketing the ground, trees swaying wildly, snapped willow branches trailing in the water. Had *I* done this?

"Your Talent lies with Air, but you have some affinity in Fire," Teacher Daoming observed.

Through my exhilaration, something tugged at the edge of my consciousness, something she had let slip earlier. I gestured toward the glowing spheres. "Are these *all* the Talents?"

A shadow flitted across her face. "It's late. You are dismissed," she said abruptly.

Curiosity warred with courtesy. I bowed, thanking her for the lesson. But then the question burst from me, "If Life is *one* of the intrinsic Talents, what are the others?"

"It is forbidden." Without another word, she walked away.

Her strange behavior only stoked my curiosity further, weighing on me for the rest of the day. During the evening meal, I ate with little enthusiasm, barely tasting the prawns fried in red peppercorns.

"Aren't you hungry?" Liwei asked, his chopsticks poised above his bowl.

I hesitated. Teacher Daoming had said it was forbidden but . . . he was the only one who might tell me. "Beyond Life, what are the other intrinsic Talents?"

He was quiet for so long, I thought he, too, would leave me in the dark. "Are we not allowed to even speak of it?" I shook my head then. "Forget I asked. I don't want you to say anything you shouldn't."

He set down his chopsticks, his fingers tapping the table in a restless rhythm. "There's just one other: Mind, which used to be among the most powerful Talents. However, centuries ago, my father and his allies condemned this magic and banned it across the realm."

I refilled the teapot with hot water, letting the tea steep before pouring it into our cups. "Why did he do that?"

"Terrifying stories emerged regarding the practices of Mind Talents—that they drank mortal blood and feasted on the flesh of children to sustain their magic, that their powers had distorted their true forms beyond recognition." He frowned. "Rumors, perhaps? After all, they are immortals just as us. The only difference we know for sure is in their eyes, which glitter like cut stones."

"Were their powers truly evil?" I asked.

"Some Mind Talents could compel others against their will to perform their bidding. A heinous act. Imagine, being forced to attack someone? To harm those you love?"

I shuddered at the thought. "How is such a thing possible?"

"Fortunately, few are truly capable of it. The stronger one's lifeforce, the harder it is to compel them as it requires more en-

ergy. A skilled Mind Talent might only be able to control a powerful immortal for a brief period." A shadow crossed his face.
"Even if this happens once, that's once too often. Even if it's just
for a moment, one's life can be destroyed then. A prison of the
mind is far worse than that of the body."

"Do many immortals have this power? Why aren't we warned
about it?"

"My father doesn't like this to be mentioned. Besides, it is a
rare skill, not even my father wields it."

Part of me could not help wondering if that was why the
emperor hated this magic. Because he could not understand it,
because it was the one Talent that eluded him. But I buried those
thoughts, unwilling to speak them aloud. No matter how close
Liwei and I had grown, I could not let myself forget that he was
the son of the Celestial Emperor.

He continued, "Most came from the Cloud Wall, once a domain of our kingdom which bordered the Golden Desert. When
the ban was announced, a few volunteered to seal their powers
to resettle in our lands. However, most refused."

"It's a hard thing to sacrifice years of study and practice," I
ventured, thinking of my own efforts to master just a few skills.

"Those who did were well compensated. The Cloud Immortals were stirred to rebellion by an ambitious upstart, in a
gambit to seize power and declare himself king. After they pro-
claimed their separation from us, my father burned the ancient
scrolls of their magic, burying their ashes at the bottom of the
Four Seas."

A harsh retaliation. "Was that the end of it?" I asked.

"Unfortunately, the Cloud Wall King retrieved the ashes and
reconstructed the scrolls. He was weakened, but with whatever

dark arts he learned, his new powers outstripped his old. With newly forged alliances with the Northern and Western Seas, he declared war upon us. The losses were catastrophic, thousands of immortals perishing—until, at last, a truce was agreed. However, my father swore that no Cloud Immortal would ever be allowed into the Celestial Kingdom again."

I searched my memory for all Ping'er had told me of the eight kingdoms of the Immortal Realm. There had been no mention of the Cloud Wall. "Did it become part of another kingdom?"

He paused. "It's now known as the Demon Realm."

I choked on my tea, coughing and sputtering, as Liwei passed me a handkerchief to wipe my chin. The Demon Realm was said to be a land of mist and fog, home to fearsome beasts, monsters, and evil sorcerers. Somehow, it was easier to despise them before realizing—as Liwei had said—they were like us.

My mind spun with all I had learned and I could not help asking, "Did you agree with what your father did?"

He grimaced. "According to my father, there can be no respect without fear. To be a powerful leader, one needs to govern with an iron hand, to crush resistance with even greater strength. I'm a disappointment to him; he reprimands me for being too soft. But no matter what he does, I can't change who I am."

"What does he do?" A tightness formed in my gut. I had never seen Liwei look so troubled before.

His fingers curled into a fist on the table. When he spoke, his voice was low. "He only wants what's best for me. But when my turn comes to take the throne, I will not rule as he does."

Reaching out, I touched his clenched knuckles in comfort. All I knew of such matters were from our lessons, what I studied in the texts, the stories of great kings and queens—both mortal and immortal. But I was sure of one thing, that the Celestial Kingdom—*any* kingdom—would fare better under a ruler who listened with an open mind, than one who demanded unswerving obedience.

I had no love for the Celestial Empress and less for the emperor who had imprisoned my mother, although I had never met him before. From what I gleaned from gossip and learned myself, Liwei was nothing like his parents. Unlike many in positions of power, he took no pleasure in imposing his will or pushing others down. Never did he condescend to me, as far too many had. He morphed from a laughing friend to a patient instructor, and whichever role he took, his care and consideration warmed me. Whenever we debated our lessons or sparred, he drove me to improve myself, never surrendering an advantage I had not earned. Each night I went to bed aching and exhausted, yet my heart aglow to be treated as his equal.

Archery was where I shone—whether using the short bow, which was lighter and faster, or the longbow, which allowed for greater accuracy. A few commanders soon instructed their troops to watch me while I trained. Their presence unnerved me; I was afraid of making a fool of myself by dropping my arrows or missing the target. Yet the moment I drew my bow, a calm spread over me. Perhaps my control over my emotions had improved with Teacher Daoming's instruction, although it was still far from perfect.

One afternoon, I arrived at the archery station to find it set up differently, with just two targets in the distance. Liwei stood there, holding a bow in each hand. A little behind him was General Jianyun with a small cluster of soldiers, Shuxiao among them.

"It's been three months. Did you forget?" Liwei called out.

My spirits sank as I recalled my reckless wager. Still, I plastered on a bright smile as I took the bow from him. "Of course not. What are the terms?"

"Three arrows each?" he proposed. "The winner is whoever scores the most points."

I nodded in acceptance, moving to stand behind the line. His arrow whistled as it flew toward the target, but I averted my gaze. His performance was a distraction I could ill afford. Keeping my attention upon my board, I released the first arrow, piercing the target in the center. The second followed in its trail, into the crimson eye of the board. And my last arrow split the former right down its middle. Having scored three perfect strikes, my confidence swelled—until I saw Liwei's board, a mirror of my own.

General Jianyun frowned, unable to decide the victor. Striding to the weapons rack, he pulled out a clay disc, no bigger than my fist. "Our advanced archers use this to practice their skills. When the disc is released, it will soar away. The first person who shoots it down will be the winner."

I groaned inwardly. I did not have much experience with moving targets.

"Perhaps this is too difficult for Xingyin," Liwei said.

Pride got the better of me. "It's fine," I said curtly, drawing an arrow through my bow.

General Jianyun threw the disc high. It shot through the air, faster than anticipated. I blinked—half a heartbeat of hesitation—my arrow already hurtling toward the soaring disc . . . as Liwei's gold-feathered arrow shattered the clay.

I fought down my dismay. It had been a fair match. "You win," I conceded.

"I'll collect tomorrow." He flashed a grin at me, which raised my hackles. "Another month or two, I wouldn't be able to beat you. Time your battles better next time!"

As he strode away, I glowered at his retreating back, no longer caring about the dignity of losing with grace.

Shuxiao clapped me on my shoulder. "It was close. For a moment I thought you had him, but those flying targets are tricky. I miss mine half the time."

"Close is not good enough."

She pulled a face. "You're too hard on yourself. He beat you today, but you've only been training for a few months."

A little cheered by her words, I turned to General Jianyun. His head was tilted to one side, an assessing light in his eyes as he stared at the boards.

"General Jianyun, could I try that disc again?"

I would not lose a second time.

8

A loud pounding on the doors jolted me awake.

"Xingyin, are you up?" Liwei called from outside.

I groaned, my limbs and eyes still heavy with sleep. "Come back when the sun is up!"

"No." He sounded gratingly cheerful. "Must I remind you of our wager?"

I glared in his direction, a wasted endeavor when he could not see it. How tempted I was to leave him waiting outside, while I stayed in bed and ignored him—but that would be both petulant and pointless. More than the fact he *was* the Crown Prince, I had given my word. Kicking aside the covers, I dragged myself up and washed my face with cold water—too tired to even heat it—before throwing on a silk robe and gathering my hair into a low knot. When I stepped out, I found Liwei leaning by the wall, tapping his foot impatiently. He had dressed simply in plain gray brocade, his hair tied up with a black ribbon.

It was dark outside, except for the glowing rosewood lanterns. Not even the kitchen attendants had risen yet to prepare the morning meal.

"Where are we going?" I asked, as we hurried through the courtyard.

"Outside the palace. We don't have lessons this morning as our teachers will attend court for an audience with my father. Even General Jianyun has released us today because of Captain Wenzhi's return from battle."

My ears pricked up. Captain Wenzhi was one of the youngest and most celebrated warriors in the Celestial Kingdom. The soldiers spoke of his accomplishments, and his skill with the sword and bow with such reverence, my curiosity had been roused. Unfortunately, he was often away on assignment, to the dismay of his many admirers—and when he returned, it was never for long. I had hoped to meet him myself on the training field, and part of me was a little disappointed to miss this chance.

Yet a thrill coursed through me at the thought of leaving the palace, as I followed Liwei to a deserted courtyard ringed by a thick stone wall. A pulse of his energy glided over my skin, as warm as a sun-drenched breeze.

"I'm disguising our auras," he explained. "Otherwise, the guards will sense me leaving."

From Liwei's furtive behavior, this was not an official outing. Little wonder that we did not head to the main entrance as he was not permitted outside without the customary troop of guards and attendants. Only after he assumed his court duties, could he come and go as he pleased.

Struck by curiosity, I asked, "What's my aura like? I can sense yours, those around me, just not my own."

He gazed at me intently as I tensed with anticipation.

"Rain," he said finally.

"Rain?" I repeated, feeling like a bubble pricked. It sounded dismal and dull, not exciting in the least.

"A silver storm; fierce, relentless, untamed."

An unexpected warmth kindled in me at his words.

He grinned. "Do you like that explanation?"

My brief pleasure was abruptly doused. "Only if you mean it."

"I mean everything I say. Maybe that's why I displease my father so." He sounded somber now, his teasing manner gone.

Trying to lighten his mood again, I asked, "Will whatever you're doing help us walk through the wall, too?"

"Of course not. Just be patient." His eyes narrowed in concentration as the air around us shimmered once more. A gust of wind surged, sweeping us into the air. My heart plunged, my stomach turning over as we were tossed over the wall—and set back down again at the edge of a large forest.

I staggered, clutching onto a tree. My breaths came short and fast. The sensation of nothingness, of falling through the air, brought unwelcome memories crashing down. The terror of the moment when I had leapt from Ping'er's cloud.

Liwei stared at me. "You're shaking. What's wrong?"

Unable to speak, I crouched on the ground, pressing my forehead to my arms.

He had been hurrying me all morning, yet now he sat beside me in companionable silence. His arm slid across my shoulders, drawing me to him. I inhaled deeply, catching his scent—like spring grass, fresh with a tinge of sweetness.

Slowly, his heat seeped into my trembling body until I was steady once more. Conscious of his nearness, I shifted away, clasping my hands around my knees and trying not to think how cold I felt without his touch.

"I'm fine. We don't need to sit here anymore," I said.

"What happened?" he asked gently.

"I . . . I don't like falling." A sliver of the truth, barely scraping its surface.

Footsteps thudded against the ground, growing louder. Guards, patrolling the area? Taking my hand, Liwei helped me up, and we sprinted into the forest.

"Was this how you got out the first time I met you?" I asked, as we ran. After the months of training, I found it easy to keep pace with him.

"Yes. I was curious about my companion. I would be spending a lot of time with this person and I wanted to make sure they weren't annoying, awful, or dull. I'd already visited six houses before the Golden Lotus Mansion."

"Why did you hold the competition?" I wanted to know.

"Friends—real ones—are hard to come by in the Jade Palace." His blunt admission took me by surprise. Countless courtiers and nobles vied for his attention. Part of my duties included sifting through the gifts and invitations which streamed into the Courtyard of Eternal Tranquility each day. Liwei ignored most of the requests, preferring to read or paint in his room than attend any banquet.

"I ask myself, sometimes," he continued in a low voice. "How many would seek my friendship if I were not the emperor's son? A position I did nothing to earn."

I would.

The words sprang to my tongue, yet I could not speak them aloud. It sounded like hollow flattery when it was nothing but the truth. How many times did I wish he were *not* the son of the Celestial Emperor? And that I did not have to lie about who I was to keep my loved ones safe.

"With the contest, I hoped to meet someone new—untainted

by ambition or greed. My mother thwarted me with her conditions, but fortunately, I met you."

It was the first time he told me why he had aided my participation. "I thought you helped me because you pitied me," I admitted with a pang of shame. I had not deserved his sympathy, not when I'd misled him into thinking my family was dead. Yet how could I have corrected him without more lies?

A smile lit his face. "I helped you because I *liked* you. You speak your mind, you take pride in yourself. You're honest in what you want, and fearless in reaching for it. You don't pretend to be someone else around me. And while you didn't know who I was then, that holds true even now."

Guilt doused the glow in my chest. I found myself unable to hold his stare. I *was* pretending, I had been right from the start. I was myself and yet, I was not who he thought I was.

He continued, oblivious to my unease. "When I'm with you, I feel you see me for who I am—not the crown or the kingdom. Not the favors I can extend or withhold." He sighed then, with exaggerated heaviness. "Little did I know what I got myself into. Every night I fall asleep, worn out from your attacks, your insults ringing between my ears—"

"Nothing you didn't deserve or ask for!" I retorted. "Might I remind you that *you're* the one who insists on sparring with me day and night." I ignored the hand he extended to me, glaring at him instead.

Liwei cleared his throat meaningfully. "And might *I* remind you, you're not honoring the terms of our bet right now."

Swallowing several choice insults, I took his hand. When his strong fingers closed around mine, I tried to quell the unexpected leap in my pulse.

We strolled through the forest, only halting at the sound of voices. The air hummed as though alive, with the mingled auras of immortals.

"We're here." He pulled me through the trees into a large clearing.

Dozens of stalls were packed together, coiling into a large spiral like the whorl of a shell. They were crafted from lacquered wood in red and black, blue and yellow, with painted signs displayed on the top. Mouthwatering smells of unfamiliar and tempting foods laced the air, and there was an undercurrent of excitement among the crowd already browsing at this early hour.

"What is this place?" I breathed, in a tone of wonder.

He seemed pleased by my reaction. "This market is held once every five years. It appears at dawn and ends by noon. Immortals come from all over to trade possessions, magical items, or rare delicacies."

As we strode deeper into the clearing, heads swung toward Liwei like flowers to the sun. Even without his regal attire, his bearing and looks commanded attention. When he paid them no regard, their eyes slid to me—narrowed with speculation, widened in surprise. We were an incongruous pair, but what did I care for the opinions they wore as plainly as the ornaments in their hair? Nothing could dampen my excitement today, my exhilaration at being here with him.

As we walked past the stalls, merchants called out loudly to entice prospective customers:

"Enchanted amulets!"

"Lychees from the Mortal Realm!"

"Rubies from the Fire Valley!"

Customers purchased items by trading goods of their own— from sparkling gems and pearls the size of my thumb, to sachets of fragrant herbs and rings of precious metal. I would have lingered at every stall, but Liwei hastened me along.

"We only have a couple of hours until the market closes. The rarer items are farther down, toward the center," he explained.

"Tea from Kunlun Mountain!" called a young lady as she offered cups to those passing by. The aroma from her tea was so fragrant, she soon attracted a long line of customers—Liwei and I among them.

Kunlun was a mountain range of great mystical energy in the world below. It was the only place in the Mortal Realm where immortals were permitted to reside, as long as they kept themselves hidden from sight. The rarest plants and flowers grew there, cultivated by the unique harmony of mortal and immortal energy. Sipping the tea, I found it wonderful—rich and aromatic, with a hint of bitterness that only enhanced its flavor. Liwei pulled out a jade ring and exchanged it for several silk bags of tea.

"Why the ring?" I asked. "Why the jewels, herbs, and such?"

"Some are for ornamentation, while the rest possess special properties or power. These rings"—he lifted his pouch—"each contain a fragment of energy which can aid in the casting of enchantments."

A stall caught my attention, one piled with shells. Some were as large as my fist, and others, the size of my nail. Their colors ranged from pure white to azure, and a few with the blush of a lotus petal.

"These shells are enchanted to capture your favorite sound, melody, or even a loved one's voice. They were picked from the deepest waters in the Southern Sea," the merchant said with pride.

The Southern Sea, Ping'er's home. I picked up a beautiful white shell, tracing my finger along its curve. However, with nothing to trade, I laid it down again. Beside me, Liwei dug out a ring of red jade, offering it to the vendor. I pulled his arm back, not wanting him to buy it for me.

"Will you trade the shell for a song?" I asked the merchant. "I could play you a tune to capture into these shells which might enhance their value."

"How well do you play?" His gaze shifted, skimming the crowd for less troublesome customers.

Before I lost his attention completely, I drew out my flute and played a lively melody. One of my mother's favorites, of the rain trickling through a bamboo forest. When the song finished, I was startled to find a small group of people around me, some holding out a colored stone or a silver ring. Before I could refuse, the shell vendor swooped in and took all the items. With deft hands, he wrapped up the white shell I wanted, placing it into my palm along with half the items I had earned. The rest, he dropped into his own pouch.

"A pleasure doing business with you," the merchant said, winking at me.

My mouth fell open as Liwei clapped me on my back. "You should set up a stall here next time," he suggested, in an amused tone.

I grinned. "And what would you do? Sit beside me and sell your paintings?"

He tilted his head to one side, his eyes bright. "Perhaps. We could travel the realm, stopping where we choose and leaving when we grow bored. It would be a good life."

"Yes, it would."

The words leapt out before I could stifle them. *Impossible*, a voice whispered in my mind, telling me nothing I did not know. The Celestial Crown Prince was not destined for such a life, unfettered by responsibility or duty. And how would such aimless wanderings help my mother? How could I leave her, alone and trapped, while I indulged my selfish impulses?

A pulse of silence beat through us, the air thick with sudden tension. To distract him, I lifted my palm to show him my earnings—a couple of silver rings, two drops of amber and a small blue stone.

"Let's find some breakfast," I said, pretending our earlier words had been forgotten.

We bought fresh lychees, crisp chive dumplings, and almond cakes, eating them as we made our way through the market. Our fingers were sticky with a coating of oil, sugar, and crumbs as we began peeling away the red scaly skin of the lychees, its translucent flesh sweeter than honey. Liwei likened their delicate flavor to the Immortal Peaches, which took over three centuries to ripen, but sadly the lychees possessed none of their magical properties.

It was almost midday when we reached the end of the marketplace, the very center of the spiral of stalls. The last one was crafted from black-lacquered wood, with a small sign that read "Precious Ornaments." Its owner sat serenely among her wares, not calling out or waving to the customers. Her trays were crammed with carved pieces of jasper and jade, carnelian and turquoise, which could be fastened to one's waist. Liwei picked up two exquisite ornaments of white jade carved into endless knots, a symbol of longevity and luck. Above them, gleamed a clear gemstone shaped as a tear, and from its base hung a tassel of azure silk.

Observing his interest, the seller drew closer. "Young Lord, you have excellent taste. Those are Sky Drop Tassels. Ask a loved one or dear friend to channel a little of their energy into it.

When the stone is clear, they are safe and well. But when it turns red, they are in the utmost danger and you can use the tassel to find them."

"I will take these." Liwei counted out ten rings of grass-green jade, which he passed to her. She thanked him as she tucked the rings into her sleeve.

Liwei's thumb grazed one of the stones in his palm. His magic swirled forth, the clear gem now aglitter with golden flecks of light.

He offered it to me, but I did not take it. "What is this for?"

"Can't I give my friend a gift?" When he opened his mouth, I braced for another reminder of our wager, but all he said was "It would please me greatly if you would take it." Something in his gaze held mine fast.

I nodded, unable to find the words. He smiled at me, before bending to tie the tassel to my waist. The jade gleamed mutedly against the pale silk of my dress. How I wished I had something to give him in exchange.

"Thank you. I will treasure it always," I told him.

"You should," he said gravely. "This way you'll know when I'm in danger and you have no excuse not to come to my aid."

I laughed aloud. An inconceivable thought that the Crown Prince of the Celestial Kingdom would ever need my help.

He gave me the other tassel. "Now, you. Channel your energy into the stone."

I paused. "Are you sure?"

"Friends watch out for each other. If that is what you want, too?" The slight hesitation in his voice pricked me. Did he think I might refuse? I cherished this about him—that despite his position, he never demanded, that he always gave me the choice.

I pressed my fingers against the stone, releasing my energy

into it. It glowed just as the one tied to my waist, yet with silver lights sparkling in its depths. With a smile, Liwei fastened it to his black sash.

"The sun and the moon. A matched pair," the vendor remarked, as she picked up her trays. I looked at her—uncertain of her meaning—but as another customer approached her, we walked away.

At noon, the crowd dispersed, the marketplace obscured by swirling clouds of white and gray. The merchants packed up their stalls, stepped upon their clouds, and were swiftly whisked away. In just a few moments, all trace of the market had vanished, as though it had never existed—except for the weight of the jade dangling from my waist, the lingering sweetness of lychees in my mouth, and the warmth nestled deep in my heart.

9

In the Celestial Kingdom there were no seasons to chart the passing of time. Two years swept by so quickly, I almost lost count but for the waxing and waning of the moon. The ease I felt here reminded me of my home, except for the nagging ache in my chest whenever I thought of my mother. How I longed to see her again and not just as a distant orb in the heavens. I consoled myself that at least I'd found a sense of purpose here which I had never known before; striving to better myself, to find a way home.

Dawn till dusk, Liwei and I were together—studying our lessons or sparring on the field. Mealtimes were my favorite, when we would talk about anything that took our fancy, whether serious matters or in jest. Once, Liwei asked me about my home and how my parents had died. I had bitten down hard on my tongue, wishing I could have told him the truth. From the tightening of his lips, I knew he had been disappointed by my reticence. How it wrenched me inside—I was not heartless, laden with guilt at deceiving him. Our friendship meant more to me than anything I possessed.

Tomorrow would be his birthday. A grand celebration was planned as this year was a special one, marking the assumption of his court duties as the Crown Prince. He had invited me to attend but I'd declined, having little interest in spending an evening with Their Celestial Majesties and their court. Nonetheless, I had agonized over his gift as I owned little of value, and finally settled on composing him a song. He had a keen appreciation for music though he did not play an instrument himself. However, it took longer than anticipated as I could only work late at night or early in the morning, weaving a privacy shield around my room to prevent the music from drifting across the courtyard.

I rummaged through the drawers, pulling out the white shell I had bought from the market years ago. It gleamed in my palm, the curved whorls ending in an elegant spire. Placing the shell on the table, I cast a shred of wind into it to awaken its magic. Then I lifted the flute to my mouth, letting my breath slide into the instrument. The shell glowed as the melody poured forth, its light fading once the last note ended. Hastily, I wrapped it with a piece of silk. I had taken too long; I was already late.

I dashed across the courtyard, halting just outside his chamber. A powerful aura pulsed within—jagged, sharp, and strong— one I had done my best to avoid so far. Sweat slicked my palms as I slid the doors open and entered. The Celestial Empress sat beside Liwei, while her attendants stood behind her. Her green robe pooled on the floor like a carpet of moss, gold leaf-shaped pins gleaming from her hair. I had never seen the empress at such close quarters before. Memories of my parting from my mother flashed across my mind, cutting me as though it had been yesterday.

I knelt to greet her as etiquette demanded, folding my body over until my brow and palms touched the floor.

The empress did not give me leave to rise. "Is this the behavior of the Companion to the Crown Prince? To rise this late and leave my son to attend to himself?" Her voice was thick with censure.

I should have apologized or pleaded for forgiveness. But though my body was taut with tension, my lips stayed tightly sealed. I was no longer a cowering child, afraid of her shadow.

"Rise," Liwei said.

I lifted my head from the ground yet remained on my knees. I would give the empress no reason to dismiss me.

"Honorable Mother, Xingyin was only late this morning because of my task." Liwei looked at me. "Did you find the snow ginseng root?"

"Yes." I was glad for his quick thinking.

"Could you give it to the kitchen to be brewed into a tonic? Ask them to send it with the afternoon meal to Their Celestial Majesties."

Conscious of the watchful attendants, I pressed my forehead to the ground in acknowledgment. Rising to my feet, I hurried to the entrance, eager to escape.

The empress's voice drifted after me, a more pleasant tone now that I was gone. "Liwei, you're a filial son," she praised him. "Tomorrow's banquet will be a grand event. The Flower and Forest Immortals will join us, as will the sea monarchs—a rare chance to affirm our goodwill toward the Four Seas. We will also be honored by the attendance of Queen Fengjin and her daughter."

"Princess Fengmei?" Liwei asked, with a catch in his voice.

"Of course. The Phoenix Kingdom is our most important ally—more than ever, with the threat of that cursed Demon Realm still hanging over us." She added, in a tone laden with meaning, "I hope you'll be an attentive host. And that you know what's expected of you."

Beyond the doorway, I glanced back at Liwei in sympathy. He did not enjoy such occasions, avoiding as many as he could. But it would be impossible for him to escape his own celebration, particularly with the sharp eye of his mother watching his every move.

Liwei and I had planted a small garden in a corner of the courtyard. Grabbing a shovel, I dug up the snow ginseng root, grown from a seed just a month ago. While it usually took years to cultivate ginseng, Liwei's enchantment helped the plants mature faster. Admiring the perfectly formed root, its flesh so white that it was almost translucent, I deemed it a worthwhile sacrifice to save my hide.

In the bustling kitchen, I found Minyi, whom I had grown to know well. After passing her the ginseng, I decided to wait while she prepared our food.

She scrutinized me, her nose wrinkling. "Xingyin, you're so pale. Are you eating enough?"

"I was late this morning and Her Celestial Majesty scolded me," I told her.

She sighed in commiseration. The empress was much feared for her temper—fierce, malicious, so easily roused—and few were spared it.

"Our empress has too much fire in her. Those from the Phoenix Kingdom have such hot tempers," she remarked.

"Phoenix Kingdom? Isn't she a Celestial?"

She shook her head, casting a furtive look around. Minyi was privy to the stories and gossip from the many attendants who visited the kitchen. It was a simple matter to trade a delicacy for the latest news and in the evenings, a cup of wine loosened even the stiffest tongues. And the one thing she loved more than collecting gossip was sharing it with her friends.

"Before she wed the emperor, Her Celestial Majesty was a princess of the Phoenix Kingdom. She was not so ill-humored at first, but her disposition worsened after the death of her beloved kin."

It was the first I had heard of it. I did not think it possible, yet pity flared in me at the thought of her loss. "What happened to them?"

Minyi's face clouded over. "A tragic tale. The empress is a relation of Lady Xihe, the sun goddess who dwells in the Fragrant Mulberry Grove in the eastern sky. Lady Xihe had ten children whom she used to take upon her phoenix-drawn chariot—one at a time—to ride across the heavens. Her children were powerful creatures of pure light and heat, revered as the sun in the mortal world."

I went cold inside. "Ten children? Ten suns? The kin of the Celestial Empress?"

Minyi stirred a simmering pot of noodles, thankfully oblivious to my mounting distress. "The phoenixes are a close relation of the three-legged sunbirds."

Sunbirds. The word seared me. "What happened?" I choked out.

"Many years ago, Lady Xihe was gravely injured. To aid her, the empress sent a trusted general to the Fragrant Mulberry Grove to drive the chariot on her behalf. Only one sunbird was permitted to join him, but they disobeyed, all ten leaping into the chariot at once and flying away before the general could stop them. The sunbirds did not wish to return, soaring through the skies night and day." Minyi paused for a moment. "It was a terrible time, of blinding light and blistering heat. The mortals suffered most, their fragile world scorched to the brink of destruction."

She continued, "The Celestial Emperor sent messengers to reprimand the sunbirds, but they ignored them all. They were so swift, no one could catch them. The emperor might have struck them down himself, but the empress shielded them from attack. Under her protection, the sunbirds would have burned the world to a cinder—but they were finally shot down by a brave mortal."

My father. My legs trembled. I clutched the side of the table, my elbow knocking over a bowl of yellow plums that rolled onto the floor. Avoiding a glare from an irate cook, I bent down to pick up the fruit, glad for the opportunity to hide my face. I sifted through my faded memories of the book I had read once—my father's story as retold by the mortals. The sunbirds were said to be favored by the gods, under their protection. But the Celestial Empress's blood relations? It was little wonder that she had sought to punish my father for slaying them.

I swallowed to moisten my parched throat. "The mortal . . . what of him?"

Minyi sprinkled chopped green chives over two bowls of noodles, then lifted them onto a tray of polished wood. Almost as an afterthought, she added a small dish of vegetables and a plate of dumplings. I suppressed the urge to grab her arm and shake the rest of the tale from her.

"Oh. The mortal's deeds were praised by the emperor and he was rewarded with the Elixir of Immortality."

"Wasn't His Celestial Majesty angry with him for killing the empress's kin?" I could not conceal the urgency in my voice.

Minyi leaned closer, speaking softer now. "It was said that the emperor might have had a hand in the sunbirds' downfall.

The mortal shot them down with an enchanted bow of ice and he wore an amulet that protected him from their fire. How could a mere mortal have obtained such treasures, much less used them without His Celestial Majesty's blessing?"

Something jarred me. Why would the emperor do such a thing? Why didn't he stop the sunbirds himself? Was it just to avoid a confrontation with the empress?

"What happened next?" I asked, though I feared her answer, too.

She looked up in surprise. Perhaps, she thought, that was the end of it. The world saved from ruin. The mortal rewarded for his service to the Celestial Emperor. "Lady Xihe was furious at the deaths of her children and she severed all ties with the empress. As a relation of the sun goddess, the Phoenix Queen was incensed, too. Before, there was much talk of an engagement between her daughter and His Highness, but I heard that was called off! A shame, as it would have been a most eligible match. Some gripe that Princess Fengmei is a hundred years older than His Highness. Yet those are trifling numbers for such as us."

Liwei had never mentioned a betrothal before, though I now understood his strange reaction to the princess's name this morning. There were so many peach blossom rumors surrounding him, I had come to regard them with no more weight than the petals blown by the wind—forgotten once they landed on the ground. But that was not what I wanted to know now.

"What of the mortal's fate? After he was gifted the elixir?" I probed, hoping she would not notice my keen interest. Perhaps I might glean some clue as to my father's whereabouts.

Minyi frowned as she lifted a porcelain teapot onto the tray. Fragrant tendrils of jasmine wafted into my nostrils. "The mortal never ascended to the skies as an immortal. No one knows what became of him." Her voice trailed off as she turned away abruptly.

I did not question her further. I was not surprised at Minyi's reluctance to speak of my mother's ascension. The punishment of the Moon Goddess was not a tale shared freely. Their Celestial Majesties did not appreciate being reminded of those who had displeased them.

I thanked Minyi, clutching the tray of food as I left the kitchen in a daze. The empress disliked me, believing me unworthy to be her son's companion. I shuddered, imagining her spite if she ever discovered that my father had slain the sunbirds. I breathed deeply, trying to calm the churning in my stomach. My mother's instincts had been right; the empress *did* bear my father a grudge. She would show us no mercy, she would snatch at the chance to destroy us. I would not let her, I resolved. Though I could do nothing now, except work as hard as I could, honing my skills and searching for a way to keep us all safe.

When I returned to Liwei's room, I was relieved to find the empress had left, in no mood to feign respect and obedience. We ate in silence, neither of us inclined to idle chatter today. Minyi's dumplings were beautifully made; plump with pork and leek, its skin fried to a crisp golden brown—yet they tasted as paper on my tongue.

"Xingyin, you look tired," Liwei observed.

My hands flew to my cheeks, discreetly pinching the color back into them. He was the second person to have commented on my pallor this morning.

"I didn't sleep well." The excuse sounded limp even to my ears.

"Don't take what my mother said to heart. She seems fierce, but she's just overly concerned for me."

I nodded woodenly, not trusting myself to speak. Lifting our books from the table, I waited for him by the doors.

He took the heavy stack from me. "I've told you that you don't need to carry my things for me."

"What would your mother say?" I asked.

"Don't tell her," he said, flashing me a conspiratorial grin.

I returned his smile, though I could not discard my unease. All morning I was unsettled, barely hearing the teachers' lessons, earning myself a scowl from General Jianyun and a scolding from Teacher Daoming. And now, by the archery boards, I missed all my targets while training alongside Shuxiao.

She winced at a particularly bad shot, which left my arrow buried in the grass a foot from the board. "Xingyin, is there dust in your eyes?"

Before I could reply, General Jianyun stalked toward me, the hollows of his cheeks pulled taut. I had worn his patience out today. "Xingyin, have our practices become so easy that you no longer bother to exert yourself?"

I lowered my head, shame rising in me. General Jianyun was a diligent mentor to Liwei and me. While many of our teachers focused their efforts on the Crown Prince, he divided his attention equally between us.

Hearing the general's raised tone, Liwei glanced over from where he was sparring with a soldier. He lunged forward, his sword outstretched—and with a few well-placed thrusts, won his match in moments. He then wasted no time in striding to my side, and while I was glad for his support, I did not want him to witness my humiliation.

General Jianyun plucked a leather bag from the weapons rack. "Let's try something more challenging today. If you miss any, stay back for an extra hour of practice tonight."

With that, he flung the contents of the bag into the air. Ten small clay discs shot out, each no larger than a loquat. "Hit them all!" he barked.

Before he finished speaking, I had shot down the first two. In the same breath, I nocked my next arrow and took down another three in rapid succession. Dropping to one knee, I shot two more that soared into the sky. The final three were almost out of sight. I positioned my arrow carefully to hit one, and then another. The last disc slipped beyond my sight. I closed my eyes, straining to listen through the silence. My mind was clear, devoid of thought. A faint flutter reached my ears, a whisper of wind. I released my arrow with a twang, the disc shattering into fragments.

I stilled, unnerved by the sudden hush and the crowd which had gathered. Then a tall, lean soldier I had never seen before clapped, the sound breaking the daze. Shuxiao cheered as Liwei stepped forward, lifting me up by my waist and spinning me around.

"Liwei, put me down," I hissed, conscious of the watchful stares. For some reason, I found it hard to catch my breath, my pulse leaping in an erratic rhythm.

He laughed as he set me upon the ground, and with a parting grin, headed back to the sword fighting station.

The soldiers dispersed but General Jianyun remained, studying me for a moment. "Have you given any thought to your future? When you're no longer the Crown Prince's companion?" he finally asked.

His blunt question struck me. I had not imagined that my position would end, but Liwei would soon assume his court duties. His lessons would decrease and then, what would I do? Become his attendant, serving his meals and tea? The idea seared me like a hot coal.

General Jianyun continued, oblivious to my unease, "Your archery is unmatched. According to Teacher Daoming, your magic is strong. I think you would do very well in the army and your future could be brighter than the sun."

My mind whirled with the possibilities. My father was a soldier; it had been his path to glory, to slaying the sunbirds and saving the world. A great honor, a terrible burden. His reward had been the elixir which turned my mother and me immortal, though it parted us from him, too.

Snapping out of my stupor, I asked, "General Jianyun, how does one advance in the army?"

"Fighting for our kingdom. Performing each task to the best of one's abilities. Protecting your fellow soldiers. Hard work, obedience, loyalty throughout the years. What greater honor is there than to serve our kingdom and Their Celestial Majesties?" Pride rang in his voice.

A curt refusal sprang to my tongue which I quashed out of respect to the general, though I could not stop my lip from curling.

He did not seem to notice, adding as an afterthought, "Some also dream of winning the Crimson Lion Talisman, though such a thing is rare."

"Crimson Lion Talisman?" I had never heard of it before.

"It is the highest honor of the Celestial Army, awarded by the emperor himself. Its bearer is granted a royal favor."

A wild hope fluttered in my chest. "How is this talisman won?" I cursed the tremor in my voice, hoping he did not hear my eagerness.

"Through exceptional acts of valor, courage, or sacrifice, in service to the Celestial Kingdom." He frowned. "However, this is not something to pin your hopes upon. In my lifetime, the talisman has been awarded less than a handful of times."

General Jianyun must be hundreds of years old. A thousand? How could I surpass the mighty warriors here, when I had barely grasped my powers a couple of years ago? No, I could not allow myself to think so, I could not admit defeat before I tried. Among all the mortals across the centuries, it was *my* father who had caught the emperor's attention to win the Elixir of Immortality. I would strive for no less.

Yet something reined in my surging excitement. If I joined the Celestial Army, I would have to leave the Courtyard of Eternal Tranquility. I was safe there. As happy as I could be, away from my mother. Ah, I was becoming muddled inside. I could never forget why I was here—that I had been torn from my home, and that I had come to the Jade Palace to find my way back. General Jianyun's talk of honor and service did not move me. This was not my home; I had no loyalty to this place. I even bore a grudge against Their Celestial Majesties, which I was willing to swallow for my own ends. And yet, this offer gave me a glimpse into a future where I could advance through my own merit, a chance to grasp at my mother's freedom. Better by far than my wild fantasies of soaring to the moon and shattering the enchantment which bound her there. What life would await us after that? An eternity of being hunted and living in fear.

General Jianyun cleared his throat, perhaps wondering at my prolonged silence.

I cupped my hands as I bowed to him. "Thank you for your confidence in me, General Jianyun. I promise to consider it." His offer tempted me more than I cared to admit. I was already inclined to accept, though I could not do so before speaking to Liwei.

Over our meal that night, Liwei asked, "What did you and General Jianyun talk about? It seemed to be a serious conversation."

Surprised that he had noticed, I lifted my chopsticks to stuff a lump of rice into my mouth. For some reason, I was reluctant to tell him about the general's offer. A few excuses drifted through my mind, but I had only lied to him once before and that had been out of necessity.

"General Jianyun suggested that I join the army, after my role here comes to an end."

"End?" He sounded confused. "Who told you it was ending?"

I placed my chopsticks down on the table and fixed him with a somber stare. "Liwei, how long will things go on this way? Once you take on your responsibilities, you will have less time for lessons. You won't need a companion."

For once, he appeared at a loss. "But . . . you're my friend."

How those words tore at my conscience, yet I could not think of myself alone. "I *am* your friend. Here, or wherever I go."

"Do you want to leave me? To join the army?" There was a note of incredulity in his voice and, buried beneath, hurt.

"There are things I want which you know nothing of. I do have my own dreams." My voice was hoarse with emotion. The years I had spent here, training and studying, were happy ones. And yet, these were just the rungs of the ladder that scaled my ambition.

Perhaps Liwei sensed me drawing away, the hardening of my resolve. He leaned toward me, as he asked, "What are your dreams? Let me help, however I can."

The words hovered at the tip of my tongue. To confide in him. To tell him the truth. He was a Celestial Prince, powerful and favored. But I stifled the urge. I was unsure of how things might change between us if he knew who I was. That I had lied to him. That I was the daughter of the disgraced goddess who had defied his father's wishes, and of the mortal who had slain his mother's beloved sunbirds.

"No, you can't help me," I said softly. "But I thank you for wanting to."

His hand covered mine, an unexpected tingle shooting through my arm. "My offer stands. Anytime, whatever you need. Think about it and don't make any hasty decisions."

I had believed my mind made up. Yet pinned by the intensity in his gaze, I could only nod in reply. *Tomorrow*, I told myself, cowardly. *I will decide tomorrow.*

10

I bolted upright, my scream piercing the night. My eyes darted
around the dark chamber as I gripped the bedcovers, crumpling them between my fingers. I was not home. I was not
too late. My mother and Ping'er were not dead.

Such nightmares had plagued me before, yet never in the
Courtyard of Eternal Tranquility—until now. Perhaps my encounter with the Celestial Empress or the uncertainty of my future had caused a relapse into the fears of my past.

Footsteps pounded across the courtyard. My doors were
flung open, the cool night air rushing in as Liwei stood in the
entrance. He crossed the room and sat down on my bed, lacing
his fingers through mine, his grip warm and strong.

"You were screaming. Are you all right?"

"A dream." My breaths were shaky and uneven. My terror
had been all too real. The image of my mother's lifeless form
flashed across my mind—my fear melding with a wrenching
longing for home. Tears, unbidden, pricked my eyes.

His other hand cradled my face, his thumb brushing my
cheek. He had only seen me cry once before, when we first met

by the river. Without hesitation, he pulled me into his arms and held me tight. I clutched him in return, his embrace awakening a need in me—unfamiliar and fierce. My guard lowered, I let myself be comforted by his strength, my body sinking against his as the dam on my emotions sprang free.

My tears drenched his clothes, the white silk damp now as I lifted my head away. Only then did I realize he wore just his inner robe; he must have come right from bed in his haste. My pulse raced, although I had seen him dressed so a thousand times before. With a corner of my sleeve, I dabbed the thin material to dry it. His heartbeat quickened against my palm as his arms tightened around me, kindling a heat which surged through my veins.

Our months of companionship melted away; it was like we were seeing each other for the first time. No longer was he the youth I had befriended, the young man who teased me. His touch inflamed my senses, his gaze stole my breath. I reached out to smooth his long hair from his face, tousled from slumber and gleaming darkly against the whiteness of his robe.

My lips parted. His eyes shifted to them, as deep as midnight pools. He bent and pressed his mouth to mine firmly, yet with an aching tenderness. I inhaled deeply, his warm clean scent laced with the fragrance of the flowers from the courtyard. One of his hands clasped the back of my head, while the other encircled my waist. My arms were wound tight around his neck, I did not know how they came to be there. We held each other so closely, his breath slipped into my mouth, hot and sweet as it mingled with my own. His lips pressed down harder, parting mine— our tongues seeking and entangling. A melting heat spread from my core all the way down to my toes. My limbs were weak as though turned to liquid, as we fell, entwined, onto my bed.

A gust of wind surged through the open doors. The pale blue curtains around my bed billowed, as soft as gossamer clouds. As the window panels rattled, I jerked upright . . . shivering from the loss of his warmth. My gaze shifted to the courtyard beyond. Anyone passing by could have seen what we were doing. Fortunately, it was still dark. The moon in the sky our only witness.

He sat up beside me, running his hands through his hair. "Xingyin, I'm sorry."

His words were a splash of cold water, a rude awakening from my daze. Of course, he would feel regret! In the darkness of night, stirred by pity and the outpouring of my emotions—it was little wonder he felt obliged to indulge me. And I had been only too eager to take advantage of his kindness.

"You have nothing to feel sorry about." My voice was light as I turned away, letting my hair veil my face. In his silence, I read agreement. "This was a mistake for us both. A moment of madness which will be forgotten by morning." A clumsy attempt to salvage my pride.

He clasped my hand tightly, pressing it to his chest. "Madness? I've never felt so sane in my life. Do you want to forget this happened? I cannot."

My heart beat wildly, as the wings of a bird against the bars of its cage. Yet fear and reason, ever vigilant, reared up. "We shouldn't be doing this."

He tilted his head toward me. "Why?"

His question was startling in its simplicity. But it was not as easy as he believed; there were too many reasons against us which he knew nothing of . . . because I had kept them from him.

He lowered his voice, as though making a confession, "I've wanted to kiss you for a long time now."

Heat suffused me again, gliding across my skin like I had

lain in the sun. His words drove my doubts away as I reached out and pulled him close, as he bent his head to mine once more. My eyes widened and then drifted shut, lost in a languid haze of desire like I was floating on a river of stars. When we finally broke apart, our breathing was harsh and ragged as we lay entangled in the moonlight, until a stirring in the stillness heralded the approach of dawn.

Remembering the day, I scrambled to my feet, digging through the drawer for my gift. As I pressed the silk-wrapped bundle into his hand, I suppressed the urge to snatch it back again. What was a humble shell to the priceless treasures he owned?

He pulled the cloth away, staring at the shell within. I picked it up and blew gently into it, the shell glowing as my song filled the room. A joyous one, rippling with promise and hope—and yearning, I realized now. The song of my heart, before I had known it myself.

He did not move until it had finished. "It's beautiful. What is it called?" he wanted to know.

I smiled, through the sudden thickness in my throat. "It's yours to name. I composed it for you."

He took the shell from me and lifted it again, but I caught his arm. "Listen to it when I'm not here."

His body stiffened as he twisted around to search my face. "Are you leaving?"

"I didn't mean it that way. It's your birthday gift, not a farewell one." My conscience pricked me at how I evaded his question.

He threaded his fingers through mine again, his tension easing. "Thank you. I've never received a more wonderful gift." He added, with a teasing smile, "And now, I don't have to plead with you to play me a song anymore."

I drew away, glaring at him with mock anger. "Am I so easily replaced?"

"I never want to find out." With a regretful sigh, he released me and rose from my bed. "I must leave before the attendants awaken."

I gathered my courage, calling after him. "Liwei, we don't have lessons tomorrow. Shall we spend the day together?"

He paused by the entrance, nodding once, his lips curved as he closed the doors after him.

Alone once more, my mind awoke from the spell I was under. Guilt assailed me, fierce and unrelenting. The Celestial Emperor had shown my mother no mercy, condemning her to eternal imprisonment. I recalled my mother's fear of the empress, her terror stabbing me with remorse. How could I feel this way about their son? Was I so weak, to betray her so easily?

I pressed my fingers to my temples, shoving them through my hair. But this was no betrayal of my mother. Even in the depths of her misery, she had not spoken a word of spite against the emperor and empress. She would not hold this against me; all she ever wanted was my happiness. I was my own person, separate from my parents—as was Liwei. And he was nothing like them. After all our time together, I knew that better than anyone. He was my dearest friend, before . . . what he was to me now. And I would not hold him to account for these events long past and circumstances beyond his control.

How I wished I could unburden my heart to him, to reveal all the parts of myself. Liwei would do nothing to hurt me, but I hesitated to entangle him in my affairs, to pit him against his parents when I knew of his tense relations with them. And the coward in me recoiled from his disappointment; a lover's deceit pierced deeper than a friend's.

I hated these lies, this fear and doubt. But all this paled at the threat of discovery. The Jade Palace was not a place for sharing such secrets. And here, my mother and I would find little mercy from the emperor's harshness, the empress's spite. More so, after all I had learned of how our families were bound. No, I would not break my promise to my mother—not until I knew it would be safe.

I lay awake in my bed until the rays of the sun slid out. In the morning light, last night's desire faded to the haze of a dream, except for the memory of his lips seared deep into my soul.

11

I stared at my reflection in the mirror. My black hair fell smoothly to my waist, my skin glowing from my afternoons in the sun. While my features might be unremarkable, I was content with what I saw—even the cleft in my chin which the Celestial Empress had criticized as a mark of ill-temper.

I reached for one of my usual dresses, but then pulled out a light blue silk instead, embroidered with colorful birds. When I slipped it on, a starling stitched in green thread spread its wings and flew once around the skirt. My lifeforce had indeed strengthened. Minyi had asked her friend, a skilled seamstress, to make this—after complaining my clothes were too plain and unbecoming. My closet was indeed filled with white garments. I had not minded, as they reminded me of my mother.

But now, life was vivid with color.

An unusual interest in my appearance gripped me today; rarely had I dressed with such care. There was a spring in my step as I walked across the courtyard, but outside Liwei's chamber, I hesitated. Had it been a dream? What if he did not remember?

Worse yet, what if he regretted all that had happened? Steeling myself, I pushed the doors open and entered.

He was already up, sitting by the table, in a brocade robe knotted around his waist with a length of black silk. A ring of silver pulled his hair up, flowing like a river of ink down his back. His eyes were as dark as they had always been, yet a hundred times more beautiful to me now.

His gaze lingered on me as he rose to his feet. "Don't look so astonished. I can get dressed without someone holding up my clothes for me." A smile tugged at his lips, as he added, "Though I much prefer it when it's you."

My treacherous mind conjured up images of all the times I had draped silk and brocade over his shoulders. How my fingers had grazed the hollow of his neck whenever I adjusted the folds of his robe, my hands encircling his waist to tie his sash. I had not given it a second thought then, yet now my heart raced as my throat went dry.

"Xingyin."

My name on his lips stirred me. I glanced at him, noticing the slender box that he held out to me. "It's your birthday, not mine."

"It's good luck to exchange gifts," he said, by way of explanation.

When I made no move to take the box, he flipped the lid open and pulled out a hairpin. Crafted from wood, it was lacquered in rich shades of blue, studded with tiny clear stones which snared and fractured the light.

My breath caught in my throat. Hairpins were traditionally gifted as a love token, but I quenched the hope that sparked in me. We had made no such promises to each other. As for last night . . . I was still unsure what it meant in the light of day.

"I made this a while ago, to match the meaning of your name. It took me a while to get the colors right."

He had made this? For me? It was exquisite, his skill capturing all the temperamental moods of the sky. And even if it were not, even if it were just a shaft of plain wood—it would mean no less to me.

He leaned forward and slid the pin into my hair. Just as he had the first time we met.

"Thank you," I managed, lifting my gaze to his.

"We only have the morning. My father has asked to see me before the banquet." He picked up a tiered basket from the table, before reaching for my hand with his other. "Will you change your mind and come tonight? It would mean a great deal to me to have you there. It would make it a lot less dull." His mouth curved into a persuasive smile.

My insides twisted at the thought of seeing Their Celestial Majesties. But this was Liwei's celebration and a part of me was curious about this side of him which I so rarely saw—that of the heir to the throne. And now, I found myself wanting to spend each moment with him, feeling an unfamiliar twinge when we were apart.

"Yes," I told him. "I will come."

In the courtyard, Liwei summoned a cloud. It struck me that he could now leave the palace at will, which meant he would assume his court duties soon. I pushed aside a wave of anxiety; I would not taint today with doubts of tomorrow or fears of the past. Although when I stared at the cloud, I could not help thinking of the last time I had flown on one with Ping'er. Stepping onto it, Liwei pulled me up behind him. The cloud was soft and cool, yet firm beneath my feet. When it darted through the air, I stumbled, but Liwei grabbed my hand to steady me and did not let go.

After a few moments, I began to relax. The cloud soared so smoothly that I soon forgot my fears. Flying in the daylight was infinitely more pleasurable than fleeing in the night. Towering mountains, shimmering lakes, and lush emerald forests unfurled like a scroll painting beneath our feet. As we darted through a light shower of rain, the droplets that grazed my skin were as refreshing as morning dew. I might have been cold with the gathering dark clouds obscuring the sun, but for Liwei's hands over mine, infusing me with warmth.

We landed in the middle of a forest, the likes of which I had never seen before. Not in the Celestial Kingdom, not even in my dreams. Peach blossom trees bloomed as far as my eye could see, their branches laden with pink and white flowers that laced the air with a heady sweetness. Whenever the wind blew, a scattering of petals drifted to the ground.

I caught one in my palm—velvet soft, lighter than air. "Where are we?"

"Somewhere in the Mortal Realm."

"The Mortal Realm?" My voice rose in alarm.

Immortals were forbidden from descending here without leave from the Celestial Emperor. Long ago, they had roamed this world at leisure. Perhaps they enjoyed the rush of power to walk among those weaker, to hear their songs of worship or terrified pleas. To the mortals, they were not just immortals; they were gods. However, this had led to great turmoil. Mortals were terrified by magic. And too many destinies were altered through such interference, causing the untimely deaths of some or saving others from fated calamities. The Keeper of Mortal Fates persuaded the Celestial Emperor to issue an edict, banning all immortals from venturing here freely. Though many lamented this outcome, none dared to challenge the command. Since then, our realm was veiled from mortal sight and with each passing year, their memories of us faded further into myth and legend. All they saw now when they looked up into the sky were the sun, moon, and stars.

"Are we allowed to be here?" I peered furtively at the sky, half expecting the Keeper of Mortal Fates to descend and haul us back for punishment.

Liwei lifted the oblong piece of jade which hung by his waist, intricately carved with a dragon. An imperial seal. "With this, we can go anywhere we wish," he assured me, dropping it down where it clinked against the Sky Drop Tassel. "One of the few benefits of attending those lengthy discussions at court."

After walking a little farther into the forest, we sat beside a gurgling stream. The soft grass was blanketed by pale petals, a few already browning at their edges. A reminder that nothing here stayed the same, each moment bringing all creatures closer to their inevitable end. I could not help thinking of my father, growing older with each passing day. A longing gripped me to search for him, to seek him out if he lived still. But Liwei knew nothing of my parents, and how could I tell him now?

I was glad he could not see my face as he unpacked the basket. Out came a porcelain wine jar, golden pears, and an assortment of steamed buns—some stuffed with sweet bean paste, others with meat. As I reached for one, my hand collided into his.

He whisked the plate out of my reach. "How about a challenge for these?"

I groaned inwardly. Without my bow, he would probably best me at any other weapon. And while I did not care much for the prize, I cared even less for losing. Oblivious to my discontent,

Liwei searched the ground until he found two sturdy sticks, tossing me one.

I caught it midair. "Don't you think the odds are weighted
in your favor? You're the better swordsman. At least for now," I
muttered under my breath.

He circled me with predatory grace. "Already conceding defeat?"

I leapt to my feet at once, my fingers tightening around the
rough bark.

A length of white silk appeared in his palm. "I'll cover one
of my eyes, but I'll still win."

"By all means," I said sweetly, trying not to gnash my teeth.
I could have spurned his arrogant offer, but I would grasp any
advantage just to dent his pride.

A breeze swept through the trees, raining flowers upon us
as we stood opposite each other. I sprang at his blindfolded side
first, hoping to take him by surprise. Liwei flung his stick up
to block mine, withdrawing quickly to strike my calf. I hissed,
whirling to stab him in the chest. A breath whooshed from his
lips as I darted out of his reach, a moment before we flew at
each other in earnest. The peace of the forest disintegrated with
the crunch of our feet against the stones and dried leaves, the
crash from our colliding sticks. I could not help a rush of admiration for his technique—his fierce attack yet swift recoil, each
move controlled and yet free. Our match was closer than expected, and I hoped with some luck I might win. Spotting an
opening, I lunged forward—but he leaned back low, my stick
slicing through empty air. Before I could retreat, his hard blow
knocked the stick from my hand.

I stifled a cry, struggling to conceal my frustration. "If it had been with the bow, I would have beaten you with *both* of my eyes closed." Grabbing a bun from the basket, I tossed it to him.

He caught it but offered it to me at once. "Here, you have it."

"It's your prize." Picking up a pear, I sank my teeth into its ripe flesh, its sweet and fragrant juice filling my mouth.

When he tried to give it to me again, I shook my head. "Do you want to challenge me for the right *not* to eat it?" I asked archly.

He shot me an icy look before biting into the soft bread. It smelled delicious, the rich fragrance of roasted pork wafting toward me.

"Make sure you don't choke on it," I said with an unfeigned smile.

Hunger was a small price to pay for the irate expression that flashed across his face. I had lost the match yet somehow gained the advantage. Gazing into the overcast sky, I marveled at how everything seemed more beautiful. Even the rain clouds were no longer gloomy and threatening, instead imbued with dark majesty.

After we had eaten, he poured me a cup of wine. As the delicate fragrance of osmanthus sprang in the air, I stilled, recalling a forest of moon-white blossoms.

My fingers clenched around the cup as I lifted it in a toast. "May you always be happy."

His gaze rested on me. "If I'm always as happy as I am now, that would be the best wish of all."

The wine slid down my throat with a heady warmth. After we had drained our cups, he refilled them and raised his to me in turn. "May all your dreams come true."

I wondered what he would think if he knew what they were.

For a long time, my dreams were about regaining what I had lost in the past. However, since last night, or perhaps even before—a hope for the future had taken root in my heart.

"What are your dreams?" he asked, just as he did yesterday, as though he had plucked the thoughts from me.

"To be with my loved ones," I said, after a pause. It was the truth, but the hollow type which was gilded in deceit.

As his eyes darkened and he leaned closer, my breathing quickened.

"But I'll settle for beating you today." I blurted the first thing in my mind, cursing myself when he drew away.

He clasped his hands behind his head as he lay down on the grass. "Care to make good on your big words from earlier?"

"Why not? I won't take it easy on you just because it's your birthday." I was not as confident as I sounded; I had never shot blindfolded before.

A golden bow materialized on the ground before us, exquisitely carved with feathers curling along its limbs.

"I wanted to show this to you," Liwei said as he rose to his feet. "One of the most powerful weapons in our treasury. This might be a good chance to test it."

I picked it up, my fingers tingling where they touched the metal. "Where are the arrows?"

Liwei moved behind me, our bodies mere inches apart. With his arms stretched out on each side of me, he guided me to raise the bow and draw its silvery string. My pulse raced and my head spun. I would miss any target in our current position, even if it were five paces away.

A flaming arrow formed in my grasp, crackling as though alive. Startled, I would have dropped the bow but Liwei's grip tightened over mine. When we finally loosened our hold over the string, the arrow vanished.

"There are few weapons as powerful in existence. Each arrow from the Phoenix Fire Bow can cause grave injury with just a single strike. But only those with a strong lifeforce can wield such a weapon effectively," he cautioned.

I stared at the bow, recalling the faded cover of the mortal book. Was it true, that my father had used a bow of ice to bring down the sunbirds? An enchanted weapon from the Immortal Realm?

"Could someone with a weak lifeforce, a mortal perhaps, use such a weapon?" I asked.

He pondered the question. "Magical items possess their own power. Most of them can be used by anyone. Even mortals. However, the stronger its user, the more powerful the item becomes—as it draws its user's energy to augment and replenish its own. If this bow is wielded by one with a weak lifeforce, not only would they find it difficult to control, but its might would be greatly diminished."

"How does this bow draw our energy? It doesn't feel any different from the others."

He leaned closer, his breath coiling into my ear. "A weapon such as the Phoenix Fire Bow forms a connection with its user, seamlessly absorbing his or her energy. This makes it powerful, but also dangerous."

"Dangerous?" I repeated, trying to think of anything but the heat from his body melding with my own.

"Dangerous, because in the tumult of battle, the users of such weapons may not realize how much energy has been expended. Until it's too late," he said gravely.

I swallowed hard, recalling Teacher Daoming's stern warning never to drain myself. Stepping out of his arms, I passed the bow to him. "You, first."

"Did you have a challenge in mind?" he asked.

"How about one of skill, not speed this time?" I suggested, thinking about my prior loss.

He bent down to pick up two withered peach blossoms. As his magic swirled over them, their color bloomed once more, the petals gleaming like they were sculpted from rose quartz. "Whoever shoots it down from the farthest distance will be the winner."

I took one of the flowers from his palm, now as hard as stone.

Gone was his teasing demeanor as he stared ahead with narrowed eyes, the bow raised, its string drawn. At his nod, I released the first blossom. It shot up, hurtling away faster than a hummingbird, spinning through the air. Several seconds passed, the flower now a speck in the horizon. With a twang, Liwei's arrow plunged forward, shattering the petals in a burst of fiery sparks.

An excellent shot. I was unsure if I could surpass it, blindfolded as I would be. It was on the tip of my tongue to retract my earlier boast, to demand a match on equal terms—but I quelled the impulse as I took the bow. Eager to test its might, I ran my fingers over the gleaming string, stiffer than those woven from silk.

As Liwei tied the white cloth over my eyes, his knuckles brushed my cheeks. A distraction I could ill afford, as I inhaled deeply to clear my mind.

Once ready, I nodded. A low thrum broke the quiet, a faint whirling, fading with every passing moment. Almost imperceptible now, yet still I waited, straining my ears. At the precise moment it slipped into silence, my arrow sprang free—whistling through the air, striking with a clink. Something shattered, catching fire with a hiss.

I raised my hand to tug the blindfold down, but strong arms encircled me, the scent of sun-warmed grass drowning my senses. His lips crushed mine, pressing them apart, his warm breath threaded with the lingering sweetness from the wine. I shivered, not from the cold, but the heat surging through my veins. Clutching his shoulders, I held him closer to me still. His mouth slid lower, trailing a scorching path down my neck with a hunger that left me breathless. With my free hand I pulled the cloth away, blinking at the sudden brightness. We fell onto the ground, the carpet of petals softer than any bed . . . my body alight with a thousand glittering sensations.

The first drops of rain were soft and frail, easily brushed aside. But they soon swelled to a torrential flood, impossible to ignore. We lay on the ground, letting the rain wash over us, drenching us as thoroughly as though we had swum in the river.

Our breaths were heavy and uneven, our fingers tangling in the wet grass.

"Who won?" I asked, drifting back to the present.

He shot me an incredulous look. "At a time like this, that is what concerns you?"

"I won." I answered my own question with a contented sigh.

"What makes you think so?"

"If you had won, you wouldn't have distracted me. You would have rubbed it in my face. Mercilessly."

He raised himself up on an elbow to stare at me. "Is that what you believe?" he asked in an aggrieved tone. "Very well. The kiss had nothing to do with how you looked when you drew the bow and hit the mark, even though it had already disappeared."

He shook his head. "Why did I fall in love with someone who takes such pleasure in grinding my pride into the dust?"

My lips parted in disbelief. "You . . . love me?"

"After all our time together, did I have a choice?"

I laid my palm against his chest, in no mood for flippancy. "Are you serious?"

The light in his eyes blazed a path to my heart, as his hand reached out to capture mine. "Yes."

As a child, my mother had cautioned me against looking directly at the sun, telling me the brightness of its glare could blind me. Perhaps it was something her own mother had told her. While it might be true for mortals, I now doubted such a thing could harm an immortal's sight. Still, her warning stuck—whenever I saw the fiery orb in the sky I would instinctively turn or shield myself. Today, I had finally dared to gaze at the sun, allowing its radiance to blaze through me unhindered, spilling through my veins until I was aglow. Never did I imagine such luminous joy existed, and never again would I be content to remain in the shadows.

After the downpour, the sky was clear once more. Liwei summoned a cloud to take us home, and on the way, we dried our clothes. Had we returned in our sodden state, we would have given rise to prying questions and unwanted gossip. As we flew back to the Jade Palace, my spirits were lighter than the clouds we passed.

In my room, I sank onto my bed in a dreamlike daze. Rest was far from my mind as the exhilaration coursing through me smothered all hope of sleep. When someone knocked, I opened the doors to find an attendant holding out a roll of paper, bound with silk cord.

"His Highness asked me to give this to you."

As I took the paper and thanked him, he added, "Someone is waiting for His Highness outside."

Wondering who it might be, I entered the courtyard to find a girl sitting in the pavilion. Her aura was warm and light, though it pulsed with strength, too. She was startlingly pretty with slender, upturned eyes in a heart-shaped face, and delicate features. Rose silk draped her tall frame, and her dark hair was held up by gold hairpins from which strands of rubies cascaded, glowing with inner flame. I bowed to her in greeting. Was she a courtier's daughter, or one of the empress's favored ladies?

"Is Prince Liwei here?" Her voice was gentle and sweet.

A sliver of unease pricked my heart, but I gave her a pleasant smile. "His Highness is with Their Celestial Majesties." As her shoulders drooped, I added, "Is there anything I can help you with?"

"I have a gift for His Highness, but I can give it to him later." The girl glanced down at the half-finished painting of a peach blossom tree on the table. A few brushes were soaking in a pitcher of water and a porcelain tray lay beside it, still wet with paint. Liwei must have worked on this just a short while ago.

"Is this Prince Liwei's work?" She traced the outline of the branches. "It's beautiful."

"His Highness has many skills," I said.

As she rose to leave, her elbow knocked over a paintbrush. Dark green paint splattered across the artwork.

She gasped as she pulled out a silk handkerchief, dabbing furiously at the paper. I rushed forward to help her, jostling the pitcher. It tipped over, water spilling onto the table, soaking the artwork in moments. Of the once exquisitely painted tree, only dark green smudges could be seen in the sodden mess.

Her fingers twisted her handkerchief into knots, her throat working with words she did not speak.

"It might have been the wind," I said solemnly.

She blinked at me. "Or a bird," she agreed quickly.

Our eyes met in a profound moment of understanding. Shortly after, she left, turning around once to stare at the courtyard.

Back in my room, I unrolled the piece of paper from Liwei. It was a painting of me, standing beneath a flowering tree—an arrow drawn through my bow, poised in the moment before flight. My gaze was intent on the target, my mouth set in determination, my back straight and tall. My pulse quickened, to think he saw me this way—strong and, somehow, beautiful.

At the bottom of the paper, a message was written in his bold brushstrokes:

You may have won the challenge, but not the greatest prize.

A slow smile spread across my face at the memory of our earlier embrace. Taking a piece of paper, I dipped my brush in the ink and wrote my reply:

There are no prizes in the game of hearts.

My mother would have been pleased; my calligraphy had improved. Folding my note up, I dropped it into my pouch. I would find a fitting moment to give it to him tonight.

12

The Hall of Eastern Light had no ceiling, opening to the starlit sky. Its white stone walls were streaked with veins of pure gold, while the floor was paved with jade tiles carved into flowers. Glowing crystal pillars illuminated the room, as did the hundreds of silk lanterns strung between them in fiery shades of crimson and vermilion. The fragrance of rare blossoms perfumed the air, mingling with the delicious aromas from the food piled onto the rosewood tables. Coveted Immortal Peaches were stacked high on silver platters, to be distributed at the discretion of the Celestial Empress. Just one of these peaches, creamy ivory with a divine blush, had the power to strengthen an immortal's lifeforce or prolong a mortal's life.

Even in the Celestial Kingdom such decadence was rare. The richly dressed guests greeted each other effusively, flushed with excitement and wine. I had only just arrived and already, I was lost in this sea of strangers.

Someone tapped my shoulder. It was General Jianyun, for once without his armor, a long coat of silver brocade draped over his gray robe. I cupped my hands and bowed, relieved to see someone I knew.

"Is this your first banquet?" he asked.

"Yes. His Highness invited me tonight."

A brief silence followed. "Well? Have you given any thought to my offer?" he asked bluntly.

My eyes fixed onto a jade tile as I fumbled for an answer. Oh, I would have snatched at this opportunity before. But now, a new fear pulsed through me at the thought of being separated from Liwei—for weeks, maybe months at a stretch. It was not that he had displaced my mother . . . but rather my heart was cleaved in two, when once it had been whole. I would do it, I knew I would—yet selfishly, I wanted a little more time here. Our love was too new, too precious to risk lightly.

I would speak to Liwei tonight, I resolved. After the festivities, I would tell him what I could without revealing my mother's name. He would understand, he would not press me for more. And perhaps, together, we would find our way.

"General Jianyun, perhaps we should not talk of such matters on His Highness's birthday." I hoped he would allow me this delay.

His brows bunched with displeasure, but he nodded as he glanced around the crowded room. "Do you recognize any of these peacocks here?"

A strangled laugh burst from my throat, which I attempted to disguise with a cough.

"I've been in the army too long. I don't flatter or say things I don't mean. Take my word for it, this lot of courtiers are only good for dressing in fine feathers and chirping empty compliments."

General Jianyun's lip curled with distaste as he jerked his

head at a man in front of us. "That one though, is more of a cunning crow. The emperor's loyal advisor, yet his advice is often self-serving."

It was rare for General Jianyun to speak so disparagingly of another, and I wondered who had earned his contempt. I could not see the man's face, just his fine purple robe and the pale gloves that covered his hands—an uncommon accessory which struck me at once. It was Minister Wu, who swung around as though sensing our eyes upon him. He ignored me, his lips pinched as he bowed to General Jianyun. The sight of the minister turned my stomach, stirring anew old misery and terror.

So wrapped up was I in my thoughts, I almost collided into the tall immortal who stopped before us, the embroidered bamboo leaves on his robe rustling in emerald silk. A gray sash was tied around his waist, his hair pulled into a glossy topknot secured with an ebony pin. His aura rushed over me, cool and fresh, yet dense and strong. Like an autumn wind thick with crushed leaves and rain. His black eyes swept over me with little interest before he greeted General Jianyun, cupping his hands together and stretching them out as he bowed.

The stranger drew the general aside, which gave me the opportunity to study him further. He carried himself with the assurance of authority, yet he appeared not much older than I—unless he was one of those powerful immortals, concealing a thousand years with his lifeforce. His face was arresting; high cheekbones with a strong jaw and a well-formed, if somewhat stern mouth. I did not recall seeing him at the training field, but I doubted he was a courtier from the way his eyes flicked impatiently around the room as though such gaiety bored him.

I took a step forward, intending to excuse myself. There was little enjoyment in being excluded, relegated to no more than a piece of furniture, though navigating this crowd alone daunted me, too.

General Jianyun started as though he had forgotten my presence. "Ah, Xingyin. Have you met Captain Wenzhi?"

The celebrated commander? One of the finest warriors in the kingdom, despite being just a hundred years older than me? Yet before I could greet him, he turned away abruptly as though eager for me to be gone. He was insufferable, I decided, biting down on my tongue. Trying not to let his discourtesy bother me, even as I was furious with myself for ever having wanted to meet him.

"Xingyin is the Crown Prince's companion," added General Jianyun.

The arrogant young captain swung to me then, his face alight with sudden interest. "The one who trains with His Highness? The archer?"

"Yes," I replied curtly, still stung by his earlier rudeness.

"I only returned a few days ago. I saw you yesterday, in the field, when you shot those discs. I've never seen such fine marksmanship before." A smile hovered on his lips.

I blinked, finally recognizing him. The tall soldier who had clapped first.

His gaze slid over the azure silk of my dress, the creamy magnolias with golden centers embroidered on my skirt. A green brocade belt, shot through with silver, was tied around my waist. Tucked in my hair was the pin Liwei had gifted me.

"I apologize for not recognizing you earlier. In this dress, you look . . ." His voice trailed off, the tips of his ears reddening.

"Like a useless peacock?" I finished his sentence for him, with a grin at General Jianyun.

Captain Wenzhi did not laugh. "I meant to say, in this dress you don't look like the warrior you are."

His compliment filled me with unexpected pleasure. Perhaps he was not as insufferable as I had thought.

"Would you like to sit with us?" he invited.

I accepted gladly. I had just caught a glimpse of Lady Meiling's father and was as keen to keep my distance from him as he was from me.

Our table was in the front with a clear view of the dais. There, a rosewood table was set before the white jade thrones, flanked by smaller ones on each side. Tonight, the visiting royalty were honored by being seated alongside Their Celestial Majesties, though they had yet to make an appearance.

A hush fell over the room then. The air thrummed with power as the royal family entered, everyone scrambling to fall to their knees. I lifted my head an inch to catch a glimpse of the emperor who had imprisoned my mother. Even surrounded by the most powerful immortals of the realm, the Celestial Emperor dazzled. His aura blazed with impenetrable might; that of a stone mountain, an endless glacier. Scarlet and azure dragons were embroidered upon his brilliant yellow robes, darting through swirling clouds. The ornate gold frame of his crown was set into a jewel-encrusted base, from which strands of lustrous pearls cascaded. They swayed before his brow, catching the light with his every move. His face was ageless, even for an immortal, his smooth skin bearing neither the vitality of youth nor the cares of time. In the darkness of his pupils, I found a fragment of resemblance to his son—though their opaque depths were devoid of warmth. He did not look particularly terrifying, but something about him turned my insides to ice.

Liwei stopped before me, inclining his head in greeting. Yet his smile was guarded and his eyes, dulled. Did he wish himself back in his room? I wanted to ask him, but not here. Not now.

Just by acknowledging my presence he had flouted the protocol that required him to greet the honored guests first. As he walked away, my pulse fluttered as I stared after him like some moon-eyed girl. He looked magnificent tonight, his coat of midnight brocade parted to reveal his silver-white robe, shining as though woven from starlight. His hair was pulled into a gold and sapphire crown, held in place by an ornate pin.

"The monarchs of the Four Seas." General Jianyun nodded toward the dais, mistaking my keen interest. "It's rare to see them together. Relations have been strained since the Western and Northern Sea's support of the Demon Realm. However, that is in the past; perhaps this heralds a new beginning."

Each of them wore flowing robes in varying shades of blue and green, but there the resemblance ended. The King of the Eastern Sea's long hair glistened as spun silver against his dark skin, while the Queen of the Southern Sea's green eyes gleamed from her pale face. The remaining two monarchs sat stiffly upon their chairs, one wearing a crown of coral, the other of turquoise and pearl.

"Who sits beside them?" I stared at the striking immortal with jeweled blossoms sparkling from the coils of her hair.

"The Flower Immortal. Our exquisite gardens are the results of her endeavors. I've seen her revive a withered garden with a flick of her wrist, although she's not as powerful as her predecessor," General Jianyun remarked.

"What happened to her predecessor?" It was rare for an immortal to surrender their position.

"Lady Hualing chose to live away from the Celestial Kingdom, in the Eternal Spring Forest. A place she cultivated to her liking."

I waited for him to continue—curious about this immortal—but he fell silent, drumming his fingers on the table.

Captain Wenzhi spoke then. "The Celestials don't like to speak of her. Perhaps it reminds them of what can happen to even the most powerful, should they lose the emperor's favor."

General Jianyun scowled. "Even such as you from the Four Seas would not wish to anger our emperor."

I was about to ask Captain Wenzhi which of the Four Seas he was from, when he spoke again. "It was said Lady Hualing grew distracted and neglected her duties for decades, until the court petitioned His Celestial Majesty to take away her position. Since then, she has not been seen. Not for hundreds of years."

I wondered, why did the emperor not remove Lady Hualing from her duties sooner, when he seemed not to tolerate the slightest disobedience in others? But then all heads swung to the entrance, eager whispers rustling through the crowd. I turned to see two immortals approaching the dais.

"Queen Fengjin and her daughter, Princess Fengmei, from the Phoenix Kingdom," Captain Wenzhi told me.

Her name hit me like a blow. The princess rumored to have been betrothed to Liwei? Gleaming cloaks of gold feathers were clasped around their shoulders, over their long robes of crimson brocade studded with pearls. A crown of fire rubies glittered on the queen's hair. When the princess lifted her head, something in my chest contracted. She was the girl I had met in the courtyard earlier, my partner in the inadvertent destruction of Liwei's painting. The empress greeted them warmly, rising as she gestured to their seats. Something coiled tight around my heart when the princess took the chair beside Liwei, who sat there with a face carved from stone.

I breathed deeply, determined to keep my spirits high. Fortunately, General Jianyun knew plenty of interesting facts about the noble guests and did not hesitate to share them. For the most part, Captain Wenzhi was silent but solicitous of my needs, ensuring my wine cup was always full and placing the choicest delicacies on my plate.

Whenever I looked up, I found Liwei staring at me. As the night progressed, his expression grew darker than a moonless night, more thunderous than a spring storm. At this moment he appeared more fearsome than the Celestial Empress.

Captain Wenzhi leaned toward me. "Why is His Highness glowering at you?"

"You must be mistaken," I said quickly, trying to conceal my discomfort.

The look he shot me was one of disbelief. But then he shrugged. "In that case, he must be staring at me."

Perhaps it was the wine loosening my tongue or the informal way he spoke, as I replied, "Do you think your appearance so pleasing? Not everyone is struck with admiration at the sight of you."

"I would be interested to hear what you think of me." His brows were arched in a seeming challenge.

"Even if it does not please you?"

"Especially, if so," he said, his voice deepening.

I laughed, a hollow sound—unable to banish this feeling of unease, that something was not quite right. Why *was* Liwei glowering at me? There was no other way to describe his clamped lips and his eyes, burning like coals into mine.

Unfortunately, the empress noticed it, too. She crooked her finger at me, the pointed gold sheath glinting in the light. Only now did I realize that these were no mere ornaments, but Phoenix Talons, said to be laced with a potent poison.

Dragging myself to my feet, I walked to the front of the dais and knelt, awaiting her command.

Her piercing gaze reminded me of a hawk swooping down upon its prey. "Your hairpin is lovely, a rare treasure indeed. Where did you obtain it from?" The softness in her tone sheathed the dagger in her words.

Heat rushed into my cheeks as I fumbled for a response. A polite reply, a witty remark, anything but the yawning silence implying guilt where there was none.

Liwei rose and clasped his hands before him, folding over in a bow. "Honorable Mother, it was my gift to her."

"You're fortunate that my son is so generous. How do you plan to repay such kindness?" Her red lips parted in a mirthless smile. "Today is my son's birthday. What gift did you bring him? I can only hope it is one of equal worth."

Liwei raised his voice. "Honorable Mother, there is no need for this. If this offends you in any way, I ask that you speak to me alone."

She ignored him, the covers on her nails glinting as she tapped them on the armrest. She meant to humiliate me, announcing to everyone that I did not belong here. But I was not ashamed—I was furious. Not just for myself, but for her threats to my mother, her failed attempt to ruin my father, her selfishness in not reining in the sunbirds until tragedy had struck.

No, I would not flinch from her stare, I would not cower from her condescension. I lifted my head, a bright smile on my face. "I have given His Highness my gift. However, if you wish me to share it, I would be pleased to oblige you."

She stared at me as though I were the lowliest of insects. With an imperious nod, she gestured for me to proceed.

I drew the flute from my pouch, my fingers as cold as the jade in my hands. My tongue flicked over my dry lips as I stole a glance at the crowd, beginning to regret the reckless words that had gotten me here. Some guests appeared bored, while others glowed in anticipation of my encroaching humiliation. How could I perform before such an audience? I could barely breathe, my ribs clenching as though they were squeezed together. Behind me, footsteps clicked against the floor as someone approached. It was Captain Wenzhi, carrying a stool, which he placed before me.

Bending down, he whispered in my ear, "When the battle lines are drawn, advance with a clear mind."

I swallowed hard, nodding to him in thanks. His words were a comfort to my debilitating fear. To retreat now would indeed be worse than failure. I would rather the empress think my performance lacking than believe me to be a coward or liar. I sank onto the stool, grateful to sit and hide my shaking legs. Drawing a deep breath, I lifted the flute to my mouth. The empress, the emperor, the royal guests blurred from my vision; all I saw were Liwei's eyes looking into mine. This was his song, and to him alone I played. My notes soared clear, strong, and true—reflecting every emotion he had ever evoked in me.

The moment it ended, I bowed to the dais and fled back to my seat. I wished I could disappear into the ground amid the silence, punctured by a smattering of applause from those who had not yet realized the expression on the empress's face was not admiration, but rage—boiling over like a pot left too long on a stove. My anger had cooled and I worried how she would retaliate. Not now, but later—she would not forget this insult. I had done nothing except what she had asked and yet, we both knew my defiance lay in refusing to let her make a fool of me. While she was the Celestial Empress, she was also Liwei's mother. Through my rashness and pride, I had tangled further the ties between us.

I tried to catch Liwei's attention, but then the sweets were brought out, the guests murmuring in delight. The confections were exquisite—almond cakes pressed into the shapes of flowers, golden squares of osmanthus jelly, crisp sesame balls, and a rainbow assortment of puddings—but my appetite had vanished.

The empress whispered to her husband, who nodded once. His deep voice rumbled across the sudden hush in the hall. "Tonight, we come together to celebrate the birthday of our son, Crown Prince Liwei. As it happens, this is a double celebration. We are just as delighted to announce his betrothal to Princess Fengmei of the Phoenix Kingdom. May they forever be of one mind and find everlasting happiness together."

As though in a trance, my hand moved of its own volition, joining the others in raising our cups to our lips. I did not taste what I drank, if it were anything at all. The emperor's announcement slid into me as a blade to my chest, twisting cruelly when it struck. I heard nothing beyond the roaring in my mind—not the cheers from the guests springing to their feet, nor the clapping which resounded throughout the hall. My fingers curled on the table, my nails scratching the polished wood. Tears pricked my eyes but I fought them back, biting down on the inside of my cheek until the warm taste of metal and salt filled my mouth.

A wedding was a joyous occasion, believed to bring luck. As the guests fought to outdo each other in lavishing praise upon the couple, I sat numbly in my seat without the strength to even flee.

"What a harmonious combination of pearl and jade!"

"The Phoenix Princess and the Dragon Prince, an auspicious pairing indeed!"

"See their beauty? Truly a match made in heaven!"

Each word was a stab to my festering wound. I glanced up at Liwei in disbelief, half expecting him to leap to his feet in denial. To tell me this was just a cruel prank. He did not look at me, though, and his eyes were wintry, devoid of light. Worse yet, he accepted the congratulations from the guests with a terse nod. Princess Fengmei blushed at the attention and when she touched Liwei's arm, my insides shriveled as a dry leaf dropped into the flames.

This was real; he was betrothed to another. A desperate urge to leave gripped me. I wanted to be alone, to let my grief pour from me as a river into the ocean. But I crushed the craven impulse. I would not run, nor would I hide. Just when I thought I would surely collapse from the pain, a hand covered mine—firm and strong—the cool touch penetrating my daze. Lifting my head, my gaze collided with Captain Wenzhi's, alight with understanding. He was a stranger whom I had met just this evening, but right now he was my only anchor in this raging tempest. I accepted his silent comfort, clutching his fingers—feeling as empty as a discarded wine vessel which had been tipped over, spilling its contents into the uncaring soil.

13

The night was clear with a hint of frost, but I was already frozen inside. I sat in the courtyard, staring at the solitary moon in the sky. Could my mother see me? For the first time, I hoped she did not. I did not want her to sense my pain, to know what a fool I had been.

A shadow fell over me, but I did not look up. Not even when he sat beside me.

"Xingyin, let me explain."

My fists clenched in my lap, the veins straining against the skin. To have my love toyed with so callously, as a blossom plucked and left to wilt on the ground. I deserved more than this. I would salvage what pride remained, for I had lost too much already.

"Your Highness, do you require my assistance? If not, I'll retire for the night."

"Will you listen to me?" The light in his eyes was extinguished, drowned in an abyss.

I stood up, my legs like planks of wood. He reached for my arm but I recoiled, not wanting to be touched—least of all by him.

"Very well." His voice was taut. "You may assist me to-night."

I followed him in silence to his room. I lit the lamps, heated the coals in the brazier, warmed a jug of wine, and brought him a fresh set of clothes. On the table, I placed his books and materials for tomorrow. I had performed these tasks for him countless times before, yet never with such cold precision nor such an unwilling heart.

He stood there, watching me with those dark, unfathomable eyes. When he raised his arms, I slipped off his dark blue coat and then his white and silver robe, hanging them up on a wooden stand. I drew out the gold hairpin and plucked the crown from his head. His hair fell over his shoulders and I combed through it, careful not to let a single strand touch me.

When I finished, I bowed and turned to leave.

"I have not dismissed you," he said quietly.

"I have performed all my duties. What else do you need me to help you with?" My voice was flat, my heart leaden. I could not stomach this pretense for much longer.

"Sit. Listen." He added, "Please."

Though my pride raged at me to leave, I lowered myself onto a chair. Staring at the flickering candle on the table, I decided that I would stay until it was extinguished. No more would he have of me.

Liwei sat beside me, running his hands through his hair. I noted with detachment that my efforts with the comb had been for naught.

"My mother always wanted to strengthen our ties with the Phoenix Kingdom. They are a powerful domain, a desirable alliance, and her kin—although Queen Fengjin is a distant relation.

When the sunbirds were slain, shot down under our watch, the bond between our kingdoms was strained."

He drew a ragged breath. "It was then that she pushed harder for a betrothal between Princess Fengmei and me. I never agreed, even though it was my duty, what was expected of me. I had no wish to marry someone I did not love. Years passed and I believed she had abandoned the idea. When I left you yesterday, I went to my parents, intending to tell them of us. They informed me then that a betrothal had been settled that very day between Princess Fengmei and me. Of course, I refused! But they explained the urgency of the union. Beyond prestige, it was to ensure our survival. The Phoenix Queen is restless. According to our spies, our enemies have made overtures to her to join against us. We can't afford to lose the friendship of the Phoenix Kingdom now, much less have them as our enemy. Not when we've been weakened after the war with the Demon Realm. Not when we're threatened by them still. The truce between us hangs by the most tenuous of threads, likely to snap should they gain the advantage—and we are certain they are scheming against us, even now."

He continued in that dull, flat tone. "I must protect my kingdom and family, however I can. I cannot willfully do anything which might endanger them. I cannot be selfish, no matter how much I want to be."

Silence stretched between us, as wide as a gaping chasm.

His words were meant to be a comfort, but I was wretched inside. Perhaps I could have borne it better if he were forced. But to know he had accepted this betrothal of his own will hurt more than a fist plowed into my gut.

Yet logic was merciless and reason relentless, unsparing of my wounded heart. Would I have chosen any differently from what he had? Would I not have made any sacrifice to save my family and home?

It was not enough. Not enough to ease this ache in my chest, this lump in my throat, this queasiness churning in the pit of my stomach. He had said he loved me, and then promised himself to another. I was sick with these writhing, twisting emotions which swelled and burned and scorched from within. But he would not know my despair; I would not tell him. Not to spare his feelings but my own. To weep before him, to beg or plead—that I could not bear. Whatever happened, I would hold my head up high. My pride was what I had clung to during my most trying times, it was what I had left now.

But it was not easy. I fixed my gaze upon the wavering candlelight, fighting for calm. Why was it that the times which called for greatest strength were when we were at our weakest? I looked away from him, not from spite, but to hide my tears.

Remembering the folded note in my pouch, I pulled it out with trembling fingers. How cruelly prophetic my jest; there were indeed no prizes in this game of hearts. My grip tightened around the paper, crushing it into a ball. How foolish I had been to think everything would work out, just like in the books I had read: the lost child found by his mother, the monster defeated by a valiant warrior, the princess saved by the prince. But I was no princess and fairy tales did not exist for the likes of me, not even in heaven.

Somehow, I found the strength to say the words that needed to be said. The ones which would set him free, the ones which would break my heart. "I understand. I do. But I must leave."

"You don't have to. I'll always have a place for you here." He reached for me, but then drew back at the last moment, his fingers folding into a fist.

I would not be indebted to him further, even though some might think this was my due, now that he had broken his faith with me. But I would not weigh the shards of our love in favors. Grasping the threads of my dignity, I shrouded myself in indifference.

"What place can you offer me? As one of your attendants? Someone to play with your future children? A companion to your *wife*?" My laugh was jagged and hard. "I want more of life."

It was his turn to look away. "Where will you go? I'll help you find another position. Anywhere you wish."

"No," I said quickly, too quickly. It would have been so easy to accept, to let him ease my path. A fierce gladness clutched at me that I was not forced to accept his kindness. That I had won a position through my own merit, not his favor. I would be beholden to no one. My path forward was clear, I had no reason to delay. Perhaps being in the army would help me forget all which had transpired here. Perhaps starting anew would give me the chance to heal.

I pulled the hairpin from my hair and offered it to him, the clear stones glittering as they caught the light. When he did not take it, I placed it on the table. My fingers moved stiffly to the Sky Drop Tassel by my waist, but I hesitated. This, I would keep as a remembrance. It was a gift of friendship and no matter what, he was my friend still.

A crushing weight fell over me, sapping the strength from my limbs. Maybe it was knowing that when I left this room, I would never return. That our time had come to an end. I thought bitterly, I should be accustomed by now to tearing myself away from those I loved.

Rising to my feet, I cupped my hands together and swept him a low bow. "Your Highness, it was an honor to serve you."

Memories of our time together flashed before my mind: our years of friendship, our few stolen days of love. Then the candle flame flickered, struggling for its final seconds of life before curling into a wisp of smoke . . . the room now enveloped in darkness.

PART

II

14

The fire crackled, sparks shooting in the air. I did not flinch from where I sat on the ground, sanding the shaft of my arrows to make them leaner. Faster. The work was not necessary but it kept my hands busy and my mind, silent. A corner of my mouth tilted into a mocking smile. Just a few months ago I had been studying in the Chamber of Reflection, and now I was preparing my arrows to slay a monster.

Xiangliu, the nine-headed serpent, had fled the Immortal Realm to the world below. It plagued the nearby villages, flooding their rivers and snatching up victims to feed its insatiable appetite. While mortal warriors had long tried to bring this creature down, they were no match for its strength and cunning. I wondered why the Celestial Emperor had waited till now to send his forces, just as he let the sunbirds roam unchecked for so long. I did not think it was a conscious cruelty, but rather the detached triviality with which a mortal might view the life of an insect, unable to comprehend its suffering. It wasn't only the emperor; many immortals shared this view. Perhaps I might have been like them if mortal blood did not run in my veins. If my thoughts of my mother and father were not entwined with this place.

I stared at the mountain that rose from the ground. Shadow Peak, this place was called. In the fading light, the dark rock glistened as though coated in a layer of grease. This was nothing like how I imagined the Mortal Realm would be when I had gazed from above. No glowing lanterns, no laughing children, not even a single tree to adorn the barren land. Just a tautness in the air akin to the moment a storm breaks.

I shifted on the ground, the metal pressing against my shoulders and ribs. Shuxiao had not exaggerated its weight. It struck me as a bad joke that I was now clad in the same armor which had roused such fear in me before. But this was my choice.

I thought back to the night I had left the Courtyard of Eternal Tranquility. Determined not to delay any longer, I had sought out General Jianyun and accepted his offer to join the Celestial Army.

"Excellent." He had smiled then, a rare occurrence. "Have you informed His Highness? He should—"

"He knows." My nerves had been too frayed to traverse the winding path of courtesy. I bowed to him again, hoping the gesture would take the sting from my next words. "General Jianyun, I thank you for this opportunity, but I have a few terms."

"Oh?" The single syllable somehow conveyed both indignation and amusement at my temerity.

"I don't need an official rank or remuneration. What I want is the freedom to choose my own campaigns and to be acknowledged for my achievements." My body tensed, bracing for his disapproval.

A scowl twisted his lips. Was he displeased by my audacity? But I knew my own worth now and was no longer just grateful to be granted any opportunity. I would not plow through the ranks for a meaningless title or power I did not covet. Nor would I so readily place my future in the hands of another. Those most trusted could still let you down, even when they did not mean to—a lesson I had learned with Liwei, and one I learned well.

General Jianyun folded his arms across his chest, fixing me with a fierce stare. "That's not how it's done. The commanders form their troops for each assignment, considering each soldier's experience and skill. We *all* serve the best interests of the Celestial Kingdom."

"As will I." Such hollow words I spoke. I did not do this out of loyalty to the Celestial Kingdom; all I wanted was the Crimson Lion Talisman. But it would be no easy feat to shine brighter than the other warriors. And so, in this night filled with stars, I would chart my own path to blaze across the sky. I would pursue the opportunities which I believed would capture the Celestial Emperor's attention. I would *earn* the talisman, the key to my mother's freedom—the sole ambition that burned in me unchanged throughout the years, now unfettered by my weak heart. It shamed me, how I had hesitated before. I would never have forgotten my mother, I would have done all I could to help her . . . but happiness had a way of blunting one's edge, of dulling one's urgency. *Never again*, I vowed.

Finally, General Jianyun had relented. Awarded the nondescript rank of "Archer," I had joined Captain Wenzhi's troop—the only commander I knew and, more importantly, a celebrated one who would be assigned the most crucial campaigns.

I had cursed that decision in the weeks to follow, however—shooting targets until my fingers bruised, sparring until I could no longer stand, and weaving enchantments until I was as drained as a wrung-out washcloth. Captain Wenzhi trained his soldiers hard, and each night I had fallen into bed—my body limp and my muscles afire—eager to sink into the oblivion of slumber.

Nor was training without its dangers. Shortly after I had joined the army, Captain Wenzhi led me to an underground chamber lit by flickering torches. Gray stone lions with bulbous eyes lined the walls, their open jaws mimicking fearsome grins like they were mocking us. How my skin had crawled at the sight of them. The moment the captain left, the door slamming shut after him—darts hissed from the lions' mouths, hurtling toward me faster than rain pelting down in a storm. I dropped to the floor, rolling under a ledge. But I was too slow, pain streaking across my leg. I winced as I plucked the darts from my flesh, before drawing an arrow and firing in the direction they came from. By accident more than design, I struck a lion's mouth. Its jaws slammed shut, ending its attacks. Only after I had hit all of them—my arrows protruding from their jaws—did the barrage cease and the door swing open once more.

My blood roiled at the sight of Captain Wenzhi standing by the entrance. Had this been a test?

"Why didn't you warn me?" I demanded.

"In a real battle, would the enemy warn you before attacking?"

"You aren't my enemy."

He tilted his head to one side, pinning me with his stare. "I'm glad you think so. But Archer Xingyin, your performance was dismal."

I jutted my chin out, my pride pricked. "I shot all the lions. I escaped the trap."

His gaze lingered on the red marks dotted across my calf, blood trickling down in thin streams. "This was the first stage in the Chamber of Lions and you still got injured. If these were coated with venom, you'd be dead."

Shaking his head, he strode into the room and struck my arrows from the lions' jaws. Darts sprang toward us once more. I wanted to duck, to roll to safety—but as he held his ground, I forced myself to stay beside him, my heart thumping as the sharp points hurtled ever closer. Just as I was above to dive to the ground, he flicked his hand almost negligently. A shimmering wall of ice appeared before us, the darts slamming into it.

My pride vanished like steam in the cool air. A gust of wind, a wall of flame—any of these would have worked! While I had learned to summon my magic effortlessly, its use did not come instinctively to me. Perhaps I had managed without it for too long. When attacked, my first instinct was to retaliate with my hands and feet. Like a mortal, I thought silently. True to my roots.

His voice hardened. "The most powerful warriors are proficient in *both* combat and magic. You wouldn't survive long on fighting skills alone, nor can you rely on just magic. If you did, you would soon find your energy exhausted. A most dangerous circumstance. No matter what is happening, keep a clear mind to judge *when* to use your power for greatest impact. But don't hesitate to use it when necessary."

His words struck me. Eager to prove myself, I had returned to this chamber on my own. Each time the traps had been a little harder; sometimes spikes shot through the ground or fire erupted from the walls. I ended the sessions sore and bruised, blood dripping from my wounds. It was only later that I learned the Chamber of Lions was reserved for the army's most skilled warriors. While most had taken months, a year even to master every trap, it took me a matter of weeks.

And I was stronger, faster, more powerful than I had ever been.

But was I ready for what now lay ahead? I stared at the dark mountain, trying to quell the queasiness that rose in me, wondering if I had made the right choice in coming here—my first battle against a monster so fearsome, its very name cowed immortals into silence.

Someone approached, footsteps treading over the earth. I was glad for the distraction from my bleak thoughts.

"Archer Xingyin, I've been searching for you." Captain Wenzhi sank down beside me. "There are things you should know of Xiangliu."

I started to rise to greet him, but he gestured for me to remain seated. When we were alone, he often lapsed into such informality—rare in the Celestial Army, governed by rank and hierarchy. Was it because we had bonded at the banquet, when he lent me his strength at the moment I most needed it? Or was he at ease with me because I held no official position here, seeking neither his favor nor approval?

"Of Xiangliu's nine heads, you can only strike one," he said abruptly.

I stilled, my fingers curling around the arrow. "What do you mean?"

"The core of its power lies within its fifth skull, the middle one." He stared into the flames. "If we were anywhere else, we could attack it with magic. However, on this mountain, our powers are bound."

I had been warned about this. When I tried to reach for my energy here, it darted away just like it had when I was untrained. "Is this some enchantment?"

He shifted, the leaping flames throwing shadows across his

face. "No one knows. We only discovered this place when we hunted Xiangliu here. The serpent is both ancient and cunning; maybe it knew it would be safe here."

"Can't I shoot all its heads until I get the right one?" My flippancy disguised my unease. The thought of nine jaws gnashing their fangs at me sent a chill through my bones.

"If that were so, we could just get a dozen archers and blanket it with arrows. Xiangliu would be long dead and we wouldn't need you."

"Why don't you then?" I retorted, irked by his words.

"Its other heads are invulnerable. Striking the wrong one only antagonizes Xiangliu, raising its suspicions and making our task harder. The last time, we were forced to retreat once our archer was incapacitated. But with every battle we learn more about our enemy."

I stared at him in surprise. I had not realized they had tried before. Perhaps only victories were flaunted, defeats swiftly buried.

"Is its fifth head any different from the others?" I asked.

"It's not covered in scales as the rest, and its skin is almost like ours. To destroy Xiangliu, you must hit its eyes, clean through the skull." He paused. "Unfortunately, its eyelids can't be pierced by any weapon. At least none which we know of."

"I can only shoot its eyes when they're open?" I repeated numbly.

A terse nod. "Xiangliu protects itself well. From what we gathered the last time, these eyes only opened when it struck with acid, its most powerful attack. And even then, for the briefest of moments."

He picked up a stick and tossed it into the fire. It crackled, sparks flying high—mirroring my mounting tension.

My arrow fell to the ground. "Is *that* all?" How I prayed it was.

He nodded, as though this were a simple matter of hitting a target from ten paces away.

"Why didn't you tell me this earlier?" I cursed myself inwardly for not seeking more information before. I had not cared enough then. However, tonight . . . I found I was not so indifferent to my own survival.

"Don't doubt yourself. Xiangliu won't escape this time. We have all we need," he said with calm assurance.

"And what might that be?" I asked, a little suspiciously.

"*Two* archers," he quipped.

"You'll have one less soon," I told him darkly.

He laughed. "And speed. Your speed, to be precise. I've never seen anyone shoot as accurately and swiftly as you. That will be crucial." He spoke the last part somberly.

"I might have trained differently if I'd realized what we were up against."

"How could you have pushed yourself harder than you did?" he countered, before his tone gentled. "Don't you feel ready?"

My mouth twisted into a grimace. More than my fear of the serpent, I did not like this feeling—that I was a chess piece played to his whim. Told what he believed I should know, positioned where he thought I should go. Such was the hierarchy of command as Shuxiao had warned me, but I was no powerless recruit.

"Next time, I prefer to decide my readiness on my own."

His lips curved as he rose to his feet. "Good night, Archer Xingyin. It's late and everyone else is already asleep."

I expected him to go to his tent, but he walked toward the mountain instead, disappearing into its shadow. Where was he going at this hour? My curiosity battled with my reluctance to intrude, my desire to respect his privacy winning out. We all needed time to ourselves. The flames flickered weakly before dwindling into a smoldering heap. Without its hiss and crackle, the silence was only punctured by the steady breathing of the other soldiers. I had no idea how long I sat there, lost in my thoughts. When Captain Wenzhi finally reemerged, he stared at me, sitting alone in the dark.

"Why are you still up?" he asked, striding toward me.

"I'm not tired." My eyes flicked to his hands, streaked with dirt. "Why are *you* still up?" I repeated his question back to him.

"I needed to inspect our path for tomorrow. To make sure there weren't any surprises." He sighed. "Get some sleep. Tomorrow we have a steep climb and a hard fight."

I left him then, to find my place on the ground. The nights were the hardest. When I lay alone in the dark, the memories I drove away in the light of day came crashing down. Of warm dark eyes and a teasing smile, which wore away at the hard shell around my heart until I wrapped my arms around myself, struggling to breathe through the tightness in my chest. Perhaps it was worse tonight because I was in the Mortal Realm—where my mother and father had met, fallen in love, and been happy. Until the sunbirds. Until me.

Once, I had screwed up the courage to ask my mother how they'd met. If I had not read the book, I would never have been so bold. But it was so with all knowledge, having just a little left you with a greater thirst. And I had found that she did not mind speaking of her mortal past. It was the memories that came after which she shied from. Sometimes I felt there were two parts of her—the mortal and the immortal—of which the former belonged to my father and the latter to me.

She had glowed at my question, a flush rising to her cheeks. "We grew up together in a village by the sea," she had told me. "He was the clever one, the fastest runner and quickest with a bow. It was no surprise when the soldiers came for him just after he turned seventeen, recruiting him to join them. He did not complain, only hugging his mother as she wept over him. I tried not to cry, too, though we loved each other. Before he left, he promised he would come back for me. For five years, I waited. Sometimes I thought he had forgotten me along his path to greatness. But he did not."

A cloud had fallen over her face then, as she pressed her trembling lips together. There was no need for her to say aloud what we both knew: that they *had* parted, more irrevocably than if my father had a change of heart and never returned—with the entire sky between them now.

With a sigh, I stretched out on the cold ground. Everyone else was asleep just as Captain Wenzhi had said. I still ached, though no longer for my loss alone. My parents had been torn apart as a peach twisted into two halves. Their love was intact and yet they could not be together. Was that worse than the inevitable finality of death? I did not know.

I thought bitterly that unlike me, at least my mother had married her love. He had been true to her. And she to him, until the fateful day she had taken the elixir. Was this where all paths to love led? Heartbreak, whether through separation, betrayal, or death? Was the fleeting joy worth the sorrow that came after? I supposed it depended on the strength of the love, the memories made—which seemed enough to sustain my mother through the decades of her lonely vigil. Yet in my lowest moments a darkness had crept over me, whispering hateful things—that I was a fool, a weakling, so easily discarded. It would have eased my gnawing ache had I surrendered to the hate, letting resentment smother my grief, blaming Liwei for the hurt he caused me. It would only have been a brief respite though as what I mourned more than any injured pride was the love we had lost, the future which was no longer ours.

The aching hollow within my chest gaped wider. I instinctively searched the night for the moon, letting its soft light graze my face, the balm to my pain. Closing my eyes, I could almost imagine it were my mother's touch. My nails dug into my palms. I was *more* than this ill-fated love; I would not let it define me. I had my family to think of, my own dreams to fulfill . . . and a nine-headed serpent to slay on the morrow.

15

Sunlight set the mountain afire with an ominous glitter. I gritted my teeth as I hauled myself up, just behind Captain Wenzhi as we clambered up the slope. Sweat trickled down my brow, my neck and back, as I dug my fingers into the cold rock, to grip the slippery surface. I glanced down, the ground so far away that my head spun. For the hundredth time I assured myself that a fall in the Mortal Realm was unlikely to kill us, though how I wished I could summon a cloud now.

"We're here." Captain Wenzhi climbed onto a ledge.

The rest of us scrambled after him, with Archer Feimao the last to appear—flushed, his shining armor scuffed in places. Had he fallen? Fortunately, he appeared unharmed. At the end of the ledge loomed a dark entrance, high enough for us to walk through, unbowed. Xiangliu had chosen its home well. Not only was it protected from magic, but this rocky terrain with its narrow paths and tight openings made storming in with troops impossible.

Captain Wenzhi waited for us to gather before addressing us in a steady tone. "Be on your guard. Xiangliu is powerful and fast, its fangs are sharper than knives, and its skin is protected by impenetrable scales. With nine heads, little escapes its notice. And whatever you do, don't look into its eyes."

"Why?" I asked, already dreading his answer.

"It can paralyze you."

A tense silence fell over us, punctured by the shuffling of feet. It was of little surprise that this creature had evaded death for so long, even after earning the Celestial Emperor's ire.

He continued, speaking slower now, "Focus your attacks on its underbelly, its most vulnerable part. That won't kill it, but will cause it pain. Our aim is to distract and threaten it, until it unleashes its acid. That's when our target will be exposed, that's when the archers will strike. At my signal, we'll attack in two groups, flanking and driving it toward the entrance where the archers will station themselves." His gaze shifted to Archer Feimao and me. "Don't engage it unless you have to. Keep your arrows drawn, ready for the moment to strike. We won't get many chances. Stay steady, aim well, fight together."

As one, we bowed, our palms wrapped over our fists. When we rose again, we stood a little straighter. I was wound tight with tension as I glanced at the somber faces around me. This was no practice session that I could repeat whenever I wished. The slightest lapse would tilt the scales between life and death, and not just for me alone.

We left the safety of the sundrenched ledge, slipping into the cave. It was enormous, stretching so high I could not see the ceiling through the dark. I stood with my back to the light, as did Archer Feimao a little farther away. I inhaled deeply, almost gagging as the damp air hit my lungs—laced with salt, earth, and the stench of rotting flesh. Just ahead, Captain Wenzhi's hand shot up in warning. He gestured toward the center of the cave, submerged in inky water. The soldiers followed his lead, moving to the side, stepping over the bones that were scattered with an almost cruel abandon.

I squinted, making out a large silhouette huddled in the water, so still there was barely a ripple around it. Was the creature asleep? I wiped my palms, damp with sweat, before drawing an arrow. I had shot countless targets of metal, wood, and stone— though never a creature of flesh and blood. Swallowing hard, my eyes met Captain Wenzhi's. I nodded, as did Archer Feimao, signaling our readiness. As the captain's low whistle pierced the silence, the soldiers charged forward, their feet pounding the ground.

Red lights flickered to life like fireflies dancing over the water. Except these were embedded in heads which reared up as Xiangliu uncoiled to its full height, almost that of a young cypress. Nine heads sprang from its barrel-like body, each plucked from a nightmare, each darting with a life of its own. Eight were covered in black scales with flaming eyes and bone-white fangs, glistening with a foaming liquid. One had the skin of a fair immortal, except for the dark lines spread across like cracked porcelain. Lips parted, showing graying teeth, and where its eyes should have been were smooth hollows—like holes in the ground, not filled all the way through. It gave me the eerie sensation of an immortal's face which had been peeled off and draped over the serpent's like a glove.

Ice slid down my spine as I clutched my bow tighter. Soldiers dashed into the water, raising their swords. The creature's jaws snapped ferociously as it wrapped its spiked tail around those nearest, flinging them against the rock wall. They collapsed with a crash, their cries ringing in my ears. As one of Xiangliu's heads lunged down, its fangs sank into a soldier's neck. He screamed in agony, slashing his blade across the serpent's scaly face.

"No!" Captain Wenzhi shouted.

It was too late, Xiangliu's heads swarming to form a shield around its core, like the petals of a flower closed into a bud. The serpent leapt out of the water with surprising agility, drops spattering all around. Cold and reeking of death.

The soldiers pressed on. One thrust her sword into the creature's stomach. Xiangliu shrieked, a feral sound, as it slithered toward the entrance—rising higher until it towered over Archer Fcimao and me. Against the sunlight streaming in, its scales gleamed like onyx.

Fear cut my heart, not the insidious prickle of the unknown, but stabbing terror for my survival. A primitive instinct took over, my ears deaf to Captain Wenzhi's warnings, my fingers releasing the bowstring as the arrow sprang free. Even as it struck, I cursed myself for not staying hidden as instructed. For drawing the serpent's attention instead of emerging at the opportune moment to strike.

One of Xiangliu's heads bent to rip out my arrow, tossing it aside almost contemptuously. The rest fanned out around me, those glowing eyes boring into mine. I froze, only now noticing the tiny, pearlescent scales covering the eye sockets of its core, barely perceptible in the dark.

"Look away!" Archer Feimao yelled, gesturing wildly at me.

I stumbled back just as a soldier hurled her spear into the serpent's stomach. Xiangliu's cry pierced the air as its middle head reared up, eyelids snapping open to unveil two burning coals beneath. Its core! Xiangliu's eight jaws parted, spewing a frothing, greenish liquid across the cavern, acrid and sour. Those struck screamed in anguish, falling to the ground where they writhed in agony. The acid sprayed onto my arms, foaming as it ate through the cloth, blisters blooming over my skin like crimson poppies. I would have screamed till I was hoarse, yet the searing agony—that of my skin being peeled from my flesh—snatched the air from my lungs.

Grinding my jaws until I thought they would crack, I fumbled for another arrow, drawing it through my bow. Archer Feimao stared at me, signaling for me to attack—but I was trembling too much from terror and pain. Doubt raged through me that I would miss, that I would fail, letting down everyone who depended upon me. Archer Feimao's arrow streaked forward—just as those glowing orbs vanished—the shaft slamming against the serpent's eyelids and shattering to fragments.

Nine mouths curved into bone-chilling smiles, those red eyes gleaming with malice as they fixed upon us. Soldiers bolted forward as Xiangliu's tail whipped out, slamming them aside. Archer Feimao and I backed away, but two of the creature's heads lunged out and sank their fangs into his shoulders. He screamed, doubling over in agony, blood pouring from his wounds.

I wanted to buckle over and hurl out the contents of my stomach. To weep for his pain and those of the others, battered by this vicious creature. But terror sealed my throat shut; I could not even whimper. Xiangliu slid closer, one of its heads arching toward me with a languid grace. So close, I could see myself reflected in those crimson orbs. A strange fatigue sank over me. My grip on the bow slackened as it slipped from my fingers. The serpent's eyes flared as it opened its mouth. Pure white fangs dripped with foaming liquid. As its foul breath pierced my daze, I recoiled, blinking in confusion. My mind cleared as I swooped down to retrieve my bow.

Someone shouted—Captain Wenzhi—racing toward us, his sword arcing high. He hacked at the serpent's belly as Xiangliu shrieked in rage, its heads swiveling to him now.

"The target!" he shouted, as he raised his shield to fend off the creature's snapping jaws.

Those pearlescent eyelids flicked open. Red-hot coals flickered to life once more, embers in the dark. The monster's jaws parted, spraying acid which splattered on my hands, a little across my cheek where it burned and stung like fire and ice. Black waves of agony swept over my consciousness, dragging me under . . . yet the sight of Captain Wenzhi battling the monster lit a fierce resolve in me to not let him down again.

My leg muscles clenched as I struggled to hold my ground, fighting the urge to gag from the stench of scorched flesh. Plucking two arrows from my quiver, I drew them through the string. Xiangliu's head snapped back, my arms wavering as I fought to get a clear shot—my gaze fixing on its eyes of flame as all else blurred into the background. My arrows tore through the air, striking with a sickening squelch.

It stilled, eight pairs of ruby eyes blinking rapidly. Just when I thought I had failed, that I had missed—a great shudder rippled through its body as its heads rolled back, its necks bunching up as it collapsed onto the ground. Dust billowed in the air.

The sudden silence was startling, devoid of the screams and gasps, the rip of flesh. We exchanged stunned glances, in disbelief that the horror had ended. That we were alive. Feimao slapped me on the back, his grin morphing into a grimace as he clutched his shoulder. Someone laughed, another cheered. A wooden smile stretched across my face even though I did not feel like celebrating. My arms were blistered raw, but my insides knotted at the sight of Captain Wenzhi. The parts of his body I could see were crusted with injuries far worse than mine.

"I'm sorry." My voice was hoarse as I looked at Feimao and the other wounded soldiers. "I missed the first chance, I lost my nerve. If I hadn't, if I—"

"Archer Xingyin, stop apologizing." Captain Wenzhi sounded stern, though not unkind. "No battle is perfect; few things go as planned. What matters is that Xiangliu is dead and we all walk out of here today."

He scrutinized my injuries, his lips tightening—in disapproval, I thought. Instead of admonishing me, he pulled out a small jasper bottle, scattering several drops of a yellowish liquid onto my arms. The soothing scent of mint and herbs cut through the foul air, a coolness seeping into my skin as the pain subsided to a dull throb.

"This only numbs it." He passed me the bottle. "Don't try to heal yourself. Xiangliu's acid is laced with venom that needs to be treated properly. When we return, I'll send a healer to you."

"Send one to yourself, too. You're in worse shape than me." I nodded toward his wounds.

My legs wobbled then, belying my tough words as I sank to the ground. Struck by a wave of dizziness, I pressed my forehead against my arms. We had won, yet where was the exhilaration upon striking my target? There was undeniable relief that it was over, yes, but it was tangled with this clawing tightness in my chest. Was it pity? For the creature whose life I had taken? Even worse, and buried deeper, was there . . . shame? That I had killed so easily. And that I would do so again.

Captain Wenzhi crouched down beside me. "It gets easier," he said, as though he could read my thoughts.

"I'm afraid of that, too," I admitted haltingly.

"Xiangliu devoured countless mortals. If not stopped, he would have killed more."

His words gave me comfort. At least enough for my breathing to slow and my tension to ease. Staggering to my feet, I glanced down at the serpent's body. Blood trickled from its eyes, seeping into the ground. It *was* a monster—not because of its appearance—but what it had done. Grasping onto that, something hardened inside me. I would not mourn what I would do again, for as many times as I had to.

Just then, a strange sensation tugged at the edge of my consciousness. Swinging around, I glimpsed something bright, deep within the cave—only visible now the late sun shone through at this angle.

"Captain Wenzhi, what's that farther in?"

His gaze followed mine. "Is it the glare from the light?"

"I don't think so. Do you *feel* anything, coming from there?" I asked.

When he shook his head, I bit my lip, wondering if I was mistaken. Yet there it was still, that pull on my mind. That faint, elusive awareness.

"I'll inspect it and make my way back later," I decided.

"I'll join you. What if Xiangliu has a sibling?" He cracked a smile.

I shuddered. "As long as it doesn't eat mortals, we can leave it in peace."

We slipped through the narrow passageway at the end of the cave, crossing a shallow stream before emerging in a cavern. A shaft in the ceiling allowed the sunlight through unhindered, striking a heap of glittering treasure. Ropes of pearls, jade ornaments, and gems the size of my fist were piled onto the ground, as carelessly as though they were twigs, leaves, and stones.

"What is this?" I asked, finding my voice.

"Plunder from Xiangliu's victims?" Captain Wenzhi bent down to inspect a few of the items. "No, some of these are from our realm. Xiangliu must have brought them here."

Picking up a small chest, I flipped its lid open. Inside lay a gold necklace studded with chunks of amber.

He lifted it up. "An amulet of Earth magic."

"How do you know?" I asked curiously.

"Amber is a sacred treasure of the trees," he explained, dropping it back into its box. "I'll present this to His Celestial Majesty."

We opened a few more chests, tossing aside a magnificent necklace of rubies, a smooth orb of lapis lazuli thickly veined with gold, and a silver hair ornament shaped like a wind chime. When I ran my fingers over it, a tinkling melody filled the cavern.

I gestured toward the gleaming horde. "What should we do with all this?"

Immortals had little need for material wealth apart from ornamentation or vanity. Magic, rank, and bloodlines—these were the true determinants of power in the Celestial Kingdom.

Captain Wenzhi shrugged. "I'll bring a few pieces for Their Celestial Majesties' collection, and each soldier is welcome to souvenirs from a hard-won battle. As for the rest, feel free to dispose of them as you wish."

It was then I saw it, a large wooden box in a corner of the cave, its simplicity a stark contrast to the priceless treasures surrounding it. As I approached it, the unseen tug on my mind grew stronger—like sensing an immortal's aura, one which called to me alone. Bending down, I pried the lid off, my pulse racing as I stared at what lay within: a bow strung with shining gold cord and carved of green jade. A dragon, from its magnificent head at the tip, arching to its tail at the lower limb. When I touched the cool stone, a thrum of power surged through me like I had thrust my arm through a raging waterfall. Something clicked inside me, as though I'd found something I did not realize I had lost. Lifting the bow, I drew back its string, almost dropping it when a frail beam of light formed between my fingers. It did not hurt, emitting instead a pleasant tingle that crackled before it vanished.

"Sky-fire," Captain Wenzhi breathed.

The bow fell from my hands. This was said to be a great power—one the Celestial Emperor possessed—of which a single bolt could injure us greatly, even ending our lives.

His eyes were bright as he bent to pick it up. "The Jade Dragon Bow," he murmured, running his palm along its carvings.

The recognition in his tone startled me. "How do you know? Have you seen it before?"

He shrugged. "There are few weapons of Sky-fire in existence and only one bow."

"Why did the lightning vanish?" I was puzzled as I had not released the string.

A thoughtful expression crossed his face. "Perhaps your powers aren't strong enough to wield it yet."

He appeared calm though his breathing quickened. Raising the bow, he grasped its golden string. The muscles in his arm strained, yet it did not bend when it had yielded for me like a thread of silk. The moment he set it down, the bow sprang into my hands as though I had yanked it.

He raised his head, staring at me intently. Unsettled, I placed the bow back into its box and passed it to him. A loud rattling erupted from within.

He frowned as he pushed the box back to me. The clattering

ceased. "Hold on to this for now, until we decide what to do. It seems to have formed a connection with you and this is too powerful a weapon to leave lying around."

A thrill ran through me at his words. For some reason, I found myself reluctant to part with the bow, but I made myself ask, "Should we return this to the Celestial Kingdom?"

"The bow doesn't belong to the Celestial Kingdom. I heard its owner disappeared a long time ago. Keep it safe and well-hidden, until we find who we should return it to." His eyes bored into mine with sudden intensity as he added, "Speak of this to no one."

I nodded, despite the uneasiness clenching my stomach. Did he fear the Celestial Emperor might claim the bow? Yet it was surely the right thing to do, to restore the bow to its owner.

As I stared at the rest of the hoard, an idea formed. "Let's distribute this to the villages Xiangliu plagued. While nothing can compensate for the loss of their loved ones, at least their lives will be made easier."

He nodded. "Make your selection. I'll call the others."

I crouched down, picking up a gold bangle studded with coral, its bright colors reminding me of Shuxiao. I tucked it into my waistband. "My friend will like this."

"Nothing for yourself?" he asked.

I hesitated, before gathering up a necklace of sapphires, the blue fire of its stones like that of Liwei's crown. Then it slipped through my grasp, clinking as it fell to the ground. "I have no banquets or grand events to attend. Even if I did, I have all I need." I thought of the pendant I wore, which I never removed. It gave me a sense of belonging, knowing it was from my father, and that my mother's fingers had clasped it around my neck.

Captain Wenzhi was silent for a moment, before striding to the cavern entrance and calling for the others. As they joined us, their eyes widened at the sight. Even to immortals, this was no ordinary treasure. While they selected jeweled hairpins, necklaces of pearl and amber, and jade bangles, the captain chose several items for the Imperial Treasury and the soldiers who had returned earlier.

Those who were still able worked through the night, packing the gold and jewels. When we finally left the cave, my gaze flicked once to the still form huddled on the ground. I held my breath, trying to block out the metallic tang of the blood-soaked earth.

The sky had lightened to a misty gray by the time we delivered the last of the treasure to the villages. I lingered behind the others, watching as a door swung open and an old woman stepped out—the first mortal I had seen up close. Her skin was wrinkled, and her yellowed eyes drooped. The ragged clothes which hung off her frame offered meager protection from the biting chill, while in her hands was a dirt encrusted shovel. Was she setting out to toil at this early hour? She stumbled over the box in the entrance, bending down to pick it up. Her jaw dropped, her eyes rounding at the king's ransom within. A shrill cry escaped her lips, the sound piercing me deep. Cradling the chest, she ran through the streets with newfound strength, yelling for her neighbors to awaken. Doors were flung open, shouts erupting over the discovery of the treasure. Some of the villagers fell to their knees muttering grateful prayers, while others wept as they clutched each other. The air pulsed with their joy and relief . . . that perhaps this winter might not be so bitter after all.

I thought we were magnanimous in gifting the fortune, but

this warmth in my heart seemed more precious still. When someone stepped beside me, I gulped down the lump in my throat. Stealing a glance at Captain Wenzhi, I saw a smile stretch across his impassive face. His black eyes reflected the golden fire of the sun as its rays swept over us, bringing forth a new dawn.

16

There were no silvery ponds or flower-filled gardens to grace my view; my small room overlooked the walls of the palace. But I had earned it through my own efforts and not by another's grace. On the nights when my restless mind drove sleep away, I would climb up to the rooftop to stare at the stars above and the glittering lights of the kingdom below. Sometimes I would fall asleep on the cold jade tiles, lulled by the silvery glow of the moon. It reminded me of the lanterns in my home, whose light had shone through my window as I lay in my bed of cinnamon-wood.

In the privacy of my room, I stripped off my clothes, eager to wash the blood and sweat from my body. Captain Wenzhi's balm was wearing off and as I sank into the warm bathwater, my arms stung. Clenching my teeth, I scrubbed myself raw. Afterward, I slipped on a white underrobe and sank onto the bed, hoping to rest before the healer arrived.

Sleep claimed me. When I awakened, the sun had darkened to amber. I sat up and stretched my arms—bracing for pain—yet there was none. Not even a twinge or a blemish remained. The healer must have come while I slept.

"Did you rest well?"

His voice startled me, one I knew as well as my own. My pulse quickened as I slowly turned.

Liwei sat by the table, calm, as though we had just seen each other yesterday and not months before, as though our last words were not choked with pain and regret. His gray robe was clasped around his waist with a chain of onyx links and his long hair was pulled through a silver ring. He looked just as I remembered except his face was leaner, his eyes darker than before—or perhaps, the light in them had been dulled.

I smoothed my features into indifference, though inside . . . I was a mess of tangled, writhing emotions. Scrambling off the bed, I bowed with stiff formality.

"You don't have to do that," he said in a strained voice.

"I wouldn't need to if you didn't come here uninvited." I tugged the lapels of my underrobe closer together. "Liwei, this is hardly appropriate. I'm not dressed. These are the soldiers' quarters and you . . . you do not belong here."

When he did not appear inclined to leave, I stalked to the wardrobe, pulling out the first garment I found—a green robe that I slipped my arms through, tying its belt around my waist. Not wanting to take the stool beside him, I sat down on the bed again.

"Why are you here, Your Highness?"

"You called me Liwei just a moment ago," he pointed out.

"A mistake," I said. "You are the Crown Prince. I am a soldier. To me, you are 'Your Highness.'"

His slender fingers toyed with the cup on the table. "I heard you had returned. I wanted to see you, to know you were unharmed." He frowned. "Your injuries were severe. Why didn't you heal yourself before?"

"My skills are at best rudimentary. And with the serpent's venom, Captain Wenzhi believed the wound should be treated by a healer." I did not meet his gaze. The sight of him fractured the shell around my heart, reviving the ache that I had long fought to suppress.

He cleared his throat. "I believe congratulations are in order. I heard you brought Xiangliu down with two arrows in a single strike." He sounded pleased. Proud, even.

"Not me, alone. If not for the others, I wouldn't have made it out alive," I said with feeling.

The color drained from his face, yet I would not let myself read too much into his concern. "Your Highness, I thank you for your visit, but I wish to rest. Please see yourself out." I stretched my hand to the doors, tempering my rudeness with a short bow.

He did not rise. He did not speak. Was he offended? The chief attendant would have had an apoplectic fit at my disrespect. But then it struck me, how could he have seen my injuries unless—

"Did *you* heal me?"

"Yes." His gaze held mine.

My traitorous mind conjured the image of him sitting on my bed, his hands sliding over my arms as he channeled his energy into them. "I didn't ask you to. But thank you."

"There is no need for thanks," he said. "Have you been well?"

I recalled the countless sleepless nights since I had left him, the grief gnawing at my heart. The tears I had swallowed until they ran dry. These were my secrets, hidden beneath my smile.

"Yes," I lied baldly. "My training keeps me busy. Captain Wenzhi is a hard taskmaster."

His jaw tightened as an unfamiliar edge cut through his

tone. "Yes, Captain Wenzhi is most solicitous of you. One wonders why he spends so much time and effort on just one recruit?"

I simmered at the insinuation. If he was jealous, he had no right to be. "Why are you here?" I asked again, in a harder voice than before.

His hand curled into a fist on the table. "I shouldn't be here. I stayed away as long as I could. But when you were in the Mortal Realm, I could not help fearing that you might be in danger. That you might not return."

His confession slashed through my carefully constructed defenses. How I hated this weakness which stirred in me, this futile yearning for what was lost. How easy it would be to admit the ache in my chest, to reach for him as I had dreamed. But he was promised to another, and I would not settle for less than I had to give.

I laughed instead, a short, harsh sound—indifference and mockery my armor in this struggle. "Do you think so little of my abilities?"

He stared at me unflinchingly. "Xingyin, that is unfair. You know how highly I regard you."

"Not enough, it would seem. Don't speak to me of what's unfair, Liwei." I cursed myself for the lapse of his name, the sudden brightness which flared in his eyes. "You made your choice clear the night you betrothed yourself to another. I made mine clear when I left. It's unfair of *you* to come to me now, when you must realize it unsettles me."

I should have stopped there, but my resentment and anger spilled from me now. "You told me you loved me. You broke my heart. You didn't even tell me of your engagement yourself. Was that *fair*?" Bitter words and yet, it was a relief to have spoken them aloud.

"No." His voice was hoarse. "You have every right to despise me. Just know, if I could choose, it would be you."

He ran a hand through his hair as he did when he was distressed. How I wished I did not know these things about him, and that he did not move me so.

"I was going to tell you. The betrothal was not meant to be announced that night, but my mother persuaded my father otherwise."

My breath shook as I drew it in. I was wrong; the empress had not waited to retaliate, and her blow struck truer than she could have ever hoped. It did not matter; nothing would have changed. He was the Crown Prince. Marriage was his duty, and I should have realized that from the start.

A heavy silence fell over us. Part of me wished he would leave, so I could sink back into the bed and lose myself in the numbness of slumber. And yet, a weaker part of me thrived on his presence still—drinking in his face, the sound of his voice, yearning for his touch—despite knowing the anguish which would come after.

I steeled myself to ask, "Has the wedding date been set?" There it was, said aloud, the bandage ripped clean from the wound. Was it not better to battle the monster in the open than leave it lurking in the shadows, unsure when it might strike?

The light leeched from his eyes. "The betrothal gifts have been exchanged, though the ceremony won't be for years. Princess Fengmei and I are still young, and I've asked for the time to devote myself to my duties. Perhaps then, things might be different."

He did not sound like an eager bridegroom. Nor did I understand the delay when the exchange of gifts was a commitment as binding as the signing of the betrothal contract. Who would dare come between an alliance of the two most powerful families in the realm? I had asked the question, invited the pain, peeling away the last stubborn shred of hope from my heart. Yet how sharp the regret which stabbed me now, the claws of jealousy which raked me.

Someone rapped on my door. Was it Shuxiao, calling me for the evening meal? I would be glad for any distraction. Striding to the doors, I wrenched them apart, a welcoming smile on my lips—

It was Captain Wenzhi who stood in the entrance, out of his armor and in a black robe. "The healer said she was sent away before she could attend to you." At the sight of Liwei, he stiffened before bowing in greeting. "Your Highness, I did not expect to find you in the soldiers' quarters."

Liwei's expression turned cool, sliding into the imperial mask he wore so easily. "Captain Wenzhi, you are most solicitous of your soldiers. Even visiting them at this late hour."

"Indeed I am, Your Highness. Particularly of those injured." He stalked into the room, unflustered by Liwei's hostility.

As they stared at each other, their gazes flat and unblinking, my head began to throb.

Finally, Liwei turned to me. "I am at ease knowing you've returned." He nodded tersely to Captain Wenzhi, who responded with another short bow. From the set of his shoulders, I knew he was displeased as he left.

"Why should your return weigh on Prince Liwei's mind?" Captain Wenzhi asked, taking the stool newly vacated. With a surge of his magic, he heated the water in the pot, brewing a fresh pot of jasmine tea and pouring me a cup.

I took a sip, relishing its delicate fragrance and soothing warmth. "We're friends. We studied together."

"He didn't seem friendly. Neither did you."

I kept my face blank, setting the cup back down. "Captain Wenzhi, did you come for a particular reason or just to stir up trouble where there is none?"

"I came to check on your injuries. How are they?"

"Healed." I stretched out my arms to show him the renewed skin, relieved to find his wounds had vanished, too.

A strange expression crossed his face. "You're fortunate to have been attended to so well."

I snatched my arms back. He knew the healer had not attended to me. "How was your audience with His Celestial Majesty?" A clumsy attempt to divert his attention.

"The emperor was pleased. You would be in line for a promotion should you decide to make this a career." His tone lifted like he was asking a question.

I cared not for that, yet this was a promising start to the journey I hoped would bring me home. "I'm not going anywhere. If they want to give me a new title, though, I wouldn't mind yours," I told him lightly.

"I'll be sure to inform Their Celestial Majesties of your wish." He added, almost as an afterthought, "The Jade Dragon Bow—did you keep it someplace safe?"

I nodded, thinking of the box tucked beneath my bed, an enchantment woven to conceal it from prying eyes.

"I'll be leaving soon to one of the Sea Kingdoms. If you join us, we might find some information on the bow there. However, it could be dangerous. It's no small matter for their king to request our aid and no favor from the Celestial Emperor comes without a price."

Something flickered across his face. Was it distaste? Or concern for the perils ahead? "I'll consider it," I said slowly.

He rose to his feet then. "I'll see you at training tomorrow. At dawn."

I resisted the urge to protest. It would do no good.

He almost collided into Shuxiao at the doorway. Trying to balance the unwieldly tray in her grasp, she bowed to him awkwardly. He gave her a curt nod in return, his expression aloof as he left.

Shuxiao set the tray on the table. "Your dinner. I heard you were hurt."

"Thank you." I was glad for her company. Her room was close to mine and we ate together whenever we could. As I glanced at the braised pork, stir-fried green beans, and ripe loquats—my stomach growled, reminding me that I had not eaten anything all day. Lifting the lid off the bamboo steamer, I took a soft pillow of bread, tucking slices of the tender meat within its folds.

"Have you seen a healer?" she asked.

"Yes." I was reluctant to elaborate.

She slanted her head back to stare at me. "You look well. Glowing, almost. Maybe you should have brought me my dinner instead." Pushing back her stool, she lifted the hem of her robe, displaying two rows of red indents pressed into her calf.

"Are those teeth marks? What happened?"

"Fox spirits. A few broke in." She grimaced. "When their magic is drained, they bite. It doesn't hurt anymore, but they itch like fire and the healer said it will take weeks for the marks to disappear. *If* they do."

"How did they get in?" I was surprised, as powerful wards protected the Celestial Kingdom from its enemies. Each night, the soldiers on duty wove shields all along the kingdom's borders, which alerted them to any intrusion.

"One took the form of a Celestial and slipped through,

undetected. Once inside, she broke the wards from within. It shouldn't have happened. Even with a transformed appearance, our wards should have detected their auras. General Jianyun is investigating the matter."

I fumbled in my pouch, pulling out the jasper bottle that Captain Wenzhi had given me. Tugging off its stopper, I shook out the last few drops over her leg.

As the redness of her injuries subsided, she sighed in relief. "What's that?"

"Just something Captain Wenzhi gave me for my injuries."

"Oh? Does Captain Wenzhi often dispense rare medicines to lowly soldiers?" Her stare bored into me.

"Just this once" was all I said.

"Or just this *one*."

I did not reply, taking a loquat and peeling it with excessive care.

She shrugged then, perhaps tired of teasing me when I did not rise to the bait. "How was Xiangliu?" she asked, as though we were speaking of a mutual friend.

"Dead. An arrow through the eye." It was easier to speak cavalierly of it. Somehow it made it less real—the danger, the life I had taken.

"How bloodthirsty," she remarked. "Was it a hard fight?"

I described the battle, knowing she would be interested in every detail. When I was done, I looked away, admitting, "I lost my nerve. Those injured . . . it was because of my mistakes."

"Anyone would have been terrified. What were you thinking—Xiangliu, for your first assignment? New recruits are typically sent on mundane tasks like inspecting the border or searching for some lost artifact."

It was precisely for the danger that I had put myself forward.

Mundane tasks were of no use to me. They would not get my name whispered into the emperor's ear; they would not earn me the Crimson Lion Talisman.

She added, "At least you recovered in time. No one died. Well, except for Xiangliu. Don't forget it was you who killed it."

I nodded, feeling a little better. "It wasn't all bad. We found a cave of treasure."

She leaned across the table. "Did you keep anything?"

I thought about the Jade Dragon Bow, more precious by far than any jewel. But it was not mine and Captain Wenzhi had cautioned me to keep it hidden and, a secret. I dug through my pouch for the bangle, pressing it into her palm.

She flicked the clasp open, slipping her hand through it. The gold and coral gleamed against her skin. "It's beautiful."

"It's just a small trinket." I was glad that she seemed to like it. "You should have seen what Captain Wenzhi brought back for the Treasury."

Her expression turned curious. "What was Captain Wenzhi doing here? Not that I'm complaining when there are so many who would envy us."

"What do you mean?"

"Haven't you noticed the crowds in the field whenever he trains—both men and woman alike? Tall, broad shoulders, clear eyes, firm mouth, straight nose," she recited, ticking each item off on her fingers. "If only he smiled more, it would put his handsome features to better use."

"Handsome?" I had thought him striking, but handsome?

She shot me a reproachful look. "How could you not have noticed? After those months you've spent training with him, walking beside him, sleeping under the stars by the glowing campfire—"

I grabbed a bun and threw it at her, which she deftly caught.

"Don't protest too much," she grinned. "Or I might start to think there's some truth to the rumors."

Were those the same ones which had reached Liwei? Was that why he had sought me out the moment I returned, to seek a denial or admission? "Those rumors you mention are ridiculous beyond measure," I said, more heatedly than intended.

"Did I strike a nerve?"

I shut my mouth at once.

Shuxiao picked a loquat from the bowl, passing it to me. A peace offering. "Few are held in as high regard as Captain Wenzhi. His fighting skills are renowned, and his magic is unusually strong for one not descended from any known lineage."

I glanced at her. "Where is he from?"

"I've heard Captain Wenzhi is from some undistinguished family line in the Four Seas. It was no small feat for him—a foreigner—to rise through the ranks, to become the youngest captain in the Celestial Army."

I felt a sense of shared companionship with Captain Wenzhi, knowing both of us were forging a new life for ourselves here. While he was far more capable than I, it gave me hope for my own ambitions—that an unknown could rise to prominence in the Celestial Kingdom.

Though I could not help thinking, even he had not won the Crimson Lion Talisman.

After the meal, I helped Shuxiao stack the empty dishes onto the tray. As I tried to pry the tray from her fingers, she snatched it away.

"It's not every day you slay a legendary monster. And it doesn't sound like Captain Wenzhi is going to go easy on you tomorrow either." Without another word, she left the room.

Sleep eluded me that night. With an impatient sigh, I tossed off the bedcovers and left the room. Climbing onto the rooftop, I settled upon the cold jade tiles. How the solitude of night reminded me of home. The lights of the Celestial Kingdom glittered below, whose borders I now defended with my life. Would my mother feel betrayed by my new allegiance? Would she think I had forgotten her in the pursuit of power? My chest cramped at the thought. If only she knew the truth—that all I did was to win her freedom, that we might be together again.

17

I stood before General Jianyun's desk, wondering why he had summoned me. I rarely saw him these days, since I began training with Captain Wenzhi and his troops. My gaze fixed upon the table, intricately crafted from rosewood and inlaid with mother-of-pearl in designs of bamboo, lotuses, and cranes. I did not expect such a delicate piece to adorn the office of so pragmatic a soldier. Although I reminded myself that despite his forbidding exterior, the general had shown me kindness I did not deserve. He had seen something in me before I realized it myself.

I shifted uncertainly beneath the weight of his stare, the gilded scales of my armor clinking. General Jianyun's brows snapped together in a wordless rebuke: a good soldier did not fidget.

I stood straighter, forcing my legs to still. Did he call me here to admonish me for some offense? To lecture me on my carelessness with Xiangliu?

A glimmer of a smile formed on his lips. "For your first assignment, you did well."

My breath came out in a rush. "Thank you, General."

"As agreed, you may decide your next assignment. There are

two in need of another recruit. One will go to the Golden Desert to harvest the rare herbs that grow there. While it borders the Demon Realm, no disturbance is expected with the peace treaty intact."

I nodded, trying to appear enthused. I had never been to the Golden Desert, but gathering plants held little appeal. Perhaps I should have been grateful for an easier assignment after Xiang-liu, except this would not gain the emperor's attention.

"Or would you prefer to accompany Captain Wenzhi again?" General Jianyun offered. "While that is his preference, this is your choice. He will lead a troop to the Eastern Sea, whose king has called for our aid to handle recent unrest."

My mind stirred with a fragment of a tale my mother used to tell me. Her voice, soft and melodious, as she had spoken of the Eastern Sea and . . .

"The dragons," I whispered, so wrapped in the memory of her cool hand stroking my cheek that I inhaled instinctively—a futile attempt to capture a whiff of cinnamon-wood. A dull ache gripped me, different from the stabbing pain of heartbreak, though both awoke a longing in me for something lost.

General Jianyun tensed, a rare slip in his composure. "Dragons?"

I laughed to cover my lapse—too shrill, too loud. "Just an old fable I had heard, that the Eastern Sea was the birthplace of the dragons. Did they cause this disturbance?"

He spoke slowly, choosing his words with care. "The dragons are no longer in the Eastern Sea. No longer in the Immortal Realm."

A dozen questions flashed through my mind. All I knew of the dragons was the story I had been told. Until now, I had believed them merely a myth, a symbol of power which the emperor seemed to favor.

Before I could speak, the general continued with a frown, "It is the merfolk, the deep-sea dwellers. They have broken the peace for the first time, ever. And while it's just petty skirmishes for now, Captain Wenzhi is preparing for any eventuality."

The tranquil exploration of the Golden Desert or the perils of the Eastern Sea? The stench of Xiangliu's cave sprang into my memory, the ominous chink of its scales casting a shiver down my spine. But such was the price of the path I had chosen. And as Captain Wenzhi had said, perhaps we might find more information on the Jade Dragon Bow in the Eastern Sea.

IN THE WEEKS BEFORE our departure, I trained more intensely than I ever had before. While I was lauded for slaying Xiangliu, deep down I felt I was a fraud—that such praise was undeserved. My fear and inexperience had endangered us all. How arrogant I had been to imagine myself ready, that I could leap into the ocean depths and miraculously learn how to swim. How rash, to think my feats in training could be easily replicated when blood thickened the air, pain and terror engulfing my body and mind. No, I would not make that mistake again. Each night I sank into bed, so exhausted I no longer feared being alone with my thoughts in the dark. I no longer sought the solitude of the roof. Why would I, when I drifted to sleep the moment my head dropped onto the pillow?

The sky was overcast from the clouds we summoned for our journey to the Eastern Sea. A mortal looking up would have been startled by the enormous cloudbanks moving swiftly across the heavens. I had finally overcome my trepidation to master this skill, no longer reliant on another to carry me. My energy flowed in a glittering surge, calling down the nearest cloud. Silver flecks wove into its voluminous folds, imbuing it with my magic as I soared into the skies.

The beauty of the Eastern Sea transfixed me. Brilliant-colored flowers and plants abounded along the shore, glowing with an inner radiance. I reached out to touch a petal, surprised to find it as firm and cool as porcelain. A lush forest grew at the far end, away from the shoreline, while houses of cedarwood and stone were built upon the sand. Their sloping roofs were paved with turquoise and mother-of-pearl, and in the morning light, they glittered like the cresting waves of the sea. A crystal walkway arched from the beach to the palace, which rose from the midst of the ocean.

My gaze fixed on the endless horizon as I wandered toward the shoreline, my boots sinking into the soft sand. All thought of work forgotten, I crouched down and dipped my hands into the cold water, startling the tiny, silvery fish swimming in the shallows. When a shadow fell over me, I spun around, squinting against the bright sunlight.

Captain Wenzhi towered above, an amused smile on his lips. "Have you never been to the sea?"

I straightened, shaking the droplets from my hands. A few scattered over him but he did not seem to mind. "I've seen it when flying above or in pictures. And . . . someone told me it was beautiful." My mother's wistful words echoed in my mind, her hopes for the life she had envisioned for me.

Footsteps crunched the sand as several soldiers approached. Beneath their watchful stares, I wrapped my palm over my fist and bowed. "Captain Wenzhi, I await your command."

"See to your responsibilities before you acquaint yourself with our surroundings." His tone was stern, yet his smile did not waver as he turned and strode to the waiting soldiers.

I kept my head down, hiding my face. An onlooker might think I was ashamed to be reprimanded, but as I gazed at the ever-changing waters my spirits were lighter than the wandering breeze. And for the first time in months, I sensed the stirrings of anticipation.

After the camp was organized, I accompanied Captain Wen-zhi across the crystal bridge for his audience with the king. The palace gleamed against the sea and sky—a shimmering edifice of rock quartz, turquoise, and mother-of-pearl, with a two-tiered roof of gilded tiles. The large entrance doors were crafted from ash wood and inlaid with gold, over which hung a plaque inscribed with the characters:

幽珊宫

FRAGRANT CORAL PALACE

All around were more of the exquisite flowers and plants I had seen on the beach—sprays of vermilion branches, bright green flowers shaped like fans, pink tubular stalks, and smooth rocks covered with glowing red moss. An enchanted garden plucked from the heart of the ocean.

Through the doors, an attendant guided us down a long flight of stairs. The lower levels of the palace were built underwater, crafted from the same clear stone as the bridge. It was like walking on the ocean floor, surrounded by shifting water and coral reefs all around. As we entered a crowded hall with soaring ceilings, silence fell over the gathered immortals. Only then did I hear the melodious clink from the strands of ivory shells which swayed behind the agate thrones. I had only seen King Yanzheng of the Eastern Sea once before, at Liwei's banquet. Silver hair framed his smooth, unlined face and his eyes glowed against his dark skin. His teal silk robe was embroidered with waves, edged by glistening curves of white thread. A gold fan-shaped crown, studded with pearls, rested upon his hair.

Captain Wenzhi and I knelt on the floor, stretching out our clasped hands, as we bowed. "The Celestial Kingdom has answered the Eastern Sea's call for aid," he intoned formally. "Our swords will be drawn, and our bows stretched in your service."

"Rise," the king commanded, sounding pleased. "We are grateful for the assistance of the Celestial Kingdom during these troubled times. The merfolk's attacks caught us unaware as they had always lived peacefully among us before. Captain Wenzhi, your reputation has reached even our ears in the Eastern Sea and we thank the Celestial Emperor for sending us his finest warrior."

Captain Wenzhi bowed again. "Your Majesty is kind, but I do not deserve such praise. It is my honor to serve to the best of my abilities."

King Yanzheng stroked his beard, "Humility accompanying such talent is rare." He gestured toward me. "Is this lady your wife?"

Strangled noises slid from my mouth as Captain Wenzhi's ears reddened. "No, Your Majesty. This is . . . First Archer Xingyin of the Celestial Army."

My ears pricked up at his introduction. *First Archer?*

The king glanced at my armor. "Ah," he nodded, with a bemused smile. "We do not have female warriors here."

Several courtiers tittered, some smothering their laughter

behind raised sleeves. My insides churned from the unwanted scrutiny, even as my fingers curled at their disdain.

Captain Wenzhi swept a chilling gaze around the room, which silenced their mirth more effectively than a sword. "First Archer Xingyin is the highest ranked archer in our army. She will be of great assistance to this campaign." He spoke in clipped tones. "Your Majesty, could you advise us on the situation with the merfolk?"

The king gestured to the young man beside him. "My eldest son, Prince Yanxi, will brief you."

A tall immortal stepped forward, clad in a shimmering sky-blue robe. Tiny fish, embroidered in crimson and silver, darted from their folds. His dark brown hair was coiled up into a top-knot, secured with a turquoise hairpin. This close, I sensed his aura, cool and steady, thrumming with power.

"Captain Wenzhi, First Archer Xingyin. Since the beginning of time, we have lived in harmony with the merfolk. While we, Sea Immortals, prefer to stay on both land and sea—the merfolk chose to dwell deep underwater, only surfacing on rare occasions. They revered the dragons who used to live there and desired to be close to them. The dragons were wise and gentle creatures, helping to maintain the harmony in our waters."

His tone changed, growing taut. "When the Celestial Emperor banished the dragons from our realm, the merfolk grew restless. Over time, their dislike of land grew greater, preferring to keep solely to themselves in the depths of the ocean. Years ago, my father allowed them to choose a governor to represent them at our court. Unfortunately, Governor Renyu is dangerous, his ambitions stretching far beyond his mandate. We received reports that he had recruited a large army from among the merfolk, training them in weaponry and magic. When my father requested his presence to answer these accusations, he refused."

I thought to myself, training an army without a mandate was treasonous indeed. And Governor Renyu's guilt was compounded by his refusal to meet the king.

Prince Yanxi rubbed his brow, his expression darkening. "Since then, the merfolk turned outright hostile. Sea Immortals who ventured too deep into the waters were attacked. The homes closest to the shore were raided. Each time, the perpetrators fled before our soldiers could apprehend them."

"Petty banditry is unlikely to be all the governor intends. Do you have any knowledge of his plans?" Captain Wenzhi asked.

"Recently he issued his own edict, banning all Sea Immortals from the ocean depths. A grave insult to us. We believe he wants to overthrow my father and take the throne for himself. Under Governor Renyu's command, the merfolk army has grown strong and powerful, while I fear the reverse can be said of ours. We are a peaceful nation, unaccustomed to battle, which is why we appealed to the Celestial Kingdom for aid."

Would we have to fight the merfolk underwater? My stomach twisted at the thought. Like many Celestials, I had not learned how to swim—what need was there when we could fly? Once, in my childhood, I had fallen into the river near my home. Cold water had pressed all around me, clogging my nose and mouth. I had flailed, kicking out—my frantic movements only dragging me deeper into the river's embrace. It was my mother who had plunged into the water, pulling me out. She had scolded me in a trembling tone, even as her arms wrapped tight around me, the comforting beat of her heart silencing the last of my terror.

How sharp the remembered fear which pierced me now. But

I pushed it aside to say, "Celestial soldiers are unused to being underwater. If there is a battle, we should try to draw the mer-folk to land."

Something flashed across Prince Yanxi's face, akin to surprise. "Indeed. We would be greatly disadvantaged underwater. The merfolk are excellent swimmers and are accustomed to the darkness. However, they will be reluctant to challenge us on land. We will need a plan."

King Yanzheng leaned forward. "The captain and his troops just arrived today. We are being inhospitable, keeping them here when they need to settle themselves." His smile was gracious and warm. "Captain Wenzhi, we have planned a banquet tonight in your honor. I hope you will grace us with your presence, along with First Archer Xingyin."

"We would be honored." Captain Wenzhi hesitated, his throat working. "Your Majesty, the library of the Fragrant Coral Palace is renowned throughout the Immortal Realm. May I have your permission to visit it? I hope to learn what I can about the merfolk to aid us."

The king inclined his head. "An attendant will bring you there whenever you wish."

As Captain Wenzhi and I left the hall, I grinned at him. "'First Archer?' 'The highest ranked archer in our army?'" I repeated his earlier words back to him. "Does this mean we're closer in rank now?"

He shot me an exasperated glare. "It's not an official position as you're not an official recruit. And since when have our ranks mattered to you?"

I laughed, not protesting his claim. I had never been disrespectful to him, but neither had I treated him with the deference his position called for.

Without breaking his stride, he continued, "You *are* the first ranked archer in the army. Although, if you slack off and lose your position—you'll have to make do with 'Second' or 'Third Archer,' which sounds a lot less impressive."

"Hah!" I was stung by his insinuation. "Care to challenge me yourself?" He was known to be a skilled archer and yet, the moment the words left my mouth, I wanted to snatch them back. They evoked too many unsettling memories . . . of a peach blossom forest, of someone I desperately wanted to forget.

A shadow of a smile formed upon his lips. "Not with the bow. But you're welcome to try me on any other weapon."

I did not reply, forcing myself onward, one step after the other, as silence fell between us now.

He stopped by the entrance doors, tilting his head as he scrutinized me. "You look pale. Tired. You've been training too hard. Why don't you return to the camp and rest? I'll go to the library to see if I can find anything of use." He gestured to the waiting attendant who hurried over at once.

"I'm fine," I protested, eager to visit the library, too. But he stared at me unrelentingly until I nodded. I could not defy his order in front of the attendant.

"I'll tell you what I find," he said, perhaps seeing my crestfallen face. "Rest, while you can. Tonight, will be a long affair."

18

An attendant from the Fragrant Coral Palace arrived, bearing a tray of garments for the banquet. Glad for their gracious hospitality, I pulled on the yellow satin dress with turquoise beads thickly sewn onto its hem and cuffs. A sea-green sash went around my waist, its silken tassels falling to my knees. The style of this garment was different from those in the Celestial Kingdom, leaving my jade pendant bared below the hollow of my neck. My only other adornment was a comb of pearls tucked into the crown of my head, as my dark hair flowed loosely down my back.

Captain Wenzhi waited for me outside. My pulse leapt un-expectedly as I walked toward him. He was striking tonight in a forest green robe, with a gleaming length of black silk knotted around his waist. His hair was gathered into a carved jade ring, falling over his shoulder like waves of night. It was as though my eyes were rinsed, finally seeing with startling clarity all the fine features which Shuxiao had described.

The wind blew gently that evening. I inhaled the cool air, drowning my senses in the fragrance of the sea—a bewitching mixture of sunshine and salt, laced with an undercurrent of excitement. The rays from the setting sun painted the waters crimson and vermilion, the Fragrant Coral Palace glowing like a jewel in the horizon.

In the banquet hall, hundreds of lanterns were strung across the ceiling, luminous and bright. Low wooden tables and brocade-padded chairs were arranged around the walls, leaving an empty space in the center of the room. In one corner sat an elegant lady playing a pipa, the four-stringed wooden instrument shaped like an elongated pear. As she plucked its strings, the melancholy strains of her song filled the air. Her playing was masterful; from the twang of a single string she wrung a river of sorrow and an ocean of grief.

The king and queen sat on a dais at the far end of the hall. A magnificent gold flower with a pearl the size of my palm gleamed from the queen's hair. The petals fluttered around the pearl, which glowed white one moment, morphing to deepest black the next. A little boy stood beside her, clutching her hand. His head barely came up to the armrest of her throne and his dark eyes were large and solemn. Beside him stood an elegant lady in apricot silk with strands of round pink pearls looped around her neck. Her delicate chin was tilted up as she scrutinized the hall with an expression of regal aloofness.

"Is that His Majesty's daughter?" I asked Captain Wenzhi, as we went to greet our hosts.

"His Majesty has only two sons—Prince Yanxi whom you've met, and Prince Yanming." Following my gaze, he added, "The lady standing with Prince Yanming is Lady Anmei, his governess. She's the daughter of a powerful nobleman and her family holds great influence at this court."

After we paid our respects to the royal family, an attendant showed us to our table. Captain Wenzhi filled our cups and I took a sip of the wine, the mild sweetness of the fermented grains lingering on my tongue. The silver plates before us were piled with exotic foods, most of which I had never seen before: glossy red crustaceans, golden jellyfish, and black spiked spheres. I thought those looked particularly unappetizing, although the other guests ate it with relish.

Captain Wenzhi took one and sliced it open, passing half to me. I scooped up its flesh and slid it into my mouth, savoring its creamy yet briny taste.

"Is the food to your liking?" Prince Yanxi asked, appearing before us unexpectedly.

I choked on my mouthful, coughing loudly. Grabbing my cup, I took a large gulp of wine before hastily rising to greet him.

He inclined his head in acknowledgment, saying, "Captain Wenzhi, my father wishes to speak with you. He asked if you would join him at his table? I will accompany First Archer Xingyin until your return."

A frown flitted across Captain Wenzhi's face, only to vanish in the next instant. He bowed to the prince, before walking toward the dais. I could not help noticing how Lady Anmei brightened when he took the empty seat at their table.

Prince Yanxi lowered himself onto the chair as he looked intently at me. For some reason, I did not find his interest offensive. Perhaps it was the open curiosity in his expression or the humor as I boldly returned his stare, determined not to be the first to break the silence.

"First Archer, where did you learn your skills?" The candid way he spoke reminded me of General Jianyun.

"I trained alongside Prince Liwei when I was his companion." I responded in a similar vein, hoping he did not catch the quiver in my voice.

Recognition dawned. "Of course. I remember you from the banquet. You played the flute well. Do you still?"

"No." I looked away from him. I had not played since that night.

Perhaps sensing my unease, he asked, "Why did you join the Celestial Army? Was this your family's wish?"

"The general who mentored my early training offered me a position."

His fingertips played with the rim of his cup. "Surely there must have been many other opportunities available to one who had served the Crown Prince?"

"Not where I would have the freedom to make my own way. I have no family to advance me and only my skills to depend on." I lifted the cup to my mouth and took a long drink. "But this is my choice, I would not seek another," I added, thinking of the Crimson Lion Talisman.

A smile played upon his lips, his eyes crinkling. They were not black as I had imagined, but the deep, opaque blue of uncut sapphires. He picked up the porcelain jug to refill my cup. "Your candor is refreshing."

The wine was going to my head, loosening my tongue. "Why does Your Highness have so many questions for someone like me?"

"Because there aren't many like you. Captain Wenzhi holds you in high esteem. You must be exceptionally skilled to be ranked the First Archer. Yet you look like no warrior I've ever encountered."

I returned his smile. "As there are no women in your army, I'm not surprised."

He threw back his head and laughed. "I apologize. I'm not usually so inept in my compliments."

Had I heard him correctly? Growing aware of the sudden lull in conversation, I glanced around the hall. Many of the Eastern Sea Immortals were staring at us, whispering among themselves.

"Your presence with me is causing quite a stir. Perhaps Your Highness should attend to your other guests," I suggested, belatedly realizing one does not dismiss a prince of the realm.

Fortunately, he appeared amused rather than incensed. "Have I made you uncomfortable? That was not my intent. I merely wanted to get to know you better. People interest me, as much as books, music, or art interests others."

My fingers twisted the soft fabric of my skirt as I searched in vain for an appropriate response.

His eyes gleamed as they fixed upon my throat. "Your pendant—the amulet is a rare one. Could you tell me its origin?"

My throat went dry. I had been asked about my family enough times that there was a ready answer on the tip of my tongue. However, no one had ever asked me about my father's pendant, usually tucked beneath my robe. I thought it a common jewel, its only value to me in its heritage.

"I found it in the marketplace. The one that appears every five years in the Celestial Kingdom," I said quickly.

"A fortunate find." He drew out each word.

I shifted in my seat, wondering if he had seen through my lie. I was tempted to change the subject, to venture to safer ground, but his interest had piqued my own. Perhaps he knew something of my father's pendant. "Why did you call it an amulet?"

"Because it is one. A powerful one, too, of protection."

My fingers reached up to stroke the jade. Had my father worn this to challenge the sunbirds? Had it protected him from their deadly flame?

Prince Yanxi leaned closer to scrutinize the stone. "Unfortunately, it seems to have been damaged."

The crack in the rim. "Can it be restored?" I asked, a little too eagerly.

The corners of his mouth dipped. "From its carving, this appears to be a talisman of the dragons. If so, only they can restore it."

My spirits sank as I released the pendant. The dragons were no longer in the Immortal Realm. Banished, Prince Yanxi had said, echoing the tale I had heard as a child.

"You know a lot about the dragons. In the Celestial Kingdom there is little information on them," I remarked.

"The Venerable Dragons, as they were called, were born in the Eastern Sea and lived here until their banishment. Though they were never under our rule, our historians, scholars, and scribes gathered all the information they could find on them. Despite their fearsome appearance, the dragons were wise and benevolent, using their might to aid those in need and maintain the peace in our waters. Many revered them—the merfolk, Sea Immortals, even the mortals. Many mourn their loss still. If you are interested to learn more, you are welcome to visit our library."

"Thank you." I was grateful for his generous offer. According to Captain Wenzhi, it was not one made lightly. My curiosity was pricked, especially after missing my earlier opportunity and I longed to immerse myself in the library, if only I had the leisure to do so.

"Your Highness, have you heard of the Jade Dragon Bow?" I asked, trying to keep my voice light.

His body stiffened, almost imperceptibly. "Why do you ask?"

"I heard someone speak of it and I wondered who wielded such a powerful weapon."

"No one," he said gravely. "It was lost along with its owner, even before the dragons were banished, and will probably never be found again."

It was on the tip of my tongue to confide in him that the bow was not lost, that it was in my keeping. But I knew little of the prince and I had promised Captain Wenzhi to not speak of it. Moreover, he seemed to know nothing of its owner's whereabouts.

The chime of bells drew my attention, with their ringing, silvery tones. Dancers entered, gliding to the center of the hall in a swirl of blue and green silk. A string of golden bells dangled from their waists and their ornate headdresses were studded with precious gems. Each performer carried a polished jade stick to which a wide red ribbon was attached. When the pipa player struck up a new song, a livelier melody with rippling strains, they lifted their sticks and danced. Their graceful bodies twirled and dipped and spun, their ribbons streaming after them as bright as living flames. Sighs of appreciation swelled through the crowd, my own among them.

Two dancers sprang into the air, their ribbons spinning around their bodies in a graceful spiral. When they landed, another leapt up high, arching toward the thrones in a remarkable display of agility. As my eyes followed her, wide with admiration, something bright slid from the base of her stick. The softness of her expression morphed into the ruthlessness of a predator.

My gut clenched with dread. On instinct, I darted for a

weapon—finding none, I snatched up a silver plate instead, hurling it at the leaping dancer. It struck her in the temple, knocking her headdress askew. She cried out as she fell to the ground in a tangled heap of silk and ribbon.

Guests shot to their feet, shouting in alarm. A few glared at me as though I had lost my mind, disrupting the performance with my uncivil conduct.

"She has a weapon," I warned Prince Yanxi.

He sprang up at once, barking orders to the guards to apprehend the dancer.

After a few tense moments, a guard ran toward us. His face was grim as he held out a cluster of sharp needles, glistening with the viscous remnants of a greenish liquid.

"Sea scorpion venom," Prince Yanxi hissed. "It spreads swiftly, paralyzing the entire body. Too much would be fatal."

The music had stopped when the dancer fell, leaving the hall in ominous silence. The guests exchanged confused glances, their mutterings no longer outraged, but anxious and urgent. The air shifted, taut with strain. Something thudded against the wall. Metal clashed, a bloodcurdling cry ringing out. Beside me, Prince Yanxi drew his sword. The doors were flung open, a guard standing in the entrance, his blue and silver armor streaked with blood.

"Merfolk! We're under attack!"

A spear hurtled through his chest with a wet crunch, its tip now drenched with blood. The soldier's eyes bulged as he lurched forward, before falling to his knees and keeling over.

Guests stumbled to their feet, overturning tables and chairs as they scrambled to the back of the room. Captain Wenzhi leapt down from the dais, his blade already unsheathed. I cursed that my hands were empty, but the prince stripped a bow and quiver from a nearby guard and tossed them to me. Plucking an arrow, I drew it through the string, its red shaft as hard and cool as stone.

"Fire coral. Merfolk are vulnerable to it," Prince Yanxi said tightly, his knuckles white around the hilt of his sword.

Assailants swarmed into the hall. Their armor was woven from small scales that gleamed like mother-of-pearl. They raced toward us, turquoise pupils bright, their braided hair flying behind them. Their fair skin was coated with an iridescent sheen as though I were looking at them through a pane of colored glass. My skin crawled at the sight of their curved swords, coated with the same venom as on the needles. Those cut by their blades froze where they stood, their limbs jerking unsteadily, their eyes wide with horror.

As Prince Yanxi rushed into the fray, a merman lunged at him. At once I released an arrow, striking the attacker in the shoulder. He fell to the floor, clutching the shaft embedded in his flesh. I hardened myself to the sight, to his gasps. Remorse, I could ill afford, as I shot arrow after arrow at the invaders—though I aimed for their limbs when I could. Captain Wenzhi would have rebuked me had he realized this. To him, an enemy was an enemy, and to show mercy in a battle was to leave your back unguarded. Yet I could not help wondering *why* the merfolk had risen against the Sea Immortals. I was learning that kings were not always as just as in the stories, and the mercy of gods was sometimes flawed.

Blood splattered the floor, and my palms were slick with sweat. My arrows plunged forth in a relentless stream, the agonized cries of those struck beating at my conscience. I forced my attention back to the weapons the merfolk bore, the harm they had inflicted. But for as many who fell beneath our arrows and blades, more poured through the doors. Our own forces dwindled as we formed a protective ring around the royal family and guests.

The merfolk's eyes gleamed with anticipation as they closed in on us. They had the advantage; we were outnumbered. They raised their hands, the smell of brine thick in the air as torrents of water gushed into the hall. Captain Wenzhi flung his power out, shards of ice plunging toward the merfolk. Several fell, yet the water swirled higher, drenching our shoes and robes, swelling until a towering wave loomed above. King Yanzheng's energy rippled from him, dispersing the wave—though others surged in its place. More and more, springing up around us until we were hemmed in by quivering walls of water, on the cusp of breaking and washing us away. A soft cry from behind pierced me, that of a child, muffling his fear. Was he Prince Yanming?

Grasping my energy, I summoned a wind that hurtled into the hall, arching over us like a translucent dome—glistening ice streaking across it as Wenzhi threw his energy alongside mine. Just in time as the waves fell, crashing across our barrier. I staggered beneath the crushing weight, my limbs aching as I fought back my exhaustion. Just when I thought I would collapse, Prince Yanxi's power surged forth, sweeping the water up and hurling it over the merfolk.

Footsteps thudded, from a distance. I stiffened, bracing for a fresh onslaught as I raised my bow, my sore hands already drawing an arrow at the ready. More soldiers streamed into the hall, this time clad in the blue and silver armor of the Eastern Sea. I sagged with relief, lowering my weapon. The merfolk charged at the soldiers, fighting valiantly, but were soon overwhelmed.

The captured leader was dragged forward. Blood trickled

from a wide gash across his cheek as his pupils glowed with blue flame.

"Assassins masquerading as dancers with poisoned needles to kill our king. What other despicable tactics has Governor Renyu stooped to?" Prince Yanxi asked scathingly.

"All tactics are honorable when dealing with a dragon-killer," the merman spat.

"What do you mean? Explain yourself!" King Yanzheng demanded, his voice thick with outrage.

Such hatred emanated from the merman's gaze. "Governor Renyu told us how you were jealous of the dragons' power and resented their refusal to bow to your rule. You conspired with the Celestial Emperor to imprison and slay them!"

Prince Yanxi shuddered as though repulsed. "A vicious pack of lies! We revered the dragons. We honor them still. We never sought to rule them, it sufficed that they graced us with their presence." His tone hardened. "To accuse my father of this is obscene and unworthy of your intelligence."

The merman snarled, "You lie as well as your father."

Prince Yanxi lunged at him, but Captain Wenzhi grabbed his arm, pulling him back.

"Beyond your governor's claims, what proof do you have that the dragons were murdered?" Captain Wenzhi wanted to know.

Confusion flashed across the merman's face, though he remained obstinately silent.

King Yanzheng spoke calmly. "Your governor has shown you no proof because none exists. His claims are meritless, his accusations false. Nothing more than empty words to stir you to do his bidding."

The merman bared his teeth. "Governor Renyu swears he

will avenge the death of the dragons. Once the unworthy king is deposed, he will restore the merfolk to our glory, he will—" He shut his mouth, turning away. Was he afraid to let something slip, or had an enchantment prevented him from doing so?

Captain Wenzhi did not seem to notice as he laughed, a mirthless sound. "Does the governor intend to take the crown after murdering your rightful ruler? How noble of him, to ascend the throne in the name of seeking retribution for the dragons."

The merman shook his head vehemently. "No, Governor Renyu is honorable! He only wishes to—" Again, his words cut off.

King Yanzheng sighed. "I wished we could have done more to aid the dragons. We pleaded with the Celestial Emperor to rescind their punishment, to release them, but he refused. They had indeed challenged his authority and our hands were tied. The dragons would not have wanted us to go to war with the Celestial Kingdom. They valued peace above all."

"Dragons have not been seen for centuries!" the merman cried.

"That does not mean they're dead," Prince Yanxi countered. "We would sense it if such light faded from our world."

As the merman sneered, I bit my lip, staring at him. Something felt wrong. His eyes blazed with conviction and he spoke with passion, yet why did he stake his life and honor on hollow claims alone?

Captain Wenzhi's voice broke through the silence, soft and low. "What was your purpose today? To kill the king and heir? Yet the Eastern Sea's allies would never accept Governor Renyu as king. What was the governor's plan?"

The merman raised his chin in defiance. "Do your worst. I will tell you nothing."

"Oh, you will," Captain Wenzhi said, each word ringed with steel. "I have found there are ways to extract even the most precious secrets. Not just fire and ice, but those from the mortal world. Limbs severed, skin flayed. Flesh boiled in oil."

A chill sank through me, though I kept my face still.

The merman flinched as Captain Wenzhi leaned toward him. "If you will not speak, one of your friends might be persuaded to. If not, your people will suffer the wrath of the Celestial Kingdom. They will be banished from the Eastern Sea, exiled to the Golden Desert. Left to wander and wither beneath the heat of the sun, for eternity upon the parched sands."

Prince Yanxi inhaled sharply as his father turned pale. To a Sea Immortal, such a fate must be worse than death. They had maintained their composure through the grim talk of torture, yet I did not think they possessed the stomach for *this* harsh a punishment. But what mattered was what the merman believed. I had heard Captain Wenzhi was skilled at extracting answers from stubborn prisoners without resorting to physical cruelties. The rumors had not been exaggerated. Already the merman showed signs of caving, his breathing quickening, his eyes darting around yet always returning to the captain.

I had witnessed Captain Wenzhi's unwavering resolve in battle, his fearlessness in charging to the fore. His honor and bravery were revered by the soldiers—but this . . . this was a new facet of his personality. Perhaps they were two sides of the same coin; one could not achieve all he had done without a certain ruthlessness.

The merman cowered away. Still, Captain Wenzhi held his gaze, his pupils obsidian dark.

Finally, the merman slumped, shaking uncontrollably. "No more," he pleaded, in a thin rasp. "Leave my people alone. Don't hurt them." He gasped as though the words were torn from him. "Prince Yanming . . . even if we failed to kill the king, we were to capture his son."

King Yanzheng lurched to his feet. He searched the hall for the young prince, who was huddled beside the queen in a far corner, his head resting upon her shoulder. Blissfully unaware of the threat to his family and life.

Prince Yanxi clutched the hilt of his sword, struggling for composure. "A contemptible plan. Governor Renyu must want to crown my brother while he rules as the power behind the throne. *After* he disposes of the rest of us." He nodded curtly at the guards, who hauled the prisoner away. There was no more fight left in the merman, who drooped like washed-up seagrass.

Just a short while ago, the hall had been filled with gaiety and laughter. Now armored soldiers replaced the elegant guests who had fled, the groans from the wounded a poor substitute for the soothing strains from the pipa.

"I apologize for the abrupt end to our festivities. It was not quite the welcome we had intended," Prince Yanxi said ruefully.

Captain Wenzhi's expression was somber. "Perhaps not, but we've gained valuable information on Governor Renyu's ambitions. And how far he's willing to go to achieve them."

Prince Yanxi nodded. "We will plan our path forward tomorrow, with our commanders. I promise it will be less eventful than tonight, now that we're on the alert. Regardless, we have an ample supply of arrows in the palace." His eyes gleamed as he added, "Plates, too, if the First Archer prefers."

My lips curved in a hollow smile, though I welcomed his attempt to lighten the mood.

Prince Yanxi inclined his head to Captain Wenzhi. "Your aid tonight was invaluable, and my father will be sure to commend you to the Celestial Kingdom. Your reputation is indeed well deserved." He glanced in my direction, "As is yours, First Archer."

I bowed in acknowledgment of his praise. Yet my smile faded as I gazed around the hall, at the fragments of porcelain and spilled food, mingling with crimson trails of blood.

19

Sleep evaded me that night. When we were attacked, a cold instinct for survival had enveloped me, and I shot our attackers down unflinchingly. But with the merman's accusations ringing in my ears, doubt wound its way into my heart. Were the dragons in danger? Was King Yanzheng as righteous as he was reputed to be? Was Prince Yanxi's admiration of the dragons feigned? No, I thought to myself, he did not seem to be of a duplicitous nature.

It had become a habit for Captain Wenzhi and I to eat together, and I usually enjoyed these moments of quiet companionship. Yet this morning, I picked over the meal listlessly.

"You fought well last night," he said.

I winced, feeling no pride at his praise, the agonized cries of those struck still echoing through my mind. "Do you believe any of what the merman said? About King Yanzheng betraying the dragons?"

"No," he said firmly, with such certainty that a little of my unease dispersed. "The king's reverence of them is well known. Besides, the dragons were no threat to him."

"Why do the merfolk believe the governor?" I asked.

"*That* is a mystery. Governor Renyu has the makings of a tyrant and his ruthless actions last night have only reinforced that suspicion. It's possible he gained such strong support only because the merfolk have been isolated for so long." He added darkly, "They seem to believe his every word."

I lifted a spoonful of congee to my mouth, the grains cooked till they were silken soft, the flavor infused with chicken and herbs. I chewed methodically, as another question hovered on the tip of my tongue—one I was more hesitant to ask. Looking at him, I found Captain Wenzhi had left his bowl untouched.

"What else is troubling you?" he wanted to know. "Your doubts are written plain upon your face."

I set the porcelain spoon down, turning to him. "Could you really have done it? All those things you said . . . even exiling the merfolk to the desert?"

"Do you think I could have?" His expression was grave and for some reason, I felt my answer mattered to him.

No, I wanted to say, but I pressed on. "Yesterday, you spoke of severing limbs and flaying skin so readily, like you meant it." No battle was without its cruelties, but it felt wrong to do such a thing to a captured enemy. A helpless one.

"There are parts of my work that I do not care for," he said in a low voice. "And what you saw yesterday was one of them. Not everything is as straightforward as at the point of a blade. I'm not proud of what I said, but imagine if I had not, Prince Yanming might have been taken. Hundreds of soldiers might have died in battle. King Yanzheng could have been murdered— along with your new friend, Prince Yanxi."

I started, wondering at his biting tone. Yet Captain Wenzhi's other words resonated with me. As I myself knew, sometimes we found ourselves in situations where we were forced to deceive against our will, our inclination and hearts.

He continued, as though it was a relief to him to unburden these thoughts. "The merman cared not for his own safety; threats to himself, he would have ignored. But the lives of his family and friends, he would not treat so cavalierly." A tight smile spread across his lips. "And it helped that the Celestial Emperor is not famed for mercy."

How well I knew this. I shuddered to recall the emperor's icy gaze, the dread which had enveloped me at the sight of him. I had no doubt he would eliminate those he believed were a threat.

"Thank you for telling me this." I meant it. He had not needed to explain himself, that he did so was an indication of his trust.

"Thank you for you listening," he said quietly. "I hope we will always speak like this. That you will share with me any worries you have."

He picked up his bowl though the congee had gone cool. We did not speak for the rest of the meal, but I ate with newfound relish, the burden on my conscience eased.

When Captain Wenzhi and I arrived at the Fragrant Coral Palace, an attendant showed us to a room on the highest floor. The windows opened out to the azure sea, ever shifting and boundless. Rosewood chairs were arranged around a large table, carved from a single slab of wood. Prince Yanxi and six other immortals were clustered around it, engaged in a heated discussion.

Dismissing the need for courtesies, the prince introduced us quickly to the commanders in the room. His face was grim as he said, "The merfolk never dared to storm the palace before.

They would only do so now because they believe their army strong enough to confront us. Which means we're running out of time."

Captain Wenzhi lowered himself onto a chair and gestured for me to do the same. An attendant hurried over to fill our cups with tea. "They might also wish to antagonize you into retaliating rashly," he warned.

Prince Yanxi nodded tersely. "We will be cautious. However, if we allow Governor Renyu to attack us without repercussion, this will only embolden him further." His gaze met mine across the room. "The First Archer's point about ensuring the battle is fought on land is a vital one. The merfolk would undoubtedly prefer to draw us underwater where they are strongest."

Captain Wenzhi clasped his hands together on the table. "Orchestrating the confrontation would allow us to choose the battleground. You've said the merfolk venture to shore to raid. Is there any other occasion that would bring them to land?"

"None that we know of," Prince Yanxi replied.

"Then we need to lure them to us. What can we use as bait?" Captain Wenzhi said decisively.

A few generals shifted in their chairs as though disconcerted by his suggestion. I took a sip of tea to loosen the tightness in my throat. "It should be something that would tempt Governor Renyu himself to lead the charge. This can only work once," I added quickly, before I lost my nerve.

"I agree. Has the governor led a charge before?" Captain Wenzhi asked.

"No. He's powerful but very cautious," Prince Yanxi said.

Captain Wenzhi sighed. "If I might speak plainly, Your Highness?" At Prince Yanxi's nod, he continued, "Magical items or treasure might not be enough to entice him to risk his neck. However, we are now aware that Prince Yanming is crucial to the governor's plans."

Prince Yanxi's chair scraped against the floor as he uncoiled to his full height. "You want to use my little brother as *bait*?" he ground out.

Captain Wenzhi did not flinch, appearing indifferent to the prince's wrath. "Your brother will be taken to safety at the first sign of danger. We just need him to draw the governor into our trap."

Prince Yanxi glared at him. "How can you ensure his safety?"

I recalled the young prince from last night, the one who had gripped his mother's hand so tightly and laid his face against her shoulder. It reminded me of how I had clutched my own mother during the times I had been most afraid—when I almost drowned in the river, when I learned I had to leave my home.

Something hardened inside me, a voice rising from my throat to say, "*I'll* guard Prince Yanming."

All heads swung toward me then, their surprise and skepticism marked clear upon their faces. I was in disbelief myself; until this moment, this had not been my intent.

Only Captain Wenzhi smiled. "She will be the perfect guard to watch over His Highness. I will protect him, too. We can't surround him with more guards than usual, not without arousing suspicion."

I slumped against my chair, relieved to no longer be the center of attention. Or was it because of his offer to stand watch with me?

A little of the ice thawed in Prince Yanxi's expression as he sat down again.

Captain Wenzhi plunged ahead, always quick to sense an

opening. "This plan will work. After last night's attack, Governor Renyu must realize it would be near impossible to take the prince from here. We could spread the news that Prince Yanming will be leaving soon for the Celestial Kingdom for his safety. All we need is for him to appear on the beach, to convince the governor of his presence. First Archer Xingyin and I will be with him at every moment. If this doesn't draw out Governor Renyu, nothing will."

A stout general with light brown hair frowned. "His Highness has just his governess and one guard with him at all times. Moreover"—he reddened as he shot me a furtive look—"there are no women in our army. Would not the First Archer's presence make the enemy suspicious?"

Silence greeted his astute observation.

Captain Wenzhi tucked his chin between his fingers as his gaze slid over me. "First Archer Xingyin can disguise as Lady Anmei, the prince's governess."

I froze, quelling an instinctive protest. How could I delude anyone into thinking I was the elegant lady from the banquet? My opinion was apparently shared by many as the generals exchanged incredulous glances, though they seemed too polite to voice their reservations aloud.

Captain Wenzhi had no such scruples. "I know she looks nothing like Lady Anmei, but with the right clothes and accessories, some face paint—"

"Captain Wenzhi, thank you for your confidence in me," I interjected, fighting down a flash of irritation at his callous remarks.

Prince Yanxi's expression was still grim. "My brother will be taken away before the battle begins." It was a demand, not a question.

Captain Wenzhi inclined his head. "Of course."

The prince spoke to me now. "This would be even more perilous than last night. Governor Renyu is dangerous and unpredictable. You would be the target of our enemy's attacks and to avoid raising their suspicions, you can't carry a weapon or use your magic—at least not until the trap is sprung. While I'm confident we can defeat them, no one knows the outcome of any confrontation. I fear for your safety should they reach you and find my brother not in your care."

His candor and concern touched me. "Your Highness, I will take care of your brother and myself," I assured him.

He nodded then, glancing around at the room. "Very well, we will proceed. Though we need some time to make our preparations and plant the information with the right sources. It would be prudent if you could spend some time with my brother over the next few days. If our plan is to succeed, he needs to be at ease with you."

Something turned over in my stomach. While I recognized the good sense in his suggestion, I had not spent much time with children.

After the meeting, Captain Wenzhi and I followed the prince to his brother's quarters. At the sight of us, Lady Anmei rose and bowed, her green brocade skirt grazing the floor. Up close, she was even more striking than I remembered. Her cheeks were stained pink when she saw Captain Wenzhi, but it was his courtly bow to her which made me gnaw the underside of my lip for some inexplicable reason.

Prince Yanming came forward then, executing a flawless bow to his brother. When he was introduced to me, he showed no recognition from last night. Prince Yanxi wasted no time in drawing Lady Anmei aside and speaking to her in hushed tones. Without another word, they left the room with Captain Wenzhi.

"Where did Lady Anmei go? Who are you?" Prince Yanming demanded. His cheeks were soft and round, even as his chin jutted out defiantly.

I crouched down to look into his eyes, the same blue as his brother's. "Lady Anmei had to leave for a short while, but she'll be back soon. I will stay with you for now."

His mouth pressed into a straight line. "Do you know any games?"

"How about weiqi?" I offered, already searching his room for the board with its smooth black and white stones.

He shuddered. "Can you sing? Draw? Craft animals from paper?" he rattled off.

I shook my head, my spirits sinking.

"You're the worst governess I've ever met." He crossed his arms mutinously in front of him.

I scowled at him, irked by his words. "Well, I'm not your governess and you're being very rude. Maybe if you were a little more polite, I would teach you some of the exciting things I *do* know."

His eyes squeezed tighter, his mouth pursing like a wrinkled grape. I braced myself for his tantrum and tears, thinking Shuxiao with her effortless charm would have been far better equipped for this challenge. But then he drew himself up straight and with remarkable poise, asked, "Well, what can you do?"

I racked my mind for something to say to capture his interest, something to live up to my rash boast. "I can play the flute," I offered, with more than a little pride.

He huffed impatiently, rolling his eyes—utterly unimpressed by one of my greatest skills.

"I've read a lot of books," I added quickly. "I can tell you stories!"

A sudden interest sparked in his face. "About the dragons?"

"The Four Dragons, when they bring rain to the Mortal Realm." I was relieved to have finally caught his attention. It had been one of my favorite tales as a child, and one with more truth to it than I had suspected.

"The one where the dragons get punished by the stuffy Celestial Emperor? That's the worst of them all!"

Before I could stop myself, a snort of laughter burst from me at his irreverent description of the most powerful immortal in the realm.

The corners of his lips curved up ever so slightly. "What else can you do?" The animosity had vanished from his tone.

I returned his smile. "Shoot arrows. And fight with a sword."

He lit up as he grabbed my arm and dragged me toward a large chest crammed with wooden swords and shields.

"Eldest Brother says I'm too young to learn. But you'll show me, won't you?" he asked eagerly.

Helpless before such enthusiasm, I nodded weakly, hoping Prince Yanxi would forgive my transgression.

When Lady Anmei and Captain Wenzhi finally returned, we were engaged in a mock battle, leaping over the coral in the garden, our wooden swords thudding against each other. At the sight of them, I hastily dropped the sword, smoothing back my disheveled hair.

"Your Highness, it's your bedtime," Lady Anmei said in a firm tone.

Prince Yanming's shoulders drooped, but he took her outstretched hand. "Will you come again tomorrow?" he asked me.

Something bloomed inside me at the hope in his voice. "Yes. I would like that very much."

The sky had darkened to twilight by the time we returned to the shore. Instead of joining Captain Wenzhi in his tent, I ate with the other soldiers. For some reason I did not want to be in his company tonight.

I was on edge, wound tight. After the meal I paced along the beach, climbing upon a large rock. It soothed my restlessness to watch the waves hurling themselves against the shore in reckless abandon. The rough stone pressed against my back as I lay down, staring at the sky. When the moon shone as brightly as it did tonight, I knew my mother had lit the thousand lanterns and the perpetual ache in my heart eased a little. As I imagined her arms around me, her cool cheek against mine—a smile spread across my lips.

Footsteps approached, almost drowned by the crashing waves.

"You like to stare at the moon," Captain Wenzhi said, from behind me.

"It's a better view than some." I did not bother to rise. It was rude of me, but I was in no mood for courtesy.

As he climbed up to join me, I jerked up onto my elbows, glaring at him. "Will you leave?" I fought to keep my voice steady.

"No."

"Then I will." I pressed my palms against the rock to slide down, but he covered my hand with his. His grip was as unyielding as the stone beneath my skin.

"Why are you angry?" He sounded confused.

I snatched my hand away, wrapping my arms around my

knees. In truth, I did not know the cause of this gnawing sensation whenever I looked at him.

"Was it because I suggested you dress as Lady Anmei?" he probed.

The memory of his careless words stung. "You had no concern for me when you said that."

His brow creased in surprise. "Are you afraid?" he asked, misunderstanding my meaning. "You can take care of the young prince and yourself, even without weapons and magic. And if I had no concern for you, would I stand guard with you?"

"I'm not afraid."

"Then what is the reason for your ill humor?" His voice was as soft as the evening breeze.

"I know you admire Lady Anmei and that I'm not as beautiful or elegant as her. But . . . it was not pleasant to hear it said aloud." Heat crept up my neck at the recollection.

"*Admire* her? If I was attentive to her it was only because it seemed to annoy you." He grinned wryly, before turning serious once more. "Why would you want to look like her? Why would a falcon want to be a nightingale?"

My pulse quickened. I did not know why, except I was suddenly unsure of myself. Eager to leave and yet . . . wanting to stay. "Captain Wenzhi—"

"Just, Wenzhi." His gaze held mine.

Somehow, I knew it was a moment of great import to him, a mark of trust that he did not easily relinquish.

My cowardly desire to leave vanished. I called Shuxiao by her name, but we were close friends. Peers. I had only ever addressed him as "Captain Wenzhi," as he called me "Archer Xingyin"—any other form of address here would have been unthinkable. We had teased, needled, and even argued outright with each another, but this would be crossing into unfamiliar terrain, sweeping away yet another barrier between us. One, I found, I was glad to do without.

"Wenzhi," I repeated slowly, unused to his name without his title.

A smile appeared on his lips, barely perceptible in the dark.

The last of my discomfort vanished, replaced by a warm flutter. I did not speak again and neither did he. Together, we lay on the rock in companionable silence, the waves rushing to shore the only sound in the night.

The moon rose higher. Its glow glinted on the water, the fragments of a thousand silver shards reflected on its surface. The breeze cooled my skin as the warmth in my chest spread to my veins, as though I was drunk on wine.

20

The next few days flew by, riddled with anxiety—and yet, they were happy ones, too. I taught Prince Yanming to hold a sword and let him trounce me each time we sparred. He showed me how to fold paper animals, and we sang silly songs that we made up together. When he discovered that I knew just one story of his beloved dragons—he gathered his books and together, we read of how the dragons saved the mer-folk from sea monsters, how they purified the waters when a swarm of venomous jellyfish tainted the ocean. It was little won-der their absence had left such a void in the Eastern Sea. And when he flung his arms around my neck, squeezing me with his soft arms, a warmth bloomed inside me. He slipped through the wall around my heart, becoming the childhood companion I never had, the sibling I never knew I wished for.

All too soon, the day of our ruse arrived. I sat in a room with Wenzhi, as two palace attendants fussed over me, assisting with my transformation into Lady Anmei.

"Could you try to act demure and gentle?" Wenzhi suggested.

"Take smaller steps when you walk. Your gaze should be softer. Lady Anmei is a delicate flower, so could you try not to be—"

"A thorn?" I bit out, my temper frayed thin. For the past hour, he had been lecturing me on the behavior I should emulate. I shot him a deceptively sweet smile. "Perhaps *you* should dress as Lady Anmei yourself, since you seem so well versed in her mannerisms."

A choked sound erupted from one of the attendants, which she quickly gulped back.

Wenzhi's eyes curved with humor, yet he continued as though I had not spoken. "Try to appear a little afraid or nervous. Not everyone can be as sure of themselves as you are."

I swung around, dislodging an attendant's attempt to fix a gold flower to my hair. "Since I met you, I've been afraid more times than in all my years before. Who wouldn't be—getting speared by darts, scalded by fire, attacked by monsters?"

"If you were afraid, you kept your wits about you. Most of the time." He sat down and unrolled a scroll crafted of bamboo strips, each crammed with tiny characters and bound with silk. Soon, he was engrossed in his reading like he had forgotten I was there.

His indifference bothered me, more than it should. I glanced into the mirror, a stranger gazing back at me. The attendants had drawn my brows into delicate arches, brushed my cheeks with rose powder, and colored my lips a light coral. My hair was pulled into smooth coils, adorned with jeweled flowers from which strands of turquoise beads cascaded. The lilac silk of my dress was embroidered with colorful shells and seagrass, a crimson sash tied around my waist. An open coat of azure satin flowed to my feet, encased in slippers of gold brocade.

The attendants flattered me, telling me I looked beautiful, before they left the room.

"Are you ready?" A note of impatience rang in Wenzhi's voice as he turned to me.

In the sudden quiet, I found myself holding my breath. "You look different," he said finally. "Though such as you does not need all this . . . gilding."

"Gilding?" I was torn between laughter and mortification. "Might I remind you this was your idea?"

He shrugged. "A good one, but I did not say I liked it."

It was no compliment, yet the intensity of his stare sent a tingling rush through me, like a cool breeze gliding over my skin. Before I could reply, he picked up the scroll and resumed his reading. As I rose to find a book of my own, I stumbled, tripping over the hem of my coat.

Wenzhi shot up to catch me, his fingers closing around my arms. Light kindled in his eyes, my heart racing like I had run a long way. But I had learned such feelings were dangerous and the wounds they could inflict more painful than those from a blade.

I pulled away, averting my gaze. His hands dropped to his side, an awkward silence descending over us.

Fortunately, Prince Yanming arrived soon after. At the sight of me, he burst into laughter, dousing my brief pride in my appearance. "You're wearing Lady Anmei's clothes!"

"She *is* Lady Anmei for today," Wenzhi reminded him sternly. "Remember what your brother told you, Your Highness."

The mirth vanished from Prince Yanming's face as he nodded, his body shaking a little. Of course, he was afraid, knowing he and his loved ones were in peril.

Crouching down, I clasped his shoulder. "Don't worry," I

told him. "It's a little dangerous, but you'll be safe. Your brother is waiting in the forest with his guards and we won't let anything happen to you."

His teeth gnawed his lip. "What about you? I don't want anything to happen to you either."

"Nothing will," I promised, wiping the sweat from my palm before taking his hand. "I will take care of us."

An odd look crossed Prince Yanming's face. "But . . . you're not a very good fighter. I always beat you and I only just started learning."

Wenzhi snorted while I glared at him. "Don't worry," I told Prince Yanming, his brow still wrinkled in a frown. "I'm better with the bow."

Together, we walked in silence from the palace to the shore. A large tent had been erected there for our use, far from the shoreline. A visible target for Governor Renyu's forces, and one which I hoped would prove irresistible. Once we were inside and the flap had been lowered, I set about concealing weapons, bows, and quivers of arrows around the tent.

Afterward, we took a long stroll on the beach, the noon sun beating down upon us. The residents had been escorted to safety, leaving disguised Celestial soldiers in their place—while Prince Yanxi and his army hid in the forest that bordered the beach. I did not let go of Prince Yanming's hand, as I scanned our surroundings for any sign of danger. Yet there was none, the sea tranquil and clear.

Soon after we returned to the tent, Prince Yanming fell asleep, perhaps exhausted from the strain of the day. I covered him with a blanket, watching his chest rise and fall, the serenity of his face striking me deep. I would keep him safe, I promised silently, no matter what happened today. Looking around for something to distract myself, I found some books and a weiqi board set up in a corner, its black and white stones gleaming invitingly. But I was in no mood for either. Waiting to be attacked shredded my nerves raw, unlike Wenzhi who sat in a chair, reading his scroll with unflappable calm.

An urge gripped me to disrupt his concentration. "When did you come to the Celestial Kingdom?" I asked.

"A while ago."

Undeterred by his curt response, I pressed on. "Which of the Four Seas are you from?"

He raised his head then, fixing me with a pointed stare. "Why the sudden interest?"

I sighed. "There isn't much I can do here other than talk. Unfortunately, I don't have much choice for company."

"Why don't we talk about you?" he suggested. "Where are you from?"

"The Southern Sea." Caught unaware, I said the first thing that entered my mind, what I had been schooled to say before.

"The Southern Sea," he repeated slowly, setting his scroll down. "And yet, you've never seen the ocean before?"

My face flamed. How fortunate that it was covered under a layer of powder. "I left when I was a child and don't remember anything. What of your family?" I was eager to shift the conversation away from me.

He was silent for a while. "I have kin in the Western Sea, but I haven't seen them for a long time. My responsibilities keep me well engaged."

"Do you miss them?" I asked, thinking of my mother.

"Some more than others," he replied, with a tight smile.

He picked up his scroll again, a sign that our conversation was over. I had finally met someone as reticent as me. Was he unwilling to speak of his family because the Western Sea had sided with the Demon Realm in the war? Perhaps it was prudent not to remind others of it. Though the Celestial Kingdom was now at peace with the Four Seas, immortal memories were long. I opened my mouth to ask another question, then hesitated. Not everyone's past was a path through sunlit fields. We each had our own corners that we preferred to leave in the shadows.

The sun dropped lower in the sky and still, there was no sign of the merfolk. Had our plan failed? Was Governor Renyu too cunning to fall for our ploy?

"How much longer must we stay here? Can't we leave now? Maybe the bad governor won't come." Prince Yanming had been restless since he awoke, unused to being confined.

I glanced at Wenzhi. "Shall we take another walk outside? To reassure them that we're still here?"

"They could be waiting until nightfall to attack. Merfolk are adept at seeing in the dark," he said.

"What if we spread the word that Prince Yanming is leaving soon? The guards and attendants can make a pretense of the preparations, while we walk near the water. After that, His Highness should be escorted to safety." Our danger increased with every passing moment. However, it would be better to provoke the merfolk into action than let their plan unfold as they wanted.

He nodded, calling in the guard to relay his instructions. Before we left the tent, he passed me a small dagger with a silver hilt. "Keep this on you at all times."

I took it, tucking it into my sash, concealed beneath my coat. It was more an ornament than a weapon, yet this was all I had to defend myself. No, I reminded myself. I still had my powers, and even with my bare hands, I was not helpless.

The ocean was restless now, its gray-green waters turbulent. Foaming waves crested high before crashing against the shore. Breaking free of my grasp, Prince Yanming ran ahead of me. I chased after him into the water, drenching my slippers and skirt.

An inky shadow fell over us as though night had fallen, cold dread congealing in the pit of my stomach. Towering above us was an enormous octopus, blocking out the sun itself. Giant tentacles, each twice the length of a grown man, lashed out— splashing water and flooding the beach. Riding upon the creature was a warrior in pearlescent armor that reached his knees and left his arms bare, a crown of red coral branches woven into his hair. Around his neck gleamed a large pendant, a gold disc encircling a glowing yellow stone. In one hand he held a spear and in the other, a shield studded with vicious spikes. His eyes were as pale as a glacier and when they locked on me, I froze.

Governor Renyu.

Wenzhi shouted in warning as the governor's lips curled into a smirk. The octopus—it was almost upon Prince Yanming! Dashing deeper into the water, I swept him up, clutching him tightly as we raced from the rising tide. A tentacle lashed out behind me, slicing my calf. I choked back a cry, forcing myself onward through the churning current as the stinging seawater stripped the blood from my wound. Just as we reached the shore, the water foamed with thousands of quivering jellyfish, poisoned stingers coating their translucent tentacles.

The merfolk rode the crests of the swelling waves, roaring as they stormed the beach. With an answering shout, Prince Yanxi's men surged from the forest. The Celestial soldiers threw off their disguises, their armor gleaming in the late afternoon light. A sudden tension ripped through the air, shimmering and flickering with the energies of the warriors—as the armies collided.

Bolts of fire and ice hurtled into hastily erected shields. Swords struck in a thunderous clash, ringing through the billowing sand. Prince Yanming trembled in my arms as we sprinted to the tent. But when agonized screams erupted from behind, I halted, whirling around. My heart plunged at the sight. The giant octopus was wrapping its tentacles around Celestial soldiers, hurling them into the ocean where venomous jellyfish swarmed over them, dragging them beneath the waves. Wenzhi shouted for them to move to higher ground, but his words were lost in the chaos. His energy erupted in a blaze of light, solidifying into a towering shield along the shoreline.

Yet the area was too wide, his magic spread too thin. Flanked by several warriors, Governor Renyu raised his hand, blue light streaking forth to strike the barrier. Once, twice, and then again—until at last, Wenzhi's shield shattered. I would have darted for a weapon but if I discarded my pretense, the governor might sense a trap.

The merfolk pressed on, eagerly now, as our soldiers scattered like windblown leaves. Wenzhi was shaking, I had never seen him look so distraught—so anxious, furious, and frustrated.

"Go," I urged him. "You don't need to stay with us. I'll watch over Prince Yanming."

He stilled, his eyes fixed upon the carnage. "What will you do?"

"I'll stay in the tent. It will be safe there."

Without waiting for his answer, I stalked away with Prince Yanming. Several soldiers waited inside the tent to escort him to safety. But when they tried to take him from me, he clutched me tighter.

"Aren't you coming?" His voice shook.

I brushed his cheek with my knuckle. "Your Highness needs to leave now. Your brother is waiting for you. I'll join you soon."

"Do you promise?"

A heartbeat of hesitation before I nodded. I hated lying to him, but if the governor found this place deserted, he might leave before we could apprehend him. Every moment I bought with this farce increased our chance of capturing him.

My heart thudded as I watched Prince Yanming and the soldiers slip through the back of the tent, disappearing into the safety of the forest. Only then did a little of my tension ease. I sat down to wait, agitated at doing nothing while outside, blood soaked the sand. We had hoped to trap Governor Renyu, but he had caught us unaware by the ferocity of his attack and the sea monsters under his command.

Tossing off my sodden coat, I pulled out a bow and quiver, placing them on the table within reach. Part of me wanted to clap my palms over my ears to drown the clash of steel, the screams, and groans. How much longer could I bear this? When a loud cry pierced the air, I dashed to the entrance—stumbling to a stop as the silhouette of a limp form slumped against the tent walls.

The flap lifted. A figure loomed in the entrance. I took a step back, my body stiff with anxiety.

"You must be Lady Anmei." Governor Renyu greeted me with a mockingly low bow. "Rumors of your charms were not exaggerated."

His aura filled the air, pressing around me in the confined space; strong, to be sure, yet wavering as an inconstant tide.

Was his grip on his power unsteady? I had no time to ponder as he entered, towering above me, the parts of his body I could see corded with muscle. His cold stare sent a shudder through me as did the cruel slant of his mouth and the blood sprayed across his cheek.

I darted for the bow on the table, but he swept it out of my reach and tossed it outside with a bark of laughter. "Do you know how to use it?"

I shook my head, shrinking away as my fingers inched toward the concealed dagger. If I had the bow, there would already be an arrow through his chest. But as he had the advantage for now, I would not drop my disguise. As long as he believed I was Lady Anmei, he might not harm me.

"Who are you?" I asked, trying to draw his attention from my hands.

"You have nothing to fear. All I want is the little prince. Help me and you will be well rewarded." His gaze slid across the tent. "Where is he?"

His voice was rich, deep, melodious—the most beautiful one I had ever heard. My suspicion of him melted away, replaced by warm admiration. Governor Renyu appeared honorable and kind. Why had he been so viciously maligned? The disc around his neck gleamed brighter, like the eyes of a serpent aglow in the dark.

The image jarred me, my instincts prickling in warning. I blinked, tearing myself from the tantalizing promise of his words, forcing myself to listen to the screams outside. In a flash, it struck me—how he held such sway over the merfolk. There was magic in his voice which compelled others to believe him. Had it come from the shining pendant around his neck? What-ever it was, it had almost worked on me, even overcoming my hostility. Little wonder that the merfolk were so loyal to him, willing to risk themselves to protect him, to fight for him on the mere promise of his words and illusion of his honor. I had never encountered such power before, though. Was he a Demon? One of the dreaded Mind Talents?

I dared not let my fear show. He expected my admiration, my obedience. That I would yield to his will as a blade of grass to the wind. Widening my eyes to appear guileless, I gestured to the bed where Prince Yanming had napped earlier. The covers were bunched up over the top, giving the semblance of a small body beneath.

"He's sleeping," I said.

His mouth curved into a vicious smile. "Once the Eastern Sea is mine, I'll dispose of the brat and we'll rule together. The other kingdoms will fall to me, too, and you'll be the Queen of the Four Seas." He stretched out his hand, promising what he believed I wished to hear.

Anger flared in me, to hear him speak so of Prince Yanming and his despicable plans—yet I was glad for it to bolster my wavering will. I stared at the yellow gem against his chest. This close, a strange power emanated from it, raising the hairs on my skin.

"What makes you think you'll win?"

"The merfolk obey my every command, as do the sea creatures. You have nothing to fear with me by your side."

His words spilled through me like liquid honey, even as my insides recoiled. How tempting it was to agree with him, to earn his approval. No, I could not succumb; I could not end up one of his unthinking minions. My nails dug into my palms as I channeled a surge of energy into my ears to seal off my hearing. Cloaked in sudden silence, I could barely hear my own breathing. My gut twisted at the thought of fighting him this way, but I feared more falling under his control.

I fixed my gaze upon him. There would be no telltale rustle of a step or the whistle of a sword to alert me. A risk, though a necessary one. As he moved toward the bed, I grabbed the dagger from my sash and hurled it at him. He swung aside, the blade slicing his cheek. Without a pause, he lunged forward, tearing the covers from the bed—snarling to find it empty. At once he spun to me, but I darted for the nearest bow, drawing and releasing an arrow in the same heartbeat. With a sweep of his shield, he batted it to the ground. I shot one after another in a frantic pace, until my fingers stung from the grooves riddled across their tips. He was quick, though, evading each one with startling speed. My elbow slammed into a shelf as I groped for another arrow. As his knuckles whitened around his spear, I flung up a shield—just as his weapon slammed against it.

My last arrow sank into his shoulder. I dove for a new quiver, so intent upon it that I did not sense the shift in the air until something stabbed my calf, spreading like wildfire. Two silver needles protruded from my leg, pinning the silk of my dress to my flesh, stained with the greenish liquid I had seen once before. Sea scorpion venom, rushing through my veins. My shield was no more—dispelled—leaving me as helpless as a rabbit snared in a trap while the hunter stalked ever closer.

His lips peeled back, stretching wide, yet all I heard was a faint humming. I loosened the seal over my ears, until the faintest whisper slid through. All I had left to slow him with were words.

"Coward," I hissed, trying to delay the inevitable end, to goad him to rashness. "Fight me without such tricks."

"Losers complain and winners . . . well, winners have better things to do." He spoke with a smug complacency that sent fear shooting down my spine.

The pull in his voice was still there but fainter now; I could barely hear it. I reached for my powers, struggling to steady myself against the searing agony of the poison.

The gem around his neck glowed like sunstruck gold. As I stared at it, I asked, "Your pendant, is that how you're controlling the merfolk?" My voice sounded as though it came from far away. "Such magic is despicable."

"Despicable, because you cannot wield it? Because you fear it?" He cocked his head to one side, though I did not think he expected an answer. "The merfolk have always harbored such suspicions against the Sea Immortals. I merely lit the spark of their prejudice, nudged their will to mine. How is this any different from holding a sword to your enemy's throat? Why should one victory be deemed honorable and the other, not?"

"It's not the same," I ground out. "You've taken away their freedom to choose, to judge on their own. To compel them to acts they might rather die than commit." I fixed him with a scornful stare, even as I shrank away inside. "But no enchantment is unbreakable. You'll pay when they break free."

"Death is the only release for those under my control." A cruel light gleamed in his eyes. "There were a few who angered me with their incompetence, others who were too difficult to dominate. Just before they died, such clarity shone in their faces. Rage, too, that they had been taken for fools. It made their end all the sweeter. As yours will be."

His spear flashed. Fighting through the pain, I seized my powers—but then his fist slammed into my temple. Pain engulfed me, my energy dispersing. If my feet could move, I would have fled, but I could not even choke out a scream through the crushing numbness which sank over me.

My arrows, I still had them. While my legs were rooted fast, my arms were still free—at least for now—until the poison spread. I grasped around my back, fumbling inside the quiver. As I seized one, the governor snatched it from me and snapped it into two—grinding the metal tip against my palm, until he drove it through my flesh. The agony stripped my mind bare. I could not cry out, I could hardly breathe. With a malicious sneer, he wrenched the bow from my grasp, throwing it beyond my reach. Picking up his fallen spear, he pressed it to my chest, exerting just enough pressure to pierce my skin with its venomous tip. Blood blossomed on the silk like a crimson hibiscus unfurling its petals. I gasped then, my upper body convulsing before it froze. From the curl in his lips, I knew he relished my suffering.

My heart recoiled, stabbed by regret. Would I ever see my mother and Ping'er again? Liwei's face flashed through my mind, and oddly, Wenzhi's, too. Such scorching pain raced through my veins, swifter now, my breathing turning harsh and ragged. I shut my eyes to block out the horror of being so utterly at his mercy—weaponless, poisoned, and trapped. *No*, I told myself furiously. *I still had my training. I still had my wits.*

I still had my magic.

I fought for calm, grinding my jaws until they ached. My power flew into my grasp, a gale surging into the tent and flinging him against the ground. Something fell from his head, his crown of red coral, the branches breaking into shards.

His eyes blazed with shock, then rage. He raised his hand, gleaming with his own magic—but I was relentless, reckless even, as I hurled a stream of enchantments his way—not daring to allow him a chance to retaliate. Wild gusts lashed him, coils of air bound him, bolts of flame singed his skin before they were doused. If I were not incapacitated, rooted to the spot, I might have collapsed from the strain. Never had I fought so, relying on my magic alone. Teacher Daoming's warning not to drain my energy rang through my head, yet if I stopped I would die. There would be no mercy from him, no second chance. Backed against the tent walls, the governor deflected each blow until sweat poured from his brow and his breathing was as labored as mine. A fierce pride gripped me, that I was no longer the prey he had stalked.

Someone appeared in the entrance. Wenzhi! Covered in blood, sand, and dirt, his face taut with exhaustion, or was it fury? As Governor Renyu staggered to his feet, Wenzhi charged at him—sword slamming against spear. The governor's mouth worked furiously, uttering words I could not make out. What was he saying? What if Wenzhi fell under his control?

"His pendant!" My cry dissolved into a broken whisper; I had not the strength for more. Fear clutched at me that it was not enough, that he did not hear me. And my bow was too far away, my magic almost drained. My hand throbbed with pain— there all along, yet overshadowed by the agony raging through my body. I glanced down to find the broken shard of arrow still embedded in my palm.

A muffled crash sounded as Wenzhi flung the governor into a shelf. He sprang back up, his pendant gleaming brighter. A chill swept through me that any moment now, he might unleash its power. I could not move, not even to twitch my finger; the venom had incapacitated me entirely. Yet I could not let Wenzhi fall under the governor's control. Gasping for air, I scraped my energy to form a current of wind—slender, but swift and strong—which tore the arrow shaft from my flesh and hurled it at the governor. It struck his pendant, slamming against the stone. The yellow gem cracked, the light fading from it.

Governor Renyu's mouth opened in a rage-filled shout, but it was as whispers to my ears. I was afire with pain, numbed to all else. Wenzhi whirled with deadly grace, his foot colliding into the governor's side. As the governor staggered back, Wenzhi's blade slashed across his ribs, the pearlescent scales of his armor splintering. The governor's mouth rounded as a strange expression crossed his face. Was it shock? Disbelief that his enchantment had failed? Whatever it was, I was glad for it—a vicious satisfaction flaring in me.

Governor Renyu was panting, his movements growing more frantic as he flung off Wenzhi's brutal blows. He was careless now, reeking of desperation. As Wenzhi raised his arm, the governor flung his spear at him—but Wenzhi spun to the other side, plunging his blade smoothly through Governor Renyu's armor, right through his ribs. He lunged forward, driving his sword deeper until it was buried to the hilt, its tip sliding from the governor's back, silver coated in crimson. Wenzhi's face was twisted into a feral expression as he tore his sword free. Blood sprayed in the air as Governor Renyu's body lurched, a wet wheeze slipping from his mouth as he staggered back. His hand fumbled over his gaping wound as his blood, so much of it, streamed through his fingers. The governor crumpled then, his head slamming against the ground—his eyes rolling up, his limbs twitching, before all went still.

Dead. He was dead. There was no pity in me for him, nor was there joy. Just a bone-deep relief that it was over, that we were alive.

Wenzhi dropped his sword, rushing to me. He gripped my shoulders, his eyes widening at the sight of my injuries. When his lips moved, I strained to listen. "Where are you hurt? Why aren't you moving?"

Despite the comfort of his touch, a coldness spread over me as though I was buried under a layer of snow. My vision blurred as I gazed up at him, the last thing I saw before the darkness claimed me.

21

Cracking my eyelids apart, I squinted at the brightness. Sunlight streamed through the windows, mingled with a salt-laced breeze. My body was heavy with that limpness which comes after a long slumber, each movement a struggle. I shivered, cold, except for the warmth over my hand. A strong grip, but whose? Someone sat beside me, the face a blur as I blinked to clear my vision. I did not mind the touch. It was a comfort through the memories which curled at the edge of my consciousness—of blood, of pain and terror.

I jerked upright. My eyes locked onto Wenzhi's, softer than I had ever seen them before. My skin heated as I tugged my hand away. How long had he been here? How long had I slept? I swung my legs over the side of the bed, trying not to wince from the ache.

He frowned. "You've been asleep for days. Take it slow."

"I feel fine." Despite my bravado as I lurched to my feet, I was light-headed, swaying where I stood. Pride alone kept me from sinking back down on the bed as I gripped the wooden frame to steady myself.

He slipped an arm around me, his hold light yet firm as he helped me to the nearest chair.

"Prince Yanming. Is he safe? What happened?" My questions fell out in a rush.

"You'd do better to worry about yourself next time."

He lifted the teapot and poured out a stream of reddish-brown tea into a porcelain cup, pushing it toward me. Pu'er. I inhaled its rich and earthy fragrance before taking a long sip, the liquid sliding down my throat with a reviving warmth.

"Prince Yanming is well and has been demanding to see you." He paused to refill my cup. "After Governor Renyu's death, the merfolk surrendered. Their punishment is yet to be determined."

Memories flashed through my mind—of the sick pleasure the governor had taken in tormenting me, his haunted expression as Wenzhi's sword plunged through his chest. The crimson blood which had pooled around his body, sunken in the terrible stillness of death. I was glad for it, I told myself, even as my stomach churned. The governor would have killed me, as viciously as he could. But I still found little triumph in this moment. And though he had gone, the scars of his deceit remained; the lives he had stolen, those irrevocably destroyed.

"The merfolk may not be to blame. The governor had a strange power that helped him gain their trust. His voice, his pendant . . ." I frowned, trying to make sense of my fragmented memories. "He used it on me, too."

His face darkened. "How did you resist?"

"I sealed off my hearing." I grimaced. "Stupid, perhaps. It made fighting him much harder, but I couldn't think of anything else."

His hand clenched on the table, until his knuckles were white around the joints. "Fortunately, the governor's powers were weak, coming from the pendant, as you guessed. A true Mind Talent could have bent even your will in seconds. Once in thrall, he would have held you till your end or his."

An echo of the governor's boast, rousing anew my fears from before. As though sensing my distress, he reached across the table and touched my arm. "I should not have left you. You wouldn't have been so hurt if I had stayed."

"If you had stayed, maybe we'd all be bowing to Governor Renyu now." I added gravely, "This is not your fault. My safety is in my own care. And I certainly had no intention of letting him kill me. I would have made him regret his attempts. Eventually."

"I have no doubt that you would have." He leaned forward, inspecting my face. "If you're well enough, we should leave soon. I've already sent the others back, however Prince Yanxi wants to see you before we go. He's in the audience chamber this morning."

I rose, feeling a little steadier as I smoothed down my pale green robe, only now having the presence of mind to check if I was appropriately dressed. Such plain garments might raise brows from the impeccably attired Eastern Sea Court, but after having almost died, I had greater concerns on my mind.

The moment we entered the hall, Wenzhi was called aside by an Eastern Sea general. I kept to the outskirts of the room, searching for Prince Yanxi—finally finding him deep in conversation with another immortal. The stranger was turned away from me, yet the way he stood and how his dark blue brocade robe sat across his shoulders, were oddly familiar.

When Prince Yanxi noticed me, he inclined his head. As his companion swung around, his dark eyes pierced mine.

It was Liwei, the last person I expected to see here. A quiver rippled through my heart—dread or joy, I could no longer tell apart the emotions he evoked in me. But he was dear to me still, no matter how I wished he were not.

Liwei spoke briefly to Prince Yanxi, before coming toward me. Conscious of those watching us, I bowed to him with all due ceremony.

"Rise," he said in a strained voice.

I met his gaze without a flicker of emotion, grateful for Teacher Daoming's training—that I could now slip on this mask despite the turmoil which raged within. "Why are you here? When did you arrive?"

"Three days ago." He lifted the Sky Drop Tassel by his waist. The gem was clear, the silver flecks swirling in its depths. "When it turned red, I rushed here as quickly as I could."

I clutched the stone by my waist, the twin to his. A wild urge gripped me, to toss it away, to bury it with our past—like the temptation to rip out a scab before the wound had healed. Why did I wear it? Why cling to this remembrance? *Sentimental fool,* I scolded myself, forcing my grip to loosen.

"When I got here, the battle was already over. You were unconscious, blood streaming from your wounds as Captain Wenzhi carried you from the tent. I . . . I feared the worst." He stilled, as though struggling with himself. "You were gravely injured. Prince Yanxi had you brought to the palace so the royal healers could extract the venom from your body. Any more would have killed you."

He leaned toward me now, taking my hand in his—our

palms brushing, the tips of his fingers pressing against mine. Taken aback, I stilled. Heat sparked against my skin as his power coursed through my body. My mind cleared, a reviving strength spreading through me, but I pulled away. While he was a healer, skilled in Life magic, the thought of his energy mingling with mine aroused too many unsettling emotions.

"Thank you. You don't need to do that." I groped for something else to say. Anything, in the awkward silence which descended upon us. "What were you discussing with Prince Yanxi?"

His expression turned somber, his eyelids lowering. "A grave matter. Archer Feimao, whom you know, recently reported a strange affliction. Since the battle with Xiangliu, he found difficulties wielding his magic. We believe a piece of dark ore wedged in his armor suppressed his powers."

"How is he now?" I asked, concerned.

"Once it was removed, he recovered."

"What metal is this? How did it get there?"

"No one has come across anything like it before. Archer Feimao suspects it came from Shadow Peak, a crevice which he fell into. Our scouts found traces of the ore there, but nothing beyond remnants."

"Did someone take it?" A chilling thought.

He nodded tersely. "It appears to have been mined. Such a thing could be catastrophic in the wrong hands. I've warned Prince Yanxi to be vigilant and to alert us should he discover anything."

He fell silent. In the sudden quiet, my senses sharpened. How close we stood, speaking with the same case we always had before. There it was still, that unseen cord wound around our hearts—frayed, yet intact, despite my attempts to snap it.

Perhaps it was a bond which could never be severed, rooted in our friendship before our ill-fated love. I did not want this—for my spirits to leap and plummet in the same instant, that gaping hollow in my chest to reopen. But my near death was a blunt reminder that life was precious. Precarious, even for an immortal. And right now, I felt more alive than I had in months. His scent flooded me with memories from our time in the Courtyard of Eternal Tranquility . . . I could almost hear the rumbling from the waterfall.

My fingers curled as I stepped back from Liwei, retreating a safe distance as cool air rushed between us. His mouth opened to speak, but then he glanced up as someone approached.

"First Archer."

It was Prince Yanxi, along with Wenzhi—whose face seemed hewn from stone as he bowed to Liwei.

I would have bowed, too, except Prince Yanxi raised his hand to dismiss the formalities. "I'm glad you have recovered. My family owes you a debt of gratitude for risking yourself to protect my brother. Should you ever need our aid, it would be our honor to assist you."

His gracious words touched me. "There is no debt, Your Highness. Governor Renyu's ambitions stretched beyond here to the Four Seas. If left unchecked, he would have brought great suffering to all."

Prince Yanxi shook his head in disbelief. "It's fortunate Captain Wenzhi and you put an end to this."

"What of the governor's pendant?" Liwei asked.

"Destroyed." I recalled the arrow I had ripped from my hand, used to shatter the stone.

Liwei sighed. "It's a relief that such a dangerous artifact is gone, that it can never be used again. But I can't help wishing we had the chance to study it. We know so little of this magic, I fear it's to our disadvantage. We must know what we contend against."

I understood his meaning and yet, I was glad to never see that accursed pendant again.

"What of those who served Governor Renyu? Those who attacked us? Will they be brought to justice?" Wenzhi asked, with an edge to his tone. Did he recall the Celestials who were slain in the battle? I could not forget his anguish as he saw them fall.

"Justice will be served as the Eastern Sea decides," Liwei said grimly. "Though it would appear both sides were deceived by the governor."

"Your Highness, regardless of their excuses, the merfolk rebelled against their sovereign. Your own father believes such matters should be dealt with harshly, so none will attempt it again." Wenzhi's lips curved into a mocking smile. Did he enjoy baiting Liwei? He certainly seemed to care little for the prince's favor.

I said to Wenzhi, "I felt the power of the enchantment, I almost fell under its sway. It might just as easily have been me under its spell."

He did not reply, yet his jaw clenched as though he was stricken by my words.

"Many of the merfolk appeared dazed, unsure why they had revolted," Prince Yanxi told us. "We will investigate further to determine their innocence. Those found blameless will be released, under watch at first. Some will be invited to remain at our court as the intermediaries between us and the merfolk. Closer ties will prevent this from happening again."

The merfolk would not have fared so well under the Celestial Emperor's justice. "Your father and you are indeed wise and merciful," I said, without intent to flatter.

Before he could reply, footsteps pattered across the floor as a pair of small arms was flung round my waist. Swinging around, I lifted Prince Yanming into the air, ignoring the ache in my body as he whooped in delight. When I set him down again, his expression grew solemn, the corners of his mouth turned down.

"You did not follow us. You lied." His tone was accusing.

Guilt pricked me. I crouched down, staring into his face. "I'm sorry. I couldn't go with you then, but I should not have said I would."

"I am glad you didn't die. And . . . thank you." He held out his hand to me. Nestled in his palm was a small dragon, exquisitely crafted from red paper.

I picked it up, holding it between my thumb and finger, afraid to crush the delicate paper. "Thank you. I'll cherish this always."

His lower lip wobbled. "May the dragons protect you on your journey." He dashed the back of his hand over his eyes, as he turned and ran away.

I watched until his little figure disappeared, a thickness forming in my throat.

"Wherever you go, you'll always have a place here—whether in our court or as our friend." Prince Yanxi spoke in earnest and something eased deep inside me, at the thought of having another home in this world.

"Prince Yanxi, it's time we left," Liwei said in glacial tones.

"Thank you for your hospitality, Your Highness." Wenzhi spoke with equally cold formality.

The palpable shift in their attitude was both puzzling and

unprovoked. And the way they were looking at Prince Yanxi was decidedly unfriendly. I shook my head to banish these thoughts, wondering if I had imagined it.

Fortunately, Prince Yanxi seemed oblivious to the sudden chill, a smile playing on his lips as he said, "We thank the Celestial Kingdom for coming to our aid."

22

After the Eastern Sea, Wenzhi and I went from one campaign to the next, at times not returning to the Celestial Kingdom for months at a stretch. We fought terrifying monsters, ravenous beasts, and—most recently—the fearsome spirits that plagued the eastern border, close to the forests of the Phoenix Kingdom. I was exhausted when we finally arrived at the Jade Palace, eager to retire to my room. Yet when news reached me that Shuxiao had been awarded a promotion, I set off in search of her at once.

I knocked on her door, expecting to find her celebrating with friends. But when she opened it, her smile lacked her usual warmth; she seemed a pale copy of herself. A solitary lamp lit the dark and there was a porcelain jar of wine on the table.

"Is this how you're celebrating? Drinking by yourself?" I shook my head in mock disbelief as I entered and sank upon a stool. "Aren't you glad that I came by?"

"More than you know." She tugged off the red cloth stopper from the wine jar and poured me a cup.

I lifted it in a toast. "Lieutenant Shuxiao, may this just be the beginning."

She drained her cup in a single gulp. I stared at her, my hand frozen mid-air. Shuxiao was usually a restrained drinker, but maybe this was a special occasion. When I refilled her cup, she emptied it again. Shrugging, I decided to accompany her. We drank in companionable silence—until a flush bloomed in our cheeks, the sweet scent of osmanthus infused our breaths, and the lamp took on a hazy glow. Yet Shuxiao's eyes remained blank as though her mind was far away, and not someplace pleasant either.

"What's the matter?" I finally asked, unable to restrain myself. "Is it your family? Bad news?"

Her fingers clenched around the cup. "I want to go home."

Simple words which struck me deep, which had echoed in my mind each day and night. I knew Shuxiao missed her family; she spoke of them with such longing. But she was a Celestial, and I had thought she was happy here, that she had chosen this path.

"Isn't this your home? Don't you want to be here?" I asked tentatively, wondering if the wine had dulled my mind.

"No. Home is south in the countryside, shaded by crabapple trees, a river cutting through the fields." A small smile played on her lips. "My father never sought a place at court or the emperor's favor. While our family is not weak, we are without allies. It would not have mattered if a powerful noble had not taken a liking to my younger sister. He approached my father, asking for her to be his concubine. An insult. Even if he wasn't both lecherous and ancient, with over a dozen concubines and three wives."

Such things were common among the nobility, yet the idea repelled me. How could love thrive in so unequal a circumstance?

"My sister refused the match. My father supported her, as not many would have done. The old goat was furious that we spurned the *great* honor," she snarled. "He threatened my family with ruin. That he would blacken our reputation to the Celestial Court. Who would defend us when none knew our name?"

"Is that why you joined the army?"

She nodded. "To stop the threats and bullying. To prevent this from happening again. Few would dare malign us without proof now I have General Jianyun's ear. But this is not the life I wanted, among the crowds of the Jade Palace. I want to be home with my family and friends. Maybe fall in love. Yet the higher I rise, the more I am bound. The more we have to lose." Grabbing the jar, she emptied the last of it into her cup, some of the wine sloshing onto the table.

I did not know what to say. Perhaps I was failing her through my continued silence, but neither did I wish to give misguided advice. I had always thought Shuxiao thrived here; liked by commanders and soldiers alike. Perhaps it was as Liwei had said: *Everyone has their own troubles; some lay them bare while others hide them better.*

I could not tell her to follow her heart. I could not tell her to be selfish. This was her choice to make, though I would gladly support her however she decided. We each had our own burdens to bear and we alone knew their true cost, and whether we could pay it.

"Maybe you'll find someone here?" I teased, trying to lighten her mood.

Her nose wrinkled. "Hah! You've got the best one—among the men, at least." She rummaged in the chest behind her to pull out another jar of wine.

Did she mean Wenzhi? Heat prickled along my neck yet I held my tongue, feigning indifference.

After a pause, she nudged my arm. "Xingyin, there's something I've wanted to ask you for a while now."

I took a long drink, letting the wine burn through the sudden tightness in my throat. Did she suspect anything of my family? My identity? She would not betray my confidence, but I could not risk a chance indiscretion.

"What's that ornament you always wear by your waist? The one with the teardrop-shaped stone. I've seen it on Prince Liwei, too."

I released a drawn-out breath, relieved that my mother's secret was safe—even as my insides clenched with a new anxiety. My past with Liwei was another secret buried deep, but I would not lie to Shuxiao. Not for this.

"It was a gift. From Prince Liwei." I hated the way my voice shook over his name.

As her lips stretched in a knowing grin, I added hastily, "It was nothing, just a token of friendship. He's engaged." A statement as obvious as the color of my hair.

She squinted, as though struggling to remember something in her befuddled state. "Prince Liwei is never without the tassel. And his attendants say that your song, the one you played at his banquet, is often heard drifting from his room."

He kept the shell, still? *It means nothing, it changes nothing,* a voice inside me hissed.

My fingers toyed with my cup. This time, it was I who drained it first. "I didn't think you listened to idle gossip," I told her.

"Only when it concerns my friends," she said, with a grin.

I did not speak again, and neither did she. So, we drank in

companiable silence for the rest of the night, the air between us heavy with past remembrances.

My head throbbed mercilessly the next morning. I thought a walk would ease it but my feet led me back to a familiar courtyard. I hesitated, before entering the pavilion and sitting on a stool. Yellow and orange carp darted around the lotus blooms as the waterfall cascaded into the pond with a soothing rumble. I closed my eyes, inhaling the sweetness in the air. My old room was a few steps away—was it occupied by another? This was my first time entering the Courtyard of Eternal Tranquility since I had left. It was just as I remembered, yet everything had changed.

A girl, passing through the courtyard, halted and bowed to me. In her hands was a tray of pastries, the kind which flaked and crumbled when you bit into them to get to the sweet bean filling. When she looked up, I recognized her at once.

"Minyi, it's me!" I laughed. "Why are you being so formal?"

Two dimples appeared in her round cheeks. "Who hasn't heard of the First Archer's accomplishments over the past year?" she said, coming to sit beside me. "Did you really strike down twenty spirits during your last battle?"

My lips twitched, remembering her fondness for gossip. "Twelve. They fly fast."

"What of the Bone Devil? What did it look like?"

I shuddered at the remembrance of the malevolent creature that had broken free from the Celestial prison. "Hair and pupils so pale, they were almost translucent. Powdery skin stretched as taut as a drum."

She clutched my sleeve. "How did you kill it?"

A memory flashed across my mind: Wenzhi's sword arcing through the air, sinking into the creature's neck. Its jaws—

crammed with silver needles for teeth—had snapped at him viciously. As Wenzhi evaded its attack, the monster's claws flashed above his neck, toward the throbbing vein where his lifeblood flowed. Gripped by fear, I had released an arrow that plunged into its skull. Thick, white liquid oozed from the wound, a piercing shriek stabbing the air. Its claws had clutched the shaft once before they fell away, as it collapsed onto the ground. Gone were those days when my heart had twinged with pity, though their faces haunted me still.

"Captain Wenzhi and I fought it together," I told her.

At the mention of his name, Minyi sat straighter, her eyes brightening as whenever she scented a new tale.

To forestall her next question, I hastily asked, "What news do you have of the palace? How is His Highness?" Too late, did I bite my tongue. Last night's wine must have addled my senses, to have spoken of him aloud.

Someone approached from behind me. Had the roar from the waterfall muffled the footsteps? A throat was cleared and just from that sound, I could tell who he was before I turned. Beside me, Minyi leapt to her feet and bowed. Without another word, she grabbed her tray and hurried away, leaving me alone with the intruder. Except he was no intruder; he had every right to be here. It was *I* who did not belong.

"Please forgive the trespass, Your Highness. I will leave at once." Formality was a shield I clung to against my own weakness.

"Why don't you ask me how I am yourself?" There was a warmth to his tone which I had not heard for a long time.

I would have left then, but he moved into my path. As I looked up at him, I could not deny it was there still—that ache in my heart, that thread which tugged at it whenever he was near . . . no matter how I wished it did not. A soft breeze blew through the courtyard, sweeping a lock of my hair against his cheek. He caught it between his fingers, his eyes as inscrutable as pools of night.

"Have you been well?" he asked.

"Yes."

"Why are you here?"

"Curiosity. I wanted to meet my replacement," I said with a flippancy which fell flat.

"Who could have taken your place?"

His tone, his words, affected me still. But I wrenched myself away to leave.

"Are we not friends anymore? Since the Eastern Sea, I've seen you less than a handful of times and each time you run away." He gestured toward the stools. "Why don't you sit down? Let's talk as we used to. Unless you're afraid?" A note of challenge rang in his voice.

My sense warred with my pride. The latter won as I sat back down, goaded by his taunt. "I can't stay long. My training—"

"Yes, the valiant First Archer," he interjected cuttingly. "Who else would protect the Celestial Kingdom? Still 'First Archer' after all your accomplishments though. An honorable title but without rank or power. Why not seek a command of your own instead of trailing in Captain Wenzhi's shadow?"

I clenched my teeth. "That's my choice. I want the freedom to take on the campaigns I wish. I have no desire to climb higher for ambition's sake alone."

He stared at me like he was searching for something. "Or is there more behind your relationship? There are many rumors about the young captain and the gifted archer he favors. The two brightest stars in the Celestial Army. It's fortunate you don't hold an official position in the army, otherwise this would be most improper.”

His accusation stung. “How dare you speak to me of what's 'improper' when it's *you* who is betrothed yet baiting me this way. You have no right to ask such things of me. It's no business of yours what I do and who I see. As for me, I couldn't be more indifferent to you now.”

Such reckless words I spoke, uncaring of the storm which swept over his face. Yet I would not stay to be berated by him. I'd had enough of such entanglements and the way they twisted me into knots. Rising to my feet, I stalked away—but he caught my wrist in his grip.

“I do care,” he ground out. “Despite my sense, my judgment and honor—I cannot help but care.”

Light blazed from his eyes, as scorching as the sun. Pinned by his gaze, I could not move—only noticing, too late, when he drew me to him. I should have pushed him away yet there was no strength in my limbs. His confession roused something in me which I had thought long dead. I had never seen this side of him before, filled with passion and jealousy, and a reckless part of me reveled in it.

He bent his head—slowly at first—and when I did not flee, his hand loosened over my wrist, gliding up to encircle my waist. Something smoked in the depths of his eyes, a moment before his lips pressed against mine with a hunger as though he was starved, with an urgency that stirred my blood. There were no thoughts in my mind—no anger, no shame, no fear of what this meant. Nothing beyond this heady lightness, this glittering fire that coursed through my veins. My fingers were already winding around his neck to pull him closer as I tipped my head back, drowning in the sensation of his touch and warmth, even as his arms tightened around me, locking me into an embrace from which I no longer wanted to escape.

This courtyard . . . it had been my haven once. The soothing thrum of the waterfall, the fragrance of spring blossoms in the air, the joy I had known here. Yet while the aching familiarity of this place brought back such sweet memories, the one seared deepest in my mind was when I had sat frozen and alone the night of his betrothal.

With a wrench, I shoved him away—hard—as he staggered back, his arms falling away. I fought for breath, struggling to gather the shreds of my composure. "No, Liwei. It is over. *We are over.*"

He ran a hand through his hair, his chest rising and falling in an uneven rhythm. "Let us not lie to each other, Xingyin. We're not over. Your heart still beats to mine. You still feel something for me, just as I do for you." He spoke quietly, with no trace of pride. Just a certainty which was a hundred times more galling.

"What do you want of me?" I cried out, furious both at him and myself. "You are promised to another, yet you seem intent on humbling me to admit my feelings. Does it give you satisfaction? Would it appease your royal pride to hear you were not so easily forgotten? Or do you intend to follow in your father's steps, with a concubine in every corner of the palace?"

"Never, that." He recoiled as though insulted.

I did not believe those harsh accusations myself, but a part of me—a bitter, vengeful part—wanted to strike out at him, to wound him as he had me. We glared at each other, neither of us speaking. My heart pounding so hard I prayed he could not hear it.

At last, he turned away, his hands clenched by his sides. "I don't know what I'm doing," he said in a low voice, akin to a reluctant confession. "My mind tells me to stop, to let you go—yet I can't. I see you wherever I go, you're with me in everything I do; at my table while I eat, in my room when I awaken. Your voice in the air, your smile in my eyes. I can't forget you, no matter how I've tried."

Neither of us moved, neither of us spoke. How weak I was, that I did not leave now, that his confession moved me so. I did not know how long we would have stood there, as still as the stone lions which guarded the entrance, if the doors to the courtyard had not been thrown open. I stepped away from Liwei, just in time, as a messenger ran toward him. His black hat had been knocked askew and his robe flapped in the wind.

He bowed, panting a little as he spoke to Liwei. "Your Highness, Their Celestial Majesties request your immediate presence in the Hall of Eastern Light. An urgent matter requires your attention."

Liwei frowned. "I'll go at once." He glanced at me as though wanting to say more, but then he strode away.

I fled back to my room, trying to settle my churning emotions. Yet they were roused anew at the sight of Wenzhi, sitting by the table.

"Weren't you with General Jianyun this morning?" I asked, taking the stool beside him.

"Our meeting ended early." He sounded strained. Hesitant, which was most unlike him. "Xingyin, there is something I must tell you."

I clasped my hands in my lap, a chill spreading through me in anticipation of ill tidings.

He leaned toward me, his voice rough with sudden emotion. "I've resigned from the Celestial Army. This week will be my last. I have important family matters to attend to, far from here—and I don't expect to return." He spoke with deliberate measure, as though wanting to be sure I grasped his meaning.

"You're leaving? To the Western Sea?" I managed to ask.

A terse nod. "My final assignment will be to inspect the troops at the border of the Golden Desert. They've been unsettled of late."

My chest was so tight, I found it hard to breathe. Since the Eastern Sea, something had changed between us. My heart beat quicker at the sight of him and his smile warmed me like wine. Sometimes, I thought I caught a kindling in his eyes as he looked at me. We were circumspect in our interactions, never a touch or word beyond the bounds of propriety. Yet we had become more than friends, on the cusp of something entirely new and thrilling. Or had all this been my own delusions? I dropped my gaze to the floor, feeling oddly dismayed. Disappointed. Hurt, even? Though I had no right to be, guilt stabbing me at the memory of Liwei's lips on mine.

Wenzhi was staring at me, as though waiting for my response to a question I had not heard, his voice finally infiltrating the haze of my misery.

"Will you come with me?"

"To . . . the border of the Golden Desert?" I stammered.

"That, too, if you wish," he said gravely. "I meant, would you come with me when I leave?"

My tongue darted over my dry lips. "What do you mean?" I dared not mistake his intent.

A smile lit his face, it lit the very room.

"Don't you know how I feel about you?" His voice shook, the first crack in his iron composure. "I could not speak before, but I'm free to now. I want you to come with me—to my home, to my family. For us to share our lives together." He lowered his head to mine, our brows almost touching, his breath warm on my skin. "Your dreams will be my dreams, too."

Joy coursed through me like the ripples on a pond after a burst of rain. I had thought I was done with love . . . its breathtaking beauty, its tumultuous agony. I had been happy before and believed I would be content again once I made my way home—to my true home, not this one here built upon a web of lies. Now, a future with Wenzhi beckoned, with clear skies and not a dark cloud on the horizon. One with no broken hearts or past entanglements. One where blood had not been spilled between our kin, our ties unsullied by hatred or past grudges—where I could be whole and free from guilt, remorse, and sorrow.

Only now did I dare to admit to myself, my fear that I had failed. That in my arrogance, I had miscalculated the worth of my talent, the value of my deeds. For despite my service to the Celestial Army, my hope of winning my mother's freedom was fading away, like a silk painting left out too long in the sun. A pardon from the emperor was the surest way to securing her release. However, while my accomplishments had earned praise and gifts, which I'd declined, not even a whisper of the Crimson Lion Talisman had ever been uttered. I should have heeded General Jianyun's warning, yet in my pride I believed I knew better. The emperor was not known for his generosity in dispensing such favors. Nor had anyone sentenced to eternal imprisonment ever been pardoned. So, perhaps it was time to seek a new path to help my mother. Perhaps I would find the way in Wenzhi's homeland, in the Western Sea.

Wenzhi's hand on my arm startled me now. He was still waiting for my reply, perhaps wondering at my prolonged silence. As

I stared into his strong handsome face, something shifted in my chest. I cared for him, I know I did. My dismay at his leaving was proof of that. And was it not said that love would grow between well-matched minds, over the months and years? We had eternity before us.

"Is this what you want, too?" His tone was no longer uncertain but brimming with newfound confidence, as though he had already sensed my answer.

Yes. The word formed on my lips and yet I could not say it. Something tugged at the edge of my heart, a small voice within pleading with me to reconsider. I would have asked him for more time then, except the crunch of gravel startled us. Someone was running toward my room with undue haste, as Wenzhi threw the doors apart.

A young attendant halted in the entrance. "Captain Wenzhi," he gasped. "I've been searching everywhere for you. Their Celestial Majesties have requested your immediate presence in the Hall of Eastern Light."

How strange, I thought to myself. He was the second messenger I had seen today relaying pressing news.

Wenzhi's eyes flashed with annoyance. "I'll come shortly."

The messenger shrank away but did not leave. His courage was commendable, particularly in light of Wenzhi's evident displeasure. "All the other commanders have already gathered. I . . . I was instructed to accompany you there the moment I found you."

Wenzhi sighed as he drew me aside. "Let's speak tomorrow." He might have said more, but the messenger shuffled his feet, throwing a nervous glance at us. With an impatient shake of his head, Wenzhi stalked away.

Alone in my room, I sat by the table until the golden fire

of the sun dwindled to a glowing ember. If not for my lapse of weakness this morning, I had believed my heart whole, freed from the ties that had bound it. A glorious future beckoned on the horizon. Yet I still clung to a shred of my past, as a flowering peach blossom tree yearning for its fallen bloom.

23

Shuxiao slipped into the chair across from me, setting her tray of food on the wooden table. Her eyes slid around the large dining hall, already crowded with soldiers hunched over their morning meal. "Princess Fengmei has been abducted," she said in hushed tones.

My spoon fell into my bowl, splattering congee onto the table. "How? When? By whom?" The questions rolled off my tongue. *This* must be why Liwei and Wenzhi had been called away yesterday.

"All I heard is Prince Liwei will be leading the rescue."

Beneath the table, my hand gripped my knee. If not for yesterday, this news would not have affected me so. Yet he had kissed me as though I was the only one in his heart. Such tender words he had spoken . . . and now, he was risking himself to save his betrothed? An engagement he claimed he had not wanted? A cold, prickling sensation slithered tight around my chest. I breathed in and then out, trying to unravel its hold. I was behaving like a selfish child. As her betrothed and ally, who else but he should go?

"I wish him every success. I hope he brings her back safely." If my words came out a little hollow, I was at least glad that I meant them.

"To spirit the princess away is no easy feat. I wonder who—" Shuxiao's voice cut off abruptly.

General Jianyun stood before us with his arms folded. We leapt up at once to greet him.

"Lieutenant Shuxiao, I don't need to know where you heard this from, but I want an end to this discussion, or any other regarding this matter. Is that clear?" he commanded.

She shot me a panicked look before replying with uncharacteristic meekness, "Yes, General Jianyun."

He glanced at me then. "First Archer Xingyin, follow me. I must speak with you."

I stared at him in surprise until Shuxiao kicked my shin, the pain breaking my daze as I hastened after him.

"The news is true," he said without preamble, as he sat behind his rosewood desk. "Queen Fengjin is distraught. The abductor sent terms, demanding that she break off the alliance with us. Warning that her daughter would be shown no mercy should any attempt be made to rescue her. Which is why it falls upon us to save her."

"Was it the Demon Realm?" I asked.

"We suspect so, though we have no evidence. Regardless, our priority is to retrieve Princess Fengmei safely. His Highness will lead a small team to rescue her, no more than a dozen soldiers to avoid detection. Given the threat, discretion is crucial to not jeopardize the princess's safety." He tapped the table in a steady rhythm. "Prince Liwei has requested that you join the rescue."

I could not have been more astonished if a bolt of lightning had struck me from the cloudless sky. At a loss for words, I struggled against the emotions that swelled within—tangling and twisting, burning, yet cold. But one thing was clear: I did not want to do this.

His expression darkened, perhaps reading the refusal in my face. "While I cannot command you to do this, I strongly urge you to. For the kingdom. Our alliance. Nothing matters more."

His argument did not sway me; I was neither so noble nor valiant. It was not the physical danger which repelled me, but the hurt to my heart and pride. This was not worth the rewards the Celestial Kingdom had to offer, those I had already declined. "There are many others more suitable, more skilled than me," I said.

"With the bow?" It was Liwei who spoke, from where he stood in the doorway. I had not heard him arrive.

As General Jianyun rose to greet him, I followed suit, quelling the leap in my chest. I would not linger on what had happened between us; it was no more than a momentary lapse. Perhaps being in the Courtyard of Eternal Tranquility had clouded our minds with memories. And now, we were plunged deeper into a new reality, one where Liwei and I would drift further apart until we could never find our way back to each other again.

"With Your Highness, himself, leading the rescue, surely you have all the skills you need." This was what a courtier might say, hoping to flatter the prince—if not for the edge in my tone.

Liwei crossed the room to stand before me. "Not all. You surpassed me in archery a long time ago, as we both know."

When I did not reply, he took one of the chairs opposite General Jianyun and motioned for me to do the same. I sat stiffly beside him, wishing I were anywhere but here.

"Continue, General Jianyun," Liwei said.

"We believe Princess Fengmei is being held in the Eternal Spring Forest, close to the mountains south of the Phoenix Kingdom. That was the last trace we had of her."

The name struck a chord in me. "Was that the home of Lady Hualing, the previous Flower Immortal? Before she disappeared?"

He nodded grimly. "Since then, the forest has been veiled from sight by a strange magic. No one has ventured there for centuries. We don't know what other dangers lurk there in addition to the hostile forces holding the princess. Stealth and subterfuge will be crucial, as will your skills."

General Jianyun expected me to accept with grace. I would not. Some might think me unkind, but I could not so easily cast my feelings aside. My own desires mattered, too. Guilt pricked me at the thought of Princess Fengmei's peril, but I was not so arrogant to imagine I was the only one who could perform this task.

I stood, raising my cupped hands and bowing from my waist. "General Jianyun, you promised that I would have the freedom to choose my assignments. I refuse this one."

He scowled, his mouth opening to rebuke me—but Liwei interjected, "May I speak with Xingyin, alone?"

The general threw a forbidding look my way, before bowing to Liwei and leaving the room.

"Would you like to sit?" Liwei asked, after a moment's silence.

"I prefer to stand." I was eager to leave at the first opportunity, determined to avoid any further intimacy with him.

He sighed as he rose to join me. Part of me cringed from the absurdity of our situation. Only yesterday he had pulled me into his arms with such passion, and now he was asking me to rescue his betrothed. Anger flared in me, hot and fierce.

"Do you care so little for my feelings?" I could not help asking, hating myself for it, too.

"I must do this," he said. "If we fail, if any harm befalls Princess Fengmei—not only would it be a great tragedy, but it would tilt the Phoenix Kingdom toward the Demon Realm, strengthening them and weakening us, immensely. With this advantage the Demon Realm would be tempted to break the peace, to go to war with us again."

"I understand. But why do *I* need to go with you? There are countless competent warriors you could choose from, who would be honored to accompany you."

"Because there's no one I trust more than you." His eyes held mine. "Too many things have been happening of late. Fox spirits coming through our wards. Archer Feimao's affliction. And now, this. The princess was taken on her way to the Celestial Kingdom. Only those in the inner circles of our courts knew of this trip. Which means there is a traitor either in the Phoenix Kingdom or here," he concluded gravely. "I meant what I said about your skill. This will be dangerous, and we'll need every advantage we can gather."

When I did not reply, he added in a low voice, "I'm placing you in an impossible situation. You must hate me."

My head pounded beneath the weight of my indecision. To be tasked with saving Liwei's betrothed both unsettled and hurt me. I wanted her to be rescued, but I also wanted no part of it. And a small voice inside me whispered that if the Celestial Kingdom should fall, perhaps my mother would be free . . .

I flinched from the vile thought. I had friends here whom I cared for, who would suffer if it came to war. And what if the Demon Realm ascended to supremacy? While I no longer believed them to be the monsters I had dreaded—neither did I trust their king who seemed as ruthless as the Celestial Emperor, particularly if he *had* kidnapped Princess Fengmei to force the queen's capitulation. Dare I lay our fates in such hands? If I had learned anything over these years, it was that no one won in a war, not even those who thought they did.

Princess Fengmei's face flashed through my mind now—not the royal wearing the golden cloak of feathers I had seen from afar, but the girl I had met in Liwei's courtyard. Could I not treat this as any other task I had accepted before? If not for our past, I would have leapt at this chance to aid the Celestial Crown Prince and the Phoenix Princess. It was a rare opportunity, one which would undoubtedly gain the emperor's attention—possibly bringing me within reach of the Crimson Lion Talisman and averting a disastrous war. And beyond that, could I truly refuse to help Liwei? No matter what, he was still my friend.

A hundred considerations twisted and wound through me, now all tugging me in the same direction. I would go with Liwei. Not from duty or obligation, but to protect him—my friend—and those I cared for in the Celestial Kingdom. To help save the innocent girl I had spoken with. And if this did not win His Celestial Majesty's favor and the talisman I craved—nothing ever would. This would be my final step along this path before I began anew, and I would leave with a cleared conscience.

I met his gaze. "I'll go with you."

"Thank you."

As he took a step toward me, I moved away. "I'll go with you," I repeated. "However, I ask that you conduct yourself within the bounds of propriety from now . . . as though our past does not exist." These cold words stung me, too, but I could not allow another moment of weakness to muddle my resolve.

"What if you're improper toward me?" A shadow of a smile formed on his lips.

How easily he slipped back into being my teasing friend of the past. But I could not allow even that. "We cannot continue this way," I said in a low voice, trying to stifle the lingering desire which slid into me at his nearness, the guilt and shame that burned a hole in my stomach. "I will help you and Princess Fengmei. But you have your honor and I have mine. And there is none to be found in what we did. You are betrothed now—your heart is hers." The memory of our kiss flitted through me, unbidden. Our last—I told myself fiercely—a door closed, a final farewell.

His face was ash and shadow, his eyes stripped of light. It was then, I knew I had done it . . . severed the last frayed thread of our bond. He was silent as he inclined his head to me, before walking away. I did not look up, not wanting to see him leave. My words had struck true—a fatal blow, a swift death. Yet it was a hollow triumph, leaving a bitterness in my mouth and a clawing ache in my chest.

Sleep evaded me that night. Plagued by restlessness, I clambered up the pillars outside my room. A gentle breeze stirred the air as I sat on the cold jade roof tiles, staring at the sky. The moon shone down through the darkness, its light gentle and soft.

Something rustled—Wenzhi, pulling himself over the ledge. He flicked his outer robe aside as he sank down beside me.

"I waited for you today."

"I'm sorry. Today was . . . eventful." I hated the way my words stumbled as though I had something to hide. *Oh, you do,* my mind whispered.

"I can't go with you to the border," I told him.

His jaw tightened, yet he showed no surprise. Had he already been briefed by General Jianyun?

"Don't go with Prince Liwei." He spoke with sudden urgency. "It's too dangerous. Immortals shun the Eternal Spring Forest for good reason. Since Lady Hualing's disappearance, rumors abound of the place—of dark enchantments and hostile creatures, of misery and death."

I shrugged with an indifference I did not feel. "I've faced monsters, by your side, no less."

His sigh misted the cool air. "Don't you have any regard for your own safety?"

I frowned, a little surprised by his insistence. "How is this more dangerous than Xiangliu? Governor Renyu? Or the Bone Devil?" I rattled off, trying to ease his concern.

"Because I won't be there. What if something happened to you?" He paused, "Don't you care how I feel?"

His concern touched me, though I would not be swayed. "I do. But I can take care of myself. Regardless, it's been decided. We leave tomorrow."

"Why do this?" he demanded. "It doesn't matter what General Jianyun commands when we'll soon leave this place. Why endanger yourself needlessly? Surely it's not out of loyalty to the Celestial Kingdom."

I pulled my back straight, needled by his words. I could protect myself. In the past, I had come to his aid as often as he came to mine. And his taunt that I bore no loyalty to the Celestial Kingdom . . . I needed no reminder for that. I served here because I had believed this would lead to my mother's freedom. The training I received, the reputation I built, the lives I took— all this was a means to an end, as had been my entire time here.

Yet I heard, too, the worry which wrenched his voice. I tried to explain. "I'm not doing this because I was commanded to. Prince Liwei asked me to help him. I could not refuse."

Wenzhi's face darkened. "Are you still in love with him? Is that why you're risking your life to save someone you care nothing for? Have you forgotten that he left you for another?" His harsh words lashed out like a whip.

I stared at him, anger searing my veins. He knew nothing of Liwei and me. More than our doomed love, Liwei was my friend—my only friend when I had none and those roots went far deeper than my disappointment and hurt. His kindness to me was a debt I owed him, one I would repay.

"How can you say that to me?" I seethed. "I'm no love-sick puppet, begging for a morsel of affection. I have my own dreams, my own principles, my own honor to uphold." In no mood to explain myself further, I scrambled to my feet to leave.

"Wait, Xingyin—"

His tone was cracked by a note of despair. I halted but did not turn.

He spoke so quietly that I strained to hear. "I'm sorry. I should not have said that. I was disappointed and . . . jealous." He exhaled deeply. "I thought we had come to an understanding yesterday. Was I wrong? Did you not grasp my meaning then? My hopes for our future?"

My heart softened, despite the anger which simmered in me still. All Wenzhi had seen was my despair over Liwei's engagement, and it was little wonder that he was resentful now. A hard confession for him to make, though it did not give him the right to speak to me so.

I swung around, holding his gaze. "Wenzhi, you must trust

in my judgment as I do in yours. Do not try to insult or guilt me into doing what *you* think I should do. How will we have a future together if you do not see me as your equal?"

"You are my equal. More than my equal." Wenzhi pushed himself to his feet, clasping my hand in his strong grip. "I just don't want you to be hurt."

The wind grew stronger, blowing my hair across my cheek. As I shivered, Wenzhi slid off his outer coat, draping it over my shoulders as his arm pulled me close. "Promise me you'll keep yourself safe. That you won't do anything . . . *too* reckless," he whispered into my ear.

An urge to laugh rippled through me, dispersing my ire. He knew me well, to say such a thing. And I knew him well enough to sense how he restrained himself from saying more.

The fresh scent of pine needles wafted in the air, kindling a light in my heart which banished the lingering shadows. My feelings for Wenzhi were strong, though different from mine with Liwei before. Perhaps the blazing, all-consuming passion I had known with Liwei was the headiness of a first love, suffused with the foolish innocence that nothing could tear us apart. For those that came after, one tread a little slower, a little warier— after hearts had been bruised and promises broken. And perhaps, the growing warmth of my feelings for Wenzhi was what all love evolved to.

I rested my head against his shoulder, the last of my tension easing away. "I promise. And when I return, we'll leave this place together."

We stood there in silence, his arm tightening around me the only sign he had heard my answer. For the first time today, I was at peace. An urge gripped me to spill my secrets to him, but not tonight, not here. In the Celestial Kingdom my guard was always up. One day when we were far from this place, I would tell him of my mother.

How dark the night that stretched before us, yet ablaze with the light of the moon and stars, it felt as bright as day.

24

The Eternal Spring Forest had been the most beautiful place in the Immortal Realm. It was said the Celestial Emperor himself had planted this forest in his youth, with branches cut from the first tree of the world, sprinkled with the dew from an enchanted lotus. Beneath the graceful canopy of towering trees were crystal-clear ponds and silvery rivers, gleaming with fish. Those who wandered to the heart of the forest spoke, enthralled, of trees in eternal bloom, their branches laden with flowers in all colors. Ripe fruits, sweeter than nectar, grew as abundantly as the wildflowers amid the soft grass. The idyllic perfection of the forest had attracted birds, beasts, and immortals. Even the powerful Lady Hualing, the first Flower Immortal, had been enchanted by this place, leaving the Celestial Kingdom to make her home here—peonies, camellias, and azaleas blossoming in her wake.

But this paradise did not last. After Lady Hualing had been stripped of her position, no longer did she raise her hand to plant the flowers, no longer did she revive the faded blooms. And after she had disappeared—the lush canopies browned, the shimmering ponds dried into pools of sinking mud, and the trees withered, never to bloom again.

I stepped off my cloud, struck by the deep silence of this place. Not a chirp from a single bird, not even the flutter of a dragonfly's wings. A white fog shrouded the forest, glazed with an unwelcome chill. The trees stood tall and straight, their shriveled leaves clinging to the branches in eternal death. Scattered around were murky pools which we steered clear of, to avoid being sucked into their bottomless depths. The stagnant air reeked of decay, a sad mockery of the promise in the forest's name. As we walked deeper through shadow and mist, my skin crawled as my fingers tightened around the Phoenix Fire Bow. If only I could have brought the Jade Dragon Bow along, as Sky-fire was more powerful than flame. But I was unsure if I could wield it, having never released its arrow before. And I feared, too, using the bow in front of Celestial soldiers who might claim it on the emperor's behalf.

Two soldiers ran ahead to scout the way, while the other eight remained. "It's no use to summon a cloud here," Liwei explained. "The fog is too dense and some enchantment keeps it in place."

"Can't we dispel it?"

"It's not a simple spell. Besides, the fog conceals our trail for now and we don't want to alert anyone to our presence."

"How will we find Princess Fengmei? Even with the scouts?" I asked.

"I can sense her aura, though I need to get close enough," he said.

His revelation pricked me. Was he more intimate with the princess than I had imagined? I reminded myself to avoid speaking to him, to forestall my mind spiraling into such depths.

However, he had no such qualms. "Captain Wenzhi will be leaving the Celestial Kingdom soon. What will you do then?"

While his manner was conversational, pleasant even, my reply stuck in my throat.

He continued in that low and earnest voice. "My feelings for you remain unchanged, but I will speak of them no more. What you said yesterday . . . what you asked of me. You were right."

I nodded woodenly, thinking if that was true, what was this stifling heaviness which sank over me now? I clenched my hands, furious with myself. How could I still be stirred by Liwei, despite my feelings for Wenzhi? Was I so fickle and inconstant? My future with Wenzhi was bright with hope, not mired in past regret—and I would not discard this chance at happiness.

Footsteps padded toward us, cautious and soft. I glanced up to find one of the scouts approaching. "Your Highness, there are soldiers about five hundred paces ahead. Armed and guarding a pagoda."

"Proceed with caution. They must not know we're here," Liwei warned.

We drew our weapons, making our way stealthily onward. In the clearing before us, the pagoda loomed—eight stories high, almost as tall as the surrounding trees. The tiered towers were of crumbling wood, its latticed windows and ornamental eaves, faded from what might have once been a brilliant red. How seamlessly it blended into the blighted landscape, a dilapidated blur of browns and grays. How desolate it appeared, despite the dozen soldiers surrounding it, clad in burnished bronze armor.

"Do you recognize the armor?" I asked.

"No. But that can be easily disguised." Liwei closed his eyes for a moment, his brow creasing. "Princess Fengmei is inside; I can sense her. We must take the guards out quietly, to avoid raising the alarm." He addressed us all in hushed tones. "Start with those closest to us, working our way to the pagoda. We must be quick to avoid them crying out, else the princess will be in danger."

At Liwei's signal, I released a flaming arrow, which sank into the chest of the nearest guard. As a choked gurgle rolled from her throat, I shot the one beside her, his eyes bulging as he crumpled to the ground. Liwei and his warriors moved swiftly to surround the remaining soldiers, striking them down to an ominous chorus of strangled gasps and whispered screams.

The skirmish was over. Sweat beaded my brow despite the chill that shrouded my skin. It had been easy—too easy. Liwei's gaze swung to mine, echoing my unspoken suspicion.

"The pagoda," he said. "There might be more guards there—"

A roar erupted from the forest, drowning the rest of his words. A stream of enemies swarmed toward us, the sunlight striking their bronze armor as they flooded the clearing. With a blow from his sword, Liwei struck down two of them. I shot another who raced toward him—just as an enemy soldier slumped unconscious by my feet. In the tumult, I had not heard him. He might have caught me unaware had there not been that strange black-feathered arrow protruding from his chest.

I swung around to search for the archer, but Liwei shouted, "Get the princess!"

He raised his sword, blazing with flame as he swung it in a wide arc, throwing back the assailants who surrounded him. Their weapons glinted silver and gold, while some carried dark metal chains in their hands. The sight of them infuriated me, that they were so certain of taking him prisoner. The rest of his warriors were engaged in a furious battle around him, outnum-

bered yet holding their ground. We still had a chance . . . at least
for now. If I found the princess in time.

I wanted to stay and fight, but I raced into the pagoda, leaving the battle outside to Liwei and the other Celestials. Fear
sliced my heart, even as I reminded myself fervently of Liwei's
skill with a sword and his powerful magic. He could hold them
at bay until I returned. The sooner I found Princess Fengmei, the
sooner we could all flee this accursed place.

I sprinted up the wooden stairs, half expecting to be con-
fronted by guards around every corner. Yet the place was oddly
deserted as I reached the highest floor without encountering a
single enemy. I wrenched open the thick wooden door at the top,
but it held fast. Impatient now, I summoned a blast of air that
shattered the lock.

Princess Fengmei leapt to her feet, amid the chunks of wood
and splinters scattered on the floor. Her heart-shaped face was
pale and her brown eyes wide as she stared blankly at me, as
though unsure whether to shriek in terror or weep with relief.
Her head tilted to one side as she scrutinized me, perhaps trying
to recall where we had met before.

"I'm with the Celestial Army. We're here to rescue you. Quick,
Prince Liwei is under attack!" My voice pulsed with urgency.

She brightened at the mention of Liwei's name, as she raised
her wrists to me. They were bound with black metal manacles,
joined by a thin chain. "Could you remove these?"

I drew my sword and slammed it against the delicate chain.
The blade rebounded, my arm throbbing from the effort, but
not so much as a scratch appeared on the metal. Sawing away at
the links did not work, nor did hammering at them make a dent.
All the while, my mind raged with thoughts of Liwei below, the

arrows flying toward his unprotected back, the blades thrust at his chest.

"Stand still." I drew an arrow, releasing it at the manacle around her right hand. Crimson fire rippled across the metal, cracks appearing before they shattered. With my next breath, I shot another bolt at her left wrist, the second manacle falling away.

Princess Fengmei's lips curved into a trembling smile. "You . . . you shoot very well," she said softly, brushing away the clouds of black hair which covered her face.

Her delicate beauty sent a twinge through my heart. I swallowed hard, bending to toss away the broken links of metal around her feet. They stung like ice clinging to my skin.

"What are these chains?"

Her shoulders slumped. "I have no idea. When they put them on me, I couldn't draw my energy."

My stomach churned violently. These chains . . . I had seen the soldiers below carrying them. And in the Eastern Sea, Liwei had told me of the ore from Shadow Peak that could bind an immortal's powers.

"Hurry!" I pulled her up to her feet. "Prince Liwei is in danger!"

Something whistled through the air; a sound every archer knew by heart. I threw myself to the ground, dragging the princess down. Pain slashed my arm as I stared in disbelief at the blood oozing from the cut. Scrambling to the window, I lifted my head an inch only to see a sharp glint hurtling toward me. I ducked, flattening myself on the floor as another arrow plunged into the room.

I drew a blazing bolt of flame, releasing it through the window. In the next moment, two arrows tore toward me, missing by a hair's breadth as they clattered on the floor. I ground my teeth. This archer was formidable. It was little wonder there were no guards here when any rescuer would have long been shot dead. The black fletching was familiar—identical to the arrow that had struck my attacker outside. Had I been the target all along? Had the archer missed before? It seemed improbable given this person's skill—though more improbable still was the idea that this archer had saved me, only to murder me later.

I sucked in a breath, furious at my unseen assailant. Precious time was ticking away. If those chains could seal an immortal's magic, Liwei would not stand a chance. I drew another arrow, leaping up to gain my first look at my foe. A tall figure—a man—stood on a wide tree branch, a drawn arrow at the ready. His face was concealed by a helmet, but his eyes gleamed silver bright as they bored into me. Taken aback, my fingers slackened on the string, the flame vanishing. I braced myself, expecting an arrow to plunge through me now . . . but the archer lowered his weapon. We stared at each other for a heartbeat of silence, before he stepped backward into the shadows and was gone.

There was no time to ponder this. I grabbed Princess Fengmei's hand as we raced down the stairs together, toward the fury of battle—only to emerge into the deathly quiet of a graveyard. Bodies were strewn all around, dozens and dozens in bronze armor. My spirits plunged as I counted ten in gold and white, the armor of the fallen Celestials. I raced from one to the next, searching each body for any sign of life. But their eyes were vacant, their auras faded to nothingness.

"Where is Prince Liwei?" Princess Fengmei's voice shook as she stared at the carnage in horror.

"I don't know," I whispered, numb to everything except the dread creeping over me, turning my flesh to stone.

25

The waning light filtered through the fog, throwing an eerie halo around the trees. Princess Fengmei and I wandered through the forest, searching for any sign of Liwei. With every step, my heart sank further into despair. I could barely breathe through the panic which gripped me, but my desperate need to find him drove me on.

Her muffled sobs pierced my daze. "Prince Liwei is powerful and strong. Maybe he escaped. Or he might be injured, and unable to find us." My voice rang hollow and my words, false. He would not have abandoned us while there was life in him yet.

She nodded, hiccupping from her distress as she grasped at my weak straw of comfort. "Thank you for rescuing me. But I wouldn't be able to bear it if Prince Liwei was in danger or . . . or hurt." Her voice broke as tears welled in her eyes once more.

A flash of irritation struck me, my nerves already scraped raw. I did not want to play nursemaid at this moment, I wanted to *find* him. How could I track Liwei through her cries? If any enemies were hunting us, we would already be captured or dead.

Yet I stifled the impulse to snap at her, slipping an arm around her shoulders and drawing her close instead.

"We'll find him," I told her. A promise to us both.

It seemed to calm her as her brown orbs locked onto mine. "I recognize you now. You were Prince Liwei's companion. We met the day of his banquet."

"Yes. In the pavilion." A longing clutched me for those days long past and the joy that had filled my heart then.

She sighed. "You were kind. As you are now."

I fell silent as shame crept up from the pit of my stomach, rising to my face. No, I had not been kind—not now and not then. I had not realized who she was the first time. And after, I had not wanted to learn more about her, perhaps afraid of discovering what I knew now—that Princess Fengmei *would* be a good match for Liwei. It would have been far easier if I could have disliked her.

"Are His Highness and you good friends?" she asked.

My gaze slid from hers, under the pretext of examining our surroundings. "Yes, we are." A half answer, as Teacher Daoming would have chided me.

When she stiffened, so did I, afraid that she might ask me something which would force me to lie. As she raised her head from my shoulder, she pointed at the belt encircling my waist. "Why is that glowing?"

The Sky Drop Tassel. The once clear gem shone bright red, pulsing with a strange energy. I forced myself to breathe deeply, to rein in the terror which surged in me anew. Liwei was in danger and yet, it also meant I could find him now.

I pulled the princess to a thicket of trees. "Wait here. Keep hidden. Try not to make a sound. I'll come back as soon as I can. If I don't return by dawn, head north till you're outside the forest—that way," I pointed, in case she wasn't sure. "You have your magic again. Shield yourself and attack anyone who tries to harm you. Once outside, summon a cloud to take you home."

I fumbled in my belt, drawing out a dagger and passing it to her. She took it without a word, her grip loose and uncertain.

"Wrap your fingers tight around the hilt," I instructed her. "Blade facing away from you and tilted up. If you must strike, do not hesitate."

Her eyes were wide with fright as she nodded. Guilt struck me at leaving her, but I was running out of time. As I left, I swung around once to make sure she was hidden from sight, before sprinting away until my legs burned like fire.

I followed the tug of the Sky Drop Tassel to a narrow opening in the foothills of a mountain. Without a care for the perils within, I slipped inside. Pitch dark, the glowing red gem by my waist cast a menacing light upon the walls. The dank air was stale, thick with mold and rot; I gagged when it filled my lungs. As I turned a sharp corner, I stumbled over the uneven ground, scraping my palms as I fell.

Voices filtered through, from a distance away. I crouched low, crawling along the narrow path toward the sound, moving faster when I sighted light ahead. The passage opened to a wide ledge, which I clambered upon, staring into the large chamber below.

My heart lurched. There was Liwei upon a chair, shackled with the same manacles used to restrain Princess Fengmei. Blood flowed from his matted hair, trickling onto his face. A deep gash ran across his brow, dark bruises blossoming over one cheek. His aura was somehow diminished, flickering in an erratic rhythm. Yet he held his head high, as though he sat on a throne instead of bound in chains. I searched his guards, relieved to find no trace of the strange archer in their midst—he alone, would have been a formidable opponent. Had he been slain by the Celestial soldiers before they fell?

One aura sprang out to me, far stronger than the rest—strong and earthy, jangling and discordant. Not from the soldiers, as far as I could tell, instead emanating from the lady who stood before Liwei. Her upturned eyes glittered a rich shade of bronze and while the lower half of her face was covered by a sheer veil, her skin was as fair as new snow. Crimson peonies were embroidered on her vermilion dress, unfurling their silken petals to reveal bright gold stamens. A cluster of camellias was tucked into her sash. As I crouched in the ledge above, I caught a whiff of a floral fragrance, cloyingly sweet with the barest hint of decay.

"I used a bird to snare a dragon." Her voice was thick with satisfaction. "After all the tales of your prowess, I'm disappointed at how easily you fell into my trap, Your Highness."

Liwei's jaw clenched, his muscles straining as though he was grappling with some unseen foe. "What are these chains?" he ground out at last.

"A gift from the Demon Realm. Forged with metal from the mortal world, using the arts forbidden by your father." As she watched his struggles, she said in a bored tone, "Try all you want, but your magic is useless as long as these are on you."

"Lady Hualing, why do this? Why ally yourself with the Demon Realm?" Liwei demanded.

Lady Hualing, the deposed Flower Immortal? I thought she had left the forest or vanished through some foul play. Never did I imagine her living in these dark caves.

"You were one of the greatest immortals of our kingdom

until you chose to live in seclusion. Do you truly wish to betray the Immortal Realm?" Liwei continued, his voice calm despite his peril. Perhaps he still hoped to sway her with reason.

She laughed then, a bitter and joyless sound. "*Me* betray the *kingdom*? Did you think I *chose* this life? Let me tell you the real story, little princeling. Long ago, your father and I met in this forest. He was newly wed to your mother, though that did not stop him from courting me."

Liwei jerked up from his chair, but two guards dragged him back down, clamping their palms on his shoulders.

She did not appear to notice, lost in her memories. "Whenever he could get away, he came here. He offered me a palace in the Celestial Kingdom. I refused. I was no lowly courtier grateful for his favor, but one of the most illustrious deities in the realm." A softness slipped into her face. "One spring evening when the peonies were in bloom, he made a vow to me. That once he grew powerful enough to risk angering the Phoenix Kingdom, he would wed me, raising me to the same rank as the empress."

Liwei shook his head, the blood from his wound streaking across his cheek. "My father would never have made such a reckless promise."

"Those in love often make promises they can't keep," she snarled. "When word reached your mother's ears, she paid me a visit, spitting her threats and venom. Before she left, she gave me a gift." The light in the cavern flickered as Lady Hualing lifted her veil.

In the classic oval of her face, her full lips were a vibrant red, her nose delicately arched. The thin faded scars, one across each cheek, puzzled me—yet so slight they were barely noticeable.

The veil dropped once more. "The scars left by the Phoenix Talons can never be healed. I must live with these hideous marks, forever."

I flinched, recalling those sharp gold sheaths covering the empress's fingers which might so easily rake through flesh and bone. But despite what Lady Hualing thought, she was beautiful still. It was the viciousness in her expression that turned my stomach.

"There must be an explanation. What if it was a spirit, taking on my mother's appearance?" Liwei protested.

"You ignorant child. Who else wears the Phoenix Talons? Who else had I threatened, isolated as I was?" she sneered. "Worse still, your father, the faithless coward, abandoned me. In one stroke I was robbed of my beauty, betrayed by my love, stripped of my title. Of all I cherished most. Since then, my life has been a misery, steeped in wretchedness and regret."

As she stretched out her fingers to caress Liwei's cheek, he recoiled from her, as far back as his captors would allow. "So, it is only fitting that I seize from my tormentors the one thing they prize above all. You, their son. The person most loved, by those I most hate."

"Lady Hualing, consider carefully what you do. This is treason at the highest level. You will be an outcast from the Immortal Realm, hunted by Celestials and our allies alike. They will descend upon this place and—"

Her laughter was shrill and grating. And when she stopped, her smile was that of a sated fox. "I'm no fool, Your Highness. I will not be here when they come. Once I present your lifeforce to the Demon King, I will earn his eternal gratitude. A bridal gift, if you wish to call it so. Maybe then he can defeat your accursed parents, and when he sits on the Celestial Throne it will be I who is beside him. Finally, the empress," she gloated, lifting a ring set with an oval amethyst that glowed with malevolent light.

The sight of it stirred a deep revulsion in me, inexplicable and strange. And what did she mean about Liwei's lifeforce?

He showed not a trace of fear. "Lady Hualing, a grave injustice was done to you. Release me and I give you my word, I will investigate this matter. Any wrong done to you will be righted. Don't fall for the Demon King's promises. His treachery is boundless."

"As is that of your parents," she hissed, pressing the ring to his forehead.

The cords in Liwei's neck strained as his face clenched in agony. The amethyst flared with a shimmer of gold, just before his eyelids fluttered shut like the wings of a trapped moth.

Something snapped inside me. I did not think. Consumed by rage, my hands moved of their own volition, releasing a fiery arrow which plunged into Lady Hualing's arm. She shrieked, snatching her hand from Liwei as the guards rushed to her aid. I aimed an arrow at Liwei's manacles, just as how I had shot them from the princess. But I was trembling too much from rage and instead, it struck the chain between his wrists. They snapped apart, Liwei slumping to the ground. He stirred then, my heart leaping as his eyes opened and fixed upon me, wide with shock and luminous with . . . some emotion I could not read. Before he could move, the guards surrounded him swiftly, shields gleaming over them. A coldness engulfed me, fear mingling with rage as I shot arrow after arrow at them—until their barriers broke and they fell like stalks of rice at harvesttime. Bolts of magic and arrows hurtled toward me now, as I flung myself against the stone floor, rolling to safety. I was tiring, rapidly; I had to conserve my energy. My mind raced, trying to think of some way to distract Lady Hualing and her guards below, so I could snatch Liwei and make our escape. But then, the air pulsed with magic, the rich scent of earth and metal suffusing my nostrils. A brilliant green moss crept over the ledge, spreading like spilled water—its thorny roots sinking deep, cracks streaking across the stone. I lurched up, backing away, shielding myself—a heartbeat before the ledge shattered.

I crashed through the air, falling through nothingness. Liwei's cry pierced my ears, uttering my name with wrenching desperation. Below, Lady Hualing flicked her hand toward me, dispelling my shield. No longer protected, my feet slammed against the rough cavern floor, my knees giving way as I tumbled over. Rolling to my side, I sprang to my feet as the soldiers closed around me. Fewer now, yet more than I could take on without getting hurt. I cursed my recklessness which had led to discovery. Better by far to have remained hidden, to pick them off unaware. But what could I have done with Liwei in such danger? As the guards thrust their spears at me, I hauled my energy—unleashing a gale which flung Lady Hualing and her soldiers against the rock walls.

Spinning around, I rushed to Liwei, but the soldiers—those remaining—scrambled to close around him, some holding him fast. Lady Hualing stalked closer to me, jeweled hairpins dangling askew from her coiled hair. Her veil was torn away, the scars now vivid against the pale fury of her skin.

"Who are you?" Her tone was thick with menace.

I drew my bow in reply, aiming a bolt of flame at her.

"Stop, or he dies," she said flatly, gesturing to the soldier beside her who pressed the tip of her spear against Liwei's neck.

At once, I forced my fingers to loosen, the flaming arrow vanishing.

Lady Hualing's gaze fixed on the Phoenix Fire Bow, before sliding to my face. "Ah . . . the archer. The First Archer, is that what they call you? I have heard of your accomplishments." She sounded curious. Intrigued, even. "A pity that your abilities are wasted in the service of the Celestial Kingdom."

"Who told you about me?" I was not conceited enough to believe that my fame had spread to this remote place.

She did not answer, merely tapping her chin, seemingly lost in thought. "Your zeal in protecting the Crown Prince is admirable, to venture here where nothing but death awaits you. Forget him. Join us against the Celestial Kingdom. The Demon Realm would reward you well. Any position, any honor would be yours to demand."

"Never." My refusal burst out, though I cursed myself in the next instant for revealing myself so. A wiser course would have been to feign interest in her offer and gain her trust, to have a hope of escaping. But this had always been my weakness, my inability to think clearly when my heart was clouded.

A slow smile spread across her lips. "Oh, this is more than just loyalty and duty, isn't it?" she breathed in seeming delight. "A soldier in love with a royal? What could you possibly offer the Celestial Crown Prince, except your life in his service?"

"You know nothing," Liwei bit out. "Xingyin, you must leave. Now." He spoke the last words as a plea, urgency throbbing in his voice.

But if I left, he would die. Alone.

"Ah, Your Highness. It appears your reputation is not quite as honorable as we believed," Lady Hualing sneered. "Dallying with a commoner whom you could never hope to marry. You are your father's son indeed, plucking flowers for your own pleasure and discarding them once they wilt."

She swung to me, her gaze intent and searching. "Do you know he is betrothed? To one of royal blood, with beauty, power, and charm. A prize he would risk his life to rescue—just as *you* are sacrificing yourself to save *him*."

Each word about Princess Fengmei stabbed me, just as on the night of their betrothal. I had believed myself above such feelings, yet if they could be resurrected so easily . . . would I ever be free? A terrible thought slid into me, that there was some truth to her vicious words. That I had come here to save Liwei, but would accomplish nothing except my death. And if I died, what would happen to my mother? She would never learn of my miserable fate, whiling eternity away in her futile wait—first for my father, and then for me. Why did I sacrifice everything for the one who had broken with me, who perhaps never really loved me?

It was the gleam in her eyes that gave me pause. She had goaded me well, giving voice to my cruelest thoughts—those which taunted me in the deep of night. She wanted to make me jealous, to make me doubt my own worth. To allow hatred to slither in and sink its claws into my heart. I inhaled a deep breath, trying to gather myself. I needed to hold her interest, to gain time to strike or provoke her into rashness. I dared not have her attention return to Liwei again, and the vile things she had planned for him.

"Yes, we were together once," I admitted haltingly. "Now His Highness and I have gone our separate ways."

"Was it your choice, or his?" Her lips curved like she already knew the answer.

I looked away, her question cutting deeper than I expected.

"Life would be preferable without love," Lady Hualing said with feeling, as though I were her trusted friend. As though we were of the same mind.

Her words resonated through me. Was closing one's heart to love—all love—the only way to contentment? Had I not imagined so myself, during those long months of misery? Indeed, my darkest moments were when I had left my loved ones. And yet . . . the happiest times of my life had been with them, too. But I would not disagree with her. She seemed to believe there was a connection between us. Did she see a part of herself in me? I shuddered at the idea, although now I would tread cautiously, to cultivate this illusion to better catch her unaware.

"Perhaps you are right." I said, letting a hardness edge my voice. "Love has not served me well."

"Nor I." Lady Hualing's chest heaved. "I did not ask for the emperor's love, but he beguiled me with false promises until I returned his affection. When I was hurt and frightened, I yearned for his comfort. He never came back. Because of him, I lost everything, even the happiness I had before. I would rather he had *died* than hurt me so. All I want now is to repay those who brought me low."

I recoiled inwardly from the vehemence in her words. She had not uttered her curse in the heat of anger, but as a fervent wish wrung from the depths of her heart.

"They will never change their minds," Lady Hualing continued, her tone low and intimate. "The Celestial royals are proud, cold and unyielding. Their love, once lost, can never be regained. Ask yourself, *why* do you do this? Just so he can cherish your memory after he marries his princess? Weep a tear over your grave? Such paltry thanks for so great a sacrifice. Don't throw your life away."

It hit me then, she believed our situations similar. That I, too, had been snared by a hopeless love; that I, too, had been cast aside—by the son of her cruel lover, no less. And that my actions were a desperate bid to regain what I had lost.

My teeth sank into my lip, biting down harder until a warmth of salt and iron gushed into my mouth. Like her, I had not sought love. My life had been full without it. Yet it had crept up on me, infiltrating my senses like a subtle scent—until I found beauty in a fallen blossom and delight in a thunderstorm. However, the joy it gave me, I repaid tenfold through my sorrow. Even when I believed my heart healed, the scars remained, reopening with no more than a touch from his hand.

Why did I do this? Her question echoed through me again. I had known the dangers when I followed Liwei's trail here, but not once did I hesitate. My only thought had been to come to his aid. My only fear had been for his safety. But she was wrong; I was not trying to win him back. Was it for friendship, as I had told myself? Or out of honor, to repay the debt of his kindness? The answer eluded me as it lurked on the fringes of my mind.

I looked up, my eyes colliding into Liwei's—and it struck me then with the force of a thunderbolt. What I had been struggling to understand. What I had fought so hard against before. What I had been afraid of knowing because its revelation might be my undoing. Such proud words I had spoken to him before, of honor and duty. Lies, all lies.

I was still in love with Liwei.

All this time I kept telling myself that my feelings for him were a remnant of the past, a lingering attraction. My pride did not let me cling to him, yet I did not want to let him go. I had told him to forget us, when I could do no such thing myself. Each time he came, a secret part of me rejoiced in knowing he still cared. My coldness to him was but a mask to hide my feelings, even from myself—that I loved him still and that I had never stopped.

I stepped closer to Liwei, almost trembling now. The faces of the soldiers blurred into the background; all I saw was him. With a wrench, I unearthed the secrets buried deep in my heart. If I did not tell him now, I might never have the chance again.

"I love you." Tears sprang into my eyes. These I would not conceal or blink away. "I loved you then. I love you still. I tried to forget you, to destroy my feelings. But I failed."

Something heavy loosened in my chest and fell away, a burden I had not realized I bore till now. Gazing at him, I was lost for a moment in our past. Through the stagnant air of this putrid cavern, I could almost smell the sweet scent of peach blossoms.

I yanked myself back to the present, to the danger. Liwei's eyes were fixed on mine, his lips parted to speak—but I shook my head in warning. Lady Hualing appeared transfixed, her face alight with anticipation. Was this not what she had accused me of? Did she hope Liwei might reject me? That I would join her, bitter and distraught? It would satisfy her craving for revenge to have me turn on Liwei—validating all she had done, all she had become, because of her own tainted love.

I would give her no satisfaction today. I did not want to end up like her, engulfed in spite and hungering for something I could not have . . . until it destroyed me. Those nights when my pain was at its sharpest, it would have been so easy to slide into resentment and hatred. Yet as much as I loved him, I loved myself more. And as I was discovering, there was no end to love— it was something which grew and renewed endlessly, expanding to encompass each new horizon. Family. Friends. And other lovers, too—none of them the same—yet each precious in their own way.

I spoke to Liwei, raising my voice to be heard. "I have no regrets. I will always cherish what we had together. I do not resent your happiness with another, and I could *never* wish for your death." This was the moment, there might not be another. My insides writhed as I met Lady Hualing's furious stare. "I am *not* like you."

"You stupid, sentimental fool." Bright red spots blazed from Lady Hualing's cheeks as her eyes squeezed into slits. She was shaking now, was it with disappointment or rage?

Quick as a flash, I drew my bow, flame streaking through my fingers. It struck her chest with blinding light as she staggered back—the acrid smell of burnt silk and flesh throttling the air. But then her magic surged out in a glittering stream, extinguishing the fire with a hiss. The soldiers lunged at me, their weapons gleaming in the torchlight. I ducked, whirling aside, another arrow springing from my fingers—only to strike the shield that sprang up around Lady Hualing now. As she flicked her fingers, an earthy smell wafted forth like rotting leaves in a forest. Thick vines shot out, coiling tight around my waist and slamming me against the ground. Blood gushed from my temple as my bow was snatched from me. Sprawled on the ground, I tried to catch my breath as the beaded tip of a brocade slipper prodded my face up. Lady Hualing peered down at me, her lips curled in a smirk, a charred rip in her robe where my arrow had struck—though the skin beneath was smooth, already healed over.

She was strong. I had failed. And now, she was livid.

"How *noble* you are, loving him yet releasing him to another. Cherishing your past and forgiving the pain. Are you so self-sacrificing to risk yourself for a love that is no longer yours?" she jeered, making a mockery of my confession. "Let's see how your principles fare when you're truly tested."

A guard grabbed my arm and hauled me to my feet. Two others dragged Liwei to where I stood. Black metal bands still encircled his wrists, binding his powers—and how I cursed missing my earlier shot. Liwei's gaze never left mine. Seemingly oblivious to our peril, they glowed with all the warmth and tenderness I remembered.

"You risked your life for him, but will he do the same for you?" Her tone reeked with scorn.

"Let her go. I will not fight you," Liwei said, without a moment's hesitation.

A fierce joy sang in my veins. Even as I dreaded what would come after, that his declaration would only infuriate her more.

Her mouth stretched into a mirthless smile. "Let's have some entertainment tonight. A fight. To the death. Between you two. If you win, First Archer—you'll walk free. I'll even let you keep your bow." The sweetness of her tone jarred with the abhorrent meaning of her words.

I could not have heard her right. She did not mean it; she *could* not. For Liwei and me . . . to kill the other to save ourselves? Was this some twisted jest to frighten us? But as I stared at her face—so lovely and pitiless—a shiver rippled along the length of my spine.

This was no game.

26

Liwei's eyes blazed. "I will not fight you, Xingyin. Please . . . go."

I shook my head. I would not abandon him to certain death, not even to save myself.

Lady Hualing sighed. "Refuse to fight and you'll both be killed. A most romantic end, upholding all your honorable principles, though a reckless waste."

A hopeless despair settled over me as I met Liwei's grim yet resolute gaze. Our hands remained slack by our sides in defiance of her command. We would not be her pawns in this sick game. Nor would I go quietly; I would fight until my energy was drained, until our final breaths were spent. Only then, could she tear her bloodied victory from us.

Her tongue clacked against the roof of her mouth. "How disappointing. I had hoped for more spirited entertainment. However, there are ways to ensure your cooperation." Her shield gleamed as she stepped closer to Liwei, seizing his chin between her fingers, her nails cutting into his skin.

He recoiled, horror dawning over his face. Yet she held him fast, her soldiers gripping his arms tighter behind his back.

"Liwei!" I lunged toward him, trying to shove my way through the guards who grabbed me and flung me back.

Lady Hualing's pupils glinted as shards of topaz. A recollection emerged, something Liwei had told me once of the Mind Talents: *Their eyes, which glitter like cut stones.*

Fear plunged through me, trailed by doubt. I refused to believe it, I dared not. Lady Hualing was of the Celestial Kingdom, not the Demon Realm, the Cloud Wall or wherever that place was. Once, the Flower Immortal, her Talent had to be of the Earth, not the Mind. I had seen it myself with the creeping moss and those monstrous vines. Impossible, that she should know the forbidden arts. And even if she did, surely the emperor would have sealed them from her. But what if the emperor did not know? What if she had disappeared before such magic was banned?

Beads of sweat gleamed on Liwei's skin. Still, Lady Hualing did not release her hold. I could not help recalling that she was one of the most powerful immortals in the realm. And even if Liwei's magic was not bound, he had been weakened by the battle, and the amethyst ring. If she was trying to compel him, she would fail, I tried to assure myself. Liwei was strong, too. He would not surrender, he would fight—

But when Lady Hualing and her guards released him, I no longer knew him. Something vital in him had been lost. My insides shriveled as I stared into his eyes—worse than a stranger's, they were as cold as his father's. His face was blank as he stood unmoving, even when a guard shoved a sword into his hand. Someone passed me another, my fingers closing reflexively around its hilt.

As Lady Hualing leaned toward me, I gagged as the smell of decaying flowers crowded my nostrils. "Do you regret spurning my offer? A final warning: don't be so foolish as to throw your life away for him. He will not appreciate it; the men of his family have hearts of stone."

I did not hesitate, leaping forward to thrust my sword at her. As it crashed against her shield, pain coursed through my arm. I raised it again—better to go down fighting this way—but the soldiers shoved me aside, another kicking the back of my knees as I slumped to the ground.

Lady Hualing crouched down as she brushed an icy knuckle down my cheek. I flinched, rearing away. "Don't forget, *you* still have your powers." She spoke in an intimate whisper. "If you let him kill you . . . well, his life is forfeit regardless. But if he dies, you live."

Something splintered inside me. An impossible choice, whether to die in a futile sacrifice or to kill Liwei to save myself. More than just wanting Liwei dead, she wanted *me* to kill him. Did she take a sadistic pleasure in tormenting her enemy's child? Did she relish the thought of me living in misery and regret, as she had done? Or was this to prove me wrong? That despite my claim, she and I were not so different after all   that the same viciousness in her heart lurked in mine.

Oh, I had baited her too well and now, we both would pay.

Lady Hualing clapped, the hollow sound ringing in the cavern. As though it was a signal, Liwei's body jerked, then he stalked toward me. With his sword in his hand, he circled me—in a cruel parody of the many times he had challenged me in play.

I could not move, unable to look away from his dead gaze. Even now, I did not believe he could harm me. Although I, myself, was almost compelled before in the Eastern Sea, and had seen what a sliver of such power could do.

He charged, swift as lightning. Stunned, I threw up my sword—a second too late as his blade slashed my cheek. Blood trickled from the stinging gash, yet it was nothing to the agony within. It was not that he looked at me with hatred, but with utter indifference.

Silver flashed, hard and bright. My body moved of its own volition, flinging my arm up, our blades clanging together. He bore down relentlessly as I staggered beneath the force of his blow, digging my heels into the ground. In a sudden feint, he whirled to the side. I reeled forward as he swept his sword across the scales of my armor, thrusting it deep into my shoulder. Cold iron sank through my flesh, scraping bone. With a smooth tug of his arm, his blade slid from me with a moist sucking sound. A gasp was torn from my lungs as I pressed my palm to the gaping wound, blood gushing between my fingers. Anger surged through me now—misplaced though it was—as I lunged at him, my sword piercing his armor, driving into his side. I yanked it out at once, before it went too deep, shame and remorse searing me . . . along with the horror that he did not even flinch.

Our blades clashed. Again, and again. I held back each time, though he showed no such restraint. Yet we were more closely matched than I anticipated. He had been the better swordsman, but I had the benefit of a soldier's training. I was quick, he was strong. My strikes were deft, he was ruthless. Magic would have tipped the scales, except his was bound. And I found myself unwilling to draw my own against him. A slender distinction, but to use my powers on him now felt akin to execution. Unfair, almost. My mind screamed what use was such honor, even as my heart whispered that it was *not* Liwei who attacked me so pitilessly—just the husk of his body, dancing to another's tune. He was my opponent, but he was not my enemy. And though I wanted to win, I could not kill him. It was not honor alone which restrained me but a sense of self-preservation, knowing that slaying the one I loved would destroy me, too. I would never recover, not for all eternity. Not even if I found my way home.

My foot caught on a loose rock and I stumbled. In a flash, the point of his sword pressed against the hollow of my neck. He stilled, a muscle clenching in his cheek. Was he struggling against Lady Hualing's control? I glanced at her—dazzling light pouring from her eyes, her brow coated in a sheen of sweat. Was she tiring? Hope flared in me, only to be extinguished when Liwei's hand trembled—a moment before his sword dipped and drove through my chest. I gasped, my legs buckling as I collapsed onto the stone floor, sinking into a puddle of my still-warm blood.

Darkness beckoned, a merciful void without the pain blossoming through my body, only eclipsed by the agony of knowing that it was *he* who had done this. A forgotten memory flared. My mother's arms, lifting me up from where I had fallen, her thumb brushing the tears from my cheek. How my scraped flesh had stung—my first real injury—until her cool touch and soft murmurs soothed it away.

This would not be the end.

My eyes flew open. I reached for a precious fragment of my power, sealing my wound. The healers would have cringed at my crude work, at the scar which would remain—but the pain subsided and the bleeding staunched. My mind cleared a little as I staggered to my feet, searching Liwei's face for the faintest sign of recognition. Yet there was nothing; not a flicker of love, not a speck of remorse. And in that moment, something snapped into place for me: I would not throw my life away. I would not be defeated by myself or another. I would fight to live, and while I lived there would be hope. To grasp at a chance of our survival, I would risk everything. Even our lives.

My energy was dwindling. I seized what I could, the air shimmering as I hurled my magic at Liwei. Coils of air wrapped around his body—knocking him to the ground—sealing his ears, nose, mouth, and pressing his eyelids shut. Covering every inch of his skin until he could do nothing except lay there, writhing like a trapped beast. If his powers had not been constrained, my binds could never have held him so.

Lady Hualing's delighted laugh rang through my ears. Was this not the spectacle she had forced us to perform? Had she dreamed of inflicting such torment on her own faithless lover?

Trapped in the cocoon of air I buried him in, Liwei was paler than snow. I gagged, fighting the urge to release him. Yet I hardened myself; I could not stop now. My power flowed, settling over every pore of his body until he glittered with a thousand silver lights like he was cloaked in stardust. My heart ripped from me could not have hurt more; pain had lost all meaning.

His struggles weakened until his body went limp, the steady thrum of his aura fading until I could no longer sense it. Only then did I stop. My eyes were dry, though I had wept a river inside. How wretched I was, cracked and ripped and gouged, yet I refused to shatter. Sinking onto the ground, my fingers sought Liwei's cold hand, pressing our palms together.

"I'm sorry." A ragged whisper. "Forgive me."

Loud clapping rang through the cavern, jarring amid my despair. It hit me then—the vile, unspeakable thing I had done. Lady Hualing wanted to hurt those who had wronged her, but I had struck down the one I still loved. In the cold light of victory, were my reasons hollow? Glazing my selfish desire to live?

My control broke. I fell away from him as though scalded; I did not deserve to touch him. Not after this, not after what I had done. My arms clasped tight around myself as I retched until my stomach clenched in protest. Sobs ripped from my throat—ugly and raw—echoing through the terrible silence.

But it was not over. I could not let all this be in vain. Gathering the remnants of my composure, I staggered to my feet. "My bow," I said flatly to Lady Hualing.

She inclined her head. "I gave you my word. And my offer still stands. The Demon King would be pleased to have you by his side. A good mind, a strong arm and will. Someone who does what needs to be done, when the time calls for it."

I flinched from her praise, hoping she would take it for exhaustion rather than revulsion. I had never imagined myself bloodthirsty, but I would have killed her now and rejoiced. Yet, she had spoken no lies. My hands were stained with Liwei's blood; it had been my choice to hurt him.

"You were right," I said, trying to lull her into a sense of false security. "There is no sense in dying for principles alone. And I will consider your offer, only because the Celestial Kingdom will no longer welcome me after this."

When Lady Hualing nodded, a guard thrust the Phoenix Fire Bow at me. As I clutched it, a memory flashed through me—of the first time I had held it in the peach blossom forest. A lifetime ago, when I had still been whole. I turned away, stumbling toward him once more. Lifeless and shackled, he was still every inch the regal prince. How I prayed our ordeal was almost over.

"Free him." I pointed at his manacles. The sight of them

enraged me past bearing. I would do it myself, except I did not want to rouse her suspicions.

"Why?" she asked.

I looked her full in the face. "I have done what you wished, though it hurt me greatly. Prince Liwei should be laid to rest with all the ceremony he deserves. I will do him the final service of returning his body to his parents, but I will not bring him fettered like a slave. Besides, do you want this to fall into the hands of the Celestial Kingdom?" I gestured at the metal encircling his wrists.

When she did not speak, I frowned. "Did you *not* want Their Celestial Majesties to know what you did to their son?"

"What *you* did, you mean," she taunted me with exquisite cruelty. "It would suit me well if you delivered his body to them. I only wish I were there to see it."

She jerked her head at a soldier who hurried forward. He pressed something against Liwei's manacles, which fell away, clattering onto the ground. At once, I dragged Liwei's arm across my shoulders to haul him away.

"Wait." Lady Hualing drew closer, the amethyst ring glowing on her finger. "I must drain his lifeforce as it's fading fast. It will be quicker now, without those chains."

My breathing quickened, I fought for calm. I would not let her defile him further. As she reached for him, I grasped my energy, bracing for release—but the air warmed, a powerful force hurling Lady Hualing away. She slammed against the stone wall, her shield winking out as bands of fire bound her. I swung around to find Liwei, staggering to his feet, the tip of his blade trailing on the ground. As three soldiers charged at him, he swung his sword in a wide arc, the blow sending them flying.

A guard bolted toward me with his spear outstretched, whom I dispatched with a quick arrow to his chest.

I was shaking, my heart ablaze. It had been nothing more than a wild guess, pieced together from the little I knew. In the Eastern Sea, I had sealed my hearing to fight Governor Renyu's compulsion—but his charm was of the voice alone and that would not have worked here. Yet the governor had spoken of death being the only release from those caught in the throes of such power. And so, to break Lady Hualing's control over Liwei, I had sealed off every sense he possessed—bringing him to the brink of death itself. Though if I had failed, he would have died or killed me. And we would have perished for nothing.

When I held his hand after, I had channeled my energy into him. As much as I could muster without arousing suspicion. I was no healer and all I could do then was pray it would suffice. I could not have risked his life just to save my own. But I had done it, to save us both.

I had hoped, under the guise of death, Lady Hualing would have let me take him away. And it had almost worked. But I gloated too soon; we were not out of danger yet. Too late did I sense her gathering power. In one strike, Lady Hualing dispelled her binds as vines shot out, coiling around Liwei and me—squeezing the breath from my chest, strangling my limbs to numbness. Before I could despair, Liwei's magic rippled across us, burning away the plants.

Lady Hualing raised her hands again. The damp scent of earth thickened as the air gleamed with her magic. I flung up a barrier as Liwei threw his might behind mine. I could not fight her alone, yet together, we stood a chance. Her energy crackled when it struck, transforming into endless vines which shone with a sinister light as they writhed against our shield. Sweat dripped from my brow as I tried not to imagine what they sought with such ravenous hunger.

My struggles were not lost on her. Lady Hualing's red lips curved upward as the crushing pressure on our shield intensified. The tendrils curled with renewed vigor. Time was not on our side; I was close to exhaustion, and Liwei's strength must be ebbing, too. Soon, we would fall—either from fatigue or her malevolent spell, or the soldiers closing around us, their faces alight with anticipation.

No, I would not relinquish our hard-won lives so easily. A plan formed—mad and reckless—yet the faintest glimmer of hope was preferable to certain death. My eyes met Liwei's, as I mouthed a silent instruction for him to hold the shield steady. He nodded, straining as he bore the full weight of our barrier now. I scraped the shreds of my energy into a glowing orb no larger than a marble, flinging it out to strike Liwei's shield from within. It cracked, though the web of vines held it fast. I clenched my teeth, a hiss of breath escaping my lips. Teacher Daoming's stern warning about not draining my power pounded in my mind, but I could not stop. My head throbbed as I wrung the final flecks of light from my core and hurled them out in a gust of wind.

Our shield shattered, the force flinging Lady Hualing's vines away—right onto her body, the fleeing soldiers, the ceiling and walls, where they clung as though rooted. Cracks streaked through the cavern, the stone groaning and trembling.

I crumpled onto the ground, as hollow as a paper lantern trampled by a careless foot. I was shivering, not from the chill in the cave, but from the ice spreading through my limbs. My eyelids were heavy, yearning to shut, to surrender to the darkness spreading through my body. Everything took on a hazy sheen, until I no longer knew whether I was still alive or trapped in an endless dream.

Lights swirled, golden bright—Liwei's magic flowing into my broken body. They sank into the black yet did not vanish, like sunlight glinting over the night sea. The lights streamed into the core of my lifeforce, buried deep within my head—wringing forth a single fleck of silver, the last of my energy. The cold within me thawed, my strength returning as I awoke to find Liwei's fingers entwined with mine as we lay upon the ground.

Lady Hualing's eyes were glassy, her mouth opened in a soundless scream. Her body convulsed as the vines coiled around her in a strangling hold. Tighter and tighter they wound, tearing the silk of her dress, squeezing her bulging flesh until it turned crimson and purple. I choked down my bile as I watched her struggles weaken, the camellias at her waist wilt and droop their once proud heads, the silk peonies on her gown brown and fray. The light faded from her pupils, the bitterness receding from her face . . . until just her cold beauty remained.

I could have lain there until the moon waxed and waned, unable to summon the strength to rise. But the cavern shuddered with more force than before. Rocks tumbled from above as Liwei dragged me to my feet, my muscles straining as we raced toward the entrance. A chunk of stone struck my back, knocking me to the ground. Clouds of dust descended as the ceiling fractured, crashing down—just as Liwei summoned a gale that flung us through the opening, the cave collapsing behind us with a deafening roar.

The hard ground offered scant relief to my battered body. I could not move, lying in the dirt as though pinned down. One ragged breath, and then another slipped from my lungs. Liwei's eyes were open, gazing into mine. As the color returned to his face, my fear receded. He reached out to me then, his palm cupping my cheek, wet with tears that had fallen unnoticed.

I smiled, content to feel his warmth. I had no more words; I had said everything in my heart.

The luminous glow of the moon cast a spell around the forest. In the pale light, the dead trees gleamed like polished columns of silver and jade. The fog vanished, dispersed by the night wind. Had it been cast by Lady Hualing to hide herself from the world?

Leaves rustled, branches crackling. We swung around as Princess Fengmei emerged from the woods. With a joyful cry she rushed to Liwei and threw her arms around him. His eyes darted toward me, his hand hesitating before reaching out to hold her.

I struggled to a sitting position, looking away from their reunion, though their whispers pierced my ears. Finally, Princess Fengmei touched my arm. "I hid where you told me to, until I heard a loud crash." As she scrutinized me, she pressed a fist to her mouth. "Are you all right?"

I must have been a fearsome sight, covered in blood, bruises, and grime. Yet her concern moved me. "I will be, once Your Highness gets us back to the Celestial Kingdom."

Princess Fengmei's smile faltered as she glanced at Liwei. His expression was inscrutable, but his eyes were deep pools which threatened to drown me if I stared into them for too long. Her gaze fell upon the Sky Drop Tassel by his waist. She tilted her head toward its twin, which dangled from my belt, the gem clear once more.

"A matched pair." Her voice was as soft as a breeze in a meadow.

An inexplicable urge to explain gripped me, even though she had not asked. "A gift of friendship," I said.

She did not respond, falling silent as Liwei rose and offered me his hand. I grasped it as I rocked unsteadily to my feet, fighting the urge to clutch him tighter, to revel in the feel of his skin against mine. When he helped Princess Fengmei up, I hurried ahead of them. I did not want to intrude, nor was I strong enough to withstand seeing his arm wrapped protectively around her shoulders. Not when my heart was still raw after all we had been through. After everything I had confessed, to both myself and him.

Heading north, I led the way through the trees, beyond the forest, toward the scent of lush grass and wildflowers. I inhaled deeply, relishing the freshness of the air. Princess Fengmei's magic surged forth, summoning a large cloud, which swooped down before us. I climbed upon it, eager to leave this graveyard of broken dreams. Now that it was over, pity sparked in me at the thought of Lady Hualing's fate, a tragic end to such an illustrious immortal. I recalled my mother, too, pining away for my father—living half her life in shadow, buried in memories and regret.

No, I would not choose as they had done. I would not yearn after what had been lost, impossible to regain. I would look to the days ahead, to the happiness which awaited me there . . . if only I were brave and steadfast enough to reach for it.

PART
III

27

Sunlight streamed through the crystal pillars, casting hundreds of tiny rainbows upon the carved tiles. As a cool breeze wound through the Hall of Eastern Light, the curtain of jade beads clinked gently behind the thrones. The full court was in attendance today, the weight of all their eyes upon me as I knelt on the ground. Stretching my arms out, I folded my body over, pressing my brow and palms to the floor in a formal obeisance to the Celestial Emperor and Empress.

"Rise," the emperor intoned.

Slowly, I uncoiled my legs, lifting my head to the thrones. Today, Their Celestial Majesties were resplendent in imperial yellow brocade. Lustrous pearls cascaded from the emperor's crown, while on the empress's hair rested a gold and ruby headdress shaped like the wings of a phoenix. Beside them, stood Liwei. His high-collared robe was of midnight blue brocade, embroidered with golden herons among swirling white clouds. A belt of jade links was clasped around his waist and his topknot was encased in a sapphire crown.

I searched his face, relieved to find no trace of his injuries from the Eternal Spring Forest. I had been too nervous to seek him out before. Afraid, even. In that dank cavern where death courted us both, I had laid my heart bare. While I meant every word—in the light of day without the danger looming over us—the memory of my boldness scorched me. But I had no regrets. I understood now that before I could embrace my future, I had to release myself from the binds of the past.

My gaze shifted to Wenzhi who stood by the side of the hall. He gave me a reassuring nod as I smiled, warmed by the recollection of his care since my return—commanding the healers to attend to me, bringing me rare herbs and medicines to hasten my recovery. His constant presence brought the rumors surrounding us to a fevered pitch. But after what I had just been through, I cared not what wagging tongues might say. And I could no longer claim these were mere rumors alone.

The Celestial Empress's lips were pursed like she had bitten into an unripe kumquat. While Liwei's eyes blazed so bright, I found it hard to look away. Behind me, whispers drifted in the air, my name repeated in hushed tones. I was not alone in wondering why I had been summoned today.

The Celestial Emperor spoke then. "First Archer, you have performed a great service to our kingdom. Our son would have perished without your aid, and he spoke at length of your deeds. Princess Fengmei has also expressed her gratitude for your rescue of her. We commend your courage and valor, and we thank you for your protection of our son and his betrothed."

I smiled tightly as I bowed in acknowledgment. Such gracious praise from the Celestial Emperor was rarer than the moon eclipsing the sun. Yet despite his words, his face remained cold and expressionless. If he was relieved by his son's escape or affected by Lady Hualing's death, I saw no trace of it.

"First Archer Xingyin, hear my command."

How strange it was to hear my name spoken by the emperor. My body tensed as silence shrouded the court like a blanket of snow. Something clinked, gasps swelling through the air. I looked up to find the Celestial Emperor had stretched his hand out to me, an oblong piece of blood-red jade resting upon his palm.

"I grant you the Crimson Lion Talisman." He paused, letting his words sink in. "Ask a favor for yourself and we will grant it, as long as it's in our power to do so."

An attendant rushed up to him, bearing a black lacquered tray. The emperor placed the talisman upon it, the attendant now advancing toward me with measured steps, stopping before me to offer up the tray. My hands were stiff as I took the jade, staring at it numbly. A lion was carved in its center, its bulbous eyes and curling mane chiseled with exquisite detail. From its base, hung a thick tassel of gold silk.

The emperor's voice rumbled through the chamber, yet I only caught snatches of what he said. My heart slammed until I thought it might burst forth. Had I heard him correctly? Was this really the Crimson Lion Talisman? He spoke so coolly, as though what he offered was just a common parcel of land or a chest of gold. As though this was not the fulfillment of my greatest dream, which I had all but given up on!

Glancing up, I found the emperor staring at me expectantly. Did he expect joyous weeping, or proclamations of eternal gratitude? Certainly not this yawning silence, my sudden trepidation robbing me of voice. I had only one wish . . . and it was not one which would please him.

"Do you need time to think this through?" A sharpness jutted through his tone—impatience, perhaps. Or was it a warning not to overstep myself?

Fear assailed me that I might lose this chance. The words surged up my throat, flying out in a strangled gasp, "My mother!"

A hush swept across the crowd. I drew a shaking breath, trying to steady my jangled nerves. "My wish is for Your Celestial Majesty to free my mother." I spoke slower this time, as clearly as I could.

The empress's eyes curved as a predator's claws. "Your mother? Who might that be?"

The malice in her tone gave me pause. My wish would undoubtedly incite their fury. Their Celestial Majesties would hate to appear the fool, deceived by the powerless Moon Goddess for all these years. What if I revealed all, only to have them deny my request and inflict greater punishment upon her?

I dropped to my knees again, bending my head. "Your Celestial Majesty, my mother did not ask this of me. This is all my own doing. I humbly ask for your assurance that she will not be punished for my actions, or for anything I reveal today."

"How dare you make demands of us!" the empress hissed.

The air thickened with a sudden chill. If I were a common petitioner, the emperor might have sentenced me to imprisonment—or worse—for my temerity. Yet the jade clutched in my fist reminded me that I had *earned* the right to speak today through my blood, sweat, and tears.

"Very well," the emperor said in an icy tone. "You have my word that your mother will be safe. However, *you* yourself will have no such protection should we discover that you have offended us in any way. *You* will answer for your own actions."

His threat sapped my courage. An urge to slink away gripped me, to slip into the shadows and be forgotten. Though we were parted, my mother and I were safe for now. Unharmed. Was I greedy, reaching for more than I should? But I recalled what

Wenzhi had whispered to me once, when I first stood here facing the jade thrones as I did today.

When the battle lines are drawn, advance with a clear mind.

Somehow, I had done it; I had won the talisman. Never again would I get a chance like this. I would not be a coward now, not after everything I had done to get here. A rush of emotion coursed through me as I found the words nestled deep in my heart, the ones I had whispered to myself each night before I slept, before I awakened each dawn.

"My mother is Chang'e. I am the daughter of the Moon Goddess."

The whispers began, faint rustles gathering into gasps, fervent mutterings accompanied by the nervous shuffling of feet. Liwei's eyes went wide, his jaw clenched tight, while Wenzhi's lips were drawn into a thin line. Those who knew me best, those who trusted me most, those I had kept in the dark. How betrayed they must feel by my confession.

"The *Moon Goddess*?" The empress spat each word. "If Chang'e is your mother, who is your father?"

Fear clouded my heart, like ink billowing from a brush dipped into water. My father had killed the sunbirds, her beloved kin. But my anger at her crude insinuation prodded me into raising my chin to meet her gaze, to speak with less care and more pride than I should have.

"My father is my mother's husband, the mortal archer Houyi."

The moment those words were spoken aloud, the tension knotted deep inside me for all these years unraveled. A lightness swept through me, a rush of freedom in acknowledging my parents. I had not realized the weight of this burden until now. Yet beyond my fierce relief and pride, there was no glory in the unveiling of my identity. I had been pitied before for my lack of family and connections—but in the eyes of this court, it was worse by far to be tarnished by association with those who were disgraced.

Fury mottled the empress's fair skin. Her knuckles were white, the gold sheaths on her fingers digging into the armrest of her throne.

The Celestial Emperor broke the stillness first. "Explain yourself." His tone was grim and the way he looked at me . . . it reminded me of the moment when Liwei plunged his sword through my chest.

All knew the tale of the ten sunbirds. But none knew the truth behind the Moon Goddess's ascension to immortality. To the hostile audience hanging on to my every word, I retold the story I had heard once before. The danger to my mother's life and mine. Her heartbreaking choice. The terror that had led her to conceal my existence. I could not help the tears pricking my eyes, when I spoke of the sorrow which had haunted my mother every day of her immortal life.

When I finished, I pressed my brow to the jade tiles again, swallowing my pride and resentment for this chance to be heard. "For all these years, my mother has been a prisoner, living in loneliness and misery. She took the elixir to save our lives. She was unaware that she had broken any rule, how could a mortal know such a thing? I plead for Your Celestial Majesties' mercy and understanding, to forgive my mother's transgression and lift her punishment. This is the favor I ask for."

I raised myself, placing my shaking palms upon my folded knees. My gaze collided with the Celestial Emperor's, utterly unmoved by my heartfelt plea.

The empress pointed a finger at me, almost convulsing with rage. "Such deceit cannot be tolerated. This family line, from Chang'e and Houyi to this . . . this *girl* is a treacherous one, riddled with lies, duplicity, ingratitude. It should be ended at once."

The glorious hope that had sprung up a moment ago, shriveled and died. Yet silence greeted the empress's words. There were no enthusiastic cries of support, only a few nodded—and for that I was grateful.

Someone strode out from the side, sinking to the floor to perform his obeisance. A courtier, I could tell, from his ceremonial hat and black robe, and the yellow jade ornament dangling from his waist sash. A high-ranking one to be positioned so close to the thrones, though I could not see his face from where he knelt in front of me.

"Your Celestial Majesty, may I offer my opinion?"

Those silken tones, the back of his profile, jostled my memory then. Where had I met this immortal before?

The emperor leaned back against his throne. "Rise, Minister Wu, and speak your mind. Your counsel is valued."

My heart plunged. *Minister Wu?* I should not have been surprised; he seemed ever entwined with my most challenging times here. This close, his aura pulsed around me, as dense and opaque as a bottomless lake.

The minister bowed again, before rising to his feet. When he swung around, I flinched from the hostility in his expression. "Your Celestial Majesty, neither Chang'e nor her daughter deserves your mercy. One stole your gift, the other deceived you in this contemptible manner. How brazenly the Moon Goddess lied to Her Celestial Majesty when we visited her before! Upon your command, I will return there and apprehend her, to be tried with her daughter for their offenses. If you allow them to go unpunished, this will set a dangerous precedent to others who will seek to take advantage of your kindness."

His malice stunned me. In my brief encounter with the minister before, he had only regarded me with bored disinterest. He had not known who I was then, but why should it matter? Did he despise my mortal heritage? Did he think me unworthy to be here? Why would he utter such vicious words, carefully crafted to inflame the emperor's suspicions and rage? *Kindness? Mercy?* I seethed. *When my mother had been imprisoned all these years just for drinking the elixir?*

"My mother is no threat to the Celestial Kingdom," I cried out, undoing all the good from my composed plea before. "She has harmed no one, she was only trying to protect me. She does not deserve such—"

"Enough." The emperor spoke evenly, yet the menace which sprang from that single word was worse than any roar.

I cursed myself for my rash outburst. If he struck me down now, none would fault him for it.

In the sudden quiet, Liwei stepped down from the dais, sweeping his robe aside as he dropped to his knees beside me. He threw me a warning glare before speaking, his voice exuding a steady calm. "Honorable Father, Mother. I owe First Archer Xingyin my life. She risked herself to come to my aid, far beyond duty and honor. If not for her, I would be dead. Princess Fengmei, a hostage still. Our kingdom would be thrown into disarray. As your dutiful son, I must remind you that because of her valiant deeds, the First Archer was granted the Crimson Lion Talisman today. A royal favor, not a sentencing."

A warmth sparked inside me. To know, that here— surrounded by hostility and condemnation—I had a friend in

him still. More than the fact I could never have spoken so elo-
quently, Liwei had risked his parents' wrath by reminding them
of their promise, something no one else would have dared to
do. It might not suffice to sway my fate, but to know he had
done this—despite his discomfiture at my revelation—moved me
deeply.

The empress glared at him so fearsomely, a less courageous
man would have slunk away. As for the expression in his father's
face—I shivered, looking away. Yet Liwei held his ground, remaining on his knees before them as humbly as any petitioner.

"This is no common favor she asks. Eternal imprisonment
cannot be withdrawn on a whim." A cunning note slipped into
the empress's voice as she added, "Moreover, the First Archer's
request is on behalf of her mother. Not *herself*, which is what
is due to the talisman bearer. She is more than fortunate if we
don't punish her for this deceit, pretending to be someone she is
not."

How could she haggle over my mother's life like it was
some trinket in the market? How dare she steal my victory—so
hard-won—and twist it into this hollow triumph? The blood I
had shed, the agony I had suffered . . . I squeezed my eyes shut,
stifling the urge to lash out again, to hurl my contempt and rage
into their arrogant and uncaring faces.

"Her Celestial Majesty is wise," Minister Wu agreed smoothly.
"If the First Archer's intentions were honorable, why did she
hide her identity? Who knows what trickery she was taught by
her devious mother, what plots lurk in her heart?"

Anger roiled in my veins. Insults to myself I could endure
better than those aimed at my mother. I swung to the minister,
my mouth opening to berate him—ill-advised, to be sure—when
footsteps clicked against the stone tiles.

It was Wenzhi, sinking down beside me. "Your Celestial Majesty, please consider the First Archer's valuable service. She has served loyally and bravely, helping us win victories which have strengthened the Celestial Kingdom. Moreover, First Archer Xingyin never outrightly deceived anyone. No one ever questioned whether she was the daughter of the goddess Chang'e and the mortal Houyi."

A few heads nodded. It was a shrewd argument, one I wished I had thought of myself.

The Celestial Emperor's robes rustled as he shifted on his throne. "General Jianyun, what is your opinion?"

I held my breath as the general made his way forward. From where I knelt, I could not see his face. As the emperor's most senior commander, the general might tilt the scales in my favor—if he chose to do so. If he was not incensed by my admission.

"Your Celestial Majesty, First Archer Xingyin's parentage is . . . unfortunate. However, she has been a valiant and exceptional recruit. More importantly, she has saved the lives of His Highness and his betrothed, preserving our alliance with the Phoenix Kingdom. Such bravery should not go unrewarded, as you have graciously determined before." He paused, allowing his words to sink in. "We should appreciate the flower, regardless of its roots."

The murmurs around the hall grew louder. I strained my ears to listen. Was it possible some were expressing surprise at my treatment? A whisper of cautious disapproval, even?

The emperor did not speak. My pulse raced as I sensed his gaze upon me, though I dared not move as my breath misted the tiles. Would General Jianyun's words outweigh Minister Wu's accusations? He had spoken well, offering Their Celestial Majesties a path to pardon me in the name of magnanimity and grace. But my insides clenched at the recollection of the emperor's *mercy*—which he had so callously dispensed to my mother, Lady Hualing, and the dragons.

"First Archer Xingyin," the emperor said finally.

I folded my body over once more, bracing myself for what would come. Trying not to think of the tortures and horrors which awaited those who had offended him.

"You are not to be blamed for the mistakes of your parents. Your merits should stand on their own. You are bequeathed the Crimson Lion Talisman for your service."

My head sprang up, hope thrumming through me, barely held in check as I eagerly awaited the emperor's next words.

"However, the favor you ask for—to free Chang'e, the Moon Goddess—will not be granted."

My fingers clenched around the jade, crumpling its tassel. What use was this now? There was nothing else I wanted from the Celestial Emperor. Though I was relieved not to be punished, there was neither respect nor gratitude in my heart. Not for this trick played upon me; my service won with false coin.

"Grant me this then, Your Celestial Majesty," I said, emboldened by resentment. "A favor for me alone. The right to earn my mother's freedom through a task of your choosing." A reckless offer, yet what did I have to lose? I would spell the terms out so clearly this time, none would doubt it again.

My behavior bordered on the insolent. Who was I to make demands of the Celestial Emperor? But instead of wrath, a cunning light gleamed in those fathomless orbs, a finger lifted to stroke his chin. "Very well, First Archer. We command that you perform one more task on your mother's behalf, to rebalance her offenses against us."

"What is the task, Your Celestial Majesty?" My words fell

out in my haste. I would journey to the ends of the earth, to the Demon Realm itself to free my mother.

The emperor did not speak, holding out something to me—a dark gray lump in his palm. I leaned closer, craning my neck. It was a seal, crafted from dull metal, with an intricately carved dragon on the top.

Wenzhi inhaled softly, a breath of wonder. I glanced at him in surprise.

"The Divine Iron Seal will release the four dragons, imprisoned in the mortal world for their grave crimes. Each possesses a pearl that is unique to them. I command you to retrieve the pearls from the dragons and bring them to me." The emperor's tone sharpened. "If they do not obey my command, use whatever means necessary. Once the four pearls are in my possession, I will pardon your mother and you will be free to return to her."

I recoiled, involuntarily. The Venerable Dragons! After learning of them in the Eastern Sea, I had no desire to challenge such great and noble creatures. Would the dragons surrender their pearls freely? If they did not, could I harden myself to do what I needed to? What the emperor expected of me?

"Are we in agreement?" His voice was edged with impatience.

I swallowed my unease, letting it settle in my stomach like congealed grease. I had asked this of the emperor, sought this chance. How could I hesitate now? Cupping my hands before me, I bowed in acceptance of his terms. The bargain was struck, as commonplace as those in the market, yet the stakes here were higher by far.

An attendant came forward, placing the seal into my outstretched palm. The metal was cool against my skin and when I dropped it into my pouch, the silk sagged from its weight.

The emperor nodded to me. A curt dismissal which I accepted gladly. Rising to my feet, I turned from the thrones and pushed my legs forward, each step heavier than the last. Staring straight ahead, I might have appeared indifferent to the rest of the court. Yet inside, I was a mess of writhing emotions which threatened to tear me apart. Of relief, that the truth was finally in the open, yet fury at having my hard-fought reward snatched away. Hope soared in me to be granted this second opportunity, even as it was tempered by a sinking dread . . . that the price for my mother's freedom might be one I could not pay.

28

In a daze, I stepped out of the Hall of Eastern Light. Several of the palace servants stared at me curiously as they polished the stone balustrades and swept the immaculate grounds. Shuxiao strode toward me as though she had been waiting for me all this time. I had told her of my summons, never imagining today's events to unfold the way they had.

"Is it true?" she asked. "About your mother?"

I blinked at her, surprised. I had not taken more than five paces from the hall. "How did you know?"

"Ah. Most royal audiences are terribly dull. When it was reported that raised voices were heard—" She grinned as she looked around. "You'd be surprised at how many found something that required urgent attention here."

Her smile faded as she pulled me aside, away from keen ears. "Is your mother really Chang'e, the Moon Goddess?"

Was there anger in her voice? Resentment? All those times she had spoken of her own family, I had not said a word, letting her believe mine were deceased. I could not blame her if she never wanted to speak to me again. It might be better for her if she did not. Coupled with the disfavor of Their Celestial Majesties, I was both an unworthy and dangerous friend to have.

"Yes," I said, bracing myself for harsh words.

Instead, she reached out and hugged me. "I'm sorry about your mother," she said, releasing me. "But I'm mad at you, too. I would never have told anyone."

There were other things I had told her in confidence, things she guessed that she kept to herself. "I couldn't say anything, not until I knew it would be safe."

She nodded, slowly. "I understand. Though I doubt your news was pleasing to Their Celestial Majesties."

"As pleasing as a zither with a snapped string." I frowned, recalling the empress's hissing rage, the emperor's . . . he had been angry at first, to be sure. Yet he had seemed oddly satisfied when I left. He should be, I told myself, getting twice the labor for a single wage.

"And now, I must somehow persuade four dragons to surrender their pearls to the emperor, if I want a hope of seeing my mother again." I could not help wondering then—if I failed, if I proved myself of no further use to the Celestial Kingdom, would the emperor's promise to me still hold? Would my mother be safe from the empress's malice? Would I, even as far away as I would be in Wenzhi's homeland?

"Why the pearls?" I asked aloud. "Isn't the Imperial Treasury overflowing with jewels?"

"All I've heard is the dragons guard their pearls well, that they're precious to them though the stories don't say *why*." Shuxiao gestured at the golden dragons which gleamed from the jade roof, a luminous orb resting securely within each jaw.

I blanched at the thought of those curved fangs sinking into my flesh. Was this a cunning plot to get me devoured,

Crimson Lion Talisman and all? Would that not solve the emperor's dilemma, in one stroke ridding himself of my troublesome presence and, yet, honoring his word? My gut twisted at the thought.

Shuxiao tapped my arm. "Are you all right?"

"I'm not sure." I was numb inside. In the span of a morning my heart had soared with hope, been sunken by fear, and now rocked in a sea of turmoil.

"Well, don't get yourself killed yet. I've always wanted to visit the moon," she told me with a laugh.

"I'm not planning to, although the dragons might decide otherwise," I said darkly.

"Then we'll have to ensure they don't."

"*We?*"

She folded her arms across her chest. "I'm coming with you."

Hope flared in me before it was abruptly doused. She was a Celestial; her loyalties lay here. She served the army to protect her family—how could I so selfishly undo her sacrifice, exposing her to the emperor's wrath?

"No, you can't abandon your position." When she started to protest, I continued, "Listen. My father slew the empress's kin. My mother defied the emperor. I'm in disfavor, too. You can't get drawn into this; you have your own family to protect. What if Their Celestial Majesties took their anger out on them?"

Her face fell. "I couldn't bear that."

"Neither could I. Because we are the same," I said somberly. "We will do things for our family—our loved ones—that we would not for ourselves. I only learned this about myself after I left my home. Some might call us fools. Those who don't understand, never will."

She did not protest, although she seemed troubled still. "You can't go alone. It's too dangerous. What if I joined you without anyone knowing?"

"I'm just asking the dragons for their pearls." I spoke with an assurance I did not feel. "Those of the Eastern Sea claim the dragons are peaceful. The worst thing they can do is refuse."

My composure wavered as the emperor's words echoed in my mind: *Use whatever means necessary.* Not a suggestion but a command.

"And you won't be alone," Wenzhi said, coming forward. How long had he been there? "I will go with you."

It was not in my nature to lean upon another but, oh, how relieved I was to hear this. He was not vulnerable like Shuxiao; he would be leaving this place soon. More than that, we had fought together so many times, I was glad he would be with me for this.

Shuxiao sucked in a breath. Recovering herself, she bowed hastily to Wenzhi.

"Lieutenant, would you excuse us?" he asked. "I have something to discuss with Xingyin."

She tilted her head at me in an unspoken question. I loved her for it, that she watched out for my needs first. Yet that was precisely why I could not risk her joining me, I could not risk her angering those who had the power to retaliate and hurt her.

"Shuxiao, I'll be fine."

"If you change your mind, I could tell General Jianyun I'm feeling ill for the next few days. Old fox spirit bite acting up, and all," she added earnestly.

Wenzhi scowled. "Lieutenant, I hope you don't make a practice of such irresponsible behavior."

"No, Captain." She bowed to him, again. "Only for special occasions."

I stifled a laugh as she left, sobered by the thought of what lay ahead. Wenzhi and I walked in silence, entering a familiar garden surrounding a tranquil lake. Without warning, he took my arm and drew me across the wooden bridge into the Willow Song Pavilion. I cast aside those unwanted memories of all the times I had sat here with Liwei.

He released me then, turning to stare at the mirror-like surface of the water. "Why didn't you tell me?"

I closed my eyes, thinking of the night I had fled my home—stricken with grief and terror. The urgency in my mother's voice as she had sworn me to secrecy. "I made a promise to my mother."

"After all we've been through, don't you trust me?"

"Of course, I do. But this was not a secret I could share on a whim. It would have endangered us all." I reached out to touch his wrist. "Does it matter? I'm still who I've always been."

He turned his hand around to clasp mine. "You're right; it doesn't matter. Though I wish you had told me before. Maybe I could have helped. Maybe I still can."

It touched me, his unflinching acceptance of my past. His unwavering support. Until this moment, I had not been sure of it. I leaned against him, resting my head on his chest as his arm slid around my shoulders. The scent clinging to his skin was fresh and evergreen.

"I wanted to tell you. One day, when we were far from here."

His heart thudded against my ear, quicker than before. "Does this change anything? Will you still come with me?"

"Yes." A thrill coursed through me that now, there was neither hesitation nor doubt. "But I must help my mother first. I must fulfill the emperor's task. Will you wait a little longer?"

Wenzhi's arms tightened, holding me closer. "As long as you are mine as I am yours, we have all the time in the world."

We stood, unmoving, until a prickling at the back of my

neck roused me to recall where we were, in plain sight of anyone passing by. Pulling free, I twisted around. My gaze slammed into Liwei's as he stood on the bridge, as still as one of its wooden columns. His eyes were wide, his hands fisted by his side. Something in me wrenched apart at the expression on his face—not guilt, but sadness, for the hurt I had inflicted.

With measured steps, Liwei entered the pavilion. "May I speak with you?" His manner was cold and formal, like I was a stranger, one of those courtiers he was always trying to avoid. When just days ago, we had defended each other with our lives. Was it always to be so with us: one step forward, and then three back? No, I told myself. We no longer walked together; our paths had diverged.

I nodded, even as my insides curled. More than to anyone, I owed him an explanation.

"I will come to you later," Wenzhi said to me.

I thought he would leave then, but he took my hand in his again, sliding his thumb across my palm in a deliberate stroke. My pulse quickened and despite my mortification, I did not pull away. Wenzhi's lips curved in the shadow of a smile as he released me. He bowed to Liwei, more a curt incline of his head, before striding away.

"I'm sorry," I said haltingly to Liwei. Though I owed him more than this crude apology. For all that we were to each other, for our friendship alone, he had not deserved my dishonesty.

"You lied to me from the day we met." The bleakness in his tone cut me. "Why did you tell me your parents were dead?"

"I didn't! It was you who assumed it and I . . . I let you think that way. I had no idea how to correct you, not without more lies. I promised my mother I would keep this secret. I had to protect her. Can you imagine her punishment if your parents discovered her deception? If they learned she had concealed me, too? They would have sentenced her to torture or death, as they might have done today if I had not won the talisman. If I had not secured her safety before the court." My words tumbled out harsher than intended. I was sorry to have deceived him and yet I had little choice in the matter, driven to this by his family.

"Why didn't you tell me after we grew closer?" His eyes held mine, so dark and unyielding. "You are not who I believed you to be."

His accusation stung, rousing my ire. "I've always told you the truth about me. It was just my parents whom I concealed, and I've told you why I did so. I *was* separated from my family; they *are* lost to me. Knowing the truth would have changed nothing, except endangering my mother. So, why does this matter? Why does it bother you so? Is it because they were mortal? Disgraced, for disobeying your father?" These words of mine were hateful, nor did they quite make sense. I knew him better than that. But riled now, I spoke without thinking, wanting to hurt as much as I was trying to explain.

He recoiled, glaring at me. "That means nothing to me. I just never thought you would lie. You accepted my trust and never yielded me yours."

My anger dissipated. Though I wanted to deny it, there was truth in his words. I *had* been selfish, shuttering myself away, taking what he had to give. "I wanted to tell you, so many times, but I was scared. At first, I didn't know what you might do. And later . . . I didn't want to be a burden."

"Xingyin, how could you ever think I might have harmed you? I would have helped you in any way I could." He spoke more gently now.

"Liwei, I didn't want to hide this from you. I was afraid of your parents finding out, afraid of what they might do—to my mother, to me, to you even, if you angered them. Do you think Their Celestial Majesties would have been inclined to mercy?" My lip curled in distaste.

His eyes narrowed. "Why come here if it brought you closer to those you despise? Were you seeking revenge? Was *everything* calculated to advance yourself?"

I did not look away; I was not ashamed of what I had done. "Not revenge. Not everything. Yes, I wanted the opportunity you offered, I wanted to better myself. Only the strong are favored in the Celestial Kingdom, only then might I get what I wanted. Can you blame me for seeking a new future after mine was snatched away? It didn't occur to me, until I entered the palace, who your parents were. Even then, I never wanted to set you against them. I wanted to free my mother—more than anything—but only through *my* own efforts, as I did today. Never through harming you or yours."

"More than anything?" he repeated, with a catch in his voice. "As it turned out, I was just a stepping-stone in your ambition. How well I served your needs when I urged my father to grant you his favor today." He bent his head to mine, almost tenderly, and yet his words were steeped in bitterness. "Your gamble has paid off handsomely. Now you have what you wanted, First Archer—fame, respect, the Crimson Lion Talisman. Your mother's freedom, almost within your grasp."

"All I wanted was what was taken from me!" I snarled. "You have no idea what I went through. How my mother has suffered!" My temper snapped as my hand flew up to strike him.

He caught it in his grip, his fingers burning against my wrist. For a moment we stood still, glaring at each other. Our breaths quick and shallow, my heart pounding between my ears.

"I earned all this on my own, serving the Celestial Kingdom—your kingdom—with my blood. As I will earn my mother's freedom with this final task." I yanked myself free, stepping away from him. "I'm sorry for deceiving you, I am. But I never meant to hurt you and I don't deserve your accusations."

I was almost shaking in my rage and disappointment as I added, "No matter what we had lost, I always believed we would have our friendship. Maybe I was wrong." At this moment, I could not help thinking of Wenzhi's and Shuxiao's unreserved acceptance of me. Yet, of the three, it was Liwei whom I had hurt most with my lies.

He glanced away, at the calm lake, clasping his hands behind him. When he spoke, his tone was steady once more. "Ah, Xingyin. My disappointment has made me vicious. I am a jealous fool, the sight of you both just now—" He shook his head. "This was not what I wanted to say to you when we met again. I had it all planned out—a heartfelt speech about how grateful I am that you did not leave me to die at Lady Hualing's tender hands. Although, you might be regretting that now." A rueful smile tugged at his lips.

"Perhaps," I said stiffly, unwilling to let go of my anger even as it unraveled with his words.

"In the Eternal Spring Forest, in that wretched cave . . . I rejoiced to see you, yet was terrified that you might die." He spoke slowly as though the memory pained him. "I owe you my life. Thank you for saving it."

"You don't owe me anything," I said. "It was my choice. My decision."

"You could have saved yourself, yet you stayed. While in return, I . . . I almost killed you—" His words cut off, his chest heaving. "I will never forget the look on your face when I struck the first blow. It will haunt me for the rest of my days."

A part of me—a faithless part—wanted to pull him close. To let us comfort each other until we had ripped away those vile remembrances of his sword spilling my blood. My magic, draining his life.

My chest burned like it was crammed with hot coals, but all I said was "I know it wasn't you. I know you didn't mean to."

He fell silent then, even as his eyes held mine fast. "Did you mean what you said in the cave? That you loved me?" He spoke so softly it was almost a whisper.

"Yes." I inhaled deeply, trying to quash the twinge in my heart. Perhaps it would always be there; I was learning that love could not be extinguished at will. "But I meant what I said after, too, that I will always cherish what we had. And I wish you joy in your life, though I will no longer be a part of it."

His nails dug into his palm, a drop of blood falling upon a heron's golden wing. "I thought if we survived Lady Hualing, we still had a chance to find our way back to each other. But I was mistaken, arrogant beyond belief in thinking your path led only to me."

I started at his words. Was it possible . . . did he think I might have asked for *him*, as the reward for the talisman?

He continued, his voice laden with regret. "I wish you every happiness. Though he does not deserve you. Though I cannot help wishing things were different between us."

"Thank you." The words were awkward on my tongue. Chilled, despite the sun, I crossed my arms in front of me. "Do you still hate me for not telling you?"

"I could never hate you. And it was I who was stupid,

refusing to let go when I had no right to hold on." His throat worked as though he had more to say. "You leave tomorrow?" he finally asked.

I nodded.

"I'll come with you."

"Why?"

He shrugged, his tone reverting to the polite detachment which hurt more than I cared to admit. "For the same reason you came with me to the forest. You are entwined in my life, whether we are together or not. I'll help you because I want to, not because I must. And there is no need for any accounting; what you owe to me, what I owe to you, such debts are meaningless between us."

Long after he had left, I remained on the marble stool. A gust of wind swept the willow trees down, their branches rippling the lake. The leaves rustled as though whispering the secrets I had just spilled to the world. This had seemed an impossible dream, that I would reclaim my identity and liberate myself from the pretenses of the past. And now, I was one step closer to freeing my mother, to returning home. I had believed this opportunity would bring me unmitigated joy, yet I found it was laced with an incomprehensible bitterness.

29

Round, red lanterns fringed in yellow silk were strung above the stone-paved streets. Trees rustled, throwing their shadows over the pale building walls, the diamond latticework on the doors and windows worn to muted shades of red and green. Gray roof tiles blended into the darkness, a practical choice against the temperamental weather of the mortal world. This village might have appeared dreary in the night, but the luminous lanterns lent it an enchanted glow.

A hundred aromas wafted in the air of foods, perfumes, and mortals. People thronged the streets, most dressed in plain cotton robes, while the more prosperous few were attired in gleaming brocade or silk. Ornaments hung from their waists, some adorned with jade beads or discs of precious metal. Loud popping noises startled me, as bright sparks, shreds of red paper, and thick smoke burst into the air. Firecrackers. Was there a festival tonight? The faces of the villagers were alight with excitement, just as when I had watched them from afar in the moon.

Liwei and Wenzhi stopped outside a large building. A sturdy

black plaque hung over its entrance with the characters painted in white:

西湖客栈
WEST LAKE INN

Gourd-shaped lanterns cascaded on each side of the red wooden doors. Its windows were flung open to the cool night air, music and laughter spilling onto the street. A lively establishment, though my head began to throb from the incessant noise.

We would spend the night here before journeying to the Changjiang, the river where the Long Dragon had been trapped under a mountain for centuries. When Wenzhi had proposed that we stop in this village, I readily agreed, eager for a glimpse of how the mortals lived. But for a slip of fate, I might have been one of them, too.

At the sight of us, the innkeeper shook his head to turn us away. Was the inn full? The town was certainly bustling. Wenzhi did not speak, merely placing a silver tael on the table. It worked as well as any enchantment, the innkeeper's face lighting up as he tucked it into his sleeve. He said something in a low voice to Wenzhi, but it was drowned in the burst of laughter from a nearby customer.

A young girl, his daughter perhaps, showed us to a wooden table by the window. She left, only to return shortly, carrying a tray with plates of stir-fried wild mushrooms, braised pork ribs, a small fried fish, and a large bowl of steaming soup.

"What entertainment is there tonight?" Wenzhi asked the girl, nodding toward the raised platform in the middle of the room.

She bowed to him, a blush staining her cheeks. "A storyteller, Young Master. One of the best in this region."

Young Master? I swallowed my laugh. Wenzhi must be twice her grandfather's age, though his smooth skin and chiseled features gave no hint of it.

Midway through our meal, the storyteller arrived. A long, gray beard dusted his wrinkled face, his pouched eyes gleaming beneath thick brows. As he settled onto a bamboo chair, he laid his gnarled wooden staff on the floor. Accepting a coin from a customer, he cleared his throat before beginning his tale—of a noble king who had been betrayed by his favorite concubine, a spy planted by an enemy kingdom. When the ill-fated pair died at the tragic end, the rapt audience sighed and clapped, while a few dabbed their tears away with handkerchiefs and sleeves. I stifled a yawn, feeling little but revulsion at the concubine's deceit, and impatience for the king's foolishness.

With an amused smile, Wenzhi tossed a piece of silver to the storyteller who caught it with surprising deftness, slipping it into his pouch.

"Young Master, which tale do you wish to hear?" the storyteller asked him deferentially.

"The Four Dragons," Wenzhi replied.

I sat up straighter, my ears pricking up.

"Ah! A classic. Young Master must be a scholar," the storyteller flattered.

Several occupants of the teahouse groaned, likely hoping for more salacious tales of lustful kings and beautiful maidens. But when the storyteller raised his hand, they fell silent—the silver gleaming in his beard as brightly as that which now lay in his pouch.

He began, his voice as smooth as the finest wine. "Long ago when the world was still new, there were no lakes or rivers. All the water was in the Four Seas, and the people relied upon the rain from the sky to grow their crops and quench their thirst. The Eastern Sea was the home of the four dragons. The Long Dragon was the largest of them all, its scales as red as flame, while the Pearl Dragon glowed like winter's frost. The Yellow Dragon blazed brighter than the sun and the Black Dragon was darker than night. Twice a year, they rose from the sea to fly in the sky above."

The storyteller raised his voice, startling his listeners. "One day, they heard loud crying and wailing from our world below. Curious, they flew closer, hearing the people's desperate prayers for rain after a long drought. Their clothes hung loose on their thin bodies and their lips were cracked from thirst. Distraught by their suffering, the dragons pleaded with the Heavenly Emperor to send rain to the mortals. The emperor agreed, but due to a divine calamity it slipped his mind and weeks more passed without rain."

He paused, reaching for his cup and lifting it to his mouth. When he continued, his tone was a controlled whisper. I found myself straining to listen, though I knew this tale well. It was the same one I had offered to tell Prince Yanming, the one he had scoffed at.

"Unable to bear the misery of the starving people, the dragons flew to the Eastern Sea. They filled their jaws with briny water, spraying it across the sky. Their magic transformed it into pure water which rained to the parched earth below. The people fell to their knees, rejoicing and praising the gods. But the Heavenly Emperor was furious that the dragons had overstepped their authority. He imprisoned them, each beneath a mountain of iron and stone. However, before each dragon was trapped, it sacrificed its immense power to bring forth a gushing river to ensure that our world never lacked water again. From that day, four great rivers flowed across our land, from east to west—named after the dragons in honor of their noble sacrifice."

The audience applauded, although with less enthusiasm than before. One woman quickly tossed the storyteller a coin, shouting out her request.

I did not hear it, lost in the memories which drifted over me. This tale had been one of my favorites as a child and I had often asked my mother to tell it to me. Closing my eyes, I could almost imagine myself lying in my bed of cinnamon-wood, my fingers grazing the soft white drapes that fluttered in the breeze. I had no need for a lamp as the stars glittered in the sky and the lanterns threw their pearly glow through my window.

I had loved this story, though its ending left me unsettled. One night, I had asked my mother, "Why did the emperor forget to bring rain to the mortals?"

"The emperor has many concerns and responsibilities; governing the realms above and below is no easy task. Each day he oversees countless petitions and requests."

"But why did he punish the dragons for helping the mortals instead of thanking them?" I wanted to know.

Her hand had brushed my cheek, her cool touch soothing my restlessness. "Sleep, Little Star. It's just a story," she had said, evading my question with ease.

Only now did I understand that there was no satisfactory answer. At least none to avoid offending the Celestial Emperor.

The emperor's task filled me with unease, like a thorn stabbing the underside of my heel. More so when I recalled Prince Yanxi's admiration of the dragons, the tales I had heard of their benevolence. If the dragons were unwilling, could I fight them for their pearls? Could I even *defeat* one of them, much less four? This was a hopeless task, a thankless one—where success would come at the price of my honor, and my failure would be the death of me.

"Xingyin, what's the matter?" Wenzhi's question roused me from my thoughts.

"I'm tired," I said, although I had no reason to be.

"Why don't you sleep?" Liwei suggested, not looking up from his bowl. "It will take us a full day to get to the Changjiang by foot, even without stopping to rest."

Since we had spoken in the Willow Song Pavilion, a coolness descended upon us. Had the words exchanged severed the lingering ties between us? Or was it the intimacy he had witnessed between Wenzhi and me? Whatever the cause, Liwei was unfailingly courteous but withdrawn. And while this was exactly what I had asked of him before, it left me hollow inside.

The innkeeper's daughter came to clear our table. As she lifted each plate onto her tray with painstaking slowness, she stole furtive glances at Wenzhi and Liwei. Her eyes darted back and forth, back and forth, as though she could not decide who took her fancy more. Indeed, they had little competition in this place. Even garbed in plain robes, their auras muted, Wenzhi and Liwei had the same effect on mortal hearts as they did on immortal ones.

I stood up, eager to leave. Just sharing this meal with them had rubbed my nerves raw. "Where is my room?"

Wenzhi grimaced as he gestured to the floor above. "The inn is full. The three of us will have to share." As he caught my horrified expression, he added, "You may have the bed, of course. I'm sure His Highness can do without one for a night." A hint of mockery laced his voice.

"Indeed," Liwei said coldly. "Though I intend to be present in the room nonetheless."

Was that a warning? Was I reading too much in the edge of his tone? It mattered not. Even if this inn possessed the softest beds in the kingdom, a patch of damp grass would be preferable to suffering through a night as that.

"Ahh, I'm not tired after all." I backed away from the table, coward that I was. "After eating so much, I'll go for a walk. It's my first time in a mortal village."

Wenzhi's stool scraped against the floor as he rose. "I'll join you."

I shook my head, smiling to take the sting out of my refusal. I wanted some time alone. And, for some reason, I did not want to go with Wenzhi and leave Liwei by himself.

I hurried through the inn, slipping out of its back entrance. This street was smaller than the one we had strolled through earlier, but no less lively. Several villagers watched the street performers as they spun plates on sticks or breathed out tongues of flame. I stopped to listen to an old man playing an er-hu, a two-stringed wooden fiddle. The plaintive melody suited my mood well. When it ended, I dropped a gold tael into his bowl, where it clinked against the copper coins.

Even at this late hour, children ran around, chasing barking dogs or crowding the stalls. Some carried insects and butterflies woven from dried grass, while others clutched sticks stacked with glossy balls of red sweets. Curious, I bought one for myself, crunching through the crisp candied shell to reach the tangy hawthorn berry within. As I licked the bits of sugar off my fingers, some villagers stared at me, perhaps wondering at my enthusiasm over the common treat. Had my mother liked this, too? I lifted my head to the skies, wishing I could ask her.

The luminous orb of the moon was smaller than it appeared in the Celestial Kingdom, but just as striking against the black night. It struck me, that if my father had not been gifted the elixir, if my mother had not taken it—perhaps we might be living in a village such as this. In a house with white walls, a weathered moss-green roof, and wooden doors. Our family, whole. For a moment, I could not breathe, lost in the dream. *Or perhaps, you would be dead,* my mind whispered.

Did my mother still cast her eyes here with longing? Did my father live still? Did he . . . blame my mother for her choice? Me, for endangering her life? If only I could seek him out, but I had no idea where to start. And I dared not test the emperor's patience any more than I had.

I turned into a quiet lane. Not more than fifty steps in, my skin crawled with that same prickling sensation as whenever danger was afoot—just as when the archer had shot at me in the Eternal Spring Forest. Impossible that he could be here, in the Mortal Realm. More likely, he was dead, killed by Liwei's soldiers. But it did not change the fact that I was being watched.

Feigning ignorance, I continued down the path. While I doubted anything could injure me here, I had a couple of daggers tucked away for good measure. The Jade Dragon Bow was slung across my back, wrapped in a piece of cloth to avoid attracting attention. When Wenzhi had suggested that I bring it along, it seemed a wise idea.

In the quiet of my room, I had practiced using this bow. In the beginning, I could only sustain its arrows briefly, but over time they had grown steadier in my grasp. I had longed to test its power, to let fly the crackling shaft of light—yet never dared to. Where might one release a bolt of Sky-fire unseen in the Celestial Kingdom?

As footsteps thudded behind me, I reminded myself that immortals were forbidden from using magic in the Mortal Realm unless there was a dire need. Hostile dragons were undoubtedly one—yet for now, my physical abilities would have to suffice.

"Where are you going in such a hurry?" a man called out. "Would a beautiful lady like you enjoy some company?"

Three men swaggered forward, encircling me where I stood. They wore fine clothes and headpieces of silver and jade, but the pungent fumes of wine assailed my nostrils. They must be drunk indeed to call me beautiful, I thought scathingly. From the leers on their faces, it was not hard to guess their intentions.

My fingers clenched into fists. "Not the type of company you have in mind," I replied curtly, turning away.

A meaty palm clamped down on my shoulder, spinning me around. "Don't be so shy. Why would you be wandering here, alone, if you didn't want to be found?" the taller one slurred into my face. His breath was sour, stinking with the remnants of his previous meal, his hand now fumbling at the collar of my robe. "Do you know who we are? We can afford to—"

Rage and revulsion erupted through my veins. I seized his wrist and flipped him onto his back. He screamed in agony, clutching his hand. Was it broken? I hadn't intended to, though part of me hoped it was. His two friends snarled, charging at me together. I sidestepped their grasping hands, grabbing them both by their necks and bashing their heads into each other with a resounding crack. Two kicks sent them flying into the ground. Before either of them could sit up, I held a dagger in each hand against their throats.

Pressing the blades down until a thin line of blood oozed out, I hissed, "I'm guessing this is not your first time. If any of you even *think* of committing such a vile crime again, I'll come back and sink my knives into your hearts." I raked them with a scornful look before placing my foot onto each of their spines in turn, my kicks sending them sprawling.

"Demon! Demon lady!" one of them gasped, his eyes bulging as he scrambled up and fled.

Not quite, I thought to myself. But it was a closer guess than he would ever know.

My rage unappeased, I released a surge of glittering magic which streaked after them. Perhaps my minor transgression would slip by unnoticed. It was rash of me, but I was sickened by their intent. And how they had tried to blame my choices for *their* despicable behavior.

Someone snickered. I swung around to find Wenzhi leaning against a nearby wall, his face alight with amusement. "That was well done," he complimented me. "I would have joined you, but you didn't need any help."

"I'm glad you found that entertaining." I wiped the daggers clean before sliding them back into their sheaths.

A dangerous glint sparked in his eyes. "If you hadn't taken care of them, I would have been glad to. They wouldn't have been able to walk afterward, much less run. You let them off too lightly," he chided.

"I haven't told you what else I did. Their wounds won't heal for months; every bruise aching, the blood seeping from their cuts. They won't easily forget tonight—what they tried to do and what I did to them. I don't think they'll be able to look at another girl again, much less try to attack one."

Wenzhi raised his brows. "Remind me never to get on your bad side."

He pushed himself off the wall, closing the distance between us, his hands reaching out to slide around my waist. My pulse quickened as I lifted my face to his, anticipation flaring across my skin. His eyes blazed with unfathomable emotion as he bent his head, pressing his lips to mine. Light sparked through my mind like a scattering of stars. For a moment we stood there, utterly still, our bodies molded together. Then his lips parted mine, his mouth urgent and seeking, his breath sliding in warm and sweet. Heat flashed through me—burning, molten bright— racing through my veins, setting me alight. His palm swept up the arch of my back, his fingers tangling in my hair as he pulled my head gently back. Cool lips glided to the curve of my neck, trailing a scorching path. I was afire. Undone. All thought fled my mind as I clutched him closer, pressing against him until the pounding of his heart echoed against my own.

When his hands fell away, I could not help the sigh that slid from my throat. I wrapped my arms across my chest, small comfort to the emptiness that gaped within. Our breaths came harsh in the sudden silence which fell over us.

"I wasn't following you to stalk you. I wanted to show you something," he told me.

We walked until we reached the bank of a nearby river. It was crowded with people who were lighting lanterns and releasing them into the water. Unlike the ones of silk in the village, these were made of colored waxed paper that had been artfully folded and shaped into lotuses. A candle glowed from the center of each flower, luminous in the dark.

"I thought the Water Lantern Festival might interest you," he said.

The faces of the villagers were solemn and grave, a few weeping openly. Sadness clung to the air like winter's chill.

"What are they doing?" I wondered.

"Praying for guidance from their departed ancestors. Honoring and remembering their loved ones who have passed. The lanterns are also meant to guide wandering spirits back to their realm." From his flowing sleeve he drew out a small one, offering it to me.

I looked up at him. "What is this for?"

"A dragon is no small matter. Perhaps you should ask for guidance from your own ancestors."

I stared at him, a tenderness unfurling in my chest. With this, he acknowledged my mortal roots and my place in this world, too. It was then I realized just how much he cared for me. And I, for him.

I took the lantern and lit its candle, crouching down to release it into the river. It bobbed unsteadily for a moment, before righting itself and floating away. I did not ask for guidance—*who* might I ask? I did not know whether my father was still in this world or the next. I did not even know the names of my ancestors. But I hoped wherever they were, they would see the lantern I had lit in their honor and know they were remembered.

Beneath the dark sky, we stood unspeaking. The river shone with the light of hundreds of lanterns, a stream of living fire which flowed with the current toward an unknown horizon.

30

The sun had faded to a muted orb of crimson light. In the dwindling glow, the waters of the Changjiang glittered as it wound like a fiery serpent across the emerald valley, stretching far beyond where our eyes could see.

I squinted, scanning our surroundings for where the Long Dragon, the most powerful of the dragons, was said to be imprisoned. Liwei pointed out a mountain of blue-gray rock, its peak shrouded in fog. Fields of yellow flowers bloomed at the base. Against the darkening sky, a pale light radiated from the mountain—so faint, it could not be seen by mortal eyes.

My fingers untied the cord of my pouch, pulling out the Divine Iron Seal. The metal was no longer cold, but pulsing with heat. My heart thudded as I lifted it toward the towering peak. Would it crumble to dust—the dragon soaring into the sky, grateful to be freed from its prison?

Yet nothing happened. The valley remained still with only the crickets chirping in their nightly serenade.

"How does this work?" I asked Liwei.

He took the seal, inspecting its markings before passing it back to me. "It's a key. We just need to find the lock."

I stared at the enormous mountain, wondering how long it might take to search it. "Would this count as a 'dire' need?" I ventured.

A faint smile tugged at his lips. "My father would not fault you when you're here at his behest."

Use whatever means necessary. The emperor's words echoed through me again. Brushing aside my unease, I channeled my magic, light shooting from my palm to engulf the dull metal. The carved dragon erupted into flame, writhing as though it were alive. Hot wind surged into my face as the seal shot into the air, circling the mountain like a blazing beacon—then plunging down and vanishing from sight. Before I had time to fret, it appeared again on the horizon, hurtling back to my hand with such force that I staggered, almost falling to the ground. As I stared at it, the fire dwindled to nothingness, the dragon morphing into lifeless iron once more.

The ground shuddered. I stumbled, almost dropping the seal before I slipped it into my pouch. A thunderous roar shattered the silence. My head snapped to the peak as a large crack wrenched it apart. Rocks flew in all directions, several hurtling past me as I ducked, crouching down on the ground. Crimson tongues of flame surged from the heart of the mountain, slithering through the gaping cracks like a volcano on the brink of eruption.

With an ear-splitting cry, an enormous creature burst forth, shaking clouds of blinding dust from its body. Ruby-red scales glowed as if newly forged metal. Its massive paws were tipped with gold scythe-like claws, and its mane and tail flowed with lush vermilion strands. Its face would have been terrifying—

crowned by bone-white antlers, and with those sharp curved fangs—but for its amber eyes shining with wisdom.

We stood, transfixed, as the dragon arched its neck toward the sky. Its gaze swept over the valley, fixing upon us. Without a pause, it flew in our direction, its powerful body undulating in the air. How graceful its flight, unaided by wings! Yet as the great creature drew closer, my heart thudded so hard I thought it would drive a hole through my ribs. Xiangliu, the giant octopus, the Bone Devil . . . none of those monsters had daunted me so.

Who freed me from my prison? Tell me your name. The dragon's tone was perfectly pitched, neither low nor high, neither sharp nor soft.

With a start, I realized its jaws remained shut as it spoke—its voice reverberating in my mind like we were one and the same. I swung around to stare at Liwei and Wenzhi, both equally dazed and bewildered. I had not imagined it; the dragon had spoken to them, too.

The Long Dragon cocked its magnificent head to one side. Was it waiting for an answer to its question?

I cleared my throat, trying to loosen the sudden cramp. "Venerable Dragon, I am Xingyin—the daughter of Chang'e and Houyi. I released you at the behest of the Celestial Emperor, who asks you to relinquish your pearl to him." My pride in speaking my parents' names was quashed by the shameful nature of my task.

A deep growl punctured the quiet. Its eyes narrowed with menace as smoke streamed from its flaring nostrils. No, not smoke—but mist, as crisp as an autumn dawn. Shaken by its hostility, I took a step back, tugging the Jade Dragon Bow free from its bindings.

What right do you have to demand my spiritual essence? the dragon thundered.

"Not your essence," I said quickly, trying to allay its concerns. "The emperor only wants your pearl." Even as I spoke, a seed of doubt sprouted. In the Celestial Kingdom—where jewels were as plentiful as flowers—why did the emperor covet these pearls?

Sparks shot from the Long Dragon's nostrils as its voice erupted in my mind. *Our pearls contain our spiritual essence. Whoever possesses our pearls, controls us! Do you expect us to willingly exchange imprisonment for* enslavement? *To the one who locked us away for bringing rain to the mortals? We could have fought him then, we could have fled into the oceans beyond his reach—but that would have torn the skies and up-ended the earth, pitting land and sea against each other. And that, we could not bear.*

My heart plunged as I spun to Liwei. "Were you aware of this?"

"No," he replied tersely. "Dragons disappeared from the Immortal Realm centuries ago. Nothing in our texts tell of this."

I should have known better; he would not have kept it from me. It dawned on me, then, that I had been duped by the emperor. He had asked for the pearls, without mentioning the dragons' essence. This was not what I had agreed to . . . yet this was the bargain I had struck. How could I do this? How could I make the dragons give up their freedom in exchange for my mother's?

Yet, how could I not?

It was not the same thing, I reminded myself, though it was a hard truth for me to bear. Imprisonment was not the same as enslavement. To give the emperor such power over the dragons, to force them to yield their will to him—could I do such a monstrous thing?

"You served under the Celestial Emperor before. He must have good reason to request your service again." I fumbled for a peaceable solution, clinging to this slender thread to salvage my conscience—even as I loathed myself for it.

The Long Dragon's eyes flashed, its tail lashing the air. *We never served the Celestial Emperor. We were once ruled by a far worthier immortal. To him, we gave our allegiance—until he returned our pearls into our safekeeping.*

Its words crushed my last glimmer of hope. Turning to Wenzhi and Liwei, I read grim determination in their faces.

My fingers reached for my jade pendant, pulling it out and clasping it for comfort. I could not look at the dragon, a hot, prickling tightness spreading across my chest. "I'm sorry, but I need your pearls."

The Long Dragon bared its fangs, sharper than spears. Its jaws parted, spewing a stream of white mist toward me. Light erupted from Liwei and Wenzhi, even as I threw my own shield up—too late—the mist shrouding me, clinging to my skin where it seared with the biting cold of ice. But the discomfort faded abruptly, leaving just a pleasant coolness below the hollow of my neck. My pendant? I lifted it to stare at the carving. The crack had vanished; the jade was whole once more. Had the dragon's breath done this?

The Long Dragon reared back, its eyes bulging as mist coiled from its nostrils once more. Was it attacking again? Terror clawed me as I drew the bow, Sky-fire crackling between my fingers. My stomach churned as I aimed it at the creature. I thought wildly of my mother—grasping for the strength, the ruthlessness, to do what I needed to. All I had to do was release this arrow . . .

Unbidden, the memory of the paper dragon from Prince Yanming rose in my mind. *May the dragons protect you on your journey.* My heart quailed from a sudden burst of anguish as I raised my bow higher—away from the dragon—releasing the bolt into the sky. White veins of light illuminated the heavens. A crushing disappointment descended over me, yet it was laced with undeniable relief. I could not strike it, and deep down, I knew my mother would not have wanted this either. No matter what it cost us.

Behind me, Liwei sucked in a sharp breath. The Long Dragon craned its neck toward me, staring at the bow. Something flashed in its golden gaze, akin to recognition.

The Jade Dragon Bow. How is this possible? Its voice was calm once more.

Before I could speak, Wenzhi stepped forward. He must have heard the dragon's question, too. "The bow chose her. She wields it now."

This is most unexpected. The Long Dragon's sigh was like the wind tearing through the trees. *Would you lend me the Divine Iron Seal? I would use it to free my siblings as I must confer with them. I give you my word that we will return here, and no harm will come to any of you.*

Wenzhi drew me aside and spoke in hushed tones. "Ask the dragon to surrender its pearl, first. If you give it the seal, it will free the others and you might never see it again. We've come this far—if you lose the seal now, you will end up with nothing."

His advice was sound. In any confrontation, Wenzhi was ever vigilant and ruthless—which was why he was so often victorious.

But the dragons were not my enemy.

As I looked away, my eyes met Liwei's. "Xingyin, this is your decision," he said, in a gentler tone than I expected.

I should have heeded Wenzhi's advice, but my instincts

guided me down a different path. I believed the Long Dragon would not deceive me. How could I hope to gain its trust if I hesitated to yield mine?"

Slowly, I stretched out my hand, the seal resting in my palm.

Light shot from the Long Dragon's paw, enveloping the seal, which floated into its grasp. As its claws closed around it, the dragon's massive jaws curved up. With a single bound, it soared into the night.

Wenzhi stared silently after its shrinking silhouette. Was he displeased? I had not his wealth of experience, but I trusted my own intuition.

I reached out to touch his arm, pressing my fingers against his sleeve. "It will return."

"How can you be sure?"

"Because I'm wise beyond my years." I spoke lightly, trying to conceal my own rising doubt.

He laughed, the sound rich and full. "That you are. Though you are young, for an immortal," he added pointedly.

"Then tell me, Ancient One," I said, with a smile. "What did you mean when you said the bow chose me? Why didn't you mention this before?"

He leaned over to tuck a loose strand of hair behind my ear, his hand lingering before falling away. "It was something I read in the Eastern Sea library. I didn't think it was important as it seemed obvious the bow had made its choice."

"Not to me," I admitted. "I thought it was some coincidence, that maybe I was the first person to touch the bow. That I was just its custodian."

"I should have told you, but it slipped my mind until now. The dragon's words might have pried the memory loose," he said wryly.

"Did you discover anything else?" I probed.

"Just that the Jade Dragon Bow yields to one master at a time. I wasn't sure that part was true." A pensive look crossed his face. "However, the Long Dragon's reaction appears to confirm it."

"I've never heard of this weapon before," Liwei remarked, coming toward us. "Unsurprising, perhaps, as we did not study the dragons. May I hold it?" he asked, stretching out his hand.

Before I could offer it to him, the bow quivered in my palm in seeming protest. Liwei drew back, shaking his head. "I'll not be fool enough to try to take it."

I did not know how long we waited there, until the sky had darkened to black, until the last remnant of heat from the day was stripped from the earth. Until I finally sank to the ground in exhaustion, wrapping my arms around my knees. Was I wrong to trust the dragons? Was I mistaken in their honor? I dared not look at Wenzhi. Although he would not gloat or reproach me, I would have disappointed him, nonetheless. And terror gripped me as I wondered, what would the Celestial Emperor do should I return empty-handed, with neither pearls nor seal? Just as I was about to admit defeat—the moon and stars vanished as though swallowed by the night, covered by the silhouettes of the four creatures flying above.

The dragons landed before us, the ground trembling from the might of their descent. Soil flew up as their golden claws sank in, tails lashing behind them as their long necks arched to the sky, their antlers gleaming silvery-white. Their auras were so powerful, the air itself seemed to shudder with their force. The other three were smaller than the Long Dragon, yet no less magnificent. One glowed as moonlight with a snowy mane. Another was as dazzling as the sun, a ridge of golden spikes stretching along its back. And the last, merged seamlessly into the shadows, but for its ivory fangs gleaming like daggers of bone.

On the bank of the longest river in the realm, the Venerable Dragons were united once more. They stared at me unblinkingly, their eyes ablaze with eternal wisdom. Without knowing why, I sank to my knees and folded my body over until my forehead pressed against the grass.

The Long Dragon's voice thrummed in my mind. *We are grateful to be freed, to feel the wind in our faces again. Life is precious once more.* Its eyes flashed, mist streaming from its nostrils. *However, we do not wish to serve the Celestial Emperor. We will not give him our pearls.*

A heaviness sank over me as I rose to my feet. Wenzhi stepped closer as though lending me his support. Did he think I would fight the dragons now? I could not. It was not fear which held me back—though they could probably tear me to pieces if they were so inclined—but, I *would* not. Which meant, I had failed. My mother would remain a prisoner. And everything I had striven for in the Celestial Kingdom would be for nothing.

The Long Dragon's voice resonated through me again. *We will give them to you.*

"What? Why?" I repeated in disbelief, certain I had misheard, even as Liwei and Wenzhi swung to me.

As the Long Dragon lifted its head, its mane rippled through the air like silken flame. *Long ago, when we were young, a powerful sorcerer stole our spiritual essence. We would have died, if not for a brave warrior who saved us. Yet we were too weakened to retrieve our essence and the warrior bound it to the four pearls instead. To him, we swore our loyalty. When he left the Eastern Sea, he returned the pearls to us—though we are honor-bound to yield them to him again should he ask it of us, or to the one in his stead.* Here, the Long Dragon paused. *The Jade Dragon Bow was his cherished weapon, cleaving to him alone. And now, it has chosen you.*

My mind whirled. I had known the bow was powerful, yet never did I dream it held such a revered place among the dragons. Even less so, that *I* would be its rightful owner. And that the dragons would acknowledge me as—

"But I'm not the immortal who saved you," I said hesitantly. "I know nothing of him. My mother and father are mortal-born."

Titles are inherited, talent might be blood-bound, but true greatness lies within, the Long Dragon said. *There is a reason the bow chose you. A reason that you might not even be aware of yet, which will only become clear once the clouds are parted. Our oath must be fulfilled. We will honor the bow's choice and yield our pearls to you, if that is your wish.*

The Long Dragon fixed its golden gaze upon me. *However, there is something else you must know. If you accept our pearls, we ask you to swear—as our ruler did—to never force us to act against our inclination, and to safeguard our honor and freedom. We are creatures of peace. We cannot allow our power to be harnessed for death and destruction, or our strength will wane and we will die.*

Despite the cool night, sweat broke out over my skin. Horror struck me, to imagine what the emperor might have demanded from the dragons' service, and what it would have cost them. What the dragons offered me was an immense honor and yet a terrifying burden. One I was unsure whether I was worthy to undertake or strong enough to bear.

"Venerable Dragons, could *you* free my mother, the Moon Goddess?" I asked in a small voice. If they could, I would not need the emperor's pardon. I would not need the pearls. I would not need to weigh my honor against my mother's freedom.

The Long Dragon's amber orbs darkened. *Even during our imprisonment, we had heard the tale of Chang'e and Houyi. The emperor oversees the celestial bodies in the sky, and Chang'e is bound to the moon. Her immortality is from the elixir, his gift. Hence, Chang'e is his subject and his punishment of her—while harsh—is within his right. We cannot undo the enchantment. If we attempt to release her, it would be to defy the Celestial Kingdom. An act of war. We cannot fight them as that would destroy us.*

The weight of my indecision almost crushed me. I had no wish to betray the dragons, but what if my mother was threatened? Could I resist the terrible temptation to trade them for her safety? And what if the dragons perished in the emperor's service, then? Could I live with that on my conscience?

Part of me cried out to refuse this burden, yet how could I let this chance slip by? If only there was a way to harness the dragons' power without endangering them. If only I could keep the dragons *and* my mother safe. I did not know if it was possible, but there was only one way to find out.

I cupped my hands before me, bowing to them. "I will accept your pearls."

The dragons inclined their heads. Was it disappointment that clouded their faces?

Guilt pierced me, sharp and deep. I added at once, "In return, I swear to never force you to act against your inclination, to safeguard your honor and freedom. And I *will* return the pearls to you." My voice shook with the solemnity of my vow. The dragons had not asked the last of me, but deep down I knew this was right.

The night was so still, I could hear the shiver of the grass, the snap of a leaf fluttering from its twig. Finally, the Long Dragon prowled toward me. As its enormous jaws parted, its breath misted the air. Between gleaming white fangs, upon a blood-red tongue, rested a pearl of crimson flame. As it lowered its head, its tongue lifted the pearl gently onto my palm. One by one the others followed suit until four pearls glowed in my hand, each the color of the creature who had gifted it. They thrummed with power against my skin, incandescent like they had been drenched in sunlight.

Our destinies are in your hands, daughter of Chang'e and Houyi, the Long Dragon intoned gravely. *Whenever you wish to summon us, hold our pearls and speak our names.*

My fingers closed around the pearls, the payment the Celestial Emperor had demanded. "Thank you for your trust," I whispered.

Thank you for your promise. The Long Dragon let out a sigh of longing. *Now we wish to bathe in the cool waters of the Eastern Sea, from which we have been parted for too long.* Without another word, it sprang into the air, streaking across the heavens. The Pearl and Yellow Dragon followed close behind it.

Only the Black Dragon remained, its gaze disconcertingly bright. When it spoke, its voice chimed like a bell struck hard. *Daughter of Chang'e and Houyi. During my years beneath the mountain, I heard the mortals who bathed in my river speak of the greatest archer who ever lived.*

"You have news of my father?" I dared not hope, yet I could not suppress the wild leap in my chest.

The Black Dragon hesitated. *They spoke of his grave not far from the banks of my river. At the point where two rivers merge into one, there is a hill covered in white flowers. There, you will find his resting place.*

My father . . . dead? Deep down, I had always harbored a secret hope that he was alive. Even with the short life span of a mortal, he might still be in the early winter of his life. My last lingering hope crushed, I mourned the father I had never known. As for my mother who waited for him still—this would break her heart, destroying the dream she had clung to all this time. The strength sapped from my limbs as I dropped to my knees on the dew-glazed grass, sunken in despair.

Wenzhi crouched down beside me, drawing me into his arms. From the corner of my eye, I saw Liwei reach toward me, his fingers curling before they fell back down again.

The Black Dragon sighed. *I wish I had gladder tidings. I am sorry for your loss.* With a graceful leap into the night, it flew away.

Wenzhi's arm tightened around me then. Looking up at him, I blinked in surprise. His pupils were no longer black, but a silvery gray like rainfall in winter. I jerked back, shoving against him as a cloud swept in and whisked us into the sky—soaring so quickly, I could barely breathe through the air rushing into my face. I thrashed against Wenzhi's hold, reaching furiously for my energy, despite the numbing chill that spread through my body like the frost forming on a leaf. I could not move, not even to struggle. Liwei's shout pierced my stupor, followed by the ringing clash of metal which soon faded to a dull echo.

"I'm sorry."

A drifting whisper that dissolved with the wind, so soft I might have imagined it. Eyes of silver, shadowed with regret—and then everything went dark.

31

A deep scent infiltrated my senses, opulent and sweet like a gilded forest. *Sandalwood*, my mind whispered, roused from the fog that enveloped it. My eyes flicked open. Sitting up, I pressed my fingers to my throbbing head—the ache worsening as I stared at the room with its mahogany furniture, green marble floor, and gold silk hangings. Tendrils of fragrant smoke coiled from a three-legged incense burner. Something cold seared my hands and when I glanced down, I recoiled. Dark metal bracelets encircled my wrists, crafted from the same material used to bind Liwei in the Eternal Spring Forest. I tried to slide them off, but they stuck fast, endless circles of immutable metal with neither clasp nor hinge. I grasped at my energy, yet it evaded my hold—just as when my powers were untrained. Just as in Shadow Peak.

Fear clouded me as I stumbled to the doors, tugging at them. Locked. I sank onto a barrel-shaped stool, anger kindling in the pit of my stomach. Was I a prisoner? Was my magic bound? Where was Liwei? Wenzhi? And what of the pearls? My hands shook as I untied my pouch, shaking its contents onto the table.

My jade flute rolled out, along with Prince Yanming's paper dragon. I dashed to the bed and threw the covers aside, peering beneath furniture, flinging open chests and drawers. But there was no sign of the pearls or my bow.

I recalled the glacial hue of Wenzhi's pupils, the whisper in the wind before I lost consciousness. Was he possessed by some malevolent spirit? Impersonated by one? Was he in danger, too? My chest tightened, even as a revolting suspicion crept up the fringes of my mind.

The doors slid open. My head jerked up. A young girl entered, carrying a tray. Taken aback by my grim expression, she hesitated before bowing hastily. "My lady, you're awake. I'll . . . I'll inform His Highness at once."

She dropped the tray onto the table and hurried away, shutting the doors behind her.

"Wait!" I ran to the doors and yanked at them to no avail, shouting after her, "What is this place? Who is 'His Highness'?"

There was no reply, just her footsteps fading to silence.

I sat upon the stool again, restraining the urge to pound the table in frustration. For want of anything to do, I lifted the lid off the porcelain bowl, staring with disinterest at the clear broth drizzled with golden sesame oil. Its warm, savory aroma wafted into my nostrils, but I pushed the bowl aside.

A breeze slipped into the room, cutting through the cloying incense. I ran to the window, inhaling great gulps of fresh air. The sun shone brightly, though the ground below was obscured by violet clouds. Iridescent tiles shimmered from the roof with a rainbow-like sheen. I peered closer at the obsidian walls, noticing ridges in them deep enough to grip onto. Hiking up my skirt, I swung a foot through the window—only to slam against an invisible barrier as hard as rock.

Gritting my teeth, I grabbed at my energy with more force than before. But the flecks of light darted away as though scattered by the wind. I searched the room again, emptying out the contents of the drawers and cupboards, leaving silk and brocade strewn in my wake, books piled upon the floor. If I had to fight my way out of here, I needed to arm myself—with the leg wrenched from the table if need be. Rifling through a box filled with jewelry, I dug out all the hairpins, placing two in my hair and sliding the rest into the sash around my waist.

The doors creaked behind me. I steeled myself as I whirled around, a gold pin tucked in my palm. Wenzhi stepped into the room, dressed in a green brocade robe embroidered with autumn leaves, their hue shifting from crimson to gold. His dark hair was pulled through a jade ring, falling over his shoulder. Heat fired in my veins at the sight of his eyes, no longer black but that strange silvery hue. An imposter! I hurled the hairpin at his face and raced toward the entrance. He spun to the side, catching me around my waist as I struggled and kicked at him. My foot landed hard against his thigh, his body tensing, even as his arm tightened around me. As I bent my knee to drive it into his stomach, he struck it down deftly. Frantic now, I shoved the flat of my palms against his chest, rearing away from him—as the back of my head slammed against the wall. *Stupid,* my mind hissed through the pain, sparks flashing across my eyes.

I blinked in a dazed manner, then let my body go limp like I had fainted. One of his arms slid around my shoulders, the other below my knees as he swung me up, holding me tight. He carried me a short way, before laying me down on the bed. My eyes shut, I sensed with startling clarity his callused fingertips brushing my skin, smoothing the hair from my face with unexpected tenderness. Recoiling inwardly, I kept my expression slack, even as I groped for a hairpin from my sash. As a shadow fell over me, I tensed in alarm—my eyes flying open as I yanked the pin free, stabbing at him. His fingers locked around my wrist, trapping the sharp point a hair's breadth from his neck.

His lips curved up. "Xingyin, how bloodthirsty you are this morning."

Something cold slithered down my spine. His deep voice curled into my ear with aching familiarity, yet he was a stranger to me now. As he pried the carved silver pin from my grasp with his other hand, I thrashed against his grip with renewed force.

His hands fell away, his smile vanishing. "Don't be afraid."

"Your eyes . . ." I choked out, scrambling upright, my knees pressed to my chest. How brilliantly they glittered, just as those of Lady Hualing's. A shiver rippled through me. Until I knew what he was capable of, I would have to tread cautiously.

He shrugged as though it were of no matter. "A disguise. To avoid unnecessary questions."

"Who are you?" I demanded.

"The same person you've known all this time. The same person I've always been around you."

My voice hardened. "No word games. Tell me who you are."

He studied me intently. "Did I not accept you, when you revealed yourself as the daughter of the Moon Goddess? Xingyin, you and I know everything that matters about each other."

There was a twisting sensation in my gut of a pawn who had been played. Everything he said was a defense or delay, calculated to temper my anger and prick my conscience. To link us together, to make us seem one and the same. Whatever he had done must be terrible indeed.

"Don't even compare us," I seethed. "My deceit did not

touch you, while you . . . you have locked me up and stolen my possessions."

His jaw clenched as he turned away, striding toward the window.

"What is this place?" I asked, hating the quiver in my voice. This new uncertainty I felt around him, this *fear*.

"My home. The Cloud Wall." A warmth glided into his tone, a moment before it turned cool once more. "Although others prefer to call it the Demon Realm. A clever ploy by the Celestials to brand us as the enemy, to be reviled and feared even by those we've never encountered."

Impossible. This could not be the Demon Realm. And he was no Demon—they were forbidden from the Celestial Kingdom. Surely someone would have sensed him during those years he served with the army.

"Is this a joke?" I leapt up from the bed, my elbow knocking over an enameled vase. It struck the floor hard, the clang reverberating in the room.

The doors flew open, two soldiers raced into the room, clad in black armor edged with bronze. One, with a thin nose and the pointed chin of a ferret, his taller companion with pale skin and round eyes. Inky tassels fringed the gleaming spears they clutched. At the sight of Wenzhi, they bowed, the ends of their spears thumping the floor.

"Your Highness, we heard a crash," the fair one said.

My head darted up as I registered the soldier's greeting, the serving girl's earlier words. Was his father *really* the Demon King, the conniving monarch whom all Celestials dreaded and despised? I wanted to slump back onto the bed, to close my eyes, hoping this was just a nightmare I would awaken from. But I recalled the dragon's voice ringing through my mind, their pearls tingling in my hand, the wind surging in my face as I was borne away . . .

This was no dream.

The soldiers bowed again to Wenzhi, acknowledging a command I had not heard. When they stood upright, they stared at me with blatant curiosity.

"Leave us," he said coldly. They backed out at once, closing the doors after them.

I clasped my hands, wishing I held a weapon in them. "*Your Highness*," I ground out. "How dare you bring me here against my will?"

He leaned against the window frame, facing me now. "Against your will? You agreed to come with me."

"I did nothing of the sort."

"You did. You said you would come with me, to my home."

I could barely think through the rage which throttled me. His deceit made a mockery of our promises to each other. I had believed he was from the Western Sea; never did I imagine the Demon Realm was his home! Never would I have agreed to *this*. My fists clenched but I forced them to loosen; now was not the time to indulge my wrath. He was a liar without par, however knowing this could only help me now.

I needed to find out more.

"How could you do this to me?" My voice was hoarse with swallowed rage.

He crossed the room, taking one of the stools by the table. Lifting the porcelain teapot, he poured out two cups of tea, offering me one just as he used to. I stared at him stonily, until he raised the cup to his own mouth and drank from it.

He frowned. "Good decision, it's cold." A light surge of his power enveloped the cups, the fragrance of jasmine rising as its color morphed from the dull brown of oversteeped dregs to a rich gold.

"I might have done that myself except I couldn't. What did you do to me?" I shoved myself off the bed, stretching my hands out to him, the metal gleaming darkly against my skin.

"Just a precaution, to make sure you don't do anything foolish."

An urge to strike him gripped me. "The stupidest thing I ever did was to trust you. How did you get past the wards of the Celestial Kingdom? Why the farce of joining the army? Why did you bring me here?"

"So many questions, Xingyin. I'll answer what I can, if you sit down." He gestured to the stool beside him.

I glared at him as I lowered myself onto it, my back stiffer than a plank of wood.

"The wards of the Celestial Kingdom aren't as strong as they once were. Perhaps because they no longer possess the ability to probe their enemies' thoughts? It was a simple matter to weaken them further, to conceal myself with magic."

"You're one of *them*. You practice the forbidden arts." I could not help my shudder.

"Yes, though it is not forbidden here. Here, it is a *gift*."

"You traitor," I snarled, recalling the fox spirits that had broken through the wards and injured Shuxiao. "Don't you care for the hurt you've caused?"

"What of those I saved? The monsters and enemies I helped the Celestial Kingdom vanquish?" he countered. "But we talk in circles now; this will lead nowhere. Did you not keep your own parentage a secret, Xingyin? You, more than anyone, should understand the position I was in." His tone turned mocking.

"Don't be so righteous. Your loyalties don't lie with the Celestial Kingdom."

My fragile hold over my emotions snapped. "Whatever I did, I was no spy. I had to protect my family. My life. At no time did I endanger anyone other than myself." I added scathingly, "What of *your* loyalties? How well you pretended to care for Celestial soldiers when you were inwardly rejoicing at their wounds."

His aura thickened, churning as storm clouds. "I *always* cared for those under my command, I mourned for each life lost. But I did what I had to. It did not matter whether I liked it."

"As you did with me."

"What?" he said sharply, seemingly taken aback. "No—not that. Never."

"Then, why?" I probed, glimpsing a chink in his composure.

I did not think he would answer me and even if he did, I expected more lies. Yet when he spoke, there was such tension locked in his body, whatever he was thinking affected him deeply.

"The second son of the king has few opportunities here. Everything was given to my half-brother, Wenshuang. Even though he was less capable and his powers inferior to mine —without the slightest talent in our magic, the pillar of our might. Yet he was named the Crown Prince for no other reason than he was the firstborn." His mouth twisted into a bitter smile. "So, I went to my father and we made a bargain. Not much different from the one you struck with the emperor."

"All this, just to take your brother's position?" I uttered with disbelief. Perhaps a part of me hoped that he had been driven to this against his will. But greed and ambition . . . I did not think such things spurred him so. He was not who I believed him to be; there was no honor in him. Yet that spark of ruthlessness, that desire to win at all costs had always been there—if only I had recognized it for the unfettered ambition it was.

His fingers squeezed the cup on the table, his knuckles white with strain. "You know nothing of my half-brother."

"I didn't even know you *had* a brother."

"Beyond our shared blood, he's no kin of mine. Ever since we were young, he has showed me nothing but cruelty and hate. Such suffering I endured at his hands—the beatings, punishments, and insults. I could do nothing against him, not because I was weaker, but because he was the heir. The few loyal attendants and friends I had in my youth were taken away by him, too, and I learned not to show anyone my favor. The only way I could protect myself and those I cared for was to rise above him and claim the throne."

I quashed a spurt of pity, trying to ignore the rawness in his tone. Who knew if these were more lies to elicit my sympathy? My eyes bored into his as I asked, "What does this have to do with the Celestial Kingdom? The pearls? *Me*?"

"My father's dream is to overthrow the Celestial Kingdom. His hatred of the emperor runs deep. For vilifying our magic and turning the Immortal Realm against us. For those we lost in the war. But we could not break the truce; we were not strong enough to defeat them and their allies."

"Your magic *is* despicable." Rash words, spurred by the memory of Liwei's torment under Lady Hualing's control. My own struggles with Governor Renyu.

"No, it is not. Our magic can heal ailments of the minds, soothe misery, uncover lies, detect ill intent. It *can* be used in despicable ways—just as Water, Fire, Earth, and Air have been channeled into grotesque acts of death and destruction. It is easily maligned because it's the least understood of the Talents.

Most of all, because it is feared by those in power—the emperor and his allies."

"To control someone's mind, to take their will away, is a vile thing."

His face darkened. "This magic was rarely exercised before the war, not tolerated even among us—until we were forced to use it to defend ourselves. Don't blame the instrument, but the one who directs its tune. Perhaps this was the emperor's intent to solidify his power in the Immortal Realm. There is no greater unity than a common danger. If so, he has created a self-fulfilling prophecy, one which will be his undoing. Hounding us into exile only made us stronger, giving us a cause. And in a war, the lines between right and wrong are blurred."

My thoughts wound and tangled together. Between him and the emperor, I trusted neither. Or was it simply Wenzhi's skill that made me feel this way, his ability to twist things until I could no longer discern the head from its tail?

When I remained silent, he continued, "I promised my father that if he named me heir, I would help him overthrow the Celestial Kingdom. I would seek out the most powerful weapon against its emperor—one he feared so greatly, he locked it away in the Mortal Realm."

"The dragons," I said in a strangled whisper. "You took their pearls from me. What will you do with them?"

He shrugged. "Perhaps they would be glad to avenge themselves against the one who imprisoned them for so long."

"Never!" I cried. "You heard what they said. The dragons are peace-loving. They allowed themselves to be imprisoned to *avoid* bloodshed. They will die if you force them to do such a thing."

My words fell on deaf ears. His face was set with icy determination, hewn from stone. Ignoring the writhing in my chest,

I pressed on. I had to learn how deep his treachery lay. "The ore from Shadow Peak. You took it to forge these?" I thrust the bracelets before him.

"We needed to defend ourselves, however we could."

"In the Eastern Sea, did you orchestrate the merfolk rebellion?"

His lips clamped into thin lines. "A seed planted that bore more trouble than it was worth. I had long wanted to visit the library of the Eastern Sea, but they are fiercely protective of their knowledge. Particularly of anything related to the dragons. Our spies told us of their complacent forces and the ambitious governor. We arranged for the pendant to be gifted to Governor Renyu to sow discord, knowing the Eastern Sea would call upon the Celestial Kingdom for aid at the first sign of unrest. Who could refuse a favor to a savior? But the governor's plans went beyond what we intended. We did not want him to usurp the Eastern Sea throne, to cast his ambition toward the Four Seas. Our enmity lies with the Celestial Kingdom alone."

I forced myself to listen with a detached calm, though it sickened me to think he had feigned such concern over those struck down that day. I dared not ponder his answers too deeply; I would not be able to restrain myself if I did. Glancing up, I found his gaze upon me—pale, gleaming gray. Something stirred in me, an elusive echo of recognition. That of the archer in the forest, the one with the silver eyes who had shot at me so relentlessly.

"*You* attacked me! In the pagoda." I almost folded over from the pain slashing my heart. "It was you behind Princess Fengmei's abduction."

He looked away then. Was it with shame or guilt? "I warned

you not to go. I was trying to protect you. I only shot at you to keep you safe—to keep you in the pagoda, away from the ambush. And if you were injured, you might leave to safety."

His black feathered arrow had indeed struck down my attacker, yet it did nothing to appease my rage. "How could you? Do you know the hell we went through there?"

He inhaled a ragged breath. "I ordered Lady Hualing not to harm you. She agreed—but you, Xingyin, have a knack of evoking strong emotions in those you meet. To both your benefit and detriment."

I flinched from the intimate way he spoke to me. "An honorable plan," I congratulated him with blazing scorn. "Abducting an innocent girl and manipulating the pain of an embittered immortal, getting her to do your bidding without staining your hands. Have you no shame?"

His face tightened at my taunt. "My decades of service, gaining access to the innermost circle of power in the Celestial Kingdom, had not yielded the key to the dragons. My father was impatient, so I decided to return and deliver him a gift in lieu of them."

"Liwei." A pang struck me at the thought of him. Had he made his way back to the Celestial Kingdom? Was he wondering where I was?

Wenzhi sighed. "Either would have sufficed: the Crown Prince's lifeforce or the collapse of the alliance with the Phoenix Kingdom. It was a pity you destroyed Lady Hualing's ring. My father was most displeased at its loss."

Something in me shattered at his lack of remorse, the last of . . . whatever scrap of hope I still clung to that this was *not* him, that this was not real. Everything I had done since leaving my mother, everything I had accomplished seemed to be tainted by his wickedness.

Bile rose in my throat—hot, bitter, acrid. I fought for calm, failing miserably as my rage erupted. I swung my palm into his cheek with every bit of strength I could muster. He did not flinch or block me as his head snapped to one side with a resounding crack. My hand stung like fire, though the red imprint left on his skin gave me a fierce satisfaction.

"Xingyin, I know you're angry. But don't hit me again."

"Angry? There's no word to describe how I feel right now. How much I despise you."

He leaned closer to me, his voice dropping to a sinuous whisper. "It was your choice to make. *You* took the pearls from the dragons. Don't deny that you wanted their power, too."

I flinched from the undeniable truth he spoke, but he was wrong about me. Yes, I wanted their power. But not for the reasons he craved. Yet my chest caved then at a sudden realization. "Did you pretend to care for me because you knew the Jade Dragon Bow's heritage? Because you suspected I could control it . . . and through it, the dragons?"

"No." He spoke without hesitation. "I can't deny I was intrigued by your connection with the bow. And what I learned in the Eastern Sea gave me a reason to keep you close. At first as an ally, and then—" A dull flush spread across his face. "What exists between us began before that. The first time I watched you shoot was when you moved something in me. I did not expect to feel what I did. It was partly why I decided to give up on the pearls and return home. I wanted no more lies between us."

Even now, a part of me ached at his confession, but I would not let it show. He would never know how much he had hurt me.

He continued, "I almost wish the emperor had not given you this task. I never wanted to set myself against you. Yet as fate would have it, during your audience with the emperor, he revealed the one thing for which I had been waiting all these years. A fortuitous coincidence which I could not ignore."

"Not so fortuitous for me." I searched his face, but there was no sign that doing this to me had hurt him, too. "You knew I needed the pearls to save my mother. You knew what I went through to get them, and still you took them from me." I fought to steady myself, to make one last appeal. "If you care for me as you say you do, give me the pearls and let me go."

With one step he closed the distance between us, dragging me into his arms. Against my burning skin, his hands were like ice. "The pearls are essential for my people's future, so we can throw off the perpetual threat of the Celestial Kingdom. With the dragons at our command, we'll defeat them easily. Once that happens, I swear I'll find a way to release your mother. We will have everything we ever wanted, that we never dreamed possible. Family, power, and each other. All you need to do is trust me."

I wrenched free of his hold. My skin crawled from his touch when just a day ago I had yearned for him. His vision of our future . . . how it repelled me. "I gave the dragons my word. My promise means something to me, even if yours means nothing to you." I could have said more. I could have raged, yelled, and cursed at him, but an aching weariness gripped me now, a sickness of the heart. I turned from him, wanting him to leave, unable to bear his presence a moment longer.

His sigh was heavy, cloaked in regret. "Take your time to think things through. Either way, you'll not leave here." He strode to the doors and tugged them apart. "It's useless to try to escape. If you persist in acting the fool, I'll have no choice but to treat you as one."

The doors closed after him. My anger roiling over, I snatched his cup and hurled it at the wall, the delicate porcelain shattering into countless fragments—impossible to ever be made whole again.

32

Despite his warning, I tried to escape. I had to. But the windows were sealed and the doors firmly locked. I barged through them once, when an attendant brought me my meal—only to crash into the guards outside. Unfortunately, they were seasoned veterans, not green soldiers I might catch unaware. I fought them with all my might, but they subdued me easily, tossing me back into my room.

Slumping onto the stool, my fingers drummed the table in an incessant rhythm. How could I get out of this accursed place? How could I retrieve the pearls? And my mother . . . my hope of freeing her had dwindled to a desperate fantasy, just as when I had served in the Golden Lotus Mansion. In one stroke, Wenzhi had ripped my dreams apart, along with my heart. My nails dug into the table, prying loose thin slivers of wood.

An ache clawed at me, sharp and relentless, just when I believed myself numbed from his betrayal. My mind drifted to our time together—the memories pained me, but I was in no mood to be kind to myself. I thought back on all he had said and done: his insistence that we keep the Jade Dragon Bow secret, his midnight walk at Shadow Peak, brushing off my interest in the Eastern Sea library. Nothing glaring by itself, yet taken together, they formed a more sinister whole. Even his reticence in speaking of himself should have served as a warning, to me more than anyone. But I had been so wrapped up in my own emotions, ambitions, and desires, that I was oblivious to all else. My vanity was at fault, too—I could not deny being dazzled by his reputation and flattered by his attention. I had wanted him to be honorable, someone I could trust, and so I had cast everything he did into that light. He had deceived me, but I had let him. If only I had heeded Teacher Daoming's warning, that a clouded mind would lead to disaster. And now, it was too late.

The doors slid open. I shot to my feet, scanning the room for anything I could use as a weapon. Since the last time, Wenzhi had ordered the removal of all the hairpins. I could have subdued an attendant with my hands, but after my attempt to flee, it was now the soldiers who brought me my meals.

It wasn't a guard. Wenzhi strode in, his indigo brocade robe swirling around his feet. A cloth belt studded with amber was fastened around his waist. Upon his hair rested a crown of white jade, set with a glowing emerald. My eyes narrowed at the sight of it, the price of his honor.

I sat back down, refusing to acknowledge his presence. Instinctively, my fingers clawed at the metal around my wrists. No matter how I yanked at them, or slammed them against the walls, they remained intact—although my skin was bruised and scraped raw.

As his gaze fixed upon my arms, I tucked them behind me. He stalked forward and pulled them out. A soothing coolness seeped into me from his touch, as the marks on my skin vanished.

I jerked free of his hold. I did not thank him. I did not look at him.

He sat down across from me. "Don't harm yourself again. My patience is not boundless."

I swung to him, my voice thick with venom. "What else will you do? Beyond capturing me, sealing my magic, and stealing my possessions?"

The gem in his crown flared brighter, perhaps channeling his ire. Yet his expression remained inscrutable as he leaned toward me. "What can I do to put you at ease?" he asked, as though he were a gracious host and I, his honored guest.

I lifted my shackled wrists to him.

A corner of his mouth curved up. "I'm afraid not. At least not until you come to your senses."

"I *have* come to my senses," I shot back. "Now that I see you for what you are: a liar and a thief."

He drew away, his expression shuttering. If he was wounded by my words, I was glad for it.

"Something occurred to me," I said. "You, a Demon Prince, deceived the Celestial Emperor. You infiltrated the Celestial Kingdom, the closest circles of their court, and spied upon them. Does that not violate your truce? Surely the Celestial Kingdom's allies will rise with them against you."

He shrugged, showing none of the concern I had hoped for. "One might argue that I served them well. At least while I was theirs to command."

I bit the inside of my cheek at the reminder that he had indeed been the most renowned warrior of the Celestial Army. "But it was *you* who weakened the wards, instigated the unrest in the Eastern Sea, plotted Princess Fengmei's abduction—"

"Xingyin, only you know that," he interjected with infuriating calm. "The Celestials don't know who I am here, at least not yet. They believe I'm just a spy, like those they've sent to infiltrate our court to no avail. Moreover, the emperor will be reluctant to admit to being deceived all these years; his pride is too great. For now, he will seek a way to salvage his dignity, rather than mustering his allies for a war he does not want. At least, not while the balance of power is uncertain." A smile played on his lips. "Though it is certainly weighted in our favor now."

The pearls, I seethed silently.

Seemingly oblivious to my simmering rage, he plucked a mandarin from the bowl, stripping away its peel. He offered the fruit to me, but I did not deign to respond.

"What about me?" I demanded. "Surely it would violate your precious truce to kidnap a Celestial soldier, stealing the pearls the emperor wanted for himself?" My voice rang with triumph; I was sure I had struck true this time. "Release me, return my possessions, and I won't tell them what you did." It injured my pride to bargain with him, but I was in no position to be particular.

He popped the fruit into his mouth, one wedge at a time, chewing with great concentration. Was he trying to avoid answering me? Had he not realized this before? Unlikely, given his cunning.

At last, he rested his elbows on the table, weaving his fingers together. "I would have preferred that you not know this."

"What do you mean?" A chill slid over my skin. I did not think I would like what he had to say next.

"The Celestial Court believes you are my honored guest, my future bride. The conniving trickster who persuaded the emperor to give you the seal, then took the dragons' pearls and fled here of your own will. They cannot fault me for harboring you; it does not go against the truce if I was ignorant of *your* crimes."

"You monster." I swore under my breath. "This was all *your* doing. No one would believe I would . . . that we . . ." My insides twisted at the recollection of the gossip which had surrounded us. Which I had disdained, thinking wagging tongues did not matter. I was wrong, so wrong. Words held power; they whispered falsehoods into reality, built reputations up or tore them down. It was why I had trusted Wenzhi so readily, before. It was why so many would believe this of me now—a known liar who had concealed her identity from all who knew her. Who would trust me with my honor in tatters?

"Liwei," I said. "He would believe me. He was there—" My frail hope crumbled as something jolted my memory. Those shouts I had heard as Wenzhi carried me away, the clang of metal . . . had Liwei been attacked? Was he hurt? He would have tried to help me. He would have tried to come after me. Unless he had been prevented from doing so.

"What did you do to him?" I demanded.

As an irate expression flashed across Wenzhi's face, relief flooded me. "He escaped," I said with certainty.

"Even if he spoke for you, few would believe him. The evidence against you is irrefutable and it's well known that he has a soft spot for his former companion." He paused, as though weighing his next words. "Xingyin, I'm sorry if this distresses you, but it's for the best. A clean break. Forget the Celestial Kingdom. There is nothing left for you there."

He spoke gently, and in that moment . . . I hated him. The enormity of what he had done crashed over me, my body clenching in terror. If the emperor believed I had betrayed him, what would he do to my mother? Would he still honor his promise to not harm her? I had to go back to set this right.

His mouth opened to speak again, but then a soldier rushed in. He bowed low as he said urgently, "Your Highness, the Celestial Army—"

"Not now," Wenzhi bit out.

The soldier stiffened, before turning on his heel and hurrying away, closing the doors after him.

"Celestial Army?" My tone lifted with mild interest, though I burned to know.

A heartbeat of hesitation was the only sign of his unease. "Just the usual trouble at our borders."

I feigned indifference, even as my mind spun, trying to make sense of what I had heard. That soldier had hurried to relay urgent news about the Celestial Army. And Wenzhi's sharp response was most unlike his usual self. This was no simple matter of unruly troops at the border. Something more serious was afoot, something he wanted to hide from me.

How smoothly he lied, I realized with a twinge in my chest. But I was no longer so easily deceived.

The moment he left, I rushed to the doors. They were crafted from ebony with a solid panel of wood at the bottom, the top half latticed in a pattern of interlocking circles, lined with white silk. I crouched low to hide my silhouette from the other side.

Wenzhi's voice reached my ears, low and muffled. "Double the guard. Should anything unexpected happen or if she tries to escape again, inform me at once."

Armor clinked, perhaps the soldiers bowing. The thought of having my guard doubled infuriated me. How would I ever escape now? Bunching up my long skirt, I sank onto the floor. The marble was hard and cold, but perhaps I might hear something of import.

I must have sat there for hours, with my back pressed against the doors—until my neck ached and my legs were cramped. Twice I leapt to my feet and rushed away at the creak of wood. The sun sank lower, my room falling deeper into shadow. Yet I had learned nothing beyond the favorite meals of my guards, their family histories, the immortals they fancied. With a sigh, I rose to pace the floor, trying to settle the ceaseless churning in my gut.

By the window, I paused. Over a thousand soldiers had gathered below, their black armor gleaming like an ocean of night. Wenzhi stood upon a dais in front of them, addressing the troops as he usually did before an impending confrontation — though it sickened me to think he was now plotting against those he had fought alongside before. I strained to listen, but nothing slipped through the barrier, not even the sigh of the breeze which glided through it. I pounded the shield until my fists were sore. If only I could hear what he was saying, it would answer the questions searing my mind.

Below, a group of soldiers stepped forward. When Wenzhi nodded, they raised their hands. The air glittered with magic as a stretch of violet cloud morphed to golden sand.

Why? I pressed closer against the barrier, but the soldiers dispersed soon after. An uneasiness settled over me like I was standing on a rickety bridge that might give way any moment, dropping me into the gorge. Night had fallen, so I extinguished the lamp, plunging the room into darkness. Perhaps the soldiers might be less guarded if they believed I was asleep.

I returned to my place by the doors, sinking down and

wrapping my arms around my knees. A confrontation was looming, I was sure of it. But when? How was the Celestial Army involved? And why did they transform the clouds to sand?

Footsteps thudded outside. Armor clinked.

"His Highness requests a report." A woman's voice this time.

She spoke so softly I had to close my eyes, straining to hear. Just as I had done when shooting blindfolded in the peach blossom forest.

"No trouble. She was quiet today and went to bed early. Maybe she's finally coming around."

Someone laughed. I clenched my jaws at the mocking sound.

"Captain Mengqi, we missed His Highness's address," another said in a respectful tone. "Do you have any news for us?"

My ears pricked up. A captain? She might be better informed.

"Our sources tell us the Celestial Crown Prince will join the army tomorrow. They will march the day after, at dawn."

Liwei was coming here? Why? My soaring hope plunged into fear as I wondered, what would Wenzhi do? Somehow, he would twist this to his advantage. Which meant . . . this was a trap and I, its bait.

Someone cleared his throat. "Is everything in order?" he asked, a little nervously.

"The moment they cross the border, our victory is sealed." Her voice throbbed with satisfaction, as grunts of approval met her words.

Shortly after, Captain Mengqi left. As her footsteps faded to silence, I slumped against the wall, fighting down a burst of panic. Why was the Celestial Army here? It could not be for me—the emperor would never lift a finger in my defense, especially not after the lies Wenzhi had spread. They must be here for the pearls. But why would they come, alone, without even gathering their allies? Surely, they did not mean to attack and break the truce—not for a war they were not ready for, one they did not want. More than Wenzhi's claim, I sensed the truth in this. In the Celestial Army, there seemed to be little appetite to engage with the Demon Realm again. Soldiers did not speak of the past confrontation with triumph, but in hushed voices, sunken with dread. They had gone to battle expecting a quick victory, only to limp back with a frail truce.

No, the Celestials would not cross the border. Liwei would never be so rash, not even if he were provoked. I had studied with him; I knew his mind. Reckless loss of life was not something he would accept. Was this a decoy, to distract the Demon Realm while they searched for the pearls? But Wenzhi must realize the Celestial Army did not intend to invade, he had said as much earlier. What could he be planning? With the pearls in his possession, Wenzhi controlled the dragons. It was in his greatest advantage to force a confrontation now, close to his homeland. Yet if they attacked the Celestials without cause, the rest of the Immortal Realm would rise against them.

My head throbbed as I tried to piece together the fragments of my thoughts. The Cloud Wall lay beside the Golden Desert. The soldiers had changed the violet clouds into sand. Were they creating a new border? An illusion of one? The sudden realization left me cold.

It *was* a trap, but one far worse than I had imagined.

The Celestials would be lured into the Demon Realm with a false border. Once they crossed over, they would be in violation of the truce and vulnerable to retaliation. Not even their allies could fault the Demon Realm for anything they did to defend themselves. An ambush would await the Celestials—I was sure of it—nothing would be left to chance. A devious plan, a heinous one.

My fist flew to my mouth, stifling my cry. Oh, if only I had not taken the pearls! But I had been tempted by the power, desperate for a way to free my mother without paying the emperor's price. How greedy I had been in trying to have it all. How utterly arrogant, in thinking that I could protect them when I could not even protect myself. And now, the upcoming devastation, the deaths of thousands would be on my conscience.

A wave of midnight swept over me, stealing the last of my strength. I closed my eyes yet all I could see was the ground awash with blood, glittering with the armor of fallen Celestials. Liwei's unseeing gaze. Shuxiao's lifeless body. The faces of those I had served with flashed across my mind, all marching toward their doom. I bit down hard on my knuckle until the skin split and a warm gush of iron and salt spilled into my mouth. My vision blurred from the hot tears filling my eyes as I crumpled to the ground, my body curled into a tight ball, my hands clenching into fists that could do nothing but pummel the cold marble floor.

33

I could not let Liwei and the Celestial Army walk into the deadly trap which awaited them. I could not let them die because of me.

What could I do to prevent it? If I had my magic and the Jade Dragon Bow, I might have taken my chances and stormed out. But powerless, weaponless, friendless—my hope of escaping was as slender as a mouse trapped in a tiger's claws. For now, I had only my wits to depend on. And I reminded myself, not every battle could be won with brute force; sometimes it was water that could wear down stone.

I had lashed out at Wenzhi as a child would—hurt, angry, and rash. My defiance only roused his suspicions of me, which made escape harder. I needed to convince him I had a change of heart to get him to lower his guard. Only then might I recover the pearls and escape. But he would not be easily duped. Tears might be useful, except Wenzhi had seen me slay monsters without flinching. Pleading would not work; his ambition was pitiless. Nor would it be easy to lie to him, he knew me too well. At least, he thought he did—anger searing me as I recalled his arrogant assumptions. How could he ever imagine that I would fall in with his vile plans?

But perhaps I could use what he knew of me against him, to let him think *he* had swayed me to his side. He had tried to use my mother's freedom to tempt me. He believed I would do anything to save her, just as he had done to secure his position. He was wrong, I was not like him. My honor was precious to me, and I knew it was precious to my mother, too.

It was dark still, yet I threw aside the covers and rose to ready myself, my stomach churning as it always did the morning of a battle. This time, however, I had no weapons beyond smiles and words, neither of which I was adept at wielding. And instead of armor, I would be clad in silk. I rummaged through the closet, crammed with exquisite garments in vivid colors. How trivial and wrong this felt, to worry about my attire now. Yet a polished outward appearance would distract from the hollow lies I planned on uttering. Determined on this course, I pulled out a black robe which suited well my current mood. Feathered cranes were embroidered on its skirt and when I touched a white wing, it fluttered, the bird soaring through the midnight silk. If only I could do the same.

Hours passed, the sun rising higher in the sky, still Wenzhi did not come. I thought bitterly, perhaps he was too busy planning for the slaughter tomorrow. Setting his traps, plotting and scheming, while all I had accomplished so far was to scrape a sizable hole in the table. No, I could not just sit here and wait when those I cared for were in danger. If he did not come, I would seek him out—before it was too late.

Striding to the doors, I rapped loudly upon them. Muted voices filtered through the silk-lined panel.

"Don't answer, it's another trick," one whispered.

"What if she's hurt or something is wrong?"

Another snorted. "Hurt? We'll be the ones hurt if we open the doors."

I scowled to hear their suspicions, well-founded though they were. In my attempts to escape I had clawed, kicked, and cursed them with abandon. Impatient now, I demanded, "I need to see Prince Wenzhi." His title felt awkward on my tongue.

Silence greeted my request. Just when I thought they would refuse, that I might have to pound the doors down, they slid open. A shield shimmered around the six soldiers, their spears thrust toward me.

Even in the bleakness of my predicament, I stifled the urge to laugh. Did they think me so fearsome?

"Could you take me to Prince Wenzhi?" I asked in my sweetest tone, trying not to choke over the words.

The guards exchanged flustered looks. After whispering among themselves, one of them hurried away. Was it in search of reinforcements? Not long after, a tall, female soldier appeared, stalking down the corridor. Her features were striking, despite the suspicion in her clear, brown eyes. She did not appear anything like the Demons I had expected from Ping'er's tales—none of them did. Though I hated to admit it, the word "demon" *had* altered my perceptions, making me think the worst of them when they were no different from the rest of us.

"I'm Captain Mengqi, of Crown Prince Wenzhi's personal guard. His Highness left orders not to be disturbed today," the newcomer announced with grim finality.

But I would not return meekly to my room, in no mood to be so easily deflected. "Prince Wenzhi told me I could see him whenever I wished," I lied baldly, surprised at my own glibness.

A young, pale-skinned soldier piped up, "His Highness is

meditating before the batt–" At the fierce glare from Captain Mengqi, he shut his mouth and stepped back.

I sighed, smoothing out the nonexistent creases on my skirt. "Prince Wenzhi will be most displeased to learn of this." I brightened as though struck by a sudden idea. "Why don't you take me to him? If he declines to see me, we can come back right away."

As the captain's eyes curved with suspicion, I added, "Can't seven armed soldiers restrain one weaponless and powerless captive?" My voice rang with challenge and a hint of scorn, as I raised my wrists to display the cursed metal which encircled them.

With a jerk of her head, Captain Mengqi indicated that I should follow her. She led the way at a brisk pace, while the other guards trailed after me. With every step I could feel their stares boring into my skull, their spears pointed at my back.

I hurried to keep pace with the captain, studying our path, hoping to find a way out. The heady scent of sandalwood clung to the air, wafting from the bronze, incense burners scattered along the corridor. Ornate gold latticework wrapped the ebony pillars, while the green marble floor was veined with thick streaks of silver.

Through the wooden doors at the end of the corridor, we entered a lush garden. Here, the fragrance of blooming flowers drowned the cloying incense. I paused, turning around as though entranced, as I hunted for anything I might exploit. Jasmine was sometimes used as a sedative, but it was too mild. I ripped a few leaves from the gingko tree, said to cause stomach upsets and dizziness—though I did not know yet what I intended. Despite the abundance of plants and herbs here, I could find nothing else of use, not even a single mushroom with hallucinatory properties. If only I had been a more attentive student! But then I stilled, glimpsing the blue flowers with pointed petals peeking through the grass. I had seen these before . . . the first day in the Chamber of Reflection. The memory of our irate instructor surfaced in my mind, and that of Liwei pretending to fall asleep. Crouching down, I plucked one, pretending to admire it while I bruised its petals between my fingers until they were sticky with juice. As I breathed in its scent, a drowsiness settled over me. I dropped it at once, wiping my hands on my skirt. Starlilies. Mixed with wine, they could send anyone into the deepest slumber.

Behind me, a soldier cleared his throat impatiently. I glanced up to find Captain Mengqi had already left the garden. I was glad for it as she seemed harder to dupe. Rising, I feigned a stumble—falling and grinding my palm against a rock until blood streaked across it. As the soldiers stared at it in consternation, my other hand snaked around my back to snatch a fistful of flowers.

"How clumsy of me." I shot them a rueful smile. Hard to believe that I had uttered my first lie just a few years ago. I had hated lying to Liwei and Shuxiao, but this deceit fired some thing new in me. An unexpected satisfaction, an inner glee—almost—at fooling my captors, to repay Wenzhi in kind.

I shook the dirt from my skirt, slipping the flowers into my pouch. As a shadow fell over me, I looked up to find a stranger standing before us. His clothes were magnificent, almost ostentatious, studded with precious gems which winked against the purple brocade. He seemed somewhat familiar with those high cheekbones, his strong jaw and thin lips. While some might find him attractive, the cunning restlessness in his expression repelled me.

"Your Highness." The soldiers greeted him with a bow.

Another prince? I thought to myself. Hardly surprising as the Demon King was unwed, rumored to have dozens of concubines, many of whom would be vying for children to secure their influence and position.

He ignored the others; his attention fixed on me. "And who might you be?" His tone was pleasant, but his yellowish eyes reminded me of a serpent hunting for its prey.

I did not reply, unsure of what to say—certain that I would find no allies here. Fortunately, Captain Mengqi appeared, striding toward us. She frowned at the sight of the stranger, although she bowed to him respectfully.

"Captain Mengqi. How rare to see you from my younger brother's side. Can you tell me who she is?" He gestured toward me.

Younger brother? I started, peering closer at him. Was this Prince Wenshuang? Wenzhi's hated sibling?

"She is Crown Prince Wenzhi's guest," Captain Mengqi replied in a level tone.

A sudden menace swept over the man's face. Had the mention of Wenzhi's title infuriated him so? And had Captain Mengqi done it to antagonize him, to avoid our detainment, or both?

Prince Wenshuang cast a dazzling smile at me now, all trace of his ire gone. "I heard news of this. Are you really from the Celestial Kingdom?"

Unsettled by his stare, I nodded tersely.

"Your Highness, forgive us, but we must be on our way." Captain Mengqi bowed again, her body tensing as she rose.

Prince Wenshuang's lip curled as he flicked his hand in a dismissive gesture. As we left, I could sense his gaze boring into my back.

We walked through a circular stone gateway into a courtyard, toward a large building surrounded by pine trees—tall and evergreen. The air was fresh and sweet, the scent of pine needles mingling with the night breeze . . . reminiscent of Wenzhi's own scent, though I quelled the unwanted thought. Black marble pillars flanked the entrance, carved with a swirling pattern inlaid in gold. The closed doors were solid panels of ebony, giving no hint as to what lay behind them.

Captain Mengqi rapped her knuckles against the wood.

A brief silence, then footsteps tread across the floor. "I gave clear instructions that I was not to be disturbed," Wenzhi said coldly from within.

The captain glared at me. "I apologize for the intrusion, Your Highness. We will leave at once."

I would not. "I insisted Captain Mengqi bring me here," I called out.

He did not reply. I held my breath as Captain Mengqi sighed, the soldiers exchanging anxious glances.

The doors slid open then. Wenzhi stood in the entrance, his dark green robe almost sweeping the floor. His hair fell over his shoulders, loose and unbound. At the sight of me, his eyes widened, before tightening—with suspicion, I thought. Yet, he moved aside, allowing me to enter.

I stepped into his room, hearing the doors shut behind me with an ominous thud. My back pulled straight, I glanced around the spacious quarters, taking in the stone walls, high ceilings, and tall windows. Gold incense burners flanked the entrance, thankfully unlit, as I was glad for the unscented air. A mahogany bed lay on a raised platform in the middle of the room, draped with white curtains from its wooden frame. Books and scrolls were piled onto a large desk by the window, which would offer a pleasing view of the courtyard if it were not shuttered. Several swords were hung on the far side of the room, in scabbards of gold and silver, precious woods and jade. At the sight of them, I stilled, trying to suppress a burst of excitement.

He walked toward me, his gaze pinning me where I stood. My fingers curled, yet I forced them to hang limp against my skirt. If I could keep my composure, if he believed me ignorant of his plots—I had a chance. But if I revealed my true intentions, I would be locked up once more with no hope of escape. And that would be the least of my troubles.

His eyes slid from my brocade slippers, along the length of my robe, to the jade comb in my hair. "Why . . . this? Though the color suits you."

I shrugged. "I was bored."

A smile played on his lips. "Did you miss me, today?"

I stifled the urge to snarl at him. Harsh words would gain me nothing but a moment's childish satisfaction, undoing all my efforts to get here. Instead, I lifted my chin, fixing him with a challenging stare. "Even if I did, I would not admit it."

"Why are you here, Xingyin?" he asked bluntly.

"I want answers," I returned in kind. "You have the pearls. The Jade Dragon Bow. I am no longer of use to you. Why keep me here?"

He was silent for a moment, as though trying to decide what to say. "Is it not obvious? My heart remains unchanged."

I thought I would feel nothing but loathing for him. Yet his simply spoken confession stirred something in me. Weak—that was what I was, and I cursed myself for it. Despite the tenderness of his words, I would never forget the vicious things he had done. He had claimed he cared for me, and then taken everything I held dear. If this was his love, I did not want it.

I looked down at the floor, trying to appear confused. Torn.

Undecided. "What you said before . . . about us. Our future. My mother. Did you mean it?"

He leaned closer to me, so close, a lock of his hair brushed my cheek. "Are you no longer angry with me?" Though his voice was soft, his stare was watchful and assessing.

I drew a deep breath, trying to calm myself. "I was angry before. Furious. How could I not be after what you had done?" Lifting my chin, I met his gaze. "But you were right. What matters most is my mother's freedom. It's why I joined the army, what I've worked for all these years. And there's also—" My voice trailed away then, though I hoped the implication was clear. That he would mistake the heat coloring my cheeks for desire, and not the shame it was.

"You said you could help me free her. How?" I asked urgently, like I was trying to test his sincerity rather than convince him of mine. He would not expect a disadvantaged opponent moving to attack rather than defend. It would be a reckless move, foolish, even. But what did it matter when I had nothing more to lose?

"Once we overthrow the Celestial Kingdom, with the might of the dragons behind us, nothing will be beyond our reach." His tone was guarded, though his eyes shone startlingly bright.

I forced myself to nod, inwardly seething that he believed the dragons were his to command. Even against their will, even though they might die from serving him so. As though it would be a fair battle tomorrow, instead of the devious tactics he had planned to ambush the soldiers who had fought with him before.

I buried my revulsion in the warm smile on my lips. "Do I have your word?" How it stung, letting him dangle before me the thing I wanted most in the world. More so, because it was still out of my reach.

He blinked slowly, in seeming disbelief. Yet his mind was ever sharp. "Are you willing to sever *all* your ties with the Celestial Kingdom?" he countered, seeking the slightest crack in my composure.

Did he mean Liwei? I slipped on a mask of indifference. "The Celestial Kingdom means nothing to me. The emperor imprisoned my mother. The empress treated me with spite and disdain. As for their son—" Here, I let a teasing note slide into my voice. "Are you still jealous of him? He hurt me once, and I only helped him after because I hoped he would plead for my mother." It was what Liwei had accused me of before. Just what Wenzhi might believe given his own lack of scruples.

I stepped closer to him until the silk of our robes grazed. "You were my choice, even before we left to find the dragons. My anger these days past had nothing to do with him, but *you*—what you did, how you lied to me and broke my trust." My tone gentled, now low with promise as I tossed my head back. "Oh, I haven't forgiven you yet—it will take a while. Though it depends . . ."

"On what?" he wanted to know.

"On whether you can make things right between us."

He stared at me, his arms folded over his chest. I knew that look of his, deep in thought, weighing each word spoken against what he knew. Did he recall the coolness between Liwei and me in the Mortal Realm? My promise to him on the rooftop? The best lies were indeed those steeped in truth.

Finally, he dropped his arms, his expression softening. "Stay with me, and I promise to free your mother once we defeat the Celestial Kingdom. Your family will be mine, too."

He spoke the words with the gravity of a vow, one which would have brought me such joy just days ago—but now, turned my stomach. Yet hope sparked in me, too, that he had believed my lies. That I still had a chance.

"I will hold you to that." I drew out each word softly.

His eyes shone molten silver as he raised a hand to cradle my cheek. Our embrace in the mortal village flashed across my mind, when I had craved his touch and longed for more. But I knew what he wanted of me now, and I would not give it to him. I could not kiss him again; I was not that good a liar.

"Shall we have a drink? To celebrate?" I suggested then.

"If you wish." He dropped his hand, raising his voice to call for an attendant, who entered with a deferential bow.

"Osmanthus wine," he told her, recalling my drink of choice.

Yet such consideration was irrelevant now; I needed something stronger to mask the bitterness of the star-lilies. My fingers brushed the cool skin of his wrist as I tried not to flinch. "I'm in the mood for something else. Plum wine, maybe?"

He nodded to the attendant, who bowed in acknowledgment before leaving. As the doors closed behind her, he took a step toward me, his gaze darkening with intent. My eyes darted around the room, seeking something—anything—to distract his thoughts. A qin lay upon a low table in the corner, a beautiful instrument, the red-lacquered wood inlaid with mother-of-pearl.

"Do you play?" I asked. A stark reminder that I did not know much of him at all.

"A little."

"Those who say 'a little,' usually mean 'a lot.' Are you skilled?" My voice rang with challenge.

The corners of his mouth tilted up. "A little."

He lowered himself before the instrument, his forehead creased in concentration. His song began in a tantalizing whisper, soft and sweet. As he plucked the strings, his notes rose and fell with haunting beauty. He played with such intensity, such passion, that even with all I knew of him, his music moved me deep inside.

As the last note faded, I brushed my palms against my skirt. The crumpled petals of the star-lilies fell unseen to the floor, their juice squeezed into the wine the attendant had brought. Lifting the porcelain jar, I filled a cup with wine and offered it to him with both my hands. He accepted it with a smile, but when he lifted it to his lips, he paused.

I raised my cup to him at once, "To the days ahead."

He accepted my toast, draining his cup. His expression was surprised, perplexed, even. Did he wonder at the taste?

"You play well," I said, a little too quickly, hoping to divert his attention.

"Not as well as you play the flute."

The only time he had heard me perform was at Liwei's banquet, the song I gifted him. Wenzhi had never asked me to play before and I wondered, was it because of this? To buy precious time, I pulled out my flute, tilting my head toward him in an unspoken question.

"It would be an honor," he said quietly.

I had not played in a long time. I blew several running notes to reacquaint myself with the instrument, sifting through my mind for the song I wanted. My breath slid into the hollow jade, measured and calm, the notes soothing and languid. As I played, I thought of the waterfall in the Courtyard of Eternal Tranquility, the water falling onto the rocks as it lulled me to sleep. Of the moon in the dark sky, its radiance comforting countless mortals before their eyes closed in slumber. Of the star-lilies, crushed into Wenzhi's wine, a sleeping draught more potent than a half dozen jars of wine—which even now, was racing through his blood.

His hand clamped over my flute, dragging it from my lips. My pulse raced as I shot him an innocent look. I wrenched my instrument free from his weakened grasp and dropped it back into my pouch. Hastily, I pulled the qin toward me, strumming the first song I could think of—a vibrant, lively melody. I was out of practice, less skilled than him, but it sufficed to drown his voice from the soldiers outside.

He blinked slowly, as though fighting the wave of fatigue which I prayed would soon drag him under.

"Xingyin, what did you do?" He slurred the words, his furious tone laced with hurt.

"Nothing less than you deserved." My fingers slid over the qin, plucking out rippling strains that culminated into a triumphant crescendo, a mockery of his current predicament.

A strangled gasp broke from his throat, as though he was trying to call out to the guards—even as a new melody flowed from my fingers now, a mournful one with haunting, drawn-out notes which drowned his cries.

"Why?" he rasped.

I cast him a scornful glare. "Did you really think I could forgive you for all you did? That my promise to the dragons would be so easily broken? That I could betray those I cared for to fulfill my own ends? I'm *not* like you."

He fumbled at his waist but there was no weapon by his side. Again, he tried to call to the guards, his voice nothing more than a hoarse whisper.

"This won't change anything."

"Maybe not," I hissed, my fingers gliding over the strings without a pause. "But I know all about your trap for the Celestial

Army. I had to do something or I'd never be able to live with myself."

"They're already here. It's too late." There was a hard set to his mouth as his eyes drooped. "I knew he would come. For you or the pearls. It mattered not which, but I knew he would come." His voice dropped to a strained breath. "Just as I suspected you would go to him if you could. I had hoped, but . . ." He weaved where he sat, blinking rapidly before his eyelids sank shut and he slumped onto the floor.

I continued playing until the end of the song; to stop now would invite suspicion. The plaintive melody was a fitting farewell to all we had lost.

The moment the last note faded, I leapt to my feet. I was not sure how long I had until the draught wore off. Grabbing a sword from his collection—a white jade hilt studded with rubies—I looked toward the door, only to shake my head. I could not escape before finding the pearls; I could not leave them in Wenzhi's keeping. I stole a glance at his still form, his dark green robes spread across the floor, his hair spilling around him like a pool of ink. Sleep relaxed his stern features, tugging at my conscience, shame sweeping over me in this moment.

That like him, now, deceit came so easily to me.

34

The pearls were here, I was certain of it. Wenzhi would keep so precious an item close at hand, particularly on the eve of battle. Flinging open the drawers in his desk, I found only a few seals of jade and metal, an inkstone, and loose sheets of paper. The shelves held nothing but books and scrolls, while the closet was stacked with garments that tumbled to the floor in my frantic search.

The sun descended, the room growing darker. I lit the silk-paneled lanterns which cast their soft glow across the walls. Deep in slumber, Wenzhi's rhythmic breathing broke the silence. How much time did I have until the draught wore off? He had asked not to be disturbed, yet how long would that order stand? What if someone brought him a meal, or a report? And I could not help wondering, what the guards outside believed us to be doing all this time.

My nails cut into my palms. I forced myself to calm, to think. In Xiangliu's lair I had somehow sensed the Jade Dragon Bow's presence. Closing my eyes, I focused on drowning out the powerful thrum of Wenzhi's aura, reaching out with my senses as I did when taking a particularly challenging shot. I pressed my fingers to my temples, trying to steady the thud of my heart, to silence my fear, frustration, and hope, too—just as Teacher Daoming had taught me. As the stillness descended, I breathed easier, the tension easing from my body. All around was the soothing darkness threaded with glimmers of light.

My eyes flew open. There it was, that elusive sensation grazing my awareness—a whisper, a brush of wind. Calling to me, just as it had when it drew me to the hidden cavern in Shadow Peak. Surely the pearls would be kept in the same place as the Jade Dragon Bow.

It was like feeling my way blind in the night, but for a thread of spider silk between my fingers as a guide. Step by step, I traced the pull to a small, lacquered cabinet in a corner of the room. In my frantic search, I must have missed it—or had it been enchanted to stay out of sight? I dashed to it and tugged the handles, only to find it secured with a heavy brass lock. Impatient now, I snatched up my sword and sawed at the hinges as hard as I could. The wood was sturdy and it took time, splinters piercing my skin before the panel broke and swung free.

Someone cleared his throat behind me, a deliberate sound crawling with menace. I spun around, afraid to find Wenzhi waking up, only to look into the gloating yellow orbs of Prince Wenshuang.

I had not heard him enter, so intent was I on my task. Only now did I perceive the shift in the air, pulsing with the heat of his aura. He shut the doors behind him as I smothered the urge to cry out. Dread sank over me at his presence, but I feared more alerting the guards. If they came in, nothing I uttered would convince them of my innocence. But he was just one man and I was so close now, if only I could rid myself of him.

"Does my dear brother know what you're doing?" He spoke in a pleasant tone, a smile playing on his lips.

I did not reply, my mind drawing a blank. His finger tapped his chin as his stare swept the room. It had been immaculate when I entered, yet now appeared as though a tornado had swept through, scattering Wenzhi's possessions with abandon.

"I think not." He answered his own question.

My pulse quickened as I took a casual step to the side, trying to block Wenzhi's sleeping form from his sight. His eyes followed me, an eerie light flaring in them as they alighted on his brother. Despair surged in me, that surely he would cry out. I would have no choice but to attack him, as guards poured into the room at the first clash of metal. I would be imprisoned or killed, leaving the dragons to be enslaved, and my mother trapped forever. And Liwei and the Celestial Army would perish.

Without warning, his magic surged through the air, the walls of the room shimmering with a translucent light that sank into the crevices between the windows and doors. A coldness formed in the pit of my stomach like I had swallowed a chunk of ice. I knew this enchantment; I had woven it once before, to prevent my music from drifting across the Courtyard of Eternal Tranquility. Even if I screamed until my throat was hoarse, the guards outside would hear nothing but the rustling wind.

The thought heartened yet terrified me.

"What are you doing?" I was glad my confusion masked my fear and it helped that it was unfeigned. Even though the room was silenced and my bow was just a quick lunge away, I dared not risk him discovering the pearls. Not while his magic rippled off him while mine was still bound.

"You have my deepest thanks. I've long wished for this moment. It wasn't enough for my little brother to be revered and praised by all, he had to steal my birthright, too." His hands bunched into fists by his sides.

I stepped away from him, closer to the lacquered cabinet.

He cocked his head at me. "I'm so grateful, I'll even let you flee. It would save me the trouble of disposing of you and it would strengthen my story."

I froze. "Story?"

"Everyone will weep at the tragic tale. How the Celestial spy, the one my stupid half-brother fell in love with, betrayed and killed him." His lips curved wider into a vicious smile.

"You're . . . going to kill him? Your brother? And blame me for it?" Despite my anger at Wenzhi, my heart twisted at the thought.

"*Half*-brother," he corrected me coldly, echoing Wenzhi's own disdain at their kinship. "What's the matter? Don't you want to escape? Don't you hate him? Isn't that why you did all this?" His arm swept across the room.

Without waiting for my answer, he drew his sword and stalked toward Wenzhi.

Chaos erupted in my mind. I hated Wenzhi, I reminded myself. For all he had done, for all he planned to do. I loathed and despised him and wanted nothing more than to escape. Yet could I really stand by and let him get murdered without a chance to defend himself? He was only vulnerable because I had tricked him. His death would be on my conscience, as surely as though I had plunged the sword into him myself. Unbidden, memories flooded me—of when he had defended me against Governor Renyu, when he had borne the brunt of Xiangliu's attack, the many times we had watched over and protected each other. Oh, how he had lied to and deceived me; we could never go back to what we once were. But neither could I pretend that everything had been erased between us. I hated him now because I had loved him then.

I moved in front of Prince Wenshuang, blocking his path. My fingers clutched the jade hilt of my sword so tightly, the rubies dug into my palm. "I can't let you do this."

His pupils were slits of yellow flame. "Perhaps it would be best if you didn't survive after all."

I lunged at him, my sword raised high. He slammed it away with his blade, before flying toward me. I spun aside, whirling to kick at him. He dodged, I missed. As my sword arced toward his chest, he ducked —too slow—my blade slicing his ear. As blood trickled down his neck, a snarl erupted from his throat. I dove at him again—the air thickening with his energy as a gleaming shield encased him now. My sword crashed into his barrier, my arm throbbing as I staggered from the rebound. Before I could recover, he seized my wrist, twisting it roughly as my weapon clattered to the floor.

His fist plowed into my temple, his rings cutting into my flesh. I gasped as pain exploded through my head. Darkness bloomed, as I fought against the beckoning void. If I fainted now, Wenzhi *and* I would die. Prince Wenshuang charged at me—so quick, I was caught unaware—his arms locking around my waist, jerking my body against his, forcing me into a repulsive embrace. The fury in his expression morphed into something more sinister, which made me want to hurl up the contents of my stomach. If only I had my powers, I would have flung him against the wall until every bone in his immortal body broke. And still, it would not be enough.

My legs lashed out instead, my knee driving into his abdomen. He flinched, but did not loosen his hold. As I thrashed against him, he twisted my arms behind me and spun me around, shoving me against the ground with blinding force. My head slammed into the marble—stinging—as my blood splattered across the floor. As he crouched over me, he held me firmly down by my shoulder blades as I writhed in his grip.

"If only I could tell my little brother about this. Unfortunately for him, he'll never awaken." He was so close to me, flecks of his spittle sprayed across my cheek.

I gagged, trying to twist away from him. His fingers dug into my flesh with bruising force, his breath was hot and thick against my neck. Fear racked me as a thought flitted across my mind . . . that maybe death might be a mercy after all.

No, I banished it at once, sucking in a mouthful of air and screaming as loudly as I could. *Let the guards come,* I thought wildly, *let them capture me.* I would rather be a prisoner than at the mercy of this monster. But it was futile, the prince's privacy shield swallowing the sound. Yet I did not stop—what had begun as a hollow cry of fear morphing into a bellow of white-hot rage, burning away my terror, kindling the fire in me . . . that I would fight.

Prince Wenshuang jerked away, perhaps disconcerted by the ferocity in my voice. Just for a heartbeat, but it was enough. I struck then, bashing the back of my head into his face with all the force I could muster. A crack ripped the air. He released me with a curse, pressing his hand to his nose to stem the gush of blood. Leaping to my feet, I grabbed my sword from the ground and swung it at him. He went scarlet with rage as lights sparked from his palm, a bolt of flame already streaking my way. My sword flashed up, blocking his attack—tendrils of fire crackling along the blade which shattered into silver shards. I did not pause, dropping down to slide across the marble floor, kicking his legs out from under him. He fell with a thump, groaning where he lay. I searched frantically for another weapon, not daring to look away from him—already he was scrambling up, his expression one of murderous fury. My blade was destroyed, yet the jade hilt in my grip was heavy and crusted with gems. Raising it high, I smashed it against his temple with all my might—and then, again. It struck with a sickening crunch, his eyes widening before they fluttered shut.

I panted, fighting the urge to retch as I dropped the hilt. Blood poured from the gash on his forehead. If he were mortal my blow would have crushed his skull like a soft-boiled egg. I felt no pity for him though for planning to murder his sleeping brother, for what he had tried to do to me. A part of me wondered, should I kill him? All it would take was a single arrow from my bow.

Racing to the cabinet, I pried the remnants of its door apart—carefully, as I could not drop my guard. With the prince unconscious, his privacy shield was no more. My fingers closed around the jade of my bow, which I snatched up at once. Sweeping aside the debris, I plunged my hand in deeper to find a small wooden box. As I flipped the lid open, the pearls glowed back at me, luminous and bright. I could have laughed aloud from relief. Plucking out the one that gleamed with midnight fire, I held it up, whispering the Black Dragon's name—praying the wind would carry my words swiftly to the Eastern Sea.

A groan pricked my ears. I whirled to see Wenzhi stirring, his head swinging from side to side like he was suffering some restless dream. The draught was wearing off! My fingers tightened around the bow, even as I recoiled from the temptation. I would be no better than his brother if I did. And surely, the guards would barge in at the sound, trapping me inside the room. Bracing myself, I barreled through the doors, sprinting across the courtyard. Startled cries erupted behind me, from the soldiers caught unaware by my sudden dash. Their stupor didn't last; the coils of their power already surging forth to catch me. Worse yet, a familiar voice called my name in a desperate cry. Wenzhi. Fully awake now and racing after me, his long legs outpacing mine with every step. The air shimmered with his magic, flecks of ice glistening in the air—

I swung sharply down another path, evading his enchantment— but a wall loomed before me, its smooth stone impossible to scale. Footsteps thudded louder; they were almost upon me. Leaping onto one of the marble pillars, I clambered up it, using the ornate latticework as a foothold. I had enough practice doing so in the Jade Palace.

On the rooftop, I drew the Jade Dragon Bow, almost weeping at the familiar crackle of its power. With my energy still bound, the string was stiff as it cut into my fingers, the Sky-fire a shadow of its former might. I could only pray it would suffice as I aimed it downward, at the enemy who would emerge at any moment— my insides wound tight at the thought of having to release it.

But then, the pine trees shuddered, bent over by a gust of wind which tore their fragrant needles free, blanketing the grass. The waning moon vanished, hidden behind the shadowy crea- ture that descended toward me, its amber eyes glowing like two stars in the sky. The Black Dragon, its immense form undulating as it hovered above.

Wenzhi appeared, climbing up with agile grace. He moved toward me, only halting at the sight of the blazing arrow aimed at his chest.

"I should sink this into your wicked heart."

His gaze burned into mine as he took a step closer. "Why don't you then?"

I gripped the bow tighter, holding the arrow steady. It would be so easy to release it. He was awake, he was baiting me; there was no dishonor in this. Yet why did I hesitate? Shouts from below, caught my attention. Clouds swooped down from the sky, summoned by his soldiers. Soon, they would ascend and give chase.

The sky was no longer impenetrably dark, splintered by slivers of light. Dawn was almost upon us. Soon, the Celestial Army would march . . . and I was running out of time.

My fingers loosened on the string. The arrow disappeared. I spun on my heel, racing across the roof, leaping off the end as my legs arced in the air. My hand grasped a golden claw, straining to hold on as the dragon's tail coiled around my waist to lift me upon its back. Through the delicate fabric of my robe, its scales were as hard and cold as stone.

The Black Dragon soared into the sky, faster than any bird, faster than the wind itself. Looking down, I caught my first glimpse of the Demon Realm, the city resting on an endless bank of violet clouds. Silk lanterns floated around, casting an ethereal glow over the houses of ebony and stone. Their roofs were arched with upturned eaves on each corner, glazed in brilliant shades, like jewels in the night. Towering above them was the palace I had fled from, its iridescent stone tiles shimmering with the elusive beauty of a rainbow.

The city was quiet, snared in the throes of slumber. Yet try as I might, I could not drown Wenzhi's voice from my mind, and the anguish with which he had called my name. The Black Dragon's powerful body covered vast distances in mere moments. Soon the Demon Realm vanished from my sight, as though it were a nightmare I had awakened from—except for the memories etched deep, and the pain shadowing my heart.

35

The air thrummed with power like that of a roiling storm. Glancing below, a chill sank into my limbs. A thousand or more black-armored soldiers sailed upon violet clouds, a creeping shadow across the sky. They were eerily silent, with neither a clank nor rustle, and I cursed their shrewdness in shielding their movements.

The dragon flew ahead until we had almost passed them. The soldiers at the front wore gleaming bronze helmets studded with onyx. As they raised their palms, shimmering waves of light streaked forth. The energy pulsing through the air thickened, an opaque mist forming with crimson glints tucked in its folds like scattered drops of blood. It swirled through the night, thin tendrils clawing at my skirt. A heavy sweetness suffused my senses, laced with the unpleasant tang of spoiled fruit—my lungs clogging as though I had choked on smoke. A dullness settled over my mind. I shivered, wrapping my arms around myself as my head swiveled from side to side, trying to make sense of my unfamiliar surroundings.

Where was I? How did I get here? And what were those lights

darting through the sky like scarlet raindrops? My gut tightened at the sight of the creature that carried me so swiftly—of inky scales and golden claws, its whiskers streaming behind like silken ribbons. Magnificent, terrifying, though strangely familiar. A picture I had seen before, perhaps? Where was it taking me? I fumbled for my bow to defend myself, to demand an answer—but the creature swerved up, soaring higher to where the sky was black and clear. Half frozen with fright, I clutched it instinctively, the wind lashing my face as I sucked in a ragged breath. How fresh the air which filled my lungs now, expelling the cloying sweetness.

My mind cleared, though I was still reeling from shock. "I . . . I didn't know you," I told the dragon. "I thought you were an enemy. I almost shot you."

Its silvery voice chimed in my head. *The confounding mist is an enchantment of the Mind. Its victims can't distinguish friend from foe, their memories blurred for as long as they inhale it. While less powerful than compulsion, this enchantment can be spread far wider.*

"Across an army." The Celestials would be defenseless against this, trapped as butterflies in a net. "How can we protect ourselves? A shield?"

Only the strongest of shields would work; the mist can find its way through the slightest crack or crevice. Such a thing cannot be easily dispelled, but you can evade it, disperse it, or cleanse it from the heavens.

Beneath us now, the desert gleamed burnished gold—the vast crescent of land which lay between the Demon Realm and the rest of the Immortal Realm. Hundreds of lights flickered just ahead, campfires fading in the dawn. Relief swept through me that I was not too late, the Celestial Army had not yet marched. As we descended, the soldiers' heads swung to the Black Dragon—their fear mingling with awe—as we landed in a cloud of billowing sand. I slid off its back, stumbling onto the ground. Only then, did a few soldiers turn toward me, as though just noticing my presence.

Wait, the Black Dragon commanded. Its jaws parted, its pale breath rippling like frost across the bracelets which shackled me. The metal fractured, falling to the sand in shards. I rubbed my wrists to warm them. How wonderfully light they were, unbound.

"Thank you. For everything," I told it, gratefully.

The Black Dragon inclined its head in return. With a graceful leap into the air, it took flight toward the Eastern Sea, its scales glowing like embers in the light of the rising sun.

Only then did I notice the soldiers encircling me. My greeting died on my lips at the sight of their faces, wreathed in suspicion and loathing.

"Traitor," someone hissed, a soldier who had served under Wenzhi's command in the Eastern Sea. "Were you plotting to desert us all this time, while you were eating your meals in the captain's tent?"

"Why are you here?" another cried out. "Go back to the Demons where you belong!"

A chorus of agreement rose from the rest. They were not all strangers to me; I recognized several whom I had trained with, others from Wenzhi's troop. We had battled together, my arrows working in unison with their swords and spears. I did not know what I expected. There would have been surprise, of course. Questions, to be sure. But once I explained myself, would they not be glad for my escape? Yet all I saw now were their hostile glares and tightly clutched weapons. In the tumult, I had almost forgotten the rumors Wenzhi had spread. How easily they had believed those lies of me.

"You fools," a familiar voice rang out. It was Shuxiao, pushing her way through the crowd, her long hair tucked into a gilded helmet.

My spirits lifted, though I dared not run to her, I dared not taint her with my intimacy.

Yet she had no such qualms, linking her arm through mine. "Don't believe everything you hear, especially if it comes from the Demon Realm. Prince Liwei told us that Xingyin was abducted. She would never have gone there of her own will."

Shuxiao muttered for my ears alone, "At least you'd better not have." She added, "You *really* should have let me come with you to find the dragons. You might have had far less trouble."

"I wish I had," I said with feeling.

She squeezed my arm a little tighter before releasing it. "Are you all right?"

"I am, now." We were not out of danger, but it struck me that I was free. With sudden clarity, I realized how precious such a feeling was. How easily it might be taken away. And how much their captivity had cost my mother and the dragons.

The crowd of soldiers parted as Liwei strode toward me, halting a step away. His white-gold armor gleamed, a cloak of scarlet brocade flowing from his shoulders. No words sprang to my tongue, and I was content in this moment just to gaze upon him—safe, unharmed, alive. Slowly, as though awakening from a dream, Liwei closed the distance between us and folded me into his arms. His armor pressed into my skin, but I clung to him in a selfish indulgence, the warmth of his embrace driving away my distress and terror—thawing the coldness which had sprung up between us before.

In that moment, I had no thought for the impending danger or the emperor's wrath. Until a cough startled me, a reminder of the watchful soldiers surrounding us. Liwei's arms fell away as I took a quick step back.

"What happened? Who is Wenzhi?" he wanted to know.

"The Demon King's son." Even now, the claim sounded obscene to my ears.

Shuxiao's breath whistled out. "Captain Wenzhi? A Demon? But aren't you and he—" She cast a furtive look at Liwei.

"Impossible. Our wards would never have permitted a Demon to enter," he declared.

"He told me the wards are no longer as strong as before. And his own powers are formidable." I recalled his pupils, shining silvered gems. He had not stooped to controlling me through such despicable means, but after what I had done, he might not exercise such restraint again.

"What did he want?" Liwei asked grimly. "Though I can well imagine."

"The pearls, to secure his position as heir." I did not elaborate. The other things he had said . . . those were between us alone.

Liwei's jaw tightened, his throat working as though he was stopping himself from asking more.

"Wait, I must show you something." I grasped my energy— such relief to feel my senses sharpening again—the power flowing from me in a shimmering current to dispel the Demon Army's enchantment. Just a hundred paces away, the land shivered like a wind-tossed lake. Gold morphed to violet, sand churning into cloud.

"A false border," Liwei rasped, such horror in his tone.

"A trap. To get you to break the treaty."

"If we did, they could have retaliated without fear of repercussion. They would have caught us unaware. We're not prepared for battle; our presence here was intended as a diversion while we searched for you."

"Me?" I repeated in disbelief. The emperor would never have commanded the army to march on my behalf. Unless it was to haul me back to face his wrath.

His mouth lifted into a wry grin. "For Father, the imperative is to retrieve the pearls, of course. Yet for me, there is no other reason than you."

A tenderness bloomed within me, as precious and frail as the first sunshine after winter's frost. We had trod this path so many times before—just as I believed the door shut, it creaked open once more. But I would not read too much into his words; he would have done no less for Princess Fengmei. I would guard myself better this time. I was weary of heartache.

"How did you escape?" Liwei asked.

I smiled at him, my first real one since I had been taken. "Do you remember the star-lilies? From our lesson, when you gave me the answer which saved me a scolding?" That morning in the Chamber of Reflection felt like a lifetime ago. "Fortunately, you were a conscientious student. I would not have known about them otherwise."

He nodded, though somewhat uncertainly.

"I used them to put Wenzhi to sleep."

A taut silence fell over us. If he wondered how I had done it, how I enticed Wenzhi into drinking the potion, he did not ask. I was not sure I would have told him, in any case.

"It's a shame you didn't have any aconite for a more lasting slumber." His eyes flashed dangerously bright as his fingers brushed the swelling on my temple and the cuts on my cheek and lip with aching tenderness. As he took my hand, his energy flowed into me with a tingling warmth, the last of my discomfort vanishing.

"Did he hurt you?" he ground out.

"No! It was his brother." My stomach roiled, nauseated by the memory of Prince Wenshuang's flesh against mine, his breath on my neck.

Shuxiao wrapped an arm around me in silent comfort, perhaps sensing my distress.

Liwei's hands balled into fists. "This is my fault. His soldiers attacked me. I could not dispatch them quickly enough. You were gone. Only later did we discover where you were. I'm sorry . . . for not finding you sooner."

"I escaped, I'm unharmed. As are you," I said, trying to banish our unease. "And I have the pearls. That is what matters."

The air stirred, churning with power, rolling in from the west—where the Demon Realm lay.

Terror engulfed me as I grabbed Liwei's arm. It was not over. "We must leave. Now. Wenzhi's army is close. Once you crossed the border, they planned to unleash an enchanted mist upon our army—one which would confound us. He still might; he'll stop at nothing to retrieve the pearls. This far out, who would know the truth? Without witnesses, Wenzhi can claim anything he wants." I cursed myself for not thinking of this earlier.

Liwei whirled, calling for his commanders, soldiers dispatched in search of them. After a brief wait, three generals hurried toward us, the sunlight gleaming off their helmets adorned with thick tassels of red silk. They were older than Liwei, one of them a distinguished-looking immortal with white streaks in his hair—General Liutan, who had often sent his soldiers to observe my archery practices in the field. As one, they bowed to Liwei, their palms covering their fists.

"This is an ambush. Gather the troops, make for home at once." He spoke with firm authority.

The generals' eyes slid to me, creased with suspicion. I lifted my chin higher, suppressing the urge to flinch. I had done nothing wrong; I had risked my life to warn them.

The shorter of the three, stepped forward. "Your Highness, where did you hear this? Your father's command was that we remain at the border until we retrieved the dragons' pearls."

Liwei's jaw tightened almost imperceptibly. "First Archer Xingyin brought us this news."

Someone snorted, I did not know who. General Liutan cast an accusing glare my way before saying, "Your Highness, we ask you to exercise caution. She is a spy for the Demon Realm."

"I am no spy," I said as steadily as I could, though their scorn and disbelief seared me. "Those lies were spread to keep the Demon Realm blameless for the theft of the pearls."

I might as well have said nothing for all the good it did. General Liutan's expression remained unchanged as he added, "Your Highness, spies are most skilled at protesting their innocence. Your father—"

"Enough," Liwei interjected, his tone as sharp as a blade. "I trust First Archer Xingyin with my life, which she has saved more than once. Do you defy *my* command, General Liutan?"

The general's face turned a sickly gray. All three of them sank to their knees at once. "We will obey, Your Highness."

Liwei gestured for them to rise with a jerk of his hand. "There is little time to lose. The Demons will release a mist to confound us. Do not attack unless necessary. Conserve your troops' energy for flight and to shield themselves."

"The shields must be strong, woven tight." The generals did not look my way as I spoke. Anger flashed through me but I plunged onward, ignoring their contempt. "Flight is the safest way, though the mist can be cleansed with wind or rain. Don't inhale it. Just a single breath is enough to muddle you." My voice faltered at the memory of my own disorientation, and how I had almost attacked the dragon.

General Liutan hesitated. "The pearls, Your Highness. What of them? Could this be a trick so we will leave empty-handed?"

"I have them," I said, impatient to silence his doubts. Yet regretting the words when I caught the gleam in his eyes. "Not for much longer if we don't make haste."

"Spread the word. No more than two or three to a cloud, speed is essential," Liwei ordered.

The generals bowed, before turning away, almost running in their haste.

"Liwei, we should go, too," I urged.

"Not till the camp is cleared. But you . . . you must leave with the pearls," he told me gravely.

My fingers grazed my silk pouch. I did not want to leave Liwei here, in danger. But he was right, I could not let Wenzhi take the pearls again. I had undertaken this burden, and it was mine to bear.

"Be careful. Don't take too long or I'll come back for you," I said, more fiercely than intended.

"Is that a promise or a threat?" The corner of his lip quirked into a crooked smile. "I confess, my pride will be sorely wounded if you save me again."

"Better wounded than dead." My light tone masked my fear,

but I trusted him to look after himself, and greater things than us were at stake.

Clouds swooped down from above. As Celestial soldiers leapt onto them, taking flight into the heavens, I exhaled with relief. But when a familiar syrupy sweetness drifted into my nostrils—I swung around, my body clenching in terror.

We were out of time.

36

An army of night soared toward us, led by Wenzhi, stony-faced and grim. How had we come to this? Just a few weeks ago he had fought by my side—and now, he was the enemy.

"Hurry, Xingyin!" Shuxiao threw her hand out, blazing with light. As a cloud dove down, she half dragged me onto it.

The wind lashed my skin, my hair streaming behind me. As we soared farther from the border, the desert rippled before us like a bolt of unraveled satin. I craned my neck, searching for Liwei among the fleeing Celestials, my spirits sinking to find no trace of him.

"I must go back," I told her. "Something must have gone wrong."

Shuxiao glanced over my shoulder, her body stiffening. "Xingyin, something *is* wrong."

Behind us, slithering between the soldiers was the confounding mist, aglitter with bloodied stars as it streaked across the skies. With every moment, it drew closer, its tendrils grasping at all within reach. Fortunately, Shuxiao's cloud was swift; we were at the fringes of it. And yet, even at that distance, a wave of dizziness still struck me. Hastily, I wove a shield over us, sealing it tight so not a wisp of the vile enchantment could slip through. The Celestials nearest to us followed suit, gleaming shields arcing over them as they sped away. But I watched in horror as the bulk of the army behind us—where the mist swirled thickest—ground to a stuttering halt.

"Shield yourselves!" I shouted to them, though my words were lost in the tumult.

Their eyes took on a glassy sheen, their movements jerking and uncertain. Ice glazed my insides, as a few of them began shaking their heads in seeming confusion, clawing at their throats. Some fell, writhing as they ripped their helmets away, tearing at their hair. One staggered to the edge of the cloud, and then—without hesitation—beyond, plummeting into the emptiness beneath. My scream slashed the air, even as I threw my power out to catch her. But I was too late as she vanished from sight, a dull thud rising from the ground.

I lowered my hand, shaking now. "Shuxiao, we must—"

As though she had read my thoughts, our cloud swerved, racing back toward the mist.

She shuddered, gesturing ahead. "What is this?"

"Mind magic. One of its more grotesque manifestations."

"No wonder it's forbidden," she said fervently.

As we drew closer, the true extent of the horror revealed itself. I fought the urge to flee from the unfolding nightmare. Amid the roiling mist, some Celestials hurled bolts of ice and flame at each other, others attacking with weapons. One thrust his spear through his companion's shoulder, its blood-drenched tip jutting from her flesh. But the victim neither cried out nor flinched, barreling forward to hurl her weight against her attacker as they fell, rolling right to the edge. On another cloud, three Celestials hacked away at each other with methodical abandon, their faces blank—seemingly numb to the pain—though their cloud was speckled with blood.

Sick to my stomach, an urge to retch gripped me. No matter what Wenzhi had claimed, there was a viciousness to this magic beyond any other. With friend turning upon friend, the cruelties inflicted were twice as sharp. A wicked torment that those fortunate enough to survive would be doomed to a lifetime of remorse and grief.

Why did they not protect themselves, where were their shields? Why was there no attempt to banish the mist? Were they too slow, caught in its throes, before they had a chance to secure themselves? Or had the generals not conveyed my warning? Their suspicious faces flashed across my mind. Perhaps they truly believed me a traitor and Liwei a trusting fool.

The fog thickened, spreading its malevolent glow until the sky seemed soaked in blood. In a moment it would engulf those at the fringes, infiltrating their shields and throwing them into disorder. More screams rent the air, alongside cries of terror. I was free of the mist and yet, this helplessness sank over me anyway. I hated that there was no monster to slay here, no target to strike. What use was my bow against this wretched enemy? A nebulous, shifting thing, with a hunger nothing could sate.

Shuxiao clutched me, her fingers digging into my arm. "General Liutan!" she cried, pointing ahead.

I spun to find the white-haired general, the one who had accused me of being a spy, surrounded by dozens of confounded soldiers. A shield encased him, even as the others pressed closer, leaving no opening for escape. My gut recoiled as they attacked the general, his face clenched from the effort of sustaining his shield.

A Celestial soared toward us then, his scarlet cloak streaming after him. Liwei. I could have wept with relief at the sight of him.

"I'll help General Liutan. Take as many as you can to safety." He paused, his gaze lingering on me. "Be careful."

Without waiting for an answer, he flew toward the soldiers, the sunstruck gold of their armor lighting the sky. Yet nothing but chaos reigned in their midst; Celestials writhing in confusion, attacking each other with magic, fists, and weapons. Never had I imagined this calamity. Such brutal violence. When I had been confounded, I only wanted to defend myself, not to hurt another. Yet now, their bloodlust emanated in waves. Had the turmoil aggravated their confusion, knowing they were in a battle yet unable to distinguish enemy from friend?

They suffer because of you, a harsh voice inside me hissed. *You should never have taken the dragons' pearls. See what your greed and arrogance have spawned.* Remorse stabbed me like a knife thrust deep, but there were other forces at play, too—the emperor's craving for power and Wenzhi's relentless ambition. I would not pay the price alone in my conscience. And I would not wallow in guilt now, not when there was still a chance to end this.

An insidious thought slid into me, that I could so easily make this right. The dragons—what if I called them to aid us? I had summoned the Black Dragon to carry me to safety before. Why not harness them to drive away the enemy? In a single stroke I could save the Celestial Army *and* repay Wenzhi for his treachery. With their power at my command, I could wrest my mother's freedom from the emperor. My vision shifted: I saw myself with a crown on my head, raising high those loyal to me, tearing down all who had caused me harm. Only then, would I relinquish the pearls. All I had to do was speak the dragons' names . . .

My hand drifted to my pouch. Struggling against its lure, I snatched it back. No, such a thing would destroy the dragons, it would destroy me. I could never forgive myself. I had made a promise to them—one I meant, one I would keep. I dared not venture down a path I might never find my way back from, at least not until every other lane had been traversed.

I turned to Shuxiao. "Wind. Rain. Anything to cleanse the skies."

She nodded, squeezing her eyes tight in concentration, the veins straining from her neck. I grasped as much of my energy as I could muster, the power coursing through my body.

"Now!" I cried.

Magic streamed from our palms. A gust of wind surged through the clouds, snatched from a summer storm in the mortal world, laced with dust and heat. Something jolted our cloud and I stumbled, steadying myself to feed the hungering wind— the churning air transforming into a howling gale which hurtled through the sky, dispelling the mist from those closest to us.

Yet our reach was not wide enough; hundreds were still in danger. Worse still, the Demons began countering our efforts, forcing the mist back upon us. It writhed thicker now, trapped between both sides. How much longer could we sustain this? Our shields would not hold indefinitely; even now, we were tiring. If we failed to banish the mist soon, it would return in greater force, engulfing us all.

Just ahead, a cluster of Demons shot by, led by Wenzhi. I

hesitated for a moment, before summoning a cloud and leaping upon it to give chase.

"What are you doing?" Shuxiao cried.

"Going after them."

"Are you mad?" she yelled, gesturing at the horde of confounded Celestials ahead.

"No, which is precisely why I'm doing this." I pointed at Wenzhi. "His presence here is no coincidence. Maybe I'll find a way to stop this."

Trailing Wenzhi through the clouds, I flew in a winding path to avoid detection—though there was little chance of him sensing my aura amid this vast tangle of immortals. I pulled the Jade Dragon Bow from my back, clutching it in readiness. Here, the mist was so dense, I could barely see beyond the shimmering haze of crimson dust. As a whiff of its cloying fragrance hit me—of honey and of rot—I held my breath at once, tightening my shield. I could not lose control now, when a moment might make the difference between life and death. Between killing an enemy or a loved one.

A short distance away was Liwei, harnessing a raging wind to clear the air. It was working, the soldiers beginning to emerge from their stupor and move away from General Liutan—but then Wenzhi swooped toward him like a hawk sighting its prey. Had Liwei been his target all this while? He would fail, I resolved, racing after him with my heart thumping in my chest.

Liwei's head shot up, as though he sensed Wenzhi's approach. For a moment, they stared at each other—eyes so bright, so dangerously narrowed—I went cold inside. Swords drawn now, they lunged at each other with unrestrained ferocity. Blades clashing, sparks raining down in a shower of fire and ice, the clouds trembling from the force of their blows. For a moment I could not move, trapped in fear's embrace—yet transfixed by the savage grace of their swordsmanship, their movements a blur in this merciless battle.

My fingers were stiff as I drew my bow, Sky-fire crackling in my grip. I steeled myself to release, reminding myself that Wenzhi was the enemy. But they were too quick, blades flashing, bodies whirling and spinning. What if I missed?

Just then, Liwei dipped low, evading Wenzhi's sword which sliced over his head—then rolling back to thrust his blade toward Wenzhi's chest. He swerved, swinging his sword in a wide arc, slashing through Liwei's armor, his blood spraying into the air. Liwei gasped, clutching his wound.

As Wenzhi loomed over him, raising his sword—something inside me snapped. Not the bow, this close, the Sky-fire might hurt Liwei, too. Coils of air sprang from my palms, striking Wenzhi. He folded over like he had been punched in the gut, stumbling to the edge of his cloud. Catching his balance, a shield closed around him now.

He swung to me. "Xingyin, you have your powers back."

"No thanks to you," I snarled.

"You're too late, though." Regret laced his tone as he raised his hand again, daggers of ice streaking toward Liwei—

I shot through the air, hurling myself between them, slamming a barrier around Liwei and me—Wenzhi's attack shattering harmlessly against it. It stirred something in my mind, a recollection of the time Wenzhi and I had stood in the Chamber of Lions, when he had instructed me to use my powers. I did not think he ever expected his lesson to be used so.

Wenzhi's face tightened, was it with anger? Disappointment? As he drew back, the air roiled with his energy, crashing against my shield. It quivered as I braced myself, holding it steady against him—but then his soldiers attacked, unleashing their magic upon us. My shield ruptured, shards of ice and wood and flame scraping me. My teeth sank into my tongue, stifling a cry. Something hissed from behind me, fire erupting over the Demon soldiers, cast by Liwei. He shifted his hand toward Wenzhi, the tongues of vermilion flame now streaking toward him—so hot, like they were torn from the sun.

Wenzhi's shield broke. He was flung back—right off his cloud, plunging into the depths below. My heart . . . it dropped. I rushed to the edge, peering down as his soldiers hurtled after him—their power dragging him to safety. A mess of tangled emotions wound through me, one of which was undeniably relief.

"You're making a habit of saving me," Liwei remarked.

"I thought we weren't keeping count." I glanced below again, half fearing to see Wenzhi emerge. "This isn't over yet, Liwei. We must hurry."

All around us, the fog swirled thicker; Liwei's earlier efforts for naught. Once more, the soldiers closed around General Liutan whose hair was slicked with sweat, his shield beginning to waver.

My magic was already flowing forth to summon a gale, Liwei's energy merging with mine in seamless streams of light. Sweat poured from my face, my knees almost buckling from the strain. Though the mist thinned a little, it still hung over the trapped Celestials who were beginning to turn their attention to us. Flames shot out from the hands of one. I ducked, barely missing a scorching. Another hurled a spear at Liwei, but he deflected the blow with ease. While General Liutan crouched on his cloud, bearing the brunt of their attacks.

Just ahead, I sighted the Demon soldiers in the onyx studded helmets. Those I had seen when flying with the Black Dragon, only now visible in the heart of the fog. The Mind Talents who had crafted the mist, their eyes aglitter as waves of crimson light swirled from their palms. Yet their faces were strained and beaded with sweat.

They were as tired as we were, which meant they could break.

Hope flared in me as I gestured to them. "Liwei, I will attack the Mind Talents. Hold the enchantment here."

Before I finished speaking, his power had swelled to shoulder my burden. Wind rolled through the air, a storm breaking upon the Celestials.

An arrow of Sky-fire hurtled from my hand, plunging into a Mind Talent. He screamed once, his body convulsing as his skin crackled with light. As he fell, the mist streaming from his hands dissipated. I did not pause—no time for either triumph or remorse—my cloud soaring through the air as I shot another and, then, a third. The Mind Talents cried out, pointing at me as torrents of their magic leapt my way. My shield trembled before it shattered, but another sprang up in its place, golden-bright.

"Xingyin, watch out!" Liwei called out.

I nodded in thanks, another arrow already streaking from my fingers. The Demon ducked, but my next shot took her in the shoulder. As I aimed at the fifth, the Mind Talents broke rank and fled.

The mist lingered in their wake. Yet more Celestials were roused from their daze, more of them joining us now. My hair was whipped free from the last of its coils, my black dress fluttering wildly as our gale strengthened—howling as it sped across the heavens, sweeping each corner of the sky. The mist thinned, its crimson lights fading like stars in the dawn, before ebbing into oblivion. The sky had the calm of a tempest just passed, as our clouds rolled toward the safety of the Celestial Kingdom.

We were safe, the Demons gone. But my pulse still raced, my breaths coming in quick bursts at the thought of what awaited me in my audience with the emperor. My options were rapidly diminishing. Now that the generals knew I had the pearls, I must either relinquish them to the emperor, or outrightly defy him by refusing. An agonizing choice, if even a choice at all. Either one would be a betrayal, a loss of something infinitely precious—whether my mother's freedom or the dragons'. Even worse was the fear that the emperor would punish my mother further for my defiance. Or that he would wrest the pearls from me by force, just as he had ordered me to take them.

My head pounded. If only I could safeguard both! Such a thing was impossible, unless . . . there was some way to fulfill my bargain without harming the dragons. An idea formed in my mind, frail and new. Wild and undoubtedly dangerous.

"Xingyin," Shuxiao called out, as she halted beside me. "Let's go."

"I can't," I replied. "Not yet." I did not say more, I dared not reveal my plan—if it could even be called one, more a haphazard string of ideas and guesses. Such information would endanger her, placing her in an untenable situation—one I was plunging toward myself—torn between my loved ones and my honor.

"Will you do something for me?" I asked her somberly.

"Anything."

"Don't tell them I didn't go back. Spread the word that you lost sight of me in the battle." Perhaps this might delay arousing the emperor's suspicions.

"Is that all? I was hoping you might give me an actual challenge," she snorted.

"Everything about me is a challenge these days. But if things don't go as planned, maybe you can think of a way to restrain His Celestial Majesty's anger?" I spoke in jest, trying to conceal my unspoken fear.

She paused, searching my face. "Stay safe. I will do what I can," she said finally.

"Thank you" was all I said, though there was so much more left unspoken. As she flew toward the Celestial Kingdom, she turned around once, her hand lifted in a wave.

"Xingyin, my father expects you."

I looked away from Liwei, brushing the hair from my forehead, as I gathered the courage to tell him, "I can't surrender the dragons' pearls to your father. I gave them my word."

He did not speak at first, his eyes so dark and solemn. "What will you do?"

I hesitated. Dare I trust him with this? Did he want the pearls for his father? And if so, would he try to stop me? But as I looked into his face, alight with the warmth that haunted me still—I knew my worries were false. He might argue with me, he might try to dissuade me, but he would never betray me.

"The dragons said it was an enchantment which bound their spiritual essence to the pearls. According to Teacher Daoming, no enchantment is unbreakable. What if this can be undone? I don't know if it's possible, but I intend to find out." I added haltingly, "This way, I will keep my bargain with your father, but just the one I struck with him and no more."

A faint smile formed on his lips. "Just the pearls and no more, do you mean?"

I nodded, despite the doubt which gnawed at me. The emperor intended to get from me more than what had been agreed. And now, he would get *exactly* what was promised, which was not what he wanted at all. It might not work; there were too many things that could go wrong. Perhaps the enchantment could not be undone. Perhaps the emperor would not accept the pearls without the essence; he would certainly be furious. But what choice did I have? None that I could stomach making.

As Liwei's cloud drifted closer, he leapt onto mine, reaching out to clasp my hand. "We don't have much time."

At that moment, I breathed easier than I had in years—ever since I left the Courtyard of Tranquility. I was not alone, and despite everything which had happened between us, he was my friend still.

Yet I took no pleasure drawing him into these plans of mine. My schemes would pit Liwei against his father, incurring his displeasure and inciting his wrath. But I would not refuse his help now, not when it was as welcome to me as the rain on parched soil. Not when so much hung in the balance.

"Where are we going?" he asked.

"To where the dragons were born."

37

The Fragrant Coral Palace gleamed like a blushing pearl in its shell. Today, the ever-changing waters were a brilliant azure, the waves cresting with white foam. As we walked over the crystalline bridge, something caught at my heart, unwelcome memories flooding me from when I was last here.

The palace guards bowed to Liwei, recognizing him at once. While they knew me, too, his presence helped us obtain a swift audience, despite our lack of civility in appearing unannounced. We were ushered into a spacious room, as an attendant left in search of Prince Yanxi.

Liwei stared through the clear wall at a magnificent coral reef, glowing in jeweled tones. Bright-colored fish darted through it, wary of the larger shadows which passed above—the hunters in search of prey. His expression was somber, perhaps contemplating the impossible situation I had dragged him into.

"I know this is not what you want. But thank you, for coming with me," I told him.

"Many will disagree with what you're planning." His gaze

shifted to me, as opaque as the waters beyond. "But you'll always have my support."

Simple words spoken in his quiet manner, yet how they affected me.

The doors slid open as Prince Yanxi entered. His pearl-gray brocade robe was shot through with gold, a belt of lapis lazuli fastened around his waist. I surreptitiously pressed my palms against my skirt in a futile attempt to smooth out the creases. At least the dark color hid the smears of dirt, sweat, and blood.

He greeted Liwei before turning to me with a smile. "First Archer, have you decided to leave the cold Celestial Kingdom for our warm shores?"

I shook my head ruefully. "Unfortunately, we're here under less desirable circumstances, Your Highness."

The urgency in my tone banished his mirth. "If there is anything you need, you have only to ask," he assured me, sitting down and gesturing for me to do the same.

I remained standing, my fingers already untying the strings of my pouch and tipping the pearls into my palm. Tingling against my skin and pulsing with inner fire.

Prince Yanxi leaned closer to inspect them, his head jerking up. "Are these the pearls of the Venerable Dragons?"

"Yes."

"How did you get them?" he asked in wonder.

"They were given to me." The words stumbled out, halting and uncertain. I was unused to unveiling my secrets so easily. Even now, a part of me feared that I had made a mistake in coming here, that Prince Yanxi would be obligated to surrender us to the Celestial Kingdom.

Perhaps sensing my unease, he stiffened, drawing away. "Who gave them to you? Who has the right to do so?"

"The dragons themselves," I replied, a little stung by his doubt. But I recalled how greatly he cared for the dragons. And I, myself, was still in disbelief to be entrusted with their pearls.

"My father tasked Xingyin to gather the dragons' pearls for him. They were released from the Mortal Realm using his seal," Liwei explained.

Prince Yanxi leapt to his feet, his face aglow. "The dragons are freed! I must inform my father."

I moved in front of him. "Your Highness, your father will know in good time. For now, there is a more urgent matter we need your help on."

"Urgent?"

"I must ask you something about these pearls."

His gaze probed me, guarded once more as he sat back down. "I cannot help but wonder, why does the Celestial Emperor desire the pearls now? And why would the dragons relinquish them?"

"I can't speak for His Celestial Majesty's intentions. When I agreed, I did not realize what the pearls meant to the dragons. Rest assured, I have promised to protect their freedom."

He did not reply, his head tilted to one side as though he had not yet decided whether to trust us.

Inhaling deeply, I plunged ahead. "The enchantment which binds the dragons' spiritual essence to the pearls . . . can it be undone?" My heart thudded as I awaited his answer.

"Why?" He looked at me like I was a puzzle he was trying to figure out.

"I want to restore the dragons' essence to them. They will never be beholden to another again."

"Why do you want to do this? Why not just return the pearls to the dragons?" he probed, ever perceptive.

I thought of my mother, whom Prince Yanxi might still be

ignorant of. "In truth, I am being selfish, too. If I give the pearls back to the dragons, I will have failed in my task. I do not want that. The emperor has promised me something which I want very much."

He arched an eyebrow. "It must be something important, First Archer."

"Nothing is more important than family," I said in a low voice. "As you yourself know, Your Highness."

Prince Yanxi's expression softened as he leaned back against his chair. Was he thinking of his brother? His parents? "This enchantment you speak of is a powerful one." He rubbed his chin pensively, "The seal was formed through blood and magic, and through those it can be broken. But only with that of the rightful owner of the pearls."

It was possible. There was still a chance. Every enchantment required magic, though I could not help quailing at the mention of blood.

He hesitated, glancing at Liwei.

"Speak freely, Your Highness. You're among friends, none who will take offense," said Liwei.

Prince Yanxi laced his fingers together, his elbows resting on the table. "First Archer Xingyin, was it to you alone that the dragons offered their pearls?"

When I nodded, his frown deepened. "Not much is known of their ruler, the warrior who saved them. Some believe he was a relation of the Celestial Emperor. If so, why would the dragons not offer their allegiance to you or your father?" he asked Liwei.

The gold sculptures on the rooftop of the Jade Palace, the embroidery on the imperial robes . . . was the rumor true or were these merely symbols to perpetuate a powerful myth? Had the emperor coveted the might of the dragons, all this time? Had their punishment been rooted in their refusal to bow to him?

"In the Celestial Kingdom, we don't have much information on the dragons. All I know is they have no wish to serve my father. They made that clear when they were freed." Liwei paused. "Why do you ask?"

Prince Yanxi sighed. "Releasing the dragons' essence is no simple matter. It requires a great sacrifice, one which the warrior paid to bind their essence to the pearls. Half of one's lifeforce to complete the enchantment." He leaned across the table toward me, "The dragons yielded their pearls to you, which means they acknowledge *you* as their true owner. Therefore, it is you, alone, who must pay this price."

His words pounded into my mind. *Half* my lifeforce? Unlike my energy, which could be recovered through recuperation, it might take decades to regain my lifeforce. Centuries, perhaps. I would be weakened, immensely so. Drawing the Jade Dragon Bow would be a challenge. How could I protect those I loved? How could I defend myself?

Liwei seized my hand, holding it tight. "Xingyin, don't do this. There must be another way."

I pulled free from his grasp, conscious of Prince Yanxi's penetrating stare. It would be so easy to walk away, to let fate take its course. To have the decision made for me instead of grappling with it. But I had come so close to losing the pearls before, I dared not risk it again. I did not know how much longer I had. Even now, Wenzhi's troops might be closing in on us. And the emperor must be growing impatient at my absence.

I bit the inside of my lip, biting down harder until the soft flesh gave way, stinging, as the warm tang of blood filled my mouth. If Prince Yanxi was wrong, or if the enchantment failed—I would have weakened myself for nothing. And if I did not surrender the pearls to the Celestial Emperor then, I would earn his eternal enmity. Would he honor the promise not to harm my mother? As for myself . . .

A shiver coursed through my flesh.

But magic was not the only strength I possessed; I had lived without it before. I had tricked Wenzhi with my words and a fistful of petals, defeated a Demon prince with my powers bound. If this worked, in one stroke I could free the dragons *and* return with the pearls, fulfilling—in name—the bargain I had struck with the emperor. I would still have a chance of freeing my mother.

"I will do it." My hands shook as I dropped the pearls into my pouch, knotting the cord tight. "Your Highness, I'm grateful for your assistance." Now that the decision had been made, I was eager to proceed.

"You'll need a weapon. A powerful one," he said. "Blood will lift the seal and your lifeforce will open the path, but the dragons' essence needs to be expelled from the pearls. If your weapon is too weak, you'll drain yourself further. There's no turning back once the enchantment is underway." Left unspoken was his warning: *you might die.*

The Jade Dragon Bow was a comforting weight across my back. "Will this do?" I unslung it from my shoulder, laying it on the table before him.

Prince Yanxi traced its intricate carvings reverently. When the bow rattled at his touch, he drew away at once. "You wield the Jade Dragon Bow? How is that possible?"

"I'm not sure," I replied honestly. "It is the bow which allows me to wield it."

"This is why the dragons gave their pearls to you," he said.

"They did not want to," I confessed, the heat of my shame

rising in me. "But I was tempted by their power, and arrogant in believing that I could keep them safe. I was wrong."

I lifted the bow from the table. "Your Highness, I apologize for our haste, but we must go. Is there someplace secluded nearby, where we might summon the dragons?"

He rose to his feet. "The southern tip has a quiet stretch of land. If you have no objections, I will bring you there myself." A wistful smile played on his lips. "I confess, I've long desired to see the Venerable Dragons. We might be legends to the mortals, but the dragons are legends to us all."

PRINCE YANXI'S CLOUD CARRIED us to the beach, a short distance away. Hemmed in by towering cliffs and jagged rocks, it was no wonder that it was deserted despite its pristine waters. As we stood upon the white sand, I stared at the pearls in my hand. Would this work? Soon, I would find out. Drawing a deep breath, I whispered the dragons' names to the pearls, fire flaring in their lustrous depths.

For a single heartbeat, all was still; sea and sky melding as one. With a whispering rush the waters morphed from azure to green, the waves surging higher, cresting with white foam as they raced to the shore. On the horizon, a whirlpool yawned, circling wider and wider until it threatened to swallow the ocean whole. From its depths, the four dragons shot forth, soaring into the sky. Cold water splashed over us, the drops gleaming in the sunlight. The air thrummed with their might as they landed on the beach before us, gold claws buried in the sand.

Prince Yanxi staggered back, his jaw falling open. His robes were damp, his hair sticking to his brow. As I mopped the water from my own face, I tried not to smile at the sight of the immaculate prince so disheveled and drenched.

The dragons' immense bodies cast the beach into shadow, yet their steps were graceful and light as they prowled toward us.

The Long Dragon's amber gaze fixed upon me, its voice reverberating in my mind. *Xingyin, daughter of Chang'e and Houyi. Why did you summon us?*

Prince Yanxi inhaled sharply. Had the Long Dragon spoken to us all? I shot him an apologetic look. I had been a most discourteous guest, leaving him in the dark till now.

I would have been content to stand there, drinking in the sight of the dragons in their glory—but I dared not waste any more time. "Venerable Dragons. I wish to release your spiritual essence from the pearls and return it to you. Is this what you want as well?" I spoke plainly, going to the heart of the matter.

They reared their heads, the air crackling with excitement. The Long Dragon's voice rang between my ears. *We wish this more than to swim in the sea and fly in the air. We could not ask this of you before; this sacrifice must come from a willing heart.*

My chest clenched at the hope in their eyes, burning golden bright. "Then I will try."

The dragons bent their long necks in a graceful nod, their gazes fixed hungrily on the pearls in my hand.

Prince Yanxi drew out a dagger with a lapis hilt. "Are you ready?"

I nodded, holding my palm out to him. But Liwei stepped between us, catching my wrist.

His face was pale, drawn with anxiety. "Xingyin, be careful. If you don't stop when you should, I will—"

"She must do this alone," Prince Yanxi warned. "You

cannot interfere once the enchantment is underway. She will die if you do."

Liwei ignored him, speaking to me alone. "Are you sure you want to do this? You don't have to decide now."

"I have decided," I told him quietly. "This is my choice."

He fell silent, finally taking the dagger from Prince Yanxi. When I nodded, his knuckles whitened around its hilt, dragging its blade across my palm. A good cut, a clean one, neither too shallow nor too deep. The cold metal numbed the sting as my skin split, hot blood spilling forth. I curled my fingers into a tight fist and turned it over, letting it drip over the pearls like crimson rain.

My insides twisted into knots at the thought of what lay ahead. Closing my eyes, I followed the trail of lights in my body until I reached the shining core of my lifeforce, tucked deep in my head. With a wrench I clawed it apart—how wrong this felt, a violation of myself—but I did not stop, my lifeforce surging free, running through my veins like a river undammed. Strong, indomitable, roiling with power. Brighter than the infinite stars, more luminous than the moon. But when my lifeforce flowed from my hands onto the pearls, a sudden weakness swept over me, my strength snatched from my limbs. I stumbled, almost falling down. Clenching my jaw until it ached, I locked my knees into place, fighting the instinctive urge to stem the outflow. My lifeforce slid over the pearls, turning my blood aglitter—a heartbeat before it was sucked within as water into a sponge. The pearls floated from my palm into the air, the radiance within them burning brighter until each was an orb of pure flame.

Only then did I halt the flow of my lifeforce, slumping to my knees upon the sand, strangled gasps sliding from my throat. Sweat streaked down my face as a numbing exhaustion crawled up my legs and arms. Worse still was the gaping void within, an intrinsic part of me torn away. I could only hope it was enough.

Liwei crouched down and clasped my hands. His energy surged into me, coursing through my body. Unlike the other times he had healed me, though, its warmth was hollow, its comfort weak. Could I no longer channel the power he gave me, like he was pouring water into an overflowing cup?

There was no time to ponder this, I was not done. I pulled free, panting as I pushed myself off the ground. Staggering a few steps back, I raised the Jade Dragon Bow. Once it had curved in my grip as silk, but now the cord was unyielding, cutting into my fingers until it was slippery with blood. My muscles strained, yet I held fast, until—finally—a thin bolt of Sky-fire glimmered. A pang struck me at its diminished strength, but this was no time for self-pity. Aiming it at the red pearl, I released the lightning at its flaming center. It struck in a blinding flash, a cloud of gold bursting from the pearl. The Long Dragon craned its neck forward, opening its jaws wide to draw the glittering motes into its body. Its chest gleamed as though it had swallowed a star, before fading to dark.

The crimson pearl dropped onto the sand. Intact, yet its inner fire extinguished. The other dragons swung to me, their faces alight with anticipation. Three times I drew the bow, shooting three arrows at the remaining pearls. Each time the golden cloud erupted, wafting into the waiting jaws of a dragon. My energy was almost drained, my fingers cut to the bone as my blood scattered across the white sand like plum blossoms in the snow.

Four pearls lay on the ground. Bending down, I gathered them into my hands, sun-bright, fire-red, frost-white, midnight-black. They were beautiful, yet something vital in them had been lost. Once you had seen the full moon, the crescent lost its charm.

The dragons' eyes shimmered with flecks of gold as their mouths curved into a smile. Their voices reverberated as one, the sound more exquisite than any song in the world. *You have our gratitude. We are whole once more, our own masters.*

Humbled and too exhausted to speak, I bowed to them instead.

With its claw, the Long Dragon plucked a shining scale from its body, as perfect as a petal from a rose in bloom. It offered the scale to me as it inclined its head.

Should you need us, immerse this in liquid and we will come to you.

I took the scale, clutching it tight. Without another word they spun around and dove into the water. As the final ripple from their tails vanished, the sea calmed—once again mirroring the sky above.

Liwei slipped his hand over mine, his magic already coursing through me, healing my ravaged flesh—but there was nothing he could do for the gaping emptiness within. Leaning against him, I stared at the ocean, feeling strangely bereft. Prince Yanxi stood beside us, as still as a statue, his gaze fixed upon the distance.

"Your Highness, thank you for your aid," I told him.

His smile was radiant. "It is I who should thank you, daughter of the Moon Goddess. What I have seen today will warm me for eternity."

I flushed, filled with fierce pride at his unflinching address. But my mother was still a prisoner, our fates hanging in precarious balance. I had no regrets; I was glad for what I had done— yet it was shadowed by mounting dread at the confrontation that loomed before me. The Celestial Emperor was not known for his mercy, and after today, I had given him ample reason to show me none.

38

Our cloud glided through the sky, carried by a gentle breeze. It was a clear day, and we could see all the way to the mortal world below—though I stared blankly ahead. In the distance, sunlight glinted over the gold dragons poised on the roof of the Jade Palace.

Black-armored soldiers appeared on the horizon, soaring upon violet clouds to sweep between us and the Celestial Kingdom. At once, they surrounded us, only parting to let Wenzhi through. He stood before me now, his dark gray robe swirling around his ankles, the emerald in his crown flashing with jade fire. While he wore no armor, a sword was strapped to his side.

Liwei stiffened beside me, his anger rolling off him in waves. "Traitor. Are you here to confess your crimes?"

"There is nothing to confess. Nor have I heard any accusation from the Celestial Court." Wenzhi's silken tone was cultivated to infuriate.

"You know what you did, as do I. And you will pay for your offenses," Liwei snarled.

"Perhaps. But not today. And certainly not at your hands."

Wenzhi deliberately turned from him, his gaze locking onto mine. "I didn't come to fight you today."

I gestured at the arrows and spears which his soldiers aimed at us. "This would imply otherwise."

"I didn't say anything about him." His head jerked toward Liwei, though he did not look away from me. "Give me the pearls," he said, like he was asking for a pin from my hair.

I would give him nothing more of me, not now, not ever. "It's too late. The pearls are of no use to you now."

He frowned, searching my face. "What do you mean?"

"The dragons' essence is gone; returned to them."

A sharp hiss of breath. "Don't lie, Xingyin. It doesn't suit you."

"This is no lie." I spoke gravely. If he did not believe me, if he took the pearls again—he would snatch away the last hope for my mother's freedom. Digging the pearls from my pouch, I cradled them in my palm as I walked to the edge of the cloud.

"You've seen what they were before. Can you say they are the same?" My pulse leapt to an erratic rhythm. Though I wanted him to see how diminished they were, this was the very thing I feared the emperor would discover and punish me for.

He stared at the pearls, unspeaking. "Why?" he ground out, at last.

His voice throbbed with such shock, dismay, and disappointment, it was as music to my ears. I did not expect this rich satisfaction to course through me, this exulting triumph that despite everything he had done, the intricate web he had snared me in—it was all for nothing.

"Because of you," I told him.

"What?"

"I want to thank you for showing me what needed to be

done, of what would happen if the pearls fell into the wrong hands. I could not let that happen again." I tipped the pearls back into my pouch. "Now we have nothing you want, let us pass."

Instead, his cloud drifted closer, the anger easing from his expression. I braced myself for more lies.

"What if I told you I'm not here for the pearls alone?" he asked.

"I don't give a damn what you're here for." Liwei stepped closer to me, his knuckles white around the hilt of his sword.

I gripped his sleeve. "Liwei, don't attack him."

"After everything, do you still care for him?" he asked in disbelief.

"How can you think that?" I seethed, releasing him. "I am sick to my core of bloodshed, terror, and grief. Our best chance is to convince him to let us go. If you attack him, his soldiers will strike us. And if he hurts you again," I raised my voice so Wenzhi would hear, "he'll have a lightning bolt through his heart."

"You've already broken it, Xingyin. What other damage could you do?" he said quietly.

My laughter rang sharp and bright. "I shall be pleased to try." In the next moment I had unslung the bow, Sky-fire blazing between my clenched fingers—yet undeniably muted from before.

Wenzhi's gaze fixed upon the blood trickling down my hand, from old wounds torn anew. "What happened to you? Why are you weakened?" His tone was rough with urgency.

We had fought together so many times, it was little wonder he could sense my diminished strength. I did not answer, stifling a hiss of pain.

"Don't exhaust yourself," Liwei warned.

"Drop your sword, Demon Prince," I said, in my most threatening voice. "Call off your soldiers and let us go. In return, I won't sink this into your chest. Even though it's well deserved."

A heartbeat of silence pulsed through us, unbroken by word or breath.

Wenzhi's eyes flashed silvery bright. "Xingyin, have you lost your mind? If you've stripped the pearls of their power, how can you return to the Jade Palace? Do you trust so fully in the mercy of Their Celestial Majesties?"

I stiffened at his scorn, yet beneath it I detected something else—was it alarm? For my safety? It did not matter as I recalled his boundless deceit, raising my chin in defiance.

"More than in yours. What did my trust in you gain me before? Lies and captivity. My magic sealed and my possessions stolen." I could not help trembling with fury at the memory.

Wenzhi stretched his hand out to me. "You don't have to confront the Celestial Emperor. Come with me, I'll keep you safe. You'll not be a prisoner this time. I'll do what I can to help you, and your mother . . . without conditions."

His offer took me by surprise, as did his concern. But words were easily spoken. What mattered was one's conduct, and I could never trust him again. I kept my grip steady on my weapon, my gaze trained upon him. "I will not go with you. And I'll keep myself safe."

His face darkened. "Do you realize what awaits you in the Celestial Court? Count yourself fortunate if all they do is lock you up as they did your mother!"

"She has my support. Unlike you, I will never betray her," Liwei declared flatly.

Before I could speak, a hail of arrows whistled through the air, one plunging into my shoulder. Pain flashed through me as I bit back a cry, the bow slipping from my hand. Was this a trap? As Liwei pulled out the arrow and healed my wound, I glowered at Wenzhi. Yet his expression was strangely stricken.

"Hold your fire," he barked at his soldiers.

His pupils were the gray of a windswept sea as he turned back to me. "I know what my brother said to you. He offered you your freedom, and my death. You refused. Why?"

I could sense Liwei staring at me, his unspoken surprise. I had not told him of this. For some reason, I had not wanted to. "Not because of you," I said fiercely. "I couldn't let him, because not even my worst enemy deserved to be killed that way. It would not have been . . . honorable."

His lips curved into a mirthless smile. "I'm grateful for your honor. You saved me that night. In a way." He inhaled a slow breath, and when he let it out, the sound was heavy with regret. "I'll not hold you against your will again. Your hatred and resentment are not what I want."

As he glanced at Liwei, his face twisted into a sneer. "To repay my debt to her, I'll let you go free. You won't be so fortunate the next time we meet."

"Nor will you." Contempt dripped from Liwei's tone.

I stared at Wenzhi in disbelief. Was this a trick? Was he really letting us go? What of his ambition? The deal he had struck with his father? While a part of me had hoped he would do this, I never quite believed he would.

I kept these thoughts to myself as a wind surged, glittering with Liwei's energy as it bore our cloud away. And though I resisted the urge to turn around, I could feel the heat of Wenzhi's gaze trailing after us.

The closer we got to the Jade Palace, the deeper my terror sank in. My skin was like ice, my heart pounding at the thought of the emperor's fury. I had no doubt he would sense the change in the pearls, which I still hoped to claim as fulfillment of our bargain. Would he accuse me of trickery? Would he punish us? I dropped my head into my hands, my breaths sliding in and out in a frantic rhythm.

Warm fingers encircled my wrists. As gently as though holding one of his paintbrushes, Liwei drew my hands away. "You have the pearls. You fulfilled the task. I will be with you."

He did not let go of me until we landed by the Hall of Eastern Light. Sunlight shimmered over the stone walls, luminous and bright. So utterly at odds with the dread lurking within me. An urge gripped me to flee, to disappear until my very name was forgotten. But like every hard thing which had come before—Xiangliu, Governor Renyu, fighting Liwei in the Eternal Spring Forest—I would face this, too.

The moment I stepped into the hall, all heads swung my way—bodies growing taut, eyes hardening. But that was nothing to the whispers which wound around like the hissing of snakes. Snatches of "Traitor," "Liar," and "Demon," filtered through my ears. Pitying glances were cast at Liwei, as though wondering how he could have been taken in by me. My insides coiled tight at so hostile a reception, even as anger seared me to be found guilty without a chance to defend myself. On Liwei's behalf as well, in whose judgment they should have more faith.

Pulling myself as straight as a spear, I strode to the front of the dais. I did not spare a glance to the courtiers—not from arrogance—but to ensure the weight of their censure did not crush my false bravado. My only defense was that I had done no wrong, so I dared not reveal a flicker of doubt.

Before Their Celestial Majesties, I sank to my knees, folding over to touch my forehead and palms to the jade tiles. Silence greeted me; the emperor did not invite me to rise. Hesitantly, I lifted my head to the thrones—my gaze gliding over their pearl-encrusted shoes, then the hem of their brocade robes, which were the color of night. Embroidered gold dragons prowled across the skirt of the emperor's garment, while silver phoenixes danced on the empress's. The Celestial Emperor's eyes probed my face as he leaned forward, the pearl strands on his crown clicking together.

"They tell me you are a traitor. That you took the dragons' pearls to the Demon Realm, surrendering them to your lover. Not a hard tale to believe, though my son spoke so fiercely in your defense. Yet the one thing which gave me pause was how passionately you pleaded for your mother before. Surely, you would not seal her to an even worse fate with your crimes. Surely, no child could do such a thing to a beloved parent. Surely, my trust in you was not misplaced."

His voice was soft, but I was not fool enough to miss the menace in it. His threat to my mother cut me deep. Oh, I was thankful to have escaped the Demon Realm, to plead my case before him now. My instincts were right, that he would have struck out at my mother in retaliation for my imagined crimes. What was equally clear, however, was that *this* ordeal was just beginning.

"Your Celestial Majesty is wise. I would never do such a thing." It choked me to utter such flattery, but I dared not antagonize him with our lives at stake.

The emperor settled back against his throne, the air between us charged with unbridled anticipation. "Where are the dragons' pearls?"

My fingers trembled as they groped in my pouch. But I forced them to steady, stretching my hand out to display the pearls.

An attendant took them from me and gave them to the

emperor. He lifted each one in turn, between his thumb and finger, holding it up to the light. As he looked at me with those black shards of ice beneath his drawn brows, I went cold inside—with the biting harshness of winter.

"How dare you try to trick me!" he thundered.

Beneath my robe, my legs were shaking. His rage was all the more terrifying because he had always displayed such control before. But to cower and plead for mercy, would be an admission of guilt. And that I could not do.

"Your Celestial Majesty, this is no trick. These are the pearls from the dragons, as you commanded me to seek."

"They are not!"

"Honorable Father, she speaks the truth." Liwei remained beside me, instead of taking his position upon the dais.

White light flared from the emperor's palm, swirling around the lustrous orbs. "Where is the dragons' essence?" He drew out each word, quieter now—though his tone was riddled with threat.

I should have been terrified, yet anger sparked in me instead. It had been no coincidence; the emperor *had* intended to use me to force the dragons to his will. I met his gaze unflinchingly. "Returned to them, as it belongs to no other. Your Celestial Majesty, all you asked me for were the pearls in your hand. My end of the bargain is fulfilled."

His fist slammed the armrest of his throne. "The dragons belong under my rule. They should submit to my authority!"

"The dragons do not agree." Rash words, I chided myself. Though it was nothing but the truth.

The courtiers stepped away from me in a swish of silk and brocade. As though I had the plague and they were not immortal.

"Honorable Father, the dragons have no wish to be under

anyone's rule," Liwei said. "It was too dangerous to leave the pearls as they were. What if they fell into our enemy's possession again? Xingyin only recovered them at great risk to herself. Imagine the destruction the Demons would have rained upon us with the dragons at their command!"

Shocked gasps burst from the courtiers, who fell silent when the Celestial Empress pointed a finger at me.

"You have grossly overstepped yourself," she spat, her teeth bone-white against those crimson lips. "Somehow, with your conniving ways, you've tricked my son into speaking for you. But you're a traitor and should be punished as such. Did you come back because you've been discarded? Played false by your lover? Hoping to worm your way back into my son's good graces?"

Such vile words, they tore away the last shreds of my restraint. Doubly cruel because I *had* been played false, just not the way she envisaged.

I uncoiled my legs, rising to my feet. A grievous breach in etiquette, but it was nothing to the words that sprang from me now. "I'm *no* traitor. I fulfilled the task, retrieving the dragons' pearls—then risked my life to steal them back again. I did as you commanded, and all I ask now is for you to free my mother as was promised, as honor dictates."

"You speak of honor? Have you no respect for His Celestial Majesty? On your knees and beg for mercy!" A harsh voice rebuked me, adding, "Others have died for less."

I turned to see Minister Wu stepping forward, his eyes bulging in apparent outrage. My gut twisted. He had proven himself no friend of mine, nor my mother's, and this was no exception.

The minister bowed before the thrones. "Your Celestial Majesty, you have been most gracious to this liar and she has played you false, time and time again. Who knows if she really surrendered the essence to the dragons, and not to the traitor in the Demon Realm?"

For a moment I could not speak, stunned by his malicious accusation. "That's not true," I finally managed.

"How can you prove it?" Minister Wu countered.

Liwei glared at him. "Would my word suffice? Because I was with Xingyin when she was abducted, and when she fought by our side against the Demon Army. I stood beside her as she returned the essence to the dragons. Minister Wu, do you question my honor, too?" He threw each word out as a challenge.

The minister bowed to Liwei, though his expression was one of skepticism. "Your Highness, you are kind and merciful. We are all aware of your . . . special friendship with the First Archer. Is there nothing you won't say to protect her?"

Someone snickered at his insinuation. A few laughed outright. The minister's words were calculated to inflame the emperor's wrath, reminding him of what he disdained as Liwei's "weaknesses," when they were his greatest strengths. Before, I had wondered if his dislike of me stemmed from my heritage, his contempt of mortals, perhaps. But from his hostility, the way he contrived to incite the emperor against us—it had to be more than that. Had I offended him, without even realizing it? Did he bear some grudge against my parents?

The energy in the hall shifted, flecks of ice drifting in the air as I crossed my arms to cling to a fragment of warmth. Whispered murmurs died away, a moment before a stillness swallowed the room like I had been transported to the land of the dead. The Celestial Emperor's face was colder than the heart of a glacier. He raised a hand, stretching it out as white sparks crackled from his fingertips, brighter even than the light from my bow—arcing toward me with breathtaking speed. Fear engulfed me in a blizzard of frost and snow. I could not move, not even to tear my eyes from the Sky-fire's terrible beauty, a heartbeat before it hurtled into me with merciless accuracy.

Pain exploded. Scorching, searing. A thousand white-hot needles piercing my chest, again and again in never-ending agony. I did not feel myself crumple to the floor, tears falling from my eyes onto the jade tiles, unmarred by a single drop of blood. This torture was not of my body being sliced or speared, but of my nerves ripped from my flesh by the sea of lights crackling over my skin. Never had I felt such agony—not from Xiangliu's acid, the sea scorpion venom, not even when Liwei thrust his sword into me. Nothing in my worst nightmares or darkest fears could have prepared me for this wrenching torment which tore my very being apart.

Strangled gasps slid from my mouth. My body spasmed as I retched myself dry. I had come here with my head held high, but I was beyond caring that a crowd of strangers stood by to witness my utter humiliation.

My screams came then, shattering the silence. Too late did I bite down on my tongue to stifle my cries, blood spilling into my mouth. I welcomed it, a reminder that I was still alive. Through my daze, a voice drifted into my ears—Liwei—his anguish wringing my heart even as I drowned in agony.

Flashes of a life unlived, paths untrodden swept through my mind, arousing a thousand regrets and longings. If only I could have gone home to my mother. If only Liwei and I had never parted. If only Wenzhi had not betrayed me. If only . . . this was not the end.

I fought the urge to close my eyes, to sink into the beckoning oblivion. Was it possible to survive this? I waited for a flicker of anger, for my will to harden and revive my strength—but there was nothing, beyond this weariness which sank into my bones.

I would die here; I knew it now. There was neither pity nor mercy in the emperor's expression, only a callous satisfaction that his justice would be served. But I would not close myself off in blissful ignorance. I would depart with my eyes open. I would see everything, from the face of my beloved to that of my killer.

My body quivered as I pressed my palms against the floor, raising my head an inch from the ground. Each breath I drew was a shuddering torment. My pendant slipped out from the folds of my robe, the jade disc clinking against the tiles.

Had only a few seconds passed? It had been a lifetime of suffering.

"Father!" Liwei's shout pierced my ears again, along with that ominous crack in the air.

I stared at him, dazed, as a shining barrier of gold light encased me. Just as when he had protected me from the Demon soldiers—the emperor's Sky-fire splintering to nothingness when it struck. My body went limp with relief at this reprieve, despite the shield shattering a moment after. Liwei rushed forward, standing between me and the thrones —his face pale, sweat running down his brow. He had come to my aid, just as I always knew he would.

"Liwei, move aside. I'll show you no leniency if you defy me again." The emperor's voice was so hostile, it was as though he spoke to an enemy instead of his son.

The empress dashed down from the dais, stumbling in her haste. The gold flowers on her headdress shivered like they were caught in a gale. "Liwei, this deceitful girl does not deserve your protection. Her actions have threatened us all." She tugged his arm to pull him away.

As he yanked free of her grip, the emperor nodded at his guards who ran toward Liwei. I wanted to tell him to leave, yet was filled with a violent joy that he fought to stay. I was so cold, I did not think I would ever feel warm again—but as I watched his struggles, a spark kindled deep inside me, my arm stretching across the floor in a futile attempt to reach him.

The emperor's gaze flicked to me as he raised his hand. My battered body could not withstand another attack, yet I forced my eyes to open—even as his fingertips blazed once more.

Time ceased. Sky-fire streaked toward me with dazzling speed, yet agonizing slowness. Liwei's cry shattered my stupor. I shook my head, a scream erupting from my throat as he wrenched free of the guards, lunging forward to shield me with his body—even as I reached out to push him aside. Even as I knew I was too late.

"No." A broken whisper as he clasped my hands. As my eyes met his—brimming with such warmth and love—I could not regret this final sight.

White light filled my vision. I braced for death.

Yet no stabbing pain pierced my skin . . . no blistering agony ripped through my flesh. Instead, I was encased in a luminous cocoon, as soft and tender as the mist at dawn. My eyes darted to Liwei's. He was safe and alive—as was I. It was then, I felt it, a coolness rippling across my chest. I pulled my hand from Liwei's to grasp my father's pendant, tingling against my skin and sheathed in radiance. The same light which had shielded Liwei and me from harm. Yet all too soon it faded, the jade warming between my fingers as the smooth stone cracked—just as before the Long Dragon's breath repaired it.

The Celestial Emperor . . . I did not recognize him in this moment. Pale with shock, red with rage. Did he feel any remorse for almost killing his son? He would have none for me. As his stony gaze swung my way, I forced myself to hold it—I would embrace his loathing and return it with my own.

Liwei swept his robe aside, kneeling upon the floor. "Honorable Father, your command was to retrieve the pearls from the dragons in exchange for repealing the sentence of the Moon Goddess. You did not mention their spiritual essence. If we have erred, I plead for mercy on our behalf. Yet the four pearls are before you, delivered as promised. Only one side of the bargain remains to be fulfilled. Yours."

His voice carried to each corner of the hall, stirring the court from their stupor. A few courtiers, the braver ones, nodded in agreement. Whispers were exchanged behind raised sleeves. Of course, they knew little of the pearls and the great power they once held. In their eyes I had completed my task, only to be rewarded with a lightning bolt to my chest.

The Celestial Emperor stilled. Had Liwei's words reminded him of the many speculative eyes watching? Silent tongues which might withhold their judgment here might not be so restrained when they returned home. Had he been deemed just and benevolent? Or capricious and cruel? As for me, Liwei had irrevocably linked our fates together. "My" choices had become "our" choices. My punishment would be his, too. I had fought for Liwei in the Eternal Spring Forest, just as he was fighting for me here. Then I shook my head to banish such thoughts. As he had told me before, there was no need for such accounting between us. No matter how our paths diverged, our bond remained intact.

"Your Celestial Majesty," the silken tones of Minister Wu slithered forth once more. "I humbly advise you to quash such defiance at once. This girl and her mother will make a mockery of the Celestial Kingdom. Do not forget how Chang'e concealed her child's existence from you, just as her daughter attempted to deceive you now. What if others believe they can trick you so and escape unscathed?"

Liwei rounded on him, pointing to where I lay slumped upon the floor. "Unscathed? Can *you* bear the Sky-fire as she did? She has more than paid for any offense—"

"Silence!" the emperor lashed out, gripping the armrests of his throne.

The air was stifling, thick with tension. No one dared to move, not even the empress, as she stared at Liwei with wide disbelieving eyes.

The Celestial Emperor's mouth clamped into thin lines. Ice glistened in the air once more as my body recoiled in remembrance of the torment, bracing for death's embrace.

The sharp click of boots against the tiles broke the stillness. An aura approached—steady, resolute, and strong—that of General Jianyun. Before the dais, he sank to his knees.

"Your Celestial Majesty. Before you pass judgment, it is your loyal servant's duty to remind you that the First Archer saved the Celestial Army from the Demon Realm's heinous trap today. The soldiers wish to show her their gratitude and even now, they await outside." He raised his head, gesturing to the entrance of the hall.

I looked up in disbelief, staggering to my feet, ignoring the pain that bloomed with each movement. Slowly, I turned, following the sweep of General Jianyun's hand. The courtiers before me parted, whispering among themselves.

Shuxiao stood near the entrance—and just behind her, beyond the hall, was a sea of Celestial soldiers, stretching out farther than I could see. As one, they bowed, sunlight rippling over their armor, a wave of golden-white fire. My heart caught in my throat as the pain in my body subsided. Tears sprang into my eyes as I lowered myself to them in return.

I was not loyal to the Celestial Kingdom. But I was loyal to my friends; those I had fought with, those I had bled with. As I straightened, my eyes met Shuxiao's. I lifted my hand to her in greeting. I suspected I had much to be grateful to her for. Who else would have informed General Jianyun and brought the army here?

The army of the Celestial Emperor.

My skin crawled along the back of my neck. Recalling myself, I spun around and sank to my knees again. I would not plead or beg; it would do no good. "Your Celestial Majesty, I am no traitor. I fulfilled the terms of our bargain and I await your justice." My words were graceless, my voice hoarse from my screams—yet whatever came after, there was a peace in knowing that I had done all I could.

The murmurs in the hall swelled louder, several courtiers shaking their heads. While the soldiers did not disperse, remaining at the entrance of the hall.

The Celestial Emperor's face was a mask of regal poise, without a trace of his vehemence and rage from a moment ago. And when he spoke, his tone was steady and calm. "First Archer Xingyin. In gratitude for your noble service, we will grant your wish. Chang'e is pardoned and will henceforth be free to leave the moon. However, she is not to shirk her responsibilities. As the Moon Goddess, it still falls upon her to ensure the moon rises each night—without exception."

A heartbeat of silence. Then the cheering erupted, within and beyond the Hall of Eastern Light. If there were those who disagreed, the empress or Minister Wu, their protests fell on deaf ears. I sank back onto my heels, feeling the tension slide from my body, even as my mind whirled. The emperor's pardon was generous. Magnanimous. Wholly unexpected. I knew as he did, that I had not truly fulfilled my quest; I had not done what he wanted. He was within his right to deny his side of the bargain, when he was also my judge. His grace was well calculated, reading the mood of the court and of his soldiers—to preserve his honor and reputation. And I heard, too, the threat in his words. All was not well. And there would be no mercy a second time.

As the emperor waved his hand, a seal appeared before me, glittering like a star. I wrapped my fingers around it, folding my body low, pressing my head to the cold stone floor. There was no humility or gratitude in my bones, but I would perform my role in this farce. Pain threaded every inch of my flesh and I could not banish the prickle of fear that this might still be a trick. Trust was something I had learned not to readily yield. Yet my joy could not be restrained—surging free, spilling through me like the rays of the sun reaching across the infinite sky.

I was going home.

39

My mind had journeyed here a thousand times, although I had traveled this path only once before. I saw first the forest of moon-white osmanthus, the glittering laurel tree in the distance. The sweeping silver roof, then the shining stone walls of the Pure Light Palace. *My home.* Closing my eyes, I inhaled a heady trace of cinnamon-wood. If this was a dream, I did not want to awaken.

I halted my cloud and leapt onto the ground, luminous from the lanterns' glow. Any moment now, Mother and Ping'er would sense the startling presence of a visitor. I had barely taken a few steps when the doors swung open and a slender woman in white emerged, a red peony tucked into her hair. She was pale, her lips drawn tight. Visitors were a rare occurrence here, usually heralding misfortune or ill tidings.

I was no longer the child who had fled, afraid of the unknown and clinging to Ping'er. Yet time had stood still here; I would have known her anywhere. A smile stretched across my face as my feet flew over the stone path. Never had they felt so light before. And my heart . . . my heart was incandescent, brighter than all the stars in the heavens.

"Mother!" I flung my arms around her, I was taller than her now. "I have returned."

Her body stiffened as she pulled away, peering into my face. Did she suspect some trick to catch her unaware? Her gaze searched me, drinking in my eyes, moving to the cleft in my chin. She sucked in a sharp breath, a moment before her fingers lifted to brush my cheek, her eyes shining as the moonlight on water. Then her arms wrapped around me, hugging me as tightly as she had in my dreams.

"Xingyin, Xingyin," she whispered. Again, and again, each time louder than the last. As though the more she said my name, the more she could believe it was true.

Another figure appeared at the entrance, perhaps drawn by the commotion. She stood by a column of mother-of-pearl, craning her neck. "Little Star?" A faint whisper slipped from her lips.

My childhood name pierced me with a sudden sweetness. The years fell away; it was as though I had never left. In truth, my heart had always been here.

"Ping'er! It's me!" I cried.

She ran to me, embracing me just as she used to. "All these years, I've been so worried!" Her words tumbled out like she had been holding them in for a long time. "I . . . I failed you that day. I was too slow. I'm so—"

"No, Ping'er. I would never have escaped if not for you." I held her tighter. "How did you get away from the soldiers?" My last glimpse of her had been her lifeless body, as her cloud soared away.

"I had almost exhausted myself, I believed myself dead.

Fortunately, a wind sprang up and blew me to safety. I had to regain my energy before I could return. I went back to the Celestial Kingdom to find you, but I didn't know where you had gone. The soldiers stopped me then." Her face was pale. "They were suspicious of me and since then, I was not allowed to leave this place without permission."

"I knew you would have tried to find me." A lightness spread through my chest. "That when you didn't, it was because you couldn't."

We stayed outside until the moonglow began to fade. The three of us laughed and wept, our hands clasped together, none of us wanting to let go. Until now, I had not realized how much I missed such a feeling—the oneness of family, of unconditional love. I did not want to move, to do anything that might shatter the perfection of this moment, this renewal of my soul. How rare are such times, even in an immortal life? When happiness is absolute, silencing the constant murmurs preying upon us. With my mother and Ping'er beside me, upon the earth of my home—I wanted for nothing more in this moment, my heart already filled to bursting.

Only when the night gave way to the pearl of dawn did we finally enter the silver entrance doors. My gaze lingered on the pale walls, the white jade lamps, each carved wooden pillar. Nothing compared to the treasures of the Jade Palace, yet a hundred times more precious to me. The stillness was deeper than I recalled, as was the tranquility which permeated the air. But after all I had been through, I was glad for it.

I sank into a chair, my fingers tracing the grains of the wood. *I'm home,* I whispered to myself, staring at my mother—afraid she might disappear if I glanced away. That all this would vanish, leaving me alone in my bed in the Celestial Kingdom. Perhaps I had been plagued by too many nightmares, perhaps I had grown accustomed to disappointment—there it was still, that tight kernel of fear in my chest that this was just an illusion. I pinched myself until red crescents appeared in my arm, relishing the sting that told me *this was real*.

Ping'er pressed a warm cup of fragrant tea into my hands. The questions flowed then: Have you been well? Happy? Where have you been all this time? What have you been doing?

I answered them in as much detail as I could, trying to satisfy years of anxiety and curiosity. While some memories as my time in the Golden Lotus Mansion were a blur, others cut sharper than I wished. When I spoke of entering the Jade Palace, my mother grabbed my sleeve and tugged it.

"Did the Celestial Emperor discover your identity?" She glanced over her shoulder, as though expecting armed soldiers to barge through our doors.

"Not then," I assured her. Before she could probe further, I quickly described my training in magic, combat, and archery.

"Archery?" There was a catch in her voice. "Just like your father," she said with pride.

A lump swelled at the back of my throat. For so long I had lived in fear of who I was—never speaking the names of my parents, pretending to the outside world that they did not exist . . . like I was some weed sprung wild in an open field. Now, I wanted to shout it to the world.

Once, my mother interrupted me. Unguarded in my home, a warmth filled my voice whenever I mentioned Liwei's name.

"What is your relationship with the Celestial Crown Prince?" she asked.

I caught the slight puckering across her brow. "We're . . . friends," I stammered, heat creeping up my neck.

"This Captain Wenzhi, is he your friend, too?" My mother's tone was deceptively mild.

"No," I cried out, more vehemently than intended.

There was an awkward pause as my mother exchanged a worried glance with Ping'er, and I was glad when they asked no more. Hastily, I began describing the battles I had been in, the creatures and enemies I fought in the service of the Celestial Army.

Better by far those monsters, than the ones that dwelled in my mind.

Ping'er shuddered at my description of Xiangliu, as she crossed her arms over her chest. "Were you afraid?"

"All the time." Some might think me a coward, but I felt no shame in admitting it. I was not one of those valiant heroes who plunged into danger so fearlessly. I had been terrified of getting hurt, of failure, and most of all—of death. To never see my mother again, or my loved ones. To regret all the things left unsaid or undone. To leave my life . . . unlived. I had been lauded for my bravery, yet I knew the truth—that I had done these things *despite* my fear. Because not doing them frightened me more.

They were stunned to hear of how I had saved Liwei's life. I did not tell them of the vicious things Lady Hualing made us do; I was not keen to unearth those painful memories, nor did I wish to distress them further. Although, my mother's face turned ashen at the reveal of my identity and the bargain I had struck with the emperor.

"How could you do such a thing? Take such a risk?" She shot to her feet and paced the room, her hands clasped so tight that their knuckles were white. "What if you were sentenced to prison? To torture? To *death*?"

"Those were all very real possibilities then," I laughed. But my mirth vanished, at the sight of her grave face. "Mother, I had won the Crimson Lion Talisman. The emperor's favor. There was no better time to ask this of him. If I did not, I would not be here today. I would be spending my days ruing this lost opportunity, wishing I had tried. And that would be a worse fate."

I paused then, searching her face. "You risked yourself, too, Mother—when you drank the elixir." She went so still, so quiet, I almost regretted the words. "You saved me then, and I thank you for it."

A faint smile formed on my mother's lips, even as tears slid down her cheeks.

"Ah, enough with this sadness," Ping'er said, wiping her eyes with a corner of her sleeve. "This is a happy day. The happiest. We will weep no more."

"And as you can see, I'm well," I assured them, rising to my feet and stretching out my arms. Their eyes lingered on me until they were satisfied that I was not suffering from any apparent injury. Though I said nothing of the web of white scars splayed across my chest. My wounds, still-tender, from the emperor's Sky-fire. I did not think they would ever go away; I was forever marked. But what did that matter? A few scars were nothing to what I had regained.

When my mother heard that the honorable Captain Wenzhi was from the Demon Realm, she recoiled with horror.

"Xingyin, how did you feel?" she asked with piercing insight.

I shook my head, at a loss for words—his deception was still hard for me to bear. Now that I was safe, the weight of Wenzhi's betrayal had sunk in fully. A different pain from when Liwei and I had parted, not that I would have suffered either willingly.

With Liwei, it had been circumstances which tore us apart. He was the Celestial Crown Prince with obligations to his kingdom. While with Wenzhi . . . it had been *his* duplicity and choices which wounded me so. My hurt was laced with remorse that I had been so careless, so imprudent as to fall for his lies. And there was bitterness, too, that he had shaken my trust in myself. That he had brought me low, to the depths of his own deceit—when I feigned my affection to drug him to escape. I was not ashamed of what I had done, but neither did I take pride in it.

Fortunately, Ping'er had more pressing questions to ask. "What happened to the pearls? The dragons?"

I fumbled for the words to do justice to their unearthly beauty, their power and grace. When I spoke of restoring the dragons' essence, my mother's hand covered mine. There were no recriminations for endangering myself and her freedom, just pride glowing in her face.

"The dragons are free," Ping'er whispered. "I had believed them lost forever."

I kept on with my story, answering their questions as well as I could, only demurring when it would hurt too much—when I was unable to conceal my feelings. By the time I finished, the sun was high, the sky an azure blue.

It was then, I untied my pouch, reaching into it. My fingers closed around the seal the Celestial Emperor had given me, as cold as a fistful of snow. My heart beat so quickly I could barely breathe as I slid from my chair and sank to my knees before my mother.

"Xingyin, why are you kneeling?" She sounded confused as she leaned forward, her hands outstretched to lift me up—

But I raised my hands to her instead. Cupped between my palms was the seal, shimmering like sunlit ice. I was trembling so hard, I did not even know why—was it with fear, excitement, hope, or all of it? Would this work? How I prayed it would.

She took the seal from my hand and held it up. "What is this?"

Before I could answer, something sparked in the metal—beams of silver-white light streaking from its depths, engulfing my mother in dazzling radiance. Ping'er and I shielded our eyes, almost blinded from the glare—which faded abruptly, the seal now darkening to a lump of dull coal.

My mother went as still as marble. When she turned to me, her eyes brimmed with wonder, shining brighter than the thousand lanterns lit.

"The enchantment is lifted. I am free."

As Ping'er scrambled to her feet, exclaiming in delight, my body went limp with relief. Until this moment I had feared a cruel trick by the emperor. But he had kept his word. A torrential rush of emotion swept through me that untangled the knots buried deep, dispelled the lurking shadows, pried away my sorrow—my entire being filled with nothing in this moment except a soaring, blazing lightness.

Finally, our lives could begin anew.

40

In my childhood, our isolation was no great burden. I had no friends or companions, and little need for them; my mother and Ping'er had sufficed for me. But now, after a few weeks immersed in such tranquility, I found myself longing for my friends in the Celestial Kingdom and beyond.

My wish was granted sooner than I imagined. Before the sun rose the next day, Ping'er called out that Liwei had arrived. My eyes were heavy with sleep, but a pulse rippled through me at the thought of seeing him. I leapt out of bed and washed my face quickly, before pulling on a blue robe—his favorite color, my treacherous mind observed before I silenced it. Dragging a comb through my hair, I coiled part of it up. My steps were quick and impatient, and I told myself it was because I was glad to see a friend—*any* friend—after this solitude. When I entered the Silver Harmony Hall, I found my mother sitting with him as they conversed with easy familiarity. Ping'er stood beside them, pouring their tea. As we usually served ourselves, I suspected her attendance today was to glean a closer look at the Celestial Crown Prince.

My breath caught in my throat at the sight of him. His dark blue brocade robe was fastened with a length of black cloth, tassels of silk and jade hanging from his waist. His long hair was gathered into a gold ring, swinging down his back. He sat with his palms resting over his knees, with an ease to his bearing that I had not seen for a while. As he rose to greet me, his smile was more radiant than the sun.

"You . . . you are here," I stammered, all coherent thought having fled me.

"Uninvited. But not unwelcome, I hope?" He reached out to take my hand.

Such intimacy caught me unaware, as did the unrestrained warmth in his gaze. "No, never that," I finally managed.

With precise timing, my mother and Ping'er declared they were needed elsewhere. By leaving me alone with him, my mother signaled her wholehearted approval of Liwei, despite her earlier reservations. He had a way with people, a sincerity that drew others to him even before they knew who he was. Just as when we had first met.

"Have you been well?" he asked.

"Better than expected," I replied truthfully. Restful sleep undisturbed by nightmares. A carefree existence without responsibilities. No one to set my heart alight or drown it with despair. Such luxuries could work wonders on one's constitution. Since my return, my lifeforce had been strengthening, too. The moon possessed a powerful rejuvenating energy which I was unaware of before, perhaps because my magic had been suppressed. It would take a while before I regained my strength, but it might be sooner than I had anticipated.

Though my body was healing, my spirit was restless. There were only so many times I could walk through the osmanthus forest. Only so many hours I could while away in reading and music.

"Have you been well?" I echoed his question. Dread gripped me as I recalled his defiance of his father. And shame seared me, too, that I had left him to bear the brunt of his parents' wrath alone. All that consumed me after that wrenching confrontation had been a desperate eagerness to return home, to leave the Celestial Kingdom, half fearing that the emperor might change his mind and demand the return of his seal.

Liwei's hold tightened, his dark eyes pinning me where I stood. "Nothing I haven't been through before."

I bit my lip, wanting to ask more. And yet the intensity of his stare, his nearness, gave me pause. Was there something different about him today? It was almost as though he had reverted to the Liwei of old, before . . . I discarded the thought. He was here, I was glad for it. And I had a favor to ask of him today, to take my mother and me to the Mortal Realm. To take us to my father.

Selfishly, I had waited to tell my mother the news. To let us enjoy a few days of unadulterated happiness, basking in our reunion and her newly regained freedom. But I knew that she longed to fly to the Mortal Realm to seek my father at the first opportunity. One evening, when I could delay no more, I had clasped her hand in mine.

"Mother, I have something to tell you." Unwelcome words filled with foreboding. Or had it been the tremor in my voice which turned her face to ash?

Her cold hand slid from my grasp. "I don't want to hear it."

Her childlike plea had pierced me. I wondered, should I let things go on as they had? Half in hope, half in denial? Something in me reared away. Better to cut the cord clean, than to let it fray toward the inevitable end.

"I'm sorry. The Black Dragon told me . . . Father is dead." My voice had cracked over the words as my throat closed tight.

She had crumpled then, her body heaving as it folded over. I held her fast, trying not to flinch from her choked cries. My words had struck all hope from her as a knife cutting down an ailing plant still clinging to life. I had lost a father I never knew, but my mother lost a husband she loved still.

Together, now, the three of us flew to the Mortal Realm. My mother's face was white as she plucked at her sleeves nervously. It had been too long since she had left the moon. Fortunately, Liwei's cloud glided as smoothly as a bird through the air.

The Black Dragon had described the place well. Where the two rivers merged, we found the small hill covered with white flowers. At the highest point rose a large circular grave crafted from marble. Characters inlaid with gold spelled out the name:

后羿

HOUYI

All around were paintings of my father's achievements; the battles he had won, the enemies he had vanquished. It was a magnificent tomb, worthy of even a king in this world. Yet it grieved me that there was no mention of his family or descendants. Had he lived alone until the very end?

My mother clutched my arm, her step faltering. She stared at the grave, her face stricken with grief.

"We can leave, if you wish," I whispered, through the ache in my chest.

"No," she cried fiercely. She pushed her long sleeves up, picked up the broom, and began sweeping with a burst of energy. For a moment, I wondered what the mortals would think, if they saw the revered Moon Goddess sweeping as industriously as any common villager. In a flash it struck me, they more than anyone would understand the respect she wanted to pay to her husband. To show him that even in death, she honored him still. I crouched down, using my handkerchief to wipe away the dust and grime from the marble, polishing the characters until they shone once more. Liwei stood apart at first, before bending to clear away the weeds.

When the site was immaculate, my mother brought out the offerings of fruit and cakes that she had prepared herself, heaped onto porcelain plates. I lit the incense sticks and passed three to her, their tips crimson with muted flame. Holding them before us, we knelt before the grave and bowed thrice. A wife and daughter, mourning our greatest loss. After the final bow, I pushed the incense sticks firmly into the small brass censer. Thin trails of fragrant smoke drifted into the sky.

I touched her hand, rousing her from her daze. "Mother, when you walk in the forest at night, what do you think about?" I had longed to ask this so many times before.

She closed her eyes, a dreamlike smile on her lips. "You, as a child. Your father. Our life together. How I wish he were with us, that he had not been left behind." She bent her head then, broken whispers falling from her mouth. "Sometimes I wonder . . . what if the physicians were wrong? What if I had not drunk the elixir? We would have lived all these years together, in the world below. My hair would be gray now, but we would have been *happy*."

Her grip tightened around mine. "As I ascended to the skies, I turned around once to see him by the window—his hand outstretched, such anguish upon his face. He had returned too late. Some nights I torment myself, wondering how he felt as he watched me fly away. Did he understand why I did it? Did he feel betrayed? Did he . . . hate me? Those nights, I hate myself, too."

She stared ahead, her throat working before she continued. "In that moment when I held the elixir, all I could think of was you and me, and how much I wanted us to *live*. When I drank it, I chose my husband's death before mine. I chose a life without him. I chose—us." Her voice throbbed with sudden emotion. "I will never be free of my sorrow. And yet, I would do it again, even knowing all which came after. Because it meant I had you."

Tears fell from her like a scattering of rain. I cursed myself for my thoughtless question. For asking it, despite knowing it would grieve her. But we could not keep hiding and burying our hurt, especially from those we loved. I had learned that through the pain lay forgiveness, growth, and the eventual healing of our wounds. It struck me then, perhaps my mother and I were more similar than I had imagined. We had both seized the opportunities which came our way, we had both chosen to live.

Slowly, her fingers slipped from my grasp like she had forgotten my presence. Her gaze fixed on the gleaming characters of my father's name on the headstone, her lips moving to mouth them in silence. His legacy and achievements carved into immutable stone. Forever ingrained in the memory of the world he had saved, for as long as there were books to read and songs to sing. He would never be forgotten. But it was an empty solace for those who loved him.

Rising to my feet, I joined Liwei by the bank of the river. We stood in silence, watching the water glistening in the sunlight as the breeze toyed with our hair. The air in the mortal world was filled with a myriad of scents; blossoming flowers, decaying leaves, the earthy river water thrumming with life.

He turned to me then. "I asked Princess Fengmei to release me from our betrothal."

I stared at him in disbelief, unsure of what to say. "Why? When?" I finally asked.

He shot me a rueful smile. "Need you ask why? After you left, I visited Princess Fengmei. I told her the truth, what I should have told her long before. She deserved more than what I had to offer: a heart that would never be hers. She was most understanding. And she asked me to tell you, she hoped we would find happiness together. I think she knew since the day you rescued her."

I recalled her clear gaze when it had fallen upon our Sky Drop Tassels, when she realized they were a matched pair. I did not wish to hurt her . . . but oh, I could not deny the joy blossoming through me now.

"What about the alliance?"

"The Phoenix Kingdom reaffirmed its support for the Celestial Kingdom. While the tie will not be as strong as one bound through marriage, they will remain our friend and ally. Both the queen and she remain grateful for our aid."

He took my hand, pressing it against his chest—where his heart pounded as loudly as my own. His eyes shone with unbridled emotion. As his other palm cupped the curve of my cheek, I leaned unconsciously against him, drawn to his remembered warmth. "My heart is yours; it has always been yours," he said. "You don't have to answer me now. I know you need time to be with your mother and to think things through. I was wrong before; I did not fight hard enough for us then. But I will never fail you again." He spoke the last words as solemnly as a vow.

The emotions suffusing me left no room for speech. It was as though the sun had emerged from behind the clouds, illuminating the sky. The shadows might return, but for now I would bask in its radiance.

As dusk crept up, we flew back to the moon. Before he left, Liwei helped me to set up the protection wards. Our home was no longer forbidden to immortals and while we welcomed visitors, we needed to exercise caution. Together, we wove our magic into threads of power which stretched all around the Pure Light Palace. When I paused, exhausted by my efforts, Liwei took over. As he closed his eyes, his energy erupted in a surge of light, circling our wards before vanishing.

"I've added another layer of protection to detect those who conceal their form, whether Demon, spirit, or Celestial. While it cannot prevent their entry, it will hopefully give you sufficient warning," he explained.

At the gravity in his tone, the blood drained from my face. "Celestial?" I repeated, stumbling over the word. I had thought we were done with the intrigue, the danger and fear.

Liwei's face darkened. "There are no plots that I am aware of. However, my parents are displeased that the army intervened to lend you their support. Whispers have reached their ears that their capitulation here is viewed by many as a sign of weakness. Some begin to question again the wisdom of their past decisions—imprisoning the dragons, exiling the Moon Goddess. Allowing the sunbirds to roam unfettered."

A chill swept over me. "All I ever wanted was to go home

and free my mother. I never intended any of this as a challenge. I just want to live here, in peace."

"We cannot control what others fear. But you won't be alone. I will be with you, for as long as you let me." Liwei took my frozen hands, lifting them to his lips and blowing his warm breath over them. "I'm just being careful. These are rumblings and rumors, nothing to worry about for now."

I nodded woodenly. Rumblings and rumors in the wrong ears could still bear dire consequences.

That night, after Liwei had left, I tossed and turned before I fell asleep. And even in slumber I found no rest—lost in a vivid dream where I stood on the balcony, gazing at the sky. The clouds were a strange color, almost violet. As a tall figure came to stand beside me, his green robe swirled in the breeze.

He stared at me with those silvery eyes, as though waiting for me to speak.

"Thank you for letting us go. But it does not erase all you did," I said stiffly.

"I meant what I said. That I would never force you against your will again." There was a wistful note in his tone, one I had never heard before. "I did not realize what we had until it was lost. If only we could start over, I would do things differently."

I did not answer him. I did not know what to say.

"There is something I want to ask you."

"You can ask but I may not answer," I countered, unwilling to be drawn deeper into a conversation that brought back too many unsettling memories.

Though he smiled, there was a hollowness about it. "Would you indulge me? I've missed your company."

"I've not missed yours." A half-truth, a half-lie. I reminded myself that whatever I missed was the illusion of our companionship, not the reality of his deception.

His eyes flashed. "On the rooftop, before the dragon carried you away—would you have shot me?"

I had asked myself that countless times before. And now, I finally knew the answer. "No." His honesty deserved no less than mine.

At that single word, he let out a drawn breath, the tension easing from his shoulders. "Could you ever care for a Demon as you did for the Celestial?"

"The Celestial never existed. It was the Demon all along." Somehow, I kept my voice flat, ignoring the twinge in my chest.

He inclined his head gravely. "Perhaps. However you see me, I will wait until you do."

"Do what?"

"Love me again." His fingers brushed the side of my head, lightly stroking my hair. "Or at least, not hate me anymore."

Before I could jerk away, a scathing retort on my tongue, he had disappeared.

I awoke the next morning, sandy-eyed and grim. My dream was so vivid, the emotions it evoked so real—I was lost in thought for a long while. Alternating between outrage that he might have infiltrated my dreams, and resentment that the thought of him still troubled me so. Finally, I rose to get dressed. In front of the mirror, I froze at the sight of the silver pin in my hair carved with a pattern of clouds. My fingers grasped the cool metal, plucking it out and hurling it into a drawer.

I picked up the Jade Dragon Bow, slinging it over my shoulder before leaving the room. My time in the army had taught me caution; to always have a weapon on hand. Walking outside, I tested once more the wards which Liwei and I had woven.

Threads of gold and silver knitted tightly together—as delicate as a spiderweb, yet stronger than iron. With a burst of defiance, I thought, if enemies lurked on the horizon, I would be ready for them.

That night, I did not dream of Wenzhi. I was unsettled, unsure of how I felt, though I sensed it was not the last I had seen of him.

MY DAYS FELL INTO a routine. Since my mother's punishment was lifted, many immortals came to visit us. Some to pay their respects, others to satisfy their curiosity—more interested in the scandal of our tale than out of any true concern. I longed to show them out after the first cup of tea, but my mother's glare restrained my ruder impulses. Yet beyond these slight irritations, it was wonderful to be home. To feel safe and free and loved. True to her promise, Shuxiao was a frequent visitor, often dropping by unannounced. I was always glad for her company and to hear her news of the realm. Minyi came, too, and even Teacher Daoming and General Jianyun. These were my favorite times—sharing my home with the friends I had made, to hear their voices and laughter spilling through our halls. Such company did not detract from the peace but enhanced it.

Yet no visitor was more frequent than Liwei. We took long walks through the white osmanthus forest, winding between the glowing lanterns, beneath the starlit sky. When I played the qin or flute, he sat beside me, sketching or painting. At times I looked up to find his dark eyes fixed on me with such intensity, my fingers would falter over the melody. But I no longer shied from his touch, nor felt that pang of guilt when my pulse quickened at the sight of him. And my mind, once more, dared to dream of our future.

Some nights, after Ping'er had gone to bed, I joined my mother as she stood on the balcony of our home. We were together, yet each of us lost in our own memories—hers, of the realm below, and mine of the skies above. I now understood, with startling clarity, why she had not wanted to be disturbed during these times. And though we did not speak, we found a kind of solace in each other's company, in sharing our sorrow—a sorrow which I had no comprehension of in my childhood. Often, I started to find myself alone, not noticing when she had left—so wrapped up was I in my own thoughts, in trying to answer the questions which whirled through my mind.

Could Liwei and I truly forget all that had transpired to tear us apart? Could the ties that were severed be remade? In the tranquility of my home, I hoped to have the time to unravel these tangled knots of my life. Yet even though we were immortal, I could not walk this path forever—shying from love, wary of making the wrong decision, afraid to be hurt. I had not believed myself fickle, but the truth was I no longer knew my own heart.

I had always thought life was a road, twisting and turning with the vagaries of fate. Luck and opportunity, gifts beyond our control. As I gazed across the endless night, it dawned on me then, that our paths were forged from the choices we made. Whether to reach for an opportunity or to let it pass by. To be swept up with change or to hold your ground. On the surface, my life had come full circle. Yet no longer did I have to hide in the shadows, burying my past and fearing for my future. Never again would I conceal who I was, and the names of my father and mother. Word had spread throughout the eight kingdoms of the Immortal Realm that I was the daughter of the Moon Goddess, and of the mortal who had slain the suns.

In the darkness, the thousand lanterns flickered to life. The sky was clear. The stars infinite. The light of the moon was full and bright. On a night as this, my heart was content, awaiting the promise of tomorrow.

ACKNOWLEDGMENTS

Daughter of the Moon Goddess began as a wild dream which would not have been possible without the love and support of my family and friends, and those who believed in the book and me. I feel truly blessed to be able to include them here.

To David Pomerico, my brilliant editor at Harper Voyager US—I will always remember our first call, which changed the course of my life, and I knew then that my book had found its home. It is an honor to work with you, and you've been an incredible champion for *Daughter of the Moon Goddess*. Your vision for the book and keen notes (the humor was appreciated) drove me to become a better writer, and the story is so much stronger because of you.

To Vicky Leech, my amazing editor at Harper Voyager UK—I am truly so glad to be working with you! Thank you for being a wonderful advocate, and for your inspiring ideas that took us down paths I never imagined we'd tread, which I am grateful that we did.

Eternal gratitude to my incredible agent, Naomi Davis, for believing in an unknown writer who lived on the other side of the world with little experience in writing, and for working with me to hone my craft. You are wonderful and fierce, my guide and partner throughout everything with your insight, experience, and empathy.

My deepest thanks to the amazing Harper Voyager US team who I am so fortunate to work with: DJ DeSmyter, Sophie Normil, Ronnie Kutys, and the HarperCollins sales team—I wish I could name everyone! I struggled for the words to express my appreciation, but please know I am so grateful for everything.

Kuri Huang, thank you so much for illustrating the exquisite masterpiece of the US cover, and to Jeanne Reina for your inspired direction. Beyond a work of art, it's the cover of my dreams! Special thanks to Angela Boutin, Virginia Norey, Rachel Weinick, Jane Herman, and Mireya Chiriboga for your invaluable help! And to the incredibly talented Natalie Naudus, thank you for being the voice of Xingyin, for bringing her to life.

I am also so grateful to the wonderful Harper Voyager team in the UK—Natasha Bardon, Maddy Marshall, Jaime Witcomb, Susanna Peden, Robyn Watts, and Marta Juncosa—your support means so much to me. Thank you to Ellie Game, the amazing cover designer, and to Jason Chuang for creating the stunning UK cover that I could not stop looking at, which is utterly perfect for the story.

To everyone else at HarperCollins worldwide who supported *Daughter of the Moon Goddess*, who helped it reach its readers, to those I was unable to include here due to timing—please know, I appreciate all you have done.

I came into publishing without knowing anyone and it was a real fear that no one would read my book. I am eternally grateful to the brilliant authors who read an early version of the manuscript: Stephanie Garber, Shelley Parker-Chan, Andrea Stewart,

Shannon Chakraborty, Ava Reid, Genevieve Gornichec, Tasha Suri, and Elizabeth Lim. I cannot tell you how moved I was by your thoughtful and generous words, and I feel fortunate to have read your beautiful books.

To Anissa de Gomery, I am so glad that we connected, and for your friendship, now. Working with you is one of the highlights of my writing journey, and I am so thankful for you and your wonderful team.

To my beloved husband, Toby—my partner in life, my first reader, fiercest critic, and most valiant supporter—I am forever grateful to you for encouraging me to pursue my dreams and putting up with me as I transitioned into this new and undeniably demanding phase of my life. For looking after our kids when I was on deadline (most of 2021), for listening to my fears when everything seemed impossible, to celebrating each milestone. I could not have done this without you.

To Lukas and Philip, for your excitement over what started out as your mum's "crazy idea," for your enthusiastic pictures and scrawls, your questions about my story, and—most importantly—for letting me work when the headphones were on. I love you both with all my heart.

I would not be where I am without my parents. Thank you to my mother, for your love and support, for cultivating my childhood fascination with Chinese fantasy dramas, and for letting me stay at home to read instead of going out. Those few flute and guzheng lessons weren't a total waste! And to my father, for working so hard to give us a better life, for your love, humor, and enthusiasm for all that we did, and for giving me the books which kindled my passion for stories. I miss you, and I wish you were still with us.

To my sister, Ee Lynn, for your love and encouragement, for

being there for me through the best and worst of times, and for reading my early work. To my cousin Swee Gaik, for your invaluable advice and cheering me on when I first voiced my wildly improbable dream of becoming an author. So much thanks to you and Dan!

Sonali, I will always be grateful to you for reading my terrible first draft and for giving me the courage to plunge into the daunting world of querying. Your belief in me was the spark that lit this. To Jacquie, for your unflinching support and kindness, and for being my voice of reason. I don't know how I could have gotten through this without you. I am so grateful to have you two in my life—the best friends I could ever have asked for, my calm through the tumult of publishing, motherhood, and life.

Regretfully, I am not skilled enough to write a Chinese poem. Special thanks to Han Lihua for his beautiful interpretation of Xingyin's couplet in the competition and for helping me to coin the perfect location names. To Yangsze Choo for her generous advice to a new author. And to Lisa Deng for her patience with my random and frequent questions, from discussing names to myths and culture.

To my dear friends in Hong Kong—those I met at BA and HKIS. I am so grateful to all of you for your encouragement and support, particularly during the insanity of my debut year. Your friendship means so much to me, and you have touched my life in so many ways.

To the most inspiring teacher I ever had, Puan Vasantha Menon—thank you for instilling in me a love for literature.

It is such a privilege to be part of the incredibly talented #22Debuts, and to have such wonderful agent siblings who helped keep me sane. Also, to Kristen (@myfriendsarefiction), Mike Lasagna, Daniel Bassett, Kelecto (@panediting), Ellie (@faerieontheshelf), CW, Kristin Dwyer, Lauren (@fictiontea)—you are all amazing, and I am grateful for your early support.

Finally, but just as importantly, my endless thanks to the readers, booksellers, librarians, bloggers, bookstagrammers, and the book community for your support of *Daughter of the Moon Goddess*. And if you are reading this, I am so grateful to you for giving this book a chance, for allowing me to share my story with you. I have loved writing it with all my heart, and I hope you find something to love in it too.

ABOUT THE AUTHOR

SUE LYNN TAN writes fantasy novels inspired by the myths and legends she fell in love with as a child. Born in Malaysia, she studied in London and France, before settling in Hong Kong with her family.

Her love for stories began with a gift from her father, her first compilation of tales from around the world. After devouring every fable she could find in the library, she discovered fantasy books—spending many of her teenage years lost in magical worlds.

When not writing or reading, she enjoys exploring the hills and lakes around her home, the temples, beaches, and narrow winding streets there. She is also grateful to be within reach of bubble tea and spicy food, which she unfortunately cannot cook.

Find her at www.suelynntan.com, or on Instagram and Twitter @suelynntan.